"Delightful! Charming! Full of characters who take up residence in your heart. Holly's stories invite me in with love and laughter. The best of 'News from Lake Wobegon' and Father Tim combined."

**Lauraine Snelling,** bestselling author of the Red River of the North series

"Restless and reluctant, Cora Matthews is back in Moonberry where she once happily lived with her grandparents until her mother stole her away. Right from the start, the locals surround Cora and help her reclaim all she's been missing—love, a sense of belonging, and a heart of peace. An uplifting novel about the power of small-town community."

**Suzanne Woods Fisher,** bestselling author of *The Sweet Life*

"Rich characters, a delightful setting, and a heartwarming story. You'll love everything about *On Moonberry Lake*!"

**Ginny L. Yttrup,** Christy Award–winning author of *Words*

# On Moonberry Lake

*a novel*

## HOLLY VARNI

Revell

a division of Baker Publishing Group
Grand Rapids, Michigan

Published by Revell
a division of Baker Publishing Group
Grand Rapids, Michigan
www.revellbooks.com

Printed in the United States of America

Library of Congress Cataloging-in-Publication Data
Names: Varni, Holly, 1972– author.
Title: On Moonberry Lake : a novel / Holly Varni.
Description: Grand Rapids : Revell, a division of Baker Publishing Group, [2023].
Identifiers: LCCN 2023001300 | ISBN 9780800744977 (paperback) | ISBN
   9780800745141 (casebound) | ISBN 9781493443604 (ebook)
Subjects: LCGFT: Romance fiction. | Novels.
Classification: LCC PS3622.A755 O56 2023 | DDC 813/.6—dc23/eng/20230207
LC record available at https://lccn.loc.gov/2023001300

Scripture used in this book, whether quoted or paraphrased by the characters, is taken from THE HOLY BIBLE, NEW INTERNATIONAL VERSION®, NIV® Copyright © 1973, 1978, 1984, 2011 by Biblica, Inc.® Used by permission. All rights reserved worldwide.

The author is represented by Illuminate Literary Agency, www.illuminateliterary.com.

Baker Publishing Group publications use paper produced from sustainable forestry practices and post-consumer waste whenever possible.

23  24  25  26  27  28  29      7  6  5  4  3  2  1

To my mother, who always believed.
And to my father, who always hoped.

*A lake carries you into recesses of*
*feeling otherwise impenetrable.*

William Wordsworth

~

*Small towns make up for their lack of people*
*by having everyone be more interesting.*

Doris "Granny D" Haddock

# *One*

Her mother knew when someone was pregnant and when someone was dying. She claimed it was a gift from God. At the briefest glance, she could determine if someone was experiencing the beginning of life or in the process of reaching the end.

She would see a woman shopping in a store, her stomach flat, and nod in her direction. "She's expecting."

A perfectly groomed man with only a hint of gray at the temples would be walking back from communion to his pew at Sunday service, and she'd whisper, "He doesn't have much time."

This powerful insight would have been challenged or mocked if it weren't for one annoying fact: she'd never got it wrong.

Not even when the premonition came about herself.

Cora Matthews thought of this as she looked down at the coffin. Her mother had saved her the hassle of choosing one by preordering and paying for it herself. The thing had been waiting for her mother's passing on a kind of death layaway plan. Ready when she was.

Just as well. It had saved Cora a lot of trouble, because this was *not* the casket she would have chosen. The glossy lacquer finish over the fire-engine red made her think of the wall of nail polish at a salon. For the briefest moment, she had the urge to smile at the thought of telling the pedicurist, "I'd like the color of my mother's coffin, please."

Cora restrained the impulse to display anything but misery. Appearing reticent wasn't difficult. She didn't want to be there. She was fulfilling her obligation as the sole child. The smallness of her family had dwindled to where she now stood alone in the world. The hollow feeling that accompanied that realization was surprisingly not all-consuming or overwhelming. She had gradually gotten accustomed to it over the years, like immersion into freezing cold water, nursed by her distant relationship with her mother. The closeness she had shared with her mother was more civil than familial. Neither ever saying what needed to be said.

Cora stood motionless, stuck in a state of graveside mourning expectation, not sure what to do next. A tiny part inside her, hidden below years of strife, imagined heaving sobs of heartache overcoming her—or, perhaps, searing grief that would squeeze all the air from her chest.

But she experienced neither.

At one moment she had even held her breath, waiting for a swell of emotion, but nothing came. Air moved freely in and out of her body, mingling with the tree overhead. She had no desire to collapse from sorrow onto the freshly mowed summer grass. She didn't need an arm to steady her. Her legs stood as wooden as chess pieces.

It shouldn't have been surprising. Loss was a companion that had become part of her long ago, like a callus on the pad of her foot that dulled sharp sensations. To anyone else, the bereavement would be tremendous. But Cora had been orphaned by family she cherished years ago.

Concentrating on the blades of grass, she tried to muster a single tear. She knew it wouldn't appear normal to all these people who once knew her mother to not see some show of emotion. This kind of loss was supposed to be deep and painful. Perhaps at a time that wasn't so public, she'd be able to summon that emotion from memories that still haunted her. However, today, she sensed the evaluation from others in penetrating gazes, whether it was real or imagined, and it only caused her to go more numb.

Making a fist with one hand over the other, she dug her fingernails into the soft flesh of her palm, hoping to elicit the slightest stinging in her eyes. *Just one tear,* she willed herself. *One stupid tear.* She kept her eyes fixed on a flower resting on the coffin. The withering blossom had fallen away from the rest of the arrangement, bedraggled and abandoned. Its pitifulness captured her attention, and with luck, onlookers would assume she was lost in her grief and leave her alone. It worked successfully until the moment the service ended.

"Would you look at that, Henry? The poor dear is in shock."

Cora glanced to her right and met the stares of an elderly couple. Both had pearly white hair and pink scalps. With the same number of wisps as her nearly bald husband, the woman had pushed her thin hair back with a wide headband that looked more like a vise for her skull. The man inched closer to Cora, keeping the same distance a person would if peering into a lion's cage.

The woman pressed one hand to her chest, eyes crinkled with concern. "She's been as quiet as a mouse this whole time. I haven't seen her talk to a single soul or make a peep. I wonder if she's hysterical."

"She doesn't *look* hysterical." The man's volume revealed his hearing loss. Scrunching his face, he examined Cora through thick glasses.

Cora stared back at them. *Who on earth are these people?*

The woman squinted in concentration. "What if it's one of those silent hysterias? Do you think someone needs to shake her out of it?"

"*I* could shake her." The man spoke as if it were the most natural thing to say. His skin creased in folds as he studied Cora with magnified eyes.

9

"You most certainly will not, Henry Gustafson! You have a reputation to uphold in this community, and I will not be married to a man who shakes women."

"Now, settle down, Martha. I wouldn't shake her *hard.*"

His wife waved him away with a flick of her hand and stepped forward. "Oh, stop it. Let me handle this."

Curiosity bubbled up like ginger ale inside Cora. It wasn't every day that an elderly person offered to shake her.

"Honey, can you hear me? Are you all right?" the woman asked, articulating each word as if Cora were hard of hearing or knew no English. To answer her own question, the woman muttered, "Of course you're not all right." She tried again at full volume. "What I mean is, do you need me to shake you out of it? Maybe give you a hug and jiggle you about? I'm not that strong, but I'll try."

With the slightest curve touching the corners of her mouth, Cora took her time answering. "No . . . I don't think that will be necessary."

The man nodded to his wife, a wide, lopsided smile reconfiguring his wrinkled features as if to say, "See, she's not crazy after all."

The woman's face lit up in silent agreement.

Cora struggled not to laugh. The pair reminded her of matching salt and pepper shakers. They seemed proof that couples married a long time could begin to resemble each other. Their mannerisms, appearances, and ping-pong conversation were interchangeable.

"We're sorry, sweetie, but you haven't moved or said anything in a long time," Martha said. "I didn't even see you blink during the ceremony. It looked like you went into one of those catatonic trances."

Henry snorted. "I don't know how you could see anything when you're as blind as a bat without your glasses!"

"Hush, now. I'm talking to her." Martha reprimanded him with a stern look before focusing watery, cornflower-blue eyes back on Cora. "We were friends of your grandparents."

The words hit Cora as though she *had* been shaken, her numbness replaced by an unwelcome sensation. The cemetery began to feel cold, though it was a warm June day. She wrapped her arms around herself to combat the chill. She shifted, aware of the throbbing pain in her feet from standing in stiletto heels a half size too small. The sunlight suddenly seemed too bright but lacked the heat she craved.

Cora stepped out of her shoes and wiggled her toes in the grass, not caring how inappropriate it appeared. Her breath grew shallow, and she swallowed hard at the discomfort of it all.

"We loved them dearly and know they would've wanted us here today," Martha continued. "We're so sorry about your mother. We watched Lydia grow up."

The pastor cleared his throat to announce his approach, interrupting before Cora could respond. His eyes grew round, staring at her bare feet. After the service, he had mingled with the people who lingered, speaking to them in hushed tones. Though the pastor flitted around, pausing to shake hands with each person, nodding in sympathy, his hurried steps suggested he wanted this shindig to be over.

Unlike the pastor, Cora felt no rush to leave. She had nowhere she needed to be. She still hadn't found a place to live. Funny how breaking off an engagement two weeks before the wedding left one scrambling to figure out what to do—and where to go—next.

Everyone had blamed her change of heart about the wedding on the loss of her mother, and Cora hadn't done anything to contradict that assumption. She couldn't explain the panic rising like bile in her throat when she and Kyle spoke about the future together. Instead of filling out a gift registry, she had packed up her apartment and her mother's house and put it all into storage.

She had felt sick in the pit of her stomach at the look of shock and hurt in Kyle's eyes when she broke the news. She was screwing up his grand plan and doing something unexpected, which he hated. He reasoned with her that losing someone close could make a person do crazy things, which became his family's mantra to everyone after the breakup: "The bride had a breakdown."

Fine, they could think whatever they wanted. Her perceived irrational behavior had served its purpose. Her mother's death had provided an opportunity to escape the commitment she'd gotten herself into, and it was seen by others as socially acceptable considering the magnitude of her loss. She was able to abandon her life in one erratic swoop because she had seen it done. She had experienced it firsthand. That was the legacy her mother had left her—the propensity to cut ties and run.

The pastor cleared his throat again. "Pardon me, but I need to get going," he said, his eyes on Cora. "You will be in my prayers for your loss." His reverent voice, surely intended to be sincere and spiritual, felt perfunctory and scripted.

Cora couldn't explain the immediate dislike she felt when she met him. If anyone else had been available to do the service, she would've taken them. But she'd been told this man with his ashen face, drooping jowls, and sad eyes that mirrored an undeniable resemblance to a basset hound was the only pastor available.

She nodded, smiling politely, and he walked away. The service hadn't brought Cora comfort or even celebrated her mother's life. The pastor's gloom had made it hard for her to breathe, and she hated every moment in his presence.

An older man with dark eyes and a rugged appearance approached her, suddenly becoming animated after he had stood like a pillar throughout the service.

"Hello. I'm Sam Klevar." He took her outstretched hand, his grasp strong but gentle. Though not as old as the elderly couple that continued to observe her, Sam had as many deep wrinkles in his face. Thick, steely hair framed his wizened appearance, and he stood with the solid build and nonchalance of John Wayne. "Welcome back to Moonberry."

His apologetic tone and sympathetic manner felt soothing. Cora recognized his voice immediately from the phone call she'd made the previous week to discuss the funeral and her obligatory return to the town from which she had been taken almost two decades ago. She mustered a weak smile. "It's nice to meet you."

"We've met before, but you were probably too young to remember. You couldn't have been more than six years old."

"Seven," she corrected him. "I was seven the last time I was here." That she knew with certainty. The last time she was here, her mother was crying and screaming at her grandparents and then she took her away. Cora was never allowed to see them again. And the ocean of tears she cried never brought them or her happy life at the lodge back. "I'm twenty-six now."

Sam frowned. "It has been a long time."

Her stomach growled loudly.

He smiled. "Can I offer you something to eat? Some folks have organized a small luncheon and would love to meet you. Besides, I need to speak with you about some business before you leave."

A handful of people milled around. Apparently, they weren't going to leave until she did. Spending time with a group of strangers was not something Cora wanted to do, but the guilt of proper etiquette weighed on her. She found it astounding that, even though her mother had been gone so many years, townspeople who had known her mother from childhood attended the funeral and gave a reception. She supposed the least she could do was show the same courtesy.

Cora nodded. "Thank you."

Sam's shoulders eased, and the lines on his face slackened.

"You can follow me in your car. The drive is short." He turned and nodded to the remaining mourners. Silently, they began to leave.

Cora lingered for a moment, taking one last look at her mother's lonely grave. It hadn't even occurred to her to bring flowers, the conventional sign of sympathy. Another indication of how removed she felt from the experience. Cora looked down at her feet with her sore red toes and the discarded heels next to them—shoes her mother would have loved and insisted Cora wear if she were here.

Cora had no flowers to leave behind. But she did have those uncomfortable shoes that more accurately represented their strained relationship.

Taking a deep breath, she let out a long sigh and left them, walking to her car barefoot.

~

After following Sam's pickup across town, Cora parked in front of a small home facing one of the area's many lakes. Riffling through her car in search of some sandals, she moved a pile of junk and saw her mother's letter. Her hand jerked away as if she'd been burned. Reaching over again, she picked up the blue envelope. The pages tucked inside were folded neatly, and her name scrolled across the top of the envelope in elaborate cursive.

So much had changed in a week.

Henny, a longtime friend of her mother, had dropped in on Lydia for lunch and found her in her recliner, lounging back as if taking a nap. The house had appeared tidy. On the kitchen table sat two envelopes, one addressed to Cora and the other to Henny, with letters tucked inside. Henny's letter outlined instructions on whom to contact. Cora was third on the list, after the mortician and the police.

Her mother had detailed and neatly organized everything, an act that only fueled Cora's anger. How could she have chosen to say nothing, knowing her death was imminent? Doctors said she couldn't have predicted the aneurism and that she died of natural causes. There was no sign of any harm or foul play. It was documented as a random, and very unfortunate, biological occurrence. But Cora knew better. The fact that her mother had updated her will and finalized allocation of her estate and belongings a few months earlier provided proof to Cora's suspicion that her mother knew her time was nearing the end.

Everything had been handled, down to her mother's request to be buried in the small northern town of Moonberry Lake, Minnesota, where her mother had lived from infancy to when she was a young, single mother. Then, one day, she took her child and left Moonberry, never to return.

Lydia Matthews had separated herself from the town without explanation, as cleanly as the swipe of a scythe, yet had chosen to return in death.

Cora's letter contained two parts. The first page was a list of six things to do, which were easy to complete:

1. *Call lawyer*
2. *Transport me back to Moonberry Lake*
3. *Bury me in plot (already designated)*
4. *Contact Sam Klevar (phone number provided)*
5. *Attend funeral reception*
6. *Ask Sam Klevar for the envelope*

The second page of the letter offered a short goodbye and an apology for not giving Cora notice about her death.

Neither gave solace.

Cora had thrown the letter in the car along with select belongings. Now, readying herself to complete task number 5, she took a deep breath. *At least it's almost over.*

Accompanied by Sam, she entered the house, where a barrage of people waited to offer their condolences.

Most were her mother's classmates, some were old neighbors, and others were friends of Cora's deceased grandparents. All told stories of remembrance, no matter how small or vague, while feasting on the typical funeral fare of hot dishes and creamy salads. An hour and a half later, feeling dazed from endless pleasantries—not to mention a bit ill from a pistachio-green Jell-O concoction and two helpings of potato and macaroni salads—Cora escaped to the patio.

Free of the crowd, she closed her eyes and filled her lungs to capacity with the fragrant lake air. The smell of algae and fish awoke a faint memory of childhood. Footsteps padded across the patio behind her. She turned and her chest dropped in relief.

*Sam.*

He had been such a gift during the reception, skillfully negotiating her through the parade of townsfolk, never letting any one person keep her too long.

"Tired?" he asked.

She nodded. "You wouldn't have any antacids by chance, would you?"

He laughed. "I think that marshmallow Jell-O salad was your downfall."

"You could have warned me."

"Are you kidding? Those women made you two other plates that *I* personally had to eat for you." Rubbing his round belly, he shook his head. "When grieved, we eat. Food is supposed to replace the emptiness in our hearts."

Cora didn't respond. Nothing would ease the emptiness in her heart.

Sam looked out at the lake and then back at her. "Thank you for coming. This is a close-knit community, and they wanted to show you the love they had for your entire family."

Cora struggled to find the right words. She changed the subject instead. "I have something to ask."

He waited. A warm wind swept through the trees, flowing past them with a light touch.

Cora looked up at him. "I don't know if this makes any sense, but my mother left me a list of things I have to do. Contacting you was number 4, and number 6 is to ask you for an envelope. Do you have any idea what I'm talking about?"

He hesitated. Though brief, Cora did not miss the sign of internal struggle that flashed across his face. Whatever he was silently debating ended with a slight nod. "I'll be right back."

When he returned, he handed her a blue envelope with his name scrawled on it.

It looked exactly like the one she had received. She looked at him. "There were instructions inside for me to pass this on to you." He coughed.

She read the paper inside and, after a minute, looked up, her brow furrowed. "What's this?"

"The deed to your grandparents' lodge."

Cora's breath caught. Just the mention of the lodge was like pressing against a bruise. She was surprised at the actual ache she felt—like when an old injury or healed broken bone throbs unexpectedly, bringing back memories of the incident that edged between ignored and forgotten.

"Actually, your mother bequeathed the lodge to you with the condition that you maintain residence there for a certain period of time."

*What? Is he serious?* She struggled for words. "W-what? My . . . grandparents' lodge? It's available? It hasn't been sold after all these years? And I'm supposed to *live* in it?"

He nodded again. "Nobody has lived there since your grandparents died."

Cora couldn't believe the building had been left empty all these years. More shockingly, she couldn't believe her mother had owned it all this time and didn't say anything when she knew what it had meant to Cora as a child. Perhaps it was the guilt that had prevented her from saying anything or selling it. Her mother knew Cora had never forgiven her for taking her away. It marked the beginning of the rift in their relationship, like a small tear in a sweater that weakens all the threads around it so the hole just keeps getting bigger. Her mouth agape, she stuttered, but no words came out.

Sam faced the lake while he spoke, talking more to the trees than to her. "The paperwork states that it is to be handed down to you on the condition that you must spend one year living there. If you leave before the full year is complete, the agreement is null and void and there is no compensation. No exceptions or leniency. I don't know if you feel you can do that, but the inheritance

17

is worth considering. It's sizable." He paused. "Before you make any decisions, you should probably take a tour of the property."

*Of course she put in a clause forcing me to stay a year. Anything to get me to stay in one place.*

Clearing her throat, Cora tried to sound casual despite her rapid heartbeat. She felt like a seven-year-old again, confused about what was transpiring. "As it happens . . ." She paused. "I'm kind of in transition at the moment. I was planning on moving after the funeral to find a place in the city." The words tumbled out. Nobody had ever understood, especially her mother, why Cora was so restless—why she switched jobs as often as she did. *"You're always on the run toward something or away from it. The time in the middle is only long enough for you to retie your shoes. Why can't you ever settle in somewhere?"*

Cora shook away the echo of her mother's voice in her head. That was one of the reasons she had said yes when Kyle proposed. To prove her mother wrong. It wasn't that she wasn't capable of settling in somewhere, it was that no place had ever felt right after the lodge. She had always divided her life into two segments: early childhood at the lodge with her grandparents that was imprinted on her as strongly as a branding mark. And then life after, which was marked by loneliness and struggle as her mother tried to survive as a single parent with no help from anyone. Where moving constantly and feeling unsettled became her norm from her mother's insistence, and aspiration, that she wanted bigger and better things for her daughter.

Sam sighed. "Then it's perfect timing. Do you have a place to stay tonight?"

"The motel in town."

"Good. You need rest after today. Why don't you sleep on it. A lot has been thrown at you. I'll meet you at the lodge tomorrow at ten and show you around. Here are the directions." Sam pulled a small piece of paper from his pocket and handed it to her. With a smile, he turned and left.

She glanced at the paper. The address on the bottom made her heart skip. She tucked the scrap into her purse, then walked to her car. The lodge would be a place to live for *free* while she figured out what to do next. There was no way she'd be able to afford to keep it long-term with the property taxes and upkeep. The very idea of owning something so large was too daunting, especially since she had no job or excess of funds. But if she managed to live frugally and stay the year and then sell the property, she would have some serious seed money and the freedom to go anywhere.

She could start over.

Again.

In the inky blackness of the motel room that night, any chance for sleep was lost. Unanswered questions about her family and Moonberry Lake—questions that had been buried deep for so long—rose up like ghosts from the grave.

Cora remembered her grandparents and begged to see them. She cried for weeks after she and her mother had left, until her mother announced one day that they had died, which ended it. It brought an abrupt stop to her pleas but not her sorrow. That lingered.

After her mother's death, as she sorted through some of her belongings, she'd found a box of old pictures that sparked dim recollections. And when she went to check the burial plot at the cemetery and saw her grandparents' gravestones next to it that clearly indicated they hadn't died when her mother said but many years later, she was overcome with a mixture of rage and confusion. Why had her mother lied about everything? Why would she deny her a relationship with her grandparents?

Something had happened. And it must have been something awful for her mother to walk away and cut every tie. Whatever it was, her mother's rash decision had altered Cora's life to one of disjointed chaos. The sudden loss of everything was a ripping. A ripping of trust in the idea of family and home. A ripping away of actual family. She learned not to hold her breath for the next thing to be taken—and instead held tightly to nothing and no one.

Cora stared into the darkness, turning from side to side, restless from the lack of answers. Nothing made sense.

Why hadn't her mother sold the lodge when they were always struggling financially? What was the secret that marked the beginning of her lost childhood and the end of her mother's relationship with her family?

And why had her mother adamantly taken the secret with her to the grave?

# Two

Cora kept her window closed as plumes of dirt kicked up around her Jeep. The well-worn road, cushioned by rich evergreens and foliage, brought a sense of calm. She admired how the skyline knelt on the tops of dense pines and cedars. Goldenrod, thimbleberry, lupines, and other wildflowers carpeted the sides of the road.

Nearly missing the deteriorated sign, she turned onto a gravel road. The local real estate magazine had called the small cabins dotting the edge of the lake "quaint cottages or cozy bungalows on the water." She'd skimmed through the magazine before leaving the motel and was shocked at the prices of even the most modest cabins. All she could think about was the possible cash value of her lakefront inheritance.

She drove along the edges of Moonface Lake, the second largest to the town's namesake, gripping the steering wheel as though it were a life preserver. Her stomach twisted into a knot.

Finally, the faded number *615* on a badly rusted, maroon mailbox came into view. Almost undetectable from the road, the entrance to a dirt driveway appeared as a small break in the greenery. Thick brush lined the narrow drive, sweeping the top and sides of her Jeep as it passed. She slowed to a crawl. The overgrown vegetation heightened her anticipation of what felt like a hidden world.

As she lowered her window, the sound of waves against the shore and the scent of the North Woods blew in and enveloped her. The moist air was laced with the heavy, pungent smell of fish, grass, and lake water.

A sense of déjà vu gripped her as the white lodge came into sight. Though timeworn, the building stood with a certain dignity and grandeur. Nestled among the woods and overlooking the lake, the lodge was a world unto itself. All Cora could do was stare before she turned off the car and got out. Her heart pounded with every step. It was one thing to imagine seeing it again and another to actually be standing before it. It looked the same as it did in the photos—bigger than she remembered—but then again, she was remembering it from a child's point of view.

She glanced at an old truck parked near a woodpile at the end of the driveway before stepping onto the porch. Holding her breath, she approached the weathered front door covered with remnants of white paint. Chipped shards like snowflakes lay scattered before it, serving as the welcome mat. She turned the tarnished doorknob, and the door opened.

She walked into the musty building, her shoes echoing against the bare wooden floor, making her feel conspicuous. The foyer loomed like an old timepiece, undisturbed and forgotten. As she peered into the enclosed family room, she noticed a crackling fire burning within the stone hearth. French doors held in the warmth and smell of cedar. A sense of familiarity wrapped around her as snuggly as a blanket. It was different, but also somehow the same. A time capsule reopened.

A flicker of hope kindled inside her at the potential of reclaiming some of what she'd lost. *I could do this*, she thought, mustering more courage. *This isn't that bad.*

"I see you found your way."

Cora jumped at the voice behind her and turned to see Sam.

"I'm sorry. I didn't mean to startle you. I was down in the kitchen and came to check on the fire. The place was feeling a little damp.

I'm the official caretaker." He chuckled. "Basically, that means your grandfather entrusted me with a set of keys."

Cora still couldn't speak as she examined the room. It was as if memories coated over with dust were being wiped clean. Her recollection of running down the stairs and long hall tingled on her skin. The enchantment of stepping back into a forgotten dream was unexpectedly spellbinding.

Sam followed her gaze. "The place has been sealed up for some time. It'll be good to have someone living here again—that is, if you've decided to stay?"

A silence settled between them. Absorbed in thought, she didn't answer right away but took in the expansive foyer that opened to the front room and showcased a long wooden staircase.

"Yes." The response didn't come out confident but quiet.

Sam nodded. "I'll bring in your bags and help you get settled."

"You don't have to do that."

He held up a hand. "It's no trouble. Go ahead and look around."

Feeling like an intruder, Cora forced herself to take a couple steps. The lodge hadn't changed from the few pictures she had found in her mother's things. The built-in desk tucked underneath the staircase stood empty. It had been used as a check-in counter in the lodge's glory days, when church groups and fishermen flocked to the place. Next to the desk, a doorway opened to the long hall leading to ground-floor bedrooms and the dining hall. In front, sitting in the middle of the foyer, sat two square game tables surrounded by heavy oak chairs. She remembered playing cards there.

Cora opened the French doors with a tug, and the scent of burning wood permeating the room washed over her. The knotty pine floor, ceiling, and walls matched the paneling around the stone fireplace. A tall bookcase, old brown couch, and scratched coffee table served as the only decor.

"You don't have a working landline, and cell service is sketchy. Wi-Fi is nonexistent, so consider yourself off-the-grid until you get a satellite." Sam already had his first armload of her things. "I prepared a room for you upstairs."

"You made a bed for me?"

He shifted, but she didn't drop her stare.

"You knew I was going to stay?"

He shrugged. "No, but I was hoping."

His answer was so unexpected, she didn't know how to respond. *Why would it be important to him whether I stay or leave?*

Sam didn't divulge any more and left to bring in another load.

Her eyes followed the dark staircase covered with a dusty blue runner. She walked past it, across the room to the hallway. Running her hand along the wall, she counted the number of doors just as she had as a little girl. *One . . . two . . . three . . . four . . .* Four rooms with large windows faced the lake, each room with a wooden door and a screen door to the inside hallway. Cora remembered how the doors would be left open during insufferably hot summer days to cool the house that had no air-conditioning. The screen door provided guests with a little sense of privacy. Although, the groups always knew each other so it wasn't like anyone locked either door. On the opposite side of the hallway were three more bedrooms and two huge, communal bathrooms. Past the bathrooms was the back staircase, which was used as a shortcut from the second floor to the kitchen.

Reaching the dining area, Cora noticed it was still set up cafeteria style. Two twelve-foot tables with benches stretched from one end of the room to the other. In the corner was the entrance to the kitchen, and to the left was a door to the porch followed by a wall of windows looking out to the lake. Cora pushed open the swinging door to the kitchen and entered. Running her fingers along the top of the enormous black iron stove, she felt a coat of aged, sticky grease. When she approached the sink to wash off the grime, the sight of the brown-stained basin took her aback. Nothing had been updated in fifty years.

"Are you hungry?"

She leapt back at Sam's voice.

"It seems all I do is startle you." He frowned apologetically.

"I'm fine."

He stared at her, seeming to consider her automatic response. "Walking into a memory must be strange."

She met his soft eyes, surprised he understood how she felt.

He cleared his throat. "I've got some walleye I have to fry tonight or it's going to go bad. You're welcome to it."

"Thank you, but I've got some food in the Jeep."

"Suit yourself. How about I bring leftovers tomorrow morning? There's nothing like cold fish to start the day."

"Thanks." She smiled at his eagerness. "But cold fish for breakfast isn't my thing."

"Give it time." He grinned. "Well, all your bags and boxes are in the foyer."

"Thank you."

"If you like, I can give you a tour and help you get reacquainted with the place."

"That's okay. I'll snoop around on my own."

He nodded. "Then I'll leave you to explore. I'll be back first thing in the morning."

"Oh. You don't have to."

"I don't mind. It's the least I can do. I'm afraid you're stuck with me until you've gotten settled." He gave a small wave before heading toward the door.

She liked Sam. He was kind, and his presence felt comfortable. He blended in. "Thanks again for bringing in my suitcases."

"See you tomorrow. And Cora . . ." He hesitated.

Her eyebrows rose. "Yes?"

"I'm sorry for the circumstance that brought you back, but I'm glad you're here."

Cora spent the rest of the day on the dock, mesmerized by the soothing ripples and dancing light on the lake's surface. She dipped her feet in the cool water, watching tiny minnows nip at her toes. Time passed quickly until the waning sun indicated twilight. Ravenous, she ate a couple apples with peanut butter, forgoing the civility of a plate and smearing the peanut butter onto the apples with a spoon.

The lodge felt different at night. It became cavernous, chilled with an eerie stillness. She checked the doors, making sure they were locked. Feeling safe in a place so enormous would take time. She grabbed some of her bags and walked upstairs to the first bedroom, then stepped inside.

Cora's suitcase sat by the entrance as if she were a guest. The two twin beds and dresser looked and smelled their age. She shut the door and turned out the light, moving next to the window to raise it a few inches. A balmy breeze filled the room, along with the steady beat of chirping crickets. She had forgotten how the warm air thumped a strong, rhythmic beat with no other competing sounds.

Sitting on one of the tidy beds, which had been made up with soft white sheets and a thin ivory blanket, she felt the mattress dip in the middle. As she lay down, she felt the bed cradle her, weariness settling into her bones. Brushing her teeth or washing her face would take too much energy.

Her body ached with exhaustion. She closed her eyes, forcing away the constriction in her chest. The last couple days had affected her more than she wanted to admit. With the betrayal of a few tears that dissolved into the pillowcase, she pushed away unspoken questions and let them float into the night air.

$\sim$

In the morning tranquility, the air had a new rhythm of life. From where she stood on the back porch, she inhaled deeply, listening to the gentle lap of waves on the shore and a loon's song in the distance. This was her favorite time of day—the moment before the rest of the world awakened. She headed for the dock. A small thrill came over her as she watched the movement of the water between the wood planks. She turned, facing the massive building that lay like a sleeping giant.

"Hey!" a voice yelled from across the yard, jarring her out of her dreamy state. "Do you want me to put on some coffee?"

She squinted at the familiar figure. "I don't have any."

Sam raised a can high in the air.

"Thanks, but I don't drink coffee."

"You'll start liking it once you've tasted mine!" With that, he went inside. Minutes later, Sam returned carrying two mugs. They each sat on a lawn chair covered in dew drops.

She lifted the mug and peered at him. "You came back to check on me."

"I told you I would."

"Yes, but I don't understand why."

Sam grinned. "You may not remember me, but I remember you. I grew up with your mother, though I was a bit older." He winked. "Your grandparents were family to me, and they would've wanted you to have a friend. I'll help you clean up the lodge."

She kept quiet. Her mother and grandparents must have had years of happy times at the lodge before the incident that tore them apart. *What could have happened?* She winced at the familiar tug of her chest over the family she had lost.

"Sam, where do you live?"

"One lake over. It takes about five minutes to get here."

"Are you married?"

He smiled. "Happily, for over thirty years. My wife, Georgie, and I have two grown daughters. No grandchildren yet. Now, enough about me. Tell me, how was your first night back on Moonface?"

She remembered that the origin of the lake's name had come from how the area's indigenous people saw how the moon reflected off the water and illuminated the darkness. The actual Moonberry Lake was larger and closer to the entrance to town.

She shrugged. "It felt a little weird." She let the mug warm her hands.

"That's to be expected. It takes time to settle into an unfamiliar bed. A new place with old memories, or vice versa, is a peculiar blanket to sleep under. You'll get used to it."

"Why are you up so early?"

"I get up at four-thirty. Always have, always will. I like to get a jump on the day without disruption." He ducked his chin toward her. "What's your excuse?"

Cora shrugged. "I wanted to watch the sunrise on my first morning. Get a jump on the day too."

The two sat staring into the dissipating fog that hovered over the water, Sam sipping his coffee, Cora holding hers.

He nodded toward her mug. "Come on, now, you've got to try it."

She brought the bitter liquid to her lips and then spluttered, "I can't do it. The only thing tolerable is the scent and warmth."

He raised his cup in a toast. "Once again, give it time. It'll grow on you, like moss on a log."

"That's about what it tastes like."

He laughed.

Cora looked at him more closely as he drank his coffee. In this light, Sam's face seemed to be carved from the same wood as the trees, wrinkles chiseled into the weathered surface. Decades in the sun had given his dark complexion a leathered look. Lines jutted from the corners of his eyes like sunrays, deepening when he smiled. He had the face of an old man but eyes that brimmed with youthfulness. He was very likable, and Cora was thankful for his kindness since she literally didn't know anyone else in Moonberry Lake who could help her.

"It's early enough to get some bread at the convent if you want. I can take you in my boat."

Her eyes widened. "There's still a convent?"

"Yep. It's much smaller, of course, with only a few nuns." The old abbey across the lake had a bakery where nuns made bread to support themselves. People from all around the lake and outside community would bring their boats right up to the dock, where the nuns waited to sell the loaves. It was a local custom and way of life for people to go to the abbey for fresh bread.

"The bread is delicious," Sam continued, "but it's the blessing people receive with each loaf that keeps the nuns with a steady congregation. The prayers from the nuns turn the simple purchase of bread into an act of communion. People leave with not only bread but also a little bit of God."

Cora smiled. "I'd love to go."

"I'll get my boat in the water and we'll head out in about twenty minutes."

"I'll be ready." She dumped her remaining coffee on the grass and jumped to her feet. She hurried to her bedroom to change clothes, then pulled her long, straight, mousy-brown hair into a ponytail, brushed her teeth, splashed ice-cold water on her face, and pinched her cheeks to bring color to her fair skin and contrast to her turquoise eyes.

When she went back outside, Sam sat perched in his boat at the end of the dock.

"How much do they charge for a loaf?" she asked, getting in.

"They go by donation. It works out pretty well because it seems no one has the heart to look at one of those old nuns and hand them a buck."

Cora appreciated that Sam took his time crossing the lake. She watched the ripples in the water made by the motor, occasionally putting her hand over the side to run her fingers through the coolness. The push of the water against her hand brought her back to when it was just her and her grandfather making the voyage on this lake.

She recalled how early they had to get up to make the trip. He loved going to the convent for "holy bread," as he called it. He would take his time driving the boat across the lake, letting his only grandchild dangle her hands in the water, never saying a word about her soaked sleeves. Later, back at the lodge, he would fix her toast with jam. He'd hand it to her with a wink and say, "Eat all your holy bread—there's a bit of Jesus in there."

Cora would eat every bite, never leaving a crumb behind. The thought of fallen bits of Jesus all over the table had worried her young mind.

Now, Cora stared ahead as they approached the convent, the memory making her chest tight.

When they got there, no other boats were moored at the dock.

"It looks like we're the first customers of the day."

Sam frowned. "People don't come by like they used to, so you have to go in to get the bread. The nuns don't wait at the dock anymore."

The first thing greeting Cora on the landing was a wooden cross about eight feet tall. The white buildings beyond the dock looked weathered with age. Inside was a table holding loaves of bread in clear plastic bags.

On the far end of the wall hung a wooden crucifix, with a life-size statue of Mary below it. A small altar and kneeling bench sat in front of the statue with a bank of candles off to the side. A nun was kneeling in prayer, rosary in hand. At the sound of footsteps, she stood with some difficulty.

"I was praying someone would come to eat our bread. The loaves turned out so beautifully this morning. I would feel terrible if only the birds were to taste them."

The nun looked to be in her midsixties, standing no more than five feet tall. Her cheeks were so round, her eyes disappeared into tiny crescent moons.

"The bread is always perfect," Sam commented from behind her as he entered.

"Dear Samuel." The nun cupped her hands over his and closed her eyes. She bowed her head and said a prayer over him, ending with a hearty "Amen!"

He bent down and hugged her, whispering, "It's good to see you."

The nun's smile was bright, her plump cheeks wide. She turned to Cora. "Did you come for bread or a blessing? Both will fill you."

Cora's voice came out uncertain. "Um, both, please?"

"Then your cup shall overflow!" She took Cora's hands, bowed her head, and said a heartfelt blessing. After she was done, she squeezed Cora's hands gently, and unexpected tears glistened in Cora's eyes.

The nun invited them to choose from the loaves. Cora chose two loaves and put a ten-dollar bill in the donation basket at the end of the table. Sam did the same but set down a white envelope, which she guessed contained a lot more money.

On the boat ride back, Cora stared at the mission until it was out of sight. "Thank you for taking me there. It's wonderful." She hadn't expected the catch in her voice.

When they arrived at the lodge, a basket brimming with tomatoes sat on the porch.

She looked at Sam, confused. "Who could these be from?"

"My guess is Joseph, your neighbor. Only he could grow tomatoes that big this early in the season."

She studied the offering. "I should say thank you."

"Come on. I'll introduce you."

Cora set one loaf by the basket, then followed Sam next door to a modest burgundy cabin. Massive trees and brush isolated the lodge from the neighbor on the opposite side, but only a sprawling lawn separated it from Joseph's home. When they arrived, they spotted him kneeling at work in his garden, which ran the length of his cabin.

As they approached, Sam yelled, "Joseph, there's someone I want you to meet."

The man stood up, and Cora recognized him. He had been in the crowd at the funeral. He wore an old T-shirt and frayed jeans and appeared to be in his forties. As he came to greet them, she noticed his sandals. *Odd choice for garden work*, she thought.

"Cora, this is Joseph Manz. Joseph, this is Cora Matthews, your new neighbor."

Joseph wiped his hands on his pants and extended a hand. He had thick brown hair in need of a cut. His face was tan, his beard trimmed, and the skin around his eyes gently creased. He was attractive, but his kind eyes were definitely his distinctive feature. The same eyes and stare as a rescue animal—a bit hesitant and apologetic, with perhaps a hint of sadness.

She smiled as she shook his hand. "Thank you for the tomatoes. They look delicious."

He gave a nod.

*Is he shy or just reserved?* When he said nothing else, she spoke again. "Thank you for the warm welcome. We went to the mission this morning to buy bread. Please take this loaf as my thanks."

He took the loaf. "Thank you."

As they walked away, Sam glanced at her. "What do you think of your neighbor?"

"He sure isn't a talker."

"Joseph's a quiet man, but you won't find a better listener or neighbor."

She shrugged. "He kind of looks like those old storybook pictures of Jesus I had as a kid. You know, with the longish dark hair and beard. He even wears the sandals."

Sam burst out laughing. "I guess there's a resemblance."

"There's also a gentleness to his disposition that I've always read about and imagined Jesus having."

Sam shook his head. "Your perception about people is really something."

When they reached the lodge, Sam mentioned having to get home to do some errands. He waved goodbye, then headed back to load his boat onto the launch, leaving Cora to enjoy the rest of her quiet morning.

Later, Cora explored the lodge, opening all the squealing screen doors and turning the knobs that wobbled on the scratched wooden doors. The air was stale and thick with dust. Curiosity turned to sadness as she examined the neglected rooms. Daylight gave a crueler testimony to the deterioration of the old building. The bed frames were rusted, the mattresses old and stained, the furniture run-down and smelling of mildew, and the walls dirty. All sixteen rooms proved the same, with the exception of copious mouse droppings in three of them.

Since life revolved around eating and sleeping, she began cleaning the kitchen and her bedroom. At the end of the day, exhausted and overwhelmed, she walked to the edge of the dock to dangle her feet in the water.

"Care for some company?"

She turned and saw Sam had returned.

"Sure."

He sat. "You look discouraged."

She slumped down, shaking her head. "Discouraged doesn't even begin to cover it. This"—she waved one hand motioning to the entire lodge—"is . . . a lot."

"I know the place is not in the best condition."

She scoffed. "Sam, it's in *horrible* condition. It needs major renovations. My mother left me some money, but it's not enough for even all the basic repairs needed. This place is a relic. It's in rough shape, and I don't know how I would pay to fix it up properly. To say that it's overwhelming is an understatement. The commitment needed is paralyzing to me. A full year! I've never lived in one place for that long since I was a child. How am I supposed to own a lodge when I haven't even owned a dog? Honestly, after going through all the rooms and seeing what needs to be done, I think raising a litter of puppies would be less work."

Sam nodded. "It needs hard work and someone with a dedicated heart to do it."

"A miracle would be more accurate."

Sam took in her words with a soft *hmm* as he looked out across the lake. A minute passed before he spoke again. "That's not too much to ask, you know. Miracles happen all the time. Maybe this lodge has been sitting here waiting for you."

Cora chewed her bottom lip, considering Sam's words. She didn't believe in miracles, and if her past was any indicator, this adventure wasn't going to turn out well. She wasn't handy and knew nothing about home improvement. She'd worked her last job as a copy-editor at a magazine. Her boss had left the option to come back whenever she was ready after she shared her mother's death, but Cora knew it probably wouldn't happen. She'd already applied for an editing position at a book publishing house as she was breaking her engagement, working toward a total separation from her old world. To her surprise, the job was offered to her. But the window for her to accept it would close quickly. All she had to do was say yes and walk away from what had just been dumped in her lap.

They sat in silence and watched the last of the sun's golden flames dissolve into a violet sky. The day was done, but her work was just beginning.

# *Three*

The next morning, Cora smiled as she caught a whiff of brewed coffee while entering the kitchen. For a moment, she wished there were people in the dining room to serve it to. Next to the half-empty coffeepot was a note.

> *Out of town for a couple days. Sending you a gem in a rock tomorrow. You'll understand when you meet her.*
>
> > *Will come by this weekend,*
> > *Sam*
>
> *P.S. Enjoy a cup of coffee!*

Disappointed she'd missed him, she turned off the coffeepot. A quick scan of the pantry shelves revealed only a box of oatmeal. Hungry enough to actually consider cooking it, she peeked inside and then put it down. The last bit of bread from the convent, Joseph's tomatoes, and the few staples she brought would have to do until she got to the store.

Opening the back door, she welcomed in the cool morning air. The silence inside was haunting, so the bird chatter made her feel less alone.

Maybe a morning walk would take her mind off the isolation she was feeling. It worked. A few steps out, and she was completely lost in the arresting beauty that lay on the other side of the door. The towering, magnificent oak trees that sheltered the lodge and offered shade had to be nearly a hundred years old. The verdant shrubs and smaller trees hemming the property gave a feeling of wild structure and privacy. She still couldn't believe this was all hers.

Feeling emboldened, she ventured over to her neighbor's property, which was located directly across the road. She remembered the "rock house," aptly named for the hundreds of rocks cemented to the outside walls. Though small, it gave the impression of being a kind of fortress, one that had withstood time and weathered many storms. It lay tucked within thick pines facing a tiny lake.

What made this house special was the small cemetery surrounding it. It had begun as a family cemetery and grew as the town developed. Now, a century later, a number of the town's long-ago deceased were buried in the back of the enchanting property. The rare visitor would park on the roadside.

Sam had told Cora that no new residents had come to occupy a plot in the old cemetery in decades. People were buried in the more conveniently located cemetery in town—Cora's mother included. This one was all but forgotten.

When she was a young girl, her grandfather had told her the woman who lived in the rock house had been caretaker of the cemetery for as long as anyone could remember. Some estimated she had lived there over fifty years. As a child, Cora had hidden behind bushes at the entrance to the property, watching as the woman hunched over the graves, looking like the witch from *Snow White*. Cora vividly remembered the tremble of excitement and terror as she crept closer to get a glimpse. The old woman would sit at the graves for hours. Children murmured that she was listening to the whispers of the dead.

Now, two decades later, Cora wanted to see what she had once considered terrifying. She marveled at the change in the air, from warm and dry to cool and moist. She glanced up at the canopy of trees overhead. They'd grown into giants, a network of interlocking branches, leaves competing for rays of light. A few pockets of sun broke through, like portals to another world. The grass had grown into a meadow. It was tall and soft, bending like feathers on the ground.

She was surprised to see the lush wisps had been cleared from each engraved headstone. Someone still cared for these otherwise-forgotten souls, fighting back the brush that threatened to cover up the last markings of a person's existence.

There were a few crosses, a statue of a church steeple, three Mary figures, and a sprinkling of stone angels "flying" in all directions. Their details were sanded down by age.

However, the writing and pictures carved on the first row of stones were remarkably clear. Each marker had different drawings. A portrait of a man in military uniform caught Cora's attention. She bent down to trace the intricate etching with her fingers.

"Can I help you find someone, dear?"

She gasped and tipped backward. The old witch stood there with her long, snowy-white hair.

The woman studied Cora. "I'm sorry. I didn't mean to sneak up on you. I'm Kitty, and I've been the caretaker of this cemetery for most my life, so I know everyone." Taking a few bobby pins from her apron pocket, Kitty pulled her hair back into a bun. Her cotton blouse was tucked into a long jean skirt that reached her ankles. Dirty red sneakers peeked out from beneath the hem. "I love to feel the fingers of wind in my hair. The older I get, the lazier I seem to be with putting my hair up properly." Kitty put her hands on her hips. "Is someone you knew buried here? I've tried to keep the identifications clear."

Though still stunned, Cora went to answer, but the woman shifted her attention.

"Oh, now, would you look at that." The woman clicked her tongue at one of the gravestones. "The letter *E* is packed with dirt. It must

be from all that rain we had last week. As soon as I think I'm caught
up, the weather creates more work for me."

Kitty knelt. Taking a small pick from her pocket, she began
scraping dirt from the letter. Flashes of the "witch" in this position came back to Cora, and her eyes widened. All those years
ago, watching her slouched over the burial plots, she had been
preserving the engravings.

Kitty's arms were as speckled as a jaguar with brown liver spots,
and her face and neck were heavily freckled too. She may have
been a little over five feet in her youth, but with the small hunch
in her back, she now appeared tiny. Her knuckles were swollen
with arthritis and her fingernails caked with soil.

"This is Thomas," she told Cora. "He died in the war. I thought
a picture of him in his uniform would be appropriate. He always
did look best in a suit—it hid his stooped shoulders. There was a
little pit in his face, which I made into a mustache." She tapped
the pick against the drawing. "He never had one before, but I think
he looks rather handsome with it. Between the uniform and the
mustache, he appears rather powerful, don't you think?"

Kitty didn't wait for an answer. She chattered on about the
others who lay next to Thomas. She spoke with such familiarity
about each individual, one would guess she was related to everyone
buried there.

"Candice, the one on the left, was Thomas's lover. She was the
bakery girl at the Piggly Wiggly and also worked checkout at the
hardware store on Saturdays. She was known for wearing tight-
fitting clothes, which is probably how she caught Thomas's eye in
the first place. Anyway, his wife is lying to his right. She was a bit
of a stiff, but a vow *is* a vow. Can you imagine lying to rest between
your mistress and your wife?"

Cora stammered. "Um . . . no, I can't. I, uh, suppose it would be
uncomfortable. Did you do all these etchings?"

"Well . . ." Kitty pursed her lips. "They started to need a little
help after a while. Nobody ever comes to visit, so I'm the closest

thing to family these people have. You see, it started when there was a crack coming from Ethel—the marker with the charcoal stone on the far right over there. The crack was extending upwards off the *L*, so I made it into a dove.

"My best work is the portrait of Beatrice. That's the marker by the replica of the church steeple." She scooted over to it. "I have her looking toward the lake, where her husband's ashes were scattered. They loved each other but got along best when they were apart."

Cora studied the marker with deeper interest now that she knew about the person below it.

"And Bea over there loved to garden, so I carved flowers on the top and tomato plants on the sides as an embellishment." Kitty traced the details on the stone before her. "That took me over three years to do, but it was worth it. She took tremendous pride in her tomato plants. She always said if heaven didn't have any, she was coming back." She chuckled and then glanced at Cora. "I'm sorry, who did you say you came to see?"

"Um, no one. I moved in across the road and came to visit. Is that okay?"

Kitty brightened. "Of course! I always enjoy company, as do they." She nodded toward the stones. "Would you like to come in for a cup of broth? I've always found broth more comforting and healing than tea. I have some simmering on the stove. I made it this morning with lots of greens.

"You'll have to help me up though. My knees don't have the same bounce they used to. I'm ready to trade them in for a new pair." She laughed.

Cora was thrilled at the possibility of seeing the inside of the famous rock house. "That's kind of you." She helped the woman to her feet.

As they crossed the yard, a breeze seemed to sweep them along, tangling Cora's hair and ruffling their clothes. The closer they got to the house, the stronger the wind blustered around them. It explained Kitty's wild appearance all those years ago. By the time

Cora and Kitty reached the stairs, Cora's hair was as untamed as Kitty's had been before she put it up. She grinned. Maybe, if children were watching, she'd be mistaken for a witch herself.

She ran her fingers through the knotted tangles. "I can't believe the wind here. Where does it come from?"

"It's the spirits. They're as excited as I am to get a visitor."

Cora stared at Kitty. *Is she serious?*

The stairs were made of cemented stones just like the rest of the house. Kitty opened the door, and an aromatic warmth embraced Cora as she stepped inside. It was only a couple steps from the door to the center of the kitchen.

On the stove, a pot of bubbling liquid and the pile of spices beside it were the only clues that this was a kitchen and not a greenhouse. Plants filled every nook. Leaves draped across the countertops and windowsills, along the floor, and on top of the appliances, including the stove. Plants hung from ceiling hooks or were jammed on shelves. Cora counted three cupboards with vines crawling out of them, and there were herbs growing in the kitchen sink. A small table with chrome legs and four yellow-vinyl chairs tucked under it was pushed against the wall. Cora squinted her eyes and noted footprints outlined in dirt on the worn, checkered linoleum.

"Sit down, dear. Make yourself comfortable." Kitty cleared a few plants from the table to make space, then replaced them with mugs. She carried planters into the next room with sprawling greenery dragging along the floor.

Something caught Cora's eye under the remaining two plants on the table. She looked closer.

Troll-like statues, about three inches tall, hid under leaves and peeked out from behind the plants. They had warty faces, long noses, and wild hair that stuck straight out. Some wore tiny stocking caps. They were sleeping, laughing, hiding, or holding tiny watering cans.

"These are . . . cute." Cora cringed at her weak compliment.

"They're gnomes. The kind you find in Scandinavian folktales.

These little guys are of Nordic descent, like me. I figure the older I get, the more I look like them." Kitty giggled. "I love them. It's like having a house full of kids. The folklore behind them is that they hoard treasures. With the number I have, I must be the richest woman in the world!" She laughed so hard she had to wipe her eyes with a red bandanna she took from her pocket.

Cora smiled politely.

Kitty placed a plate of cookies on the table. "I baked these carrot cookies yesterday. They are yummiest when you eat them straight out of the oven. I fill them with carrots, nuts, oats, raisins, and any other extras I have around the house."

"They look delicious." Cora picked one up to take a bite. It had to weigh close to a pound. The texture was rough and tasted like muesli. Not wanting to insult her host, she swallowed.

After pouring steaming broth into their mugs, Kitty settled into her chair. "It's always relaxing to take a break with a cup of broth. I'm sorry, sweetie, what did you say your name was again?"

"Cora Matthews."

"Are you related to the Matthews family who used to own the lodge across the street?"

"Yes, I'm their granddaughter."

"You're Lydia's girl?"

Cora's jaw tightened, and she gave a stiff nod.

"That's an awfully big property. Do you have a lot of children?"

"No. I'm alone." The words came out sounding hollow.

"You know, we're never truly alone." Kitty winked.

Cora shifted in her seat. "I'm going to restore the lodge." She said it so naturally, it surprised even her.

"Well, I'm tickled pink for you. And I'm overjoyed we're neighbors. That place needs some life put back into it. I'm sure you're the woman to do it. If you ever need anything, please feel free to stop by. I'm always here, except on Thursdays when I have tea with some ladies down the road."

Kitty pushed herself up with a grunt, then crossed to the bubbling pot to stir its contents. She tried a sip, then added a couple leaves from a plant hanging overhead.

Cora figured she had to try the concoction at some point. She tipped her mug back and warmth spread through her chest. "This is so tasty. What's in it?"

"A little of this and a little of that," Kitty said, giving a sly smile.

"It's delicious. Thank you for sharing it with me."

"My pleasure. Meeting you was my blessing for the day. I'll put it in my jar."

"Your jar?"

"My blessings jar. It began with an old mason jar from my days of pickling cucumbers, but as the Good Book says, 'my cup runs over,' so I switched to a clay pot that was intended to be an urn before the family of the deceased changed their minds."

"That's the second time in two days I've heard someone say something about their cup running over."

Kitty raised an eyebrow. "There's no such thing as coincidence."

Cora took another sip.

"I always write down my blessings and put them into the jar," Kitty told her. "Whenever I feel blue, I look through them to feel happy again. There's nothing like a dose of gratitude to put things back into perspective."

Cora smiled. "That's a nice idea."

Kitty stared at her. "You make such lovely company." She clapped her hands together. "Say, why don't you join me next Thursday? The ladies would love to meet you, especially before all the rumors start flying about the young woman living in that lodge all alone. We're not all as spry as you, but we have a little sass left in us."

Cora laughed. "Thank you. It's very kind of you to include me, but . . ." She hesitated, unsure how to navigate around the invite without disappointing the sweet woman. "I think I'll wait a little bit until I'm more settled." There was no way she was going to be honest and reveal the hesitancy she felt in establishing any relationships in Moonberry when things still felt so unsure. She brightened her smile. "But you can let it be known that I'm not totally alone. I have Sam Klevar if I need anything. Do you know him?"

Kitty nodded. "I've known Samuel his whole life. You'll find most of the people of Moonberry Lake consider each other family and look out for one another." Kitty patted Cora's hand. "Now that I know you have Sam helping with the lodge, I won't worry. That man is as steady as an oak."

"Speaking of the lodge," Cora said, "I should probably get back soon."

"It's been wonderful meeting you. I hope you'll visit me again."

"Oh, I'll find some excuse to come bother you."

"It would never be a bother." Kitty took a plant from the table and handed it to Cora. "Here—take this with you. Consider it a welcome home present."

*Home.*

The word stood out like the ringing of a single bell.

"You're going to love it here." Kitty winked, her eyes twinkling again.

Cora responded with a small smile. "Thank you for the plant and the snack."

As she walked back across the cemetery, the carvings on the markers seemed to come alive. The detail was extraordinary. Did anyone know what Kitty had been doing to the stones all these years? Or, for that matter, did Kitty know *she'd* been the one creating treasure, and not her gnomes?

Cora's thoughts drifted from treasures etched in stone to secrets buried in graves. If only she could uncover the truth of what had happened here with her family. Her only hope was that in restoring the lodge, something would be revealed. There had to be hints hidden within the vast space. She just wished she knew what to look for.

Distracted by her own thoughts, she didn't notice a man standing in her driveway until she looked up and was only a few feet from him. Her breath caught in surprise. "Oh!"

The older man with a prominent frown beneath his bushy white beard glared at her with squinty eyes. "This is my land, missy," he said, pointing a long finger that was curved like a talon at her. He stood tall but bent slightly, like a shepherd's crook. His hair looked like it had been pressed down, but tufts of it stood up defiantly.

Cora blinked. "W-what?"

"This is mine." He pointed to the ground.

She shook her head as if it would make the conversation less fuzzy. "I-I'm sorry, I don't understand. Who are you?"

"The land you're standing on right now is mine. So, that makes that lodge you're living in rightfully mine also . . . at least the west corner of it."

"I don't know what you're talking about. This property has been in my family for decades. I inherited this lodge."

"I've got a stake in this land, and I want you off it." The man's eyes narrowed, and his voice lowered to a menacing tone. "It was almost a done deal before you came. Leave this run-down lodge and don't return."

His threat set off something inside her. The hairs on the back of her neck rose, and her hands balled into fists. Though her breaths were shallow, she forced her voice to sound resolute. "Look, I don't know who you are, and I have no idea what you're talking about, but I want you to leave now or I'm calling the police."

He smirked. "I live right over there." He pointed in the direction of a thicket of trees. Her neighbor's house was so engulfed in full-grown pines and maples, it was hard to see. The man's property was directly across from Kitty's. "I own land that extends all the way to your front door, so *you* are the one technically trespassing, and I don't want *you* here."

Surprised not by the panic but the fury she felt growing inside her, Cora's face hardened, and she met his glare. "Get off my drive-way. If there's a problem, have your lawyers contact me."

The man's glower deepened, making his underbite pronounced and his nose scrunch up like a pug. "Your grandfather was just as thickheaded. This isn't over."

Cora watched him walk away. She didn't turn and go into the lodge until he was at the road. Her legs felt weak and wobbly. She nearly dropped the plant but managed to place it on a table in the foyer before going straight to the couch in the family room and collapsing onto it.

*Who was that guy and what was he talking about? What kind of jerk introduces himself like that?* Then it occurred to her that Sam would know. Grabbing her cell phone, she called him—or at least tried. Then she remembered—no satellite, no cell service. She groaned, vowing that to be the first investment in updating the lodge. She'd get someone out here this week.

She grabbed her keys and took off toward town in the Jeep, driving until she found reception. Pulling over to the side of the road, she called again, and this time, Sam picked up. She explained the encounter in one long breath.

Sam sighed. "Rolf Johansson." He said the name like he'd just eaten something rotten.

"What's his problem?"

"Rather than a rock in your shoe, he's more like a burr in your backside. Both cheeks."

"Is it true what he said?"

"Yes and no. It's complicated."

"That doesn't sound good."

"He's stirring up an old argument because you've come to town. When your grandparents bought the property from the previous owners, Rolf's father claimed there was a mistake with the surveying and that the lines of their property—now his—extended into yours. Rolf apparently adopted the same complaint. This is an old argument that has gone on for over sixty years. The court did settle that the plat map was correct in your grandfather's favor, and the current town map clearly shows the division of the two properties, but it seems Rolf wants to contest the decision. He has old papers he claims are the original surveys that show a different version of the markings."

45

"Wouldn't the town have those?"

"Nope. All burned in a fire decades ago, way before computers. It's his word against theirs. But the good news is that his papers were not authorized correctly, so the authenticity came into question. Rolf is probably feeling out whether or not he can scare you away."

Cora's heart sank. *Why can't things ever be easy?*

"The fact that you're so young and have moved in must've been threatening to him."

"He says he wants me gone."

"Of course he does. He's been trying to buy the lodge for years."

"What do I do?"

"Wait and see if he's full of smoke or is indeed stirring up old dirt. In the meantime, dig in your heels and make the place yours. Ignore him."

She sulked. "I don't like him."

"Nobody does."

"What do I do if he comes back?"

"Remember he's all huff and puff. He can't make you leave."

"He's kind of scary."

"That's exactly what he wants you to think. See him for what he is—an old, cantankerous man who looks like Santa."

"Yeah. An *evil* Santa who looks like he'd rather eat children than hand them presents."

Sam chuckled. "Don't worry about it. I'll see you Friday."

"What if he threatens me again?"

"He's not going to do anything overt to get himself in trouble with the law. He made his complaint known, and his words now have to settle like a bad meal. Again, don't worry."

Sam's assurance did not relieve the knot in her stomach.

# *Four*

Cora was *not* alone.

The lodge was a breeding ground for mice, something she found increasing evidence of as she cleaned. The next morning, she decided to begin in the large pantry that was stacked with dishes and heaps of pots and pans featuring a discouraging amount of mouse droppings. Everything needed to be washed—by hand, since the dishwasher was broken.

As she began, a thunderous knock made her jump and almost drop a soapy plate. It came from the back door of the kitchen. Not an entrance a visitor would use.

Wiping her hands on her pants, she opened the door and found a rugged-looking woman glaring at her, a toolbox in each hand. The stranger was dressed in denim overalls—her long underwear peeking out from the shirt neck and sleeves. A ring of keys the size of a grapefruit dangled from her waist. Whatever hair she had was mostly hidden beneath a tattered and filthy baseball cap. Where some people had laugh lines, this woman seemed to have scowl marks etched into her scrubbed, ruddy-skinned face that wore a stern expression. Her steel-toed boots, caked in dried mud, had left a mark on the door where she'd kicked it.

Cora raised her eyebrows at the stranger. "Can I help you?"

"Name's Widgy." She dropped a toolbox to pull a business card from the back pocket of her overalls.

Beneath dirty fingerprints, Cora read:

### WIDGY'S REPAIR SERVICE
### "GOOD WITH WIDGETS"

She turned the card over. Nothing. That was it.

Cora's eyebrows knitted together. "There's no phone number or address on your card."

Widgy scoffed. "I don't like people callin' me or knowin' my whereabouts. If ya need somethin', I'll know. News travels faster than the downward stench of dead skunk in this town. And I hear ya need a lotta fixin'."

"Who told you that?"

"Sam gave me a call yesterday."

Cora remembered the note. *A gem in a rock.* She eyed Widgy. "How did *he* know your number?"

The woman's eyes narrowed. "He's one of the few who have it. We've been friends for years, so I trust him. In thirty more years, you can ask for it too."

With that, Widgy pushed her way through the door, storming past with pounding footsteps, and threw the heavy toolboxes onto the small, now wobbly kitchen table.

"Sam called 'cause he has some sorta soft spot for ya and knows I'm the best repairman in these parts. If you got a problem with my age, you can get one of those young kids that don't know nothin' and they'll end up doin' more harm than good. You can dig your own hole and jump in. It's up to you."

"What's your specialty?" Cora ventured.

"What's broken is my specialty. If it worked once, I can get it to work again. Don't matter what it is." She pulled a pocketknife from her overalls and started cleaning her fingernails with the blade.

Cora did her best to feign enthusiasm. "Then you're the repair-person for me!"

Widgy put away the knife and picked up the toolboxes with a grunt.

"It's nice of you to come by, but I don't fully know what needs repairing yet."

Widgy let out a snort and shook her head, appearing amused by Cora's reply. "Here's how it works. You don't tell *me*—I tell *you*. It ain't gonna be hard. This place is as worn as my underwear." She plowed across the room to the swinging door and through the dining room to the long hallway.

"Might as well get the worst done first and start with the plumbin'. It's as old as Roosevelt." Still muttering, she disappeared into the bathroom.

Cora trailed behind her. "Would you like me to show you around?"

Widgy laughed. "I've been doin' jobs around this place since before you were born. I should be the one givin' you the *real* tour. You'd be shocked at the places I've been and what I've seen. This place is on its last legs. It's either fix it or burn it. You're gonna be seein' a lot of me." She spun to face Cora. "But before I start, I should ask if you've got the money to resurrect this place. I take cash or check. Period. No credit cards—too much of a hassle, and I don't believe in 'em. People should live within their means. With a personal check, I'll cash it the same day. If it bounces, I'll come lookin' for ya."

How could Cora answer when she had no idea what such a venture would cost? She thought of the money she got from her mother's estate and wasn't sure it was going to be enough, but she was determined not to allow this intimidating woman to see her uncertainty. She'd get the money somehow. Maybe she'd reach out to the publisher about doing some remote work. Cora squared her shoulders and jutted her chin. "I've got it."

Widgy gave a half smile. "I haven't even given you a price yet." Her smirk made her look like she was in pain. "Don't worry. I'll let you know the cost as I go along. You'll get your money's worth out of me. Sam wants me to look after ya. I guess he's tryin' to find a mother bird for ya. 'Fraid you're gonna fly away. You've taken on a lot with this ol' lodge."

Widgy lumbered to the floor and started spreading tools around the toilet. In addition to tools, her boxes contained fishhooks and tackle, three boxes of Lemonheads, and a container of tobacco chew.

"Is there anything else I should know before you get started?" Cora asked.

"I learned everythin' I know from hands-on experience. My great-grandpa, grandpa, and daddy were all repairmen. It's in my blood, so don't question my methods or work. Life has been my teacher, not any school. I start a little after dawn, and I never work past five or on Sundays."

"Is that it?"

"With me, what you see is what you get. If you've got a question, come straight out and ask. I ain't got nothin' to hide. And don't you believe a word those ole biddies down at the VFW say 'bout me. I know what they call me behind my back."

"What's that?" The question popped out before Cora could worry if it was appropriate.

"Marry-Em-and-Bury-Em Widgy."

"Why would they call you that?"

Widgy sighed. "It's not my fault every man I marry dies. I took good care of every one of 'em."

"*Every* one?"

"Yep. All five."

"Five husbands!" Cora's exclamation echoed in the bathroom. "I'm so sorry."

Widgy shrugged. "I knew Arnie had died when he stopped snorin'. That man would make the windows rattle. Clyde lay there like the stiff ole horse he was named after, so it took me a while to notice. I had an inklin' somethin' was wrong when the big oaf didn't wake up to the smell of bacon fryin'. That man was never late to the kitchen table. He could fix a toaster with his eyes closed but acted like a bloomin' idiot if he had to put a piece of bread in it to make his own toast."

She took out another tool and kept working.

"Toasters weren't even Clyde's specialty," she went on as she tinkered. "His callin' was for stuffin' animals. Made 'em look so real, we used 'em to keep guard over the house and scare away the pests from the garden. His deer were so lifelike that some hunters actually took shots at 'em. They kept shootin' till the whole head blew off. I wasn't happy they were shootin' so close to the house. But they learned their lesson as soon as they came up to check out the deer, 'cause I started shootin' at *them*. Haven't had any problems since."

Cora tried to imagine what a disturbing sight a headless deer would be as a lawn ornament.

"Clyde's best work is over at the natural history museum in the city." Widgy waved a wrench in the air, presumably pointing toward the museum miles away. "It's an enormous bear they bring out to give people a scare. There wasn't a creature that man couldn't stuff. At Halloween, he put out all his bats, rats, and any roadkill he'd resurrected to make a spooky scene. He stopped, though, after parents called 'bout their kids havin' nightmares." She shook her head. "It's a shame. He never got the appreciation he deserved. Sometimes, when he didn't have the whole animal, he'd piece 'em together and make a whole new species. I still keep a collection of 'em in the livin' room to remember him by."

Cora felt torn between horror and curiosity at what Widgy's home must look like.

"Now, George taught me everythin' I know 'bout cars. There wasn't anything with wheels that man couldn't make run. The first time I ever saw him, his legs were stickin' out from underneath his Ford like two tree trunks with boots. He never went a day without his steel-toe boots—even wore 'em to our weddin'. I didn't mind, 'cause any man with the sense to take care of his feet was good enough for me."

By this time, Widgy had removed the toilet and was shining a flashlight into the hole beneath.

"May I ask what happened to him?" Cora asked.

"He died the way he would've liked—workin' on his ole Ford. He loved that truck so much I buried him in it."

"You had him buried in a *truck*?"

"Yep. It took a bulldozer a day and a half to dig the hole and then another day to cover it up. People asked me why I did it, and I told 'em he always said, 'Widge, that darn truck's gonna kill me one day.' Turned out he was right. He was workin' on the engine when a pain shot right down his arm, and he collapsed over the carburetor. I couldn't imagine anyone else fixin' it, and *I* didn't know what to do with it, so I figured it oughtta go with him. He taught me a lot. I was indebted to him and wanted to do it right. So, I had him sittin' at the wheel with the windows down like he was goin' for a Sunday drive."

Widgy kept talking while she ran out to her truck to get another tool and Cora tagged along. She wasn't going to miss these wild stories, no matter how silly she looked following the woman like a puppy. Entertainment far outweighed pride.

"What about the others?" Cora asked when they were back in the bathroom.

"Well, Harry had a real gift with toilets and makin' things out of wood. He carved all the animals for our nativity scene. He started with a couple cows, and from that it grew to camels, ducks, sheep, dogs, pigs, bears, and giraffes. I bet I'm the only one in this town who has an aardvark in their manger scene. I bought the Mary, Joseph, and baby Jesus at a garage sale. Joseph's nose is missin', but I think the meanin's still the same."

Cora struggled not to laugh. "It sounds more like the makings of Noah's ark."

Widgy offered a deadpan glare that made Cora gulp. Comments were clearly not welcome.

"As I was sayin', Harry believed women should know how to change out a toilet and fix all the pipin' that goes with it. He always said, 'It's the most important appliance in the house. If it ain't workin', neither is no one else.' The last thing he ever made was a toilet seat out of wood. You'd think it would give splinters, but this one's soft as silk. And it keeps gettin' better with use!"

Cora closed her eyes, trying to unsee the image.

"Harry wanted a person to be comfortable while sittin'. Lord knows we spend half our lives on the toilet. He made one 'specially for me and gave it to me on our anniversary. He said, 'Here's one that should fit your caboose—I made it extra wide.' I thought that was mighty nice of him."

Widgy shook her head at the old toilet she was working on, clearly comparing it to her custom fit at home.

"Now, my other Harry—"

Cora started. "Excuse me—your *other* Harry?"

"Yeah. Harry number two, husband number five. He taught me everythin' 'bout electricity. I'm sure he wired over half the homes in this town. He had a couple bad bouts where he came home with his hair standin' on end. Not that it mattered. That man had hair on every inch of his body and shed worse than a Labrador. I told him, 'Honey, if you fry off a few hairs from those shocks, that's fine by me.' The doctor said all those years of playin' 'round outlets is what caused his irregular heartbeat. No matter what they tried, they couldn't get his ticker to beat a straight tune."

Widgy threw her flashlight back into the toolbox. "This toilet has to go. It's been leakin' for some time. You've got yourself a swamp down there. I'll redo the pipes too."

Before Cora could say anything, Widgy continued, "Fall's 'round the corner. You're gonna need a new furnace to heat this ole barn. The furnace hasn't worked for years. It's more likely to blow up than heat up. We better get that done in the next couple months. This winter's gonna be a doozy. Ya know it's gonna be a bad one by the number of dots on the back of a ladybug. I saw one the other day that was so covered it could've passed for a stink bug if ya didn't look close. That's an omen!"

Cora was still stuck on the furnace. *How much will that cost?* Thank goodness the woman was giving her a heads-up. "Can you install it?"

"Yeah, sure. Arnie taught me all about it. His specialty was heat. He knew all the insides to any furnace, stove, water heater—even those fancy electric fireplaces. He kept this town from freezin' to death in the winter. And no matter what any of those busybodies say, they never did prove he was the cause of all those fires. It didn't stop one of 'em from callin' when it was twenty below. No sirree!"

Cora didn't want to hear about huge expenses right now. The woman's life was far more interesting. "Do you have any children?" she blurted out.

"Two sons—Bob and Jake. Bob is from my marriage to Clyde and works as a park ranger, protectin' the animals instead of stuffin' 'em. He's one of them nature types, always jabberin' about trees and happy to sleep under the stars.

"Jake's from my first Harry and became a plumber like his daddy. I keep tellin' him unpluggin' pipes runs in his blood."

Cora fought to keep her lips straight.

Widgy didn't seem to notice. "They both take after their dads in looks. I would've had more kids, but the whole pregnancy thing wasn't for me. It got in the way of my work. Neither of my boys have gotten themselves a woman yet. I'm afraid I spoiled 'em too much when they were kids. You know what they say. If a man doesn't marry, it's cause he can't find a wife that measures up to his mama. There's no gettin' around that. One of my husbands used to say—though I can't remember which one—that I was a whole lotta woman! I can understand how it would be hard to find a woman with my skills and strengths." She eyed Cora up and down, then shook her head. "Yep."

Cora frowned at the not-so-subtle insult.

Widgy leaned back on her heels. "That's it. There's nothin' more to me. End of story. Anyone that fills your head with somethin' else is a liar."

Not even the most creative fib could compare to this woman's life story.

"Is there anything you want to ask me?" Cora asked.

"I know you came up here alone, Sam's your friend, and you don't know what you're doin'. That's all I need to know. What I want from you is Dr Pepper."

Cora blinked hard. "Dr Pepper? As in the pop?"

"Yep, that's the deal. Part of my compensation is you payin' for my caffeine fix. I drink five a day, so keep 'em stocked in the fridge. And it's got to be *real* Dr Pepper—no cheap substitutes. And never diet. I drink the original."

Cora was dazed by everything the woman had said. Although her brusque manner was a bit off-putting, the abysmal condition of the lodge could use such a force. Things could hardly go downhill from here.

# Five

Things did, indeed, go downhill from there.

The following week, Sam broke the rusted lock on the shed and unearthed an old aluminum fishing boat buried underneath decades of junk. It took the two of them hours to haul out the tools and clutter that had been piled to the ceiling. They dragged the boat to the dock and tied it down. Sam attached the motor. By the time they got it into the water, it was too late to take it out for a ride, and Cora was too tired to care. The boat was nothing fancy, but it floated, which was all that mattered.

However, it was a new day, and she planned to take the boat out for a ride. Peeking out the window while getting dressed, she saw Sam tinkering with the motor. She ran downstairs, stopping to turn on the coffee maker she'd set up before going to bed, and then bolted out the door.

"Good morning! I'm ready for my voyage!"

Sam finished attaching the gas hose before looking at her. "Do you even know how to work this thing?"

"Sure. You turn it on and then watch out for ducks."

He shook his head. After giving some simple instructions, he paused. "I'm not sure about this."

Cora rolled her eyes. "I've got it. Go get some of the coffee I made for you."

His eyes widened. "You made coffee?"

"I might not drink it, but I can make it. It gives the kitchen a homey smell. Now, leave me to explore the open water." She stepped into the boat.

"Aye, aye, Captain, but shouldn't you be wearing a life jacket?"

"The one I found was all ripped apart. I'll buy a new one next time I'm in town. Anyway, I'm not planning on needing it. Don't jinx me."

Sam stared at her. "I don't recall ever seeing you swim as a kid. You do know how to swim, don't you?"

"Of *course* I know how to swim. I simply prefer to do it in clean, clear, chlorinated water."

Sam's face lit up. "Now I remember! You were always too scared to go in the lake. The other kids had you convinced something would bite you." He snickered at the recollection.

She shot him a look.

"Stay along the shore so that if you run into trouble—"

"There won't be any trouble."

"Okay, then." He held up his hands in surrender. "I'll be working inside with Widgy."

"Lucky you."

Sam's grin broadened, making the creases near his eyes deepen. He glanced around and then spoke under his breath as if afraid of eavesdroppers. "I haven't had a chance to ask you how it's been going with her."

"She's gruff," Cora whispered back.

"She's good."

"She nearly breaks down the door at six-thirty every morning and hasn't spoken to me since the first day, but I hear her talking to herself all the time. Correction. It's not so much as talking, as it is a kind of passive-aggressive grumbling. I was also woken up by a phone call from a 'Private Caller' at four o'clock yesterday morning, and it was Widgy calling to let me know she had to drive to the next town over for some supplies." Cora gave Sam a pointed look. "Four o'clock. In the morning."

Sam smiled broadly. "I'm glad to hear your cell service is working. No doubt Widgy had something to do with that."

"Yeah," she mumbled. "When I tried to get someone to come out and set up satellite service, I was given a timeframe of a week. When she called, the guy was here within the hour. Apparently, her intimidation is widespread."

Sam chuckled. "Widgy definitely has a reputation, but she is also focused, talented, hardworking, and fair. There's no one better for this mammoth job. Anybody else would say you need a crew of five and a bank full of money. Trust me on this."

Cora nodded, knowing he was right. The little money she had saved, and that from her mother's estate, would not last forever. She needed to be frugal and focus on the essentials. Right now, that meant fixing the plumbing, updating the electrical, and getting a new furnace.

Sam started the motor, which coughed out a puff of smoke before settling into a steady hum. He stepped back onto the dock and sent her a concerned look. "Be careful."

He gave the boat a push.

"I'll be fine."

Sam shook his head, smiling.

Cora whooped as the boat inched away from the dock. The small five-horse motor made it seem like the boat was just dog-paddling in the vast water, but she didn't care.

After ten peaceful minutes of puttering by neighboring cabins, the motor sputtered to a stop. A tinge of fear prickled her skin. *It's probably nothing,* she told herself. *The motor hasn't been used for a long time. It just needs to be restarted.* She pulled the cord.

Nothing.

She looked for oars. There were none. She groaned. In her haste to set sail, she'd left them leaning against the shed. Taking a breath, she fiddled with the motor.

Nothing.

*No motor. No oars.* Her heart thumped in her chest.

She tried to remember what Sam had said on the dock. Something about swimming to shore. She peered into the water, murky with weeds, and groaned a second time. *No way.* Though she loved looking at the water and hearing it lap against the shore on windy days, she never entered it unless it was clear. Even then, she waded in only a few feet.

Thanks to the wind, small whitecaps were rocking the boat closer to shore. However, it was the wrong part of the shore, the part she hated most—a bog of tall reeds, undoubtedly teeming with unseen life. Using her hands as paddles, she tried to steer the boat in a better direction. It was pointless. The rhythmic sway toward the reeds continued. Her chest tightened.

"Do you need help?" she heard someone shout.

Cora peered toward land and saw a man staring from beneath his baseball cap, fishing pole and tackle box in hand. He appeared to be loading up his boat.

"The motor died," she yelled back.

"You're too far into the bulrushes. Untangle the weeds from the motor."

She leaned toward the motor but saw nothing in the water.

"Tilt it up!" he yelled.

Cora stood cautiously and tugged the motor. It seemed to have grown in both size and weight. Angling it up, she exposed a tangle of weeds around the blades. Forcing her repulsion aside, she pulled at the mass, but it wouldn't budge. Leaning slightly farther, she yanked with all her strength. The knot loosened so suddenly that she flew backwards, clump in hand, and tumbled into the water with a scream.

Everywhere she reached, she couldn't find the surface. The shock disoriented her. Panic robbed her of air and she desperately clawed at the water moving through her fingers.

She thrashed against the cold darkness pulling her under, sure she felt tentacles twisting around her waist.

But they weren't tentacles. They were arms. Arms lifting her from the water.

"Stop panicking. The water's shallow enough for you to stand."

Opening her eyes and gasping, she saw the brim of a baseball cap. The man from the shore made to let go, but she locked her arms around his neck.

"No! Don't let go!" she screeched, tightening her grip. "I don't want to touch the bottom. Something will bite me."

"Nothing's going to bite you." He tried again to set her upright. She gripped harder. "Please just help me get back into the boat."

He huffed but kept his grip tight. "Okay, but you have to help me. We'll do it together."

Cora nodded and relaxed her legs enough for him to swing them over one arm and hoist her up. She fell into the boat with a thud.

Just as she was lifting herself up onto the seat, the man spoke again. "You shouldn't go boating without a life jacket. Especially if you can't swim."

"I can swim," she corrected, wiping wet hair away from her face.

"It didn't look like it by the way you were floundering around. You were somehow staying sideways. That's why I jumped in. I thought you were going to drown."

"Well, I'm sorry you got all wet for nothing, because I *can* swim. I simply choose not to in lakes. Who knows what kinds of creatures lurk down there!"

His eyebrow raised. "There's nothing in this water that would bite you. The worst thing might be some bloodsuckers."

Cora blanched. "That is *not* reassuring," she said, examining her legs for slimy critters.

"Baby leeches are common around here. Since you're wearing shoes and were flailing so fast, I'm pretty sure they didn't have a chance to latch on." He grinned. "If you do happen to find one, you can pick it off. The bigger ones let go with a sprinkle of salt.

"I'll get the rest of the weeds out of your motor." He waded to the back and began ripping them off.

"Thank you," she said, relieved for the help.

He looked up at her, still smiling. It irritated her how he found this amusing, but she decided to keep her mouth shut since he did jump in and come to her rescue.

"You're not from here, are you?" he asked.

Trying to regain composure, Cora sat straighter, extracting a weed stuck to her shirt. Mustering all the dignity she could, she lifted her chin and lied. "As a matter of fact, I am." She bit the inside of her cheek. It wasn't entirely a fib. After all, she did live here now.

"I wouldn't go out in a boat alone without oars . . . and, in your case, a cell phone."

She sighed. Her cell phone was back at the lodge. With the oars. She felt irked that he thought her so incompetent. She got enough of that attitude from Widgy. She certainly didn't need it from a stranger. "I'm fully capable of running this boat. I merely ran into some mechanical difficulties." She saw him shake his head slightly as he removed the last of the weeds.

She continued to ramble on, not sure if she was trying to convince him or herself. "I would've gotten the weeds off the motor just fine if I hadn't fallen in."

The stranger didn't look at her but pressed his lips together as if holding in a comment. "That's all of it," he said. "You should be ready to go. I'll get you free of the bulrushes so they don't catch you again." He pushed until the water was up to his shoulders.

A wave of guilt and gratitude came over her as she watched him. *What would I have done if he hadn't shown up?* His eyelashes were wet and spiky and drew her attention to his beautiful brown eyes. She looked away when he peered up. "I'm sorry about your clothes."

"Aw, that's okay. I'll consider it my morning bath." He winked, and her stomach fluttered. Giving the boat a final push, he let her float out.

Cora sighed in relief. "Thank you again . . . though it wasn't *completely* necessary. I did have the situation under control."

"Yeah, that's what it looked like. Sorry for interfering." The man peered at her with those big brown eyes, and she found it difficult to be annoyed with his sarcasm. He had a kind face. Handsome. Older than her, but she wasn't sure how much.

She pulled the cord. Nothing happened.

"You have to squeeze the rubber ball to force gas into the motor, pull the choke, and then pull the cord."

"I know. I was simply taking my time. You know, enjoying the scenery. I'm in no hurry." Her face flushed.

He lowered his head a bit and rearranged his baseball cap so she couldn't see his expression. Cora sensed he was trying not to laugh. Slowly, she followed his instructions. The motor hummed to life.

"Thanks," she muttered, steering away.

But a few seconds later, the motor rattled to a stop. She closed her eyes and tightened her mouth to a thin line to keep from crying. Or screaming. She wasn't sure which. Apparently, being humiliated while appearing inept was just how it was going to be.

"You didn't push the choke back in. You're flooding the motor. Try again."

Heat rose in her cheeks. Her hands trembled. Taking an unsteady breath, she followed his instructions again, moving methodically. The motor purred again. Not wishing to make any more eye contact, Cora gave a short wave and headed for the lodge.

She returned tired, hungry, wet, and with an ego not wounded but demolished. As she docked the boat, Sam ran out to her.

"What happened?"

"I'm fine," she said, her words clipped. "There was a minor complication with the motor. Don't ask how I got wet." She marched past him into the lodge without further explanation, puddles forming with each step. She was grateful that Sam let her go without further questions.

She stomped into the kitchen. Food would soothe her bruised pride. She opened the fridge door and her shoulders sank.

Empty.

Driving to the grocery store improved Cora's mood. It always felt special to go into town. As she approached Main Street, she took her foot off the pedal and coasted to a pace that matched the speed of Moonberry Lake life.

The homeyness of downtown made her smile and worked to calm her after her frustrating morning. She passed the Warm & Wooly clothing store, Shoelace Café, Perfectly Pie Bakery & Bookstore, and Delphinium's Flora Emporium. Farther down the street, the sign outside the pharmacy read that they also carried birdseed and lawn furniture. Across from Mo's Pizza, there was an art deco movie theater, which advertised a movie that had come out two years ago. The cozy and nostalgic feeling of Main Street warmed her heart.

Lupine Street, which intersected Main, had more parking, so it contained the larger stores like JD Hardware, Fine Antiques, Heirlooms & Collectibles, and a furniture store showcasing Amish craftsmanship. There were no big malls. No super-plus conglomerates.

The grocery store stood at the very end of Lupine as an afterthought, not matching the uniformity of the others because of the large parking lot.

She made a mental note to pick up more Dr Pepper for Widgy. Good grief did that woman drink a lot of pop!

Relieved that the store wasn't crowded, Cora walked up to the deli. A petite woman sat on a little stool behind the counter, reading a magazine. Hot-pink reading glasses perched at the end of her nose, a stark contrast to her raven-black hair that was drawn into a bun and covered by a hairnet. Engrossed in what she was reading, she didn't seem to notice Cora's approach.

"Excuse me."

The woman jumped up from the stool. "Oh, I'm sorry!" Tucking the book into her apron pocket, she pushed up her glasses that nearly swallowed her small face. "I get so wrapped up in these *Reader's Digest* stories, I forget what's going on around me. I'm *enthralled* with them. The one I'm reading now is a real cliffhanger.

We're not supposed to read on the job, but it was so quiet, and I couldn't wait until tonight to find out if this cute couple makes it out of the storm at sea. Have you read this one?" she asked, pulling the magazine back out and showing the worn cover.

"No, I can't say I have. I don't typically read those."

"Oh, you should! They're wonderful stories. I've been a faithful subscriber for years. I never throw them away. My mother didn't either, so I have all of hers as well. As a matter of fact, this one is from 1984. I hold on to them and keep rereading. If I go back twenty years, I don't remember the story at all, so it's like receiving a new magazine."

"You certainly get your money's worth out of them."

The woman laughed. "I suppose I do. What can I get for you, honey?" She slipped on a new pair of plastic gloves.

"I'd like the biggest turkey sandwich you make and a medium container of potato salad."

"Hungry?"

"Famished."

"I'll give you the works. That includes everything you can stick in a sandwich, plus a few surprises. You'll think you've died and gone to heaven! Plus, it's big enough that you'll have some left over for dinner."

"That sounds great."

The deli woman began working. "Are you vacationing here for the summer?"

"No, I recently moved here."

"That's wonderful! Have you decided what church you'll be attending?"

"Um . . . no, not yet," Cora stammered, struck by the pivot in the conversation.

"The Lutheran pastor will have you there for a solid hour and a half. And at Christmastime they have a lutefisk fundraiser dinner. It draws in all the Scandinavians from the nearby towns. The church paid off its roof with those dinners."

She continued to build the turkey sandwich, piling on thin slices of meat and adding squares of cheese, all neatly lined across the bread. "The Catholics get down to business rather quickly. You're in and out, and there's always plenty of comfort food at their social gatherings. They love their evening Bible studies. Or is it bingo?" She thought about that for a moment before she shrugged.

"Now, nobody can beat the Presbyterian youth program. Last spring, they took a busload of kids to a convention in the Twin Cities. They spent some time at that megamall in between worship services and came back as happy as can be." She looked up from wrapping the sandwich. "Do you have any children?"

"No."

"Married?"

"No."

"Too bad. You're such a pretty thing. Let's hope the wagon hasn't passed you by. There's still time. I'll keep my eyes open for you and include you in my prayers."

Cora forced a weak "thanks" through her teeth.

"Here's your sandwich, sweetie," she said, placing the sub on the counter with a container of potato salad. The sandwich, wrapped in cellophane, looked so thick, it actually resembled a log.

The sight made Cora's mouth water. "Wow! It's enormous. Thank you."

"You're welcome, honey. You know, I hear the Methodists have started a singles group to drum up business. You could try them."

Cora formed a small smile, nodding politely as she walked away.

"You might also try going out on the lakes," the woman hollered after her. "Fishing is a great way to meet men!"

Cora winced.

Twenty minutes later, her cart was full of food and four cases of Dr Pepper. She pulled into the first checkout lane. While unloading the cart, she noticed the clerk was not only scanning the food but studying it as well.

"I see you're kind of a dairy girl with all this yogurt and cheese," she said to Cora. "You might think about buying some prunes to help move things along, if you know what I mean."

Cora stood there in disbelief, feeling grateful nobody was behind her in line. She unloaded the items faster onto the conveyor belt.

The checker went on, undeterred. "I have a delicate stomach, so I don't eat much dairy. I get my calcium from spinach, broccoli, and multivitamins. If I have a piece of cheese, it's a thin slice, and I put it on a whole-wheat cracker."

Cora focused on the gossip magazines, hoping to appear so engrossed that the woman would get the hint. It didn't work.

"What you should buy is extra-virgin olive oil. It's the only thing I cook with, and it will keep the wheels greased. I know because I read all those health magazines. I don't waste my time on that trash about celebrities and aliens."

Finally, the last item had been scanned.

"Do you have any coupons?"

"No." Cora immediately sensed it was the wrong answer.

It was.

The expression on the woman's face showed instant disappointment. "You should have coupons. You need to start saving money *now* for retirement. You'll be knockin' on your kids' door for a bed in the laundry room if you're not careful."

"I'll keep that in mind." Cora swiped her credit card, then moved to the end of the counter, where she helped bag as quickly as possible.

As she was leaving the store, the woman called after her, "Don't forget your coupons next time!"

She loaded the bags into her Jeep as fast as she could for fear of who else she might meet. Back at the lodge, she told Sam her experience as she unpacked the groceries. After he stopped laughing, he invited her to sit down at the table with him. She pulled out the sandwich and set the log between them, which set him to laughing again.

"Now, listen," he said, cutting the sandwich in thirds and picking up a hunk and peeling back the wrapper, "if you're going to live here, you have to understand the way of things in this town. The pace of life up here hasn't changed in fifty years, while the outside world spins like a top. There are two truths here that will always remain the same. One, your business *is* everyone else's business, and two, everyone is *always* interested in that business."

He took a huge bite of the sandwich before he continued. "So, instead of looking at it all from the outside, try engaging with folks and become a part of it. You'll be happier if you see them as friendly and welcoming rather than crazy. Give them a chance. Trust me." He winked, then got up to leave, sandwich in hand. "I've got to get back to work, and so do you. But first, why don't you bring Widgy a Dr Pepper." Cora opened her mouth to say something, but before she had a chance to respond, he added, "Give her a chance."

Sitting back with her arms crossed, she knew he was right. This was a different world, and she needed to adapt. Placing a chunk of the colossal sandwich on a plate and grabbing a Dr Pepper, she went to take on her greatest challenge. Perhaps food and caffeine would get the repairwoman to like her.

# Six

Cora sank deeper into the blankets, yearning to remain in morning slumber. However, any chance of going back to sleep was lost at the sudden awareness of her sore arms and back. Her body had not yet become accustomed to the hard physical work the lodge demanded. In the past month, which had flown by yet still left her feeling untethered, she had never worked so hard in her life for so little outcome.

A thorough scrubbing had removed the surface grime in the kitchen, but it hadn't produced the facelift she'd hoped it would. The linoleum floors were scuffed and discolored. Even after cleaning the stove twice, she still hadn't reached the bottom layer of grease.

Getting up with a grumble and creeping over to the window, Cora couldn't help but smile at the sight of Sam sitting in a lawn chair, looking out over the lake with a cup of coffee in hand. She put on yoga pants and a T-shirt and joined him.

He seemed excited as she sat down. "You're finally up! I've been waiting over an hour."

"It's only six-fifteen."

"I know. Of all days to sleep in!"

"What are you talking about?"

"I've got your miracle!"

"My *miracle*?"

His head bobbed. "You said you needed a miracle, and I got you one. Well, actually, I should say I got you the means to pay for the miracle you asked for. You told me how worried you were about paying for the repairs needed."

She stared at him, confused.

"Well, I found you a job!"

Cora's eyebrows scrunched together. "You found me a job?"

"Yep. As a personal assistant."

She grimaced. "A personal assistant? *That's* my miracle?"

Sam crossed his arms over his chest, shooting her a fatherly glare. "You know, sometimes miracles come in the form of opportunities you have to work for."

Cora rolled her eyes. "I'm listening."

"You'd be more of a helper—someone who runs errands and does light chores. The pay is great, and it's part-time, so you'll have plenty of time to work on the lodge. Plus, it's only ten minutes from here."

She had to admit it sounded tempting. She desperately needed to bring in some income with how much was leaving her savings account. The publisher had revoked their offer so she was desperate for a job. "I do need more money now that I have Widgy."

"Just remember, every miracle is special in its own way. Jonathan Wells is an interesting fellow." He gave her a sidelong glance. "And I *may* have scheduled your interview for this morning."

She gasped. "What? Today?"

He looked a bit sheepish. "I *might* have suggested we'd be there at eight. If, of course, that's okay with you. I guess I got ahead of myself in trying to help. But if it's too much, I can call and cancel."

Cora knew his heart was in the right place. She sighed. "It's fine, let's do it."

An hour and a half later, after a shower, eggs, and toast for her, and more coffee for Sam, they left in his car. The drive was, as he'd said, ten minutes from the lodge. He turned onto a neighborhood street lined with family homes. Tricycles and wagons were scattered across driveways that were decorated with streaks of sidewalk chalk. Children ran between yards under the supervision of a couple mothers talking on the front steps of one house.

"I can't believe how busy it is here." The lodge seemed almost shockingly quiet and isolated compared to this bustling subdivision.

Sam pulled up to a small home. In a harsh juxtaposition to its neighbors, this house had no car in the driveway, the windows were shut with curtains drawn, and the yard was barren of any decorative landscaping.

They parked and walked up the short walkway. As they reached the door, Sam stopped and turned to her. "Jon is . . . well, he's unique, like Widgy but in a different way, and he's harmless." Sam turned back to the door and was about to knock when Cora grabbed his arm and pulled it down.

"Wait a minute. What do you mean, *harmless*? You can describe a person as happy or sad, nice or mean, pleasant or grumpy, but when you say *harmless*, the implication is that he might seem *dangerous*."

"Jonathan is a nice, harmless, brilliant man. He simply doesn't fit the usual mold, that's all."

Cora's eyes narrowed. "How so?"

Sam took a deep breath. "He doesn't leave the house."

"Ever?"

"Ever." Sam shook his head sadly. "He is agoraphobic. He's also bothered by germs, but that's a separate issue."

Before Cora could say another word, Sam knocked on the door.

No response.

He knocked again.

Nothing.

Then, out of the corner of her eye, Cora saw the living room curtain sway ever so slightly.

"It's Sam," he called with his mouth close to the door.

Still no response.

Then she heard the lock on the door click.

This inside arrangement felt too suspicious. "What are you getting me into?" Cora hissed.

"Nothing bad," Sam whispered back as he opened the door and gently ushered her forward.

They stepped into a tiny entryway and then into a dimly lit living room. The blinds were pulled down so that only a few inches of light filtered in.

"Don't step on the carpet with your shoes," a voice warned. "Leave them by the door!"

Cora did as she was told. A lanky man who appeared to be in his late fifties, with pallid skin and hair buzzed short, stood in the next room, which, by design, should have been the dining room but looked nothing like one. Shoulder-high stacks of newspapers and magazines surrounded him. Beyond him was the entrance to the kitchen, where she saw a pyramid of canned fruit on the counter.

"Be sure to use some hand sanitizer!"

An industrial-size gallon jug stood sentry inside the door. Cora pumped some on her palm before entering the room.

"Have you been around any animals? I'm horribly allergic to pet dander." The man spoke in a high tone as if he were preparing to hyperventilate.

She and Sam shook their heads in unison, and the man's agitation seemed to lessen.

Sam spoke first. "Jon, this is Cora, the young woman I was telling you about."

Cora cleared her throat. "Hello."

Jonathan Wells remained expressionless, looking at her through thick, out-of-fashion glasses. The clothes on his lean frame looked equally dated but clean and pressed. He wore a necktie pushed high to the base of his throat, tied in a thick knot resembling a noose, accentuating his skinny neck and drawn face. His trousers weren't unlike the interior style of his home—a relic of years gone by.

"Why don't we all sit down and get acquainted." Sam extended his arm, directing Cora to sit.

Mr. Wells smoothed his necktie repeatedly. "Please don't touch anything. I don't want my periodicals mixed up. I have them categorized in a special order."

Cora tiptoed over to the mustard-yellow sofa, encased in form-fitted plastic cushion covers, and carefully sat down. The matching chair and even the throw pillows sported the same thick plastic coverings. *What would it be like to put your head on that?*

Everything was protected or, more accurately, untouchable.

The coffee table was decorated with two withered plants exuding a feeling of slow death. Mr. Wells fidgeted, then pulled a small notepad and pen from his shirt pocket and began taking notes. He pushed up his glasses and peered at Cora. "I don't tolerate smoking. I am highly sensitive to the scent of tobacco."

"I don't smoke."

"Do you consider yourself responsible?" He didn't wait for her to answer but kept going as he read from his notepad. "I need tasks done neatly, quietly, and with precision. They must be done exactly how I instruct. Will you be able to do that?"

She crossed her arms. "That depends, could you tell me what the job entails? What tasks need to be done perfectly?"

Mr. Wells's frown deepened. "Let's finish the interview first before I disclose the errands and my cleaning methods. Have you ever been arrested or spent time in prison?"

"No."

"Are you on drugs?"

"No." She looked at Sam and mouthed, *Let's go!*

"Now, Jon," Sam argued, "do you think I would bring you someone—"

But Mr. Wells didn't allow him to finish. He launched into an agitated diatribe. "Young people today are lazy and don't want a real job if it means they can't sleep until noon. Looking at the state of affairs in the world, you can pretty much point fingers at the youth, who recklessly spend money because they can't budget or do math and only read the newspaper for the comic strips!" Then he mumbled under his breath, "I just don't understand them at all."

"Mr. Wells"—Cora drew a loud breath—"I don't smoke, drink excessively, or take drugs. I am not lazy or irresponsible and can be trusted to work hard. I'm an early riser and do read the newspaper for information, but I admit I enjoy the *Peanuts* comic strip. I handle my finances responsibly, though, in full disclosure, I did get a C in algebra.

"And, frankly," she continued, "as your assistant, the first thing I'd do is ask if you'd mind me buying you new plants, sewing the missing button back on your shirt, and letting in a little more light to help get rid of the musty smell of all these newspapers. I assure you I mean you no harm. I'm a decent person looking for a part-time job. If nothing else, I hope you can trust Sam's opinion of me until you get to know me better." She stopped, realizing how high and breathless her voice sounded.

Mr. Wells glowered at her.

Nobody uttered a word.

The silence dragged on in agonizing discomfort.

"Whoooweeee, I *like* her!"

The voice came from the kitchen. Cora looked up to see a short, heavyset woman with the most beautiful tan skin and golden eyes come into the room, grinning from ear to ear. "Honey pie, you're hired! You're precious as can be, and I love that you're feisty. Jon, sweetheart, she's perfect for you!" She stretched out her arms and leaned down to wrap Cora in a bear hug. "I won't worry about him, knowing you're here. Sugar, all you need to know how to do is grocery shop and push a rag around, and you'll do fine."

Cora was speechless.

"Nice to see you, Nona." Sam grinned and rose to accept his own bear hug. "Cora, this is Nona. She's been Jon's personal assistant for years, but she's going to stay home to take care of her grand-daughter starting next month."

Joy shone on the woman's face. "You couldn't get me to leave this man for anyone but my grandbaby, and I know that in time you'll feel the same way, Miss Cora. He may come off as a sourpuss, but he's nothin' but butter on the inside." Nona put her hand on Mr. Wells's back. "Isn't that true, sweetie, that you're a softie?"

Cora was awestruck by the entire exchange. Mr. Wells seemingly ignored Nona and studied his notes. Cora did catch him quickly glance down at his shirt where a button was missing. After a minute of silence, he finally spoke up. "You can have the job, but only on a trial basis."

Nona laughed so that her whole chest shook. "He's priceless."

Sam seemed amused as well. Jonathan Wells was not going to be easy. But if someone like Nona got this attached, there must be something more to him than what met the eye.

"I accept," she said, not only surprising herself with the spontaneous response but Nona and Sam as well. Their faces lit up while Mr. Wells simply made notes in his little notebook.

They agreed that she would start the first Monday in August at 8:10 a.m. Not 8:00 or 8:15. 8:10.

As she and Sam walked back to the car, he put his hand on her shoulder. "I'm proud of you. Most would have fled within the first couple minutes."

"Tell me, Sam, how is it that, if miracles come in all different packages, you manage to find me the two most bizarre ones?"

Sam let out a boisterous laugh as they approached the car. Once they were settled and ready to drive away, he glanced over at her. "You know, you'll have a far more interesting and meaningful life if you open yourself up to people you have to work to understand. Take it from me—*normal* is overrated."

# Seven

The next morning Cora was drizzling local honey over a couple pieces of toast when Widgy's thunderous pounding on the door boomed loud enough to scare any creature within half a mile. The dining hall was too big for one person, so it had become Cora's ritual to eat breakfast in the kitchen and read the newspaper while waiting for Widgy. It was the best time of day to get her to talk. Once Widgy started working, she'd be in a foul mood the rest of the day.

"Come on in, Widgy."

The door flew open, and Widgy stormed in with stomping feet and a sneer.

"Good morning." Cora offered a smile.

"Yeah, same to you," grumbled Widgy as she clomped through the kitchen, grasping her toolboxes.

"You know, you don't have to knock," Cora told her. "You've been coming here at exactly the same time every day for a month now. Feel free to walk right in."

Widgy stopped dead in her tracks and let out an exasperated sigh, clearly not in the mood for small talk. She put the toolboxes down with a bang. "I *can't* because you're such a late riser that I never know if I might be catchin' you indecent!"

75

Cora scoffed. "It's six-thirty in the morning, and the only thing you've ever seen me in is a T-shirt and boxer shorts."

"That's what I mean. You're in your underwear!"

"These are my pajamas. Besides, we're both women."

Widgy's nostrils flared like a bull ready to charge. "Now, don't go lookin' at me different. I'm a worker that can do any job equal to a man. You may wear 'em as pajamas, but I wear mine respectfully hidden under my overalls, where God intended 'em to be!"

Cora smiled. "You seem to have more bite than usual this morning. Is anything the matter?"

"The dog was up all night with diarrhea. I think he might've picked up a worm. I tried givin' him some castor oil, but that made it worse and killed the grass. I'm bringin' him to the vet tonight."

"I didn't know you had a dog."

Widgy shrugged. "He was a present from my fifth husband, Harry number two. A ten-pound mutt with a lot of bark. Actually, the dog's similar to Harry. If dinner was ever late, the man started growlin'."

"What kind of dog is he?"

"He's a mix of Maltese, Chihuahua, and pit bull."

Cora's brow wrinkled. "How is that kind of blend possible?"

"You don't want to know."

Cora bit her lip to keep from laughing. "What's his name?"

"Beast."

"Why does that not surprise me? Would you like some coffee?"

"Nah, I make my own. I invented a special brew no one can beat."

"What's in it?"

Widgy went over to the cupboard and got a coffee cup. "I usually don't share, but I'll give you a sample. You've got to try it to understand." She took the thermos dangling on a loop off her tool belt, poured half a cup, and placed it in front of Cora.

*Could this offer be a breakthrough in our relationship?* She saw more of Widgy than anyone else and would feel more settled if they had some sort of friendship. It was lonely living in the lodge and not being around people—except for the repairwoman who wasn't exactly the warm and fuzzy type who enjoyed small talk. Although she enjoyed visiting Kitty, Cora missed aspects of her old life that were more social, where she was surrounded with people her age. All her previous jobs had her running around so much she didn't have time to think. Working in the lodge, she had too much time to think and not enough opportunity for interaction. She simply had to get past her dislike of coffee enough to down a sip and show Widgy that she wanted to be friends. "Thank you," she said with fake enthusiasm.

"First, I start out with strong coffee that's as black as a witch's liver. Then I add one piece of hickory bark to the grounds along with a secret ingredient from my backyard that I'm not spillin' the beans on, which gives it a lil' kick. What makes it special, though, is my pot."

Cora peered at the liquid. "What kind of pot is it?"

"It's a regular ole Mr. Coffee. The secret is that I haven't washed it out in sixteen years. That's what gives it flavor. Once in a blue moon, I'll swish it out with a lil' hot water to break up some of the muck at the bottom, but I never use soap. That strips the flavor, like turpentine to paint."

*Sixteen years?!* Cora gulped at the thought. She couldn't refuse Widgy's coffee. Trying not to cringe, she closed her eyes and lifted the cup to her mouth when Widgy spoke.

"I gotta get goin' on the sinks upstairs. They're comin' out. Have you picked the new faucets? The others were too corroded to save."

Cora shook her head. "I'll do that today," she said, putting down the cup, grateful for the distraction.

"That's what you said 'bout the toilets. Pretty soon you're gonna be relievin' yourself in a hole in the backyard."

Cora's shoulders fell. "I know. There's just so much to do," she whined. "The list never ends."

Widgy put her hand in her pocket and pulled out a matchbook. She tore off one match and threw it on the table in front of Cora. "A single match would take all of it off your hands."

Cora should have known the woman was not one for peptalks or coddling.

Picking up her toolboxes, Widgy turned to leave, but then she backtracked and fished something out of one toolbox. "Oh, and I found this on the porch yesterday." She set Cora's phone on the table. "I saw it was dead, so I used my charger to get it goin'. I figured you lost yours. You've got a lot of messages. Apparently you ignore those like you do the toilets."

Cora slumped in the chair. "Thanks." Checking messages was the last thing she wanted to do, especially if they were from her ex. Avoidance was more her style.

"You know, you could be efficient, like me, and check all those messages while *on* the toilet, doin' two businesses at once."

"Yeah . . . thanks for the suggestion."

Widgy shrugged. "Suit yourself. Don't forget to try some of that coffee. It'll put a little hair on your chest," Widgy added, heading for the door.

"It'll wake me up that much?"

Widgy turned. "No. It actually puts a little hair on your chest. I pluck mine. It's a small price to pay for such strong coffee. The darn itch is the thing I don't like." She clomped through the swinging door, whistling an off-key tune.

Cora waited until she heard Widgy working, then poured the coffee down the sink and squirted antibacterial soap in the cup. She snickered and shook her head. *Hair on your chest. Good grief.*

Going to town to pick out faucets could wait a little longer. First, Cora wanted to visit her neighbor. Entering the cemetery, she found Kitty hunched over a grave marker.

"Hello, Kitty!" Cora shouted from a distance so she wouldn't scare her.

Kitty looked up and smiled. "Miss Matthews, what a wonderful surprise! Come and tell me the exciting happenings of young people today." She tucked her chisel into her apron pocket and used the apron to wipe her hands.

Cora sat down near her. "There isn't much to tell. Widgy's making me choose toilets and faucets today, but that's certainly not exciting. That's why I wanted to sneak over here first and see whose stone you were working on."

"I'm tickled you would pay an old woman a visit and am still hoping you'll take me up on my offer to join the ladies tea one of these weeks."

Cora grinned. "I'll come to one of them soon, I promise."

Kitty stopped working to stare at her. "You look tired."

Cora moaned. "Don't get me started. When I complained to Widgy about the amount of work I have to do on the lodge, she reminded me in her own special way how I could save myself all this hassle by burning the place down."

Kitty chuckled. "That sounds like her."

Cora pointed to the marker. "What's this picture?"

"That's Millie Thurman. She was the card shark of Moonberry Lake, so I put the queen of diamonds next to her name and the joker on the back. She loved to play cards more than anything. Millie always carried a couple decks in her purse in case she ran into anyone ready for a quick game. She was in three bridge clubs, two canastas, and played poker every Friday night."

"Wow."

Kitty shook her head. "Sadly, Millie got in over her head. She was caught teaching her Sunday school class blackjack instead of Bible stories."

Cora laughed. "You're making that up!"

Kitty held up her hand. "Cross my heart! It was a real scandal. She ended up switching churches."

"What happened after that?"

"Well, she always insisted on playing with a brand-new deck of cards for every game. After many years, she had gone through countless decks. Millie would never throw them away because she believed it was bad luck. We always wondered what she did with them. It wasn't discovered until after she died that she had drained her pool and filled it with thousands of packs of cards! And there were handmade card structures stashed inside her house."

"What kind of structures?"

"You know how people create animals out of bushes?"

"You mean topiaries?"

Kitty nodded. "Yes! She did the same thing using a glue gun and old cards. Then she sprayed them with some kind of lacquer for protection. Nobody knew what to do with the sculptures once her house was sold, so they were taken to the nursing home to dress up their garden. From what I hear, the residents are rather proud of the unusual display."

The two of them laughed as Kitty moved on to the next plot.

Cora studied the marker. "Who's this?"

"Mabel Prescott, who was famous for her desserts. She loved to bake and believed everyone should enjoy some cake or pie every day of their life."

"I like her!" Cora chuckled.

"She lived joyously, baking for others and for herself. She has the only grave where I've carved words instead of a picture. I engraved her famous fudge recipe."

Cora read it out loud. "Two-and-a-half cups sugar, two teaspoon vanilla—"

"Oh, that was a little mistake." Kitty sighed. "It was *one* teaspoon of vanilla, but after the thaw last winter, the number one chipped, so I had to make it into a two. I tried the recipe with the change, and it's still the best fudge in the world."

"The whole idea is clever. I'm sure you made Mabel happy."

"I hope so. She definitely would've been pleased to give a tribute to one of her desserts. You know, she holds the record for having published the most recipes in the town newspaper. That's quite an honor."

"I'm sure it is." Cora smiled.

"God gives everyone a special talent, and sometimes it's simply to make life sweeter for the rest of us."

"Those are words to live by, Kitty."

Cora's trip to the plumbing supply store took up the majority of the day. She hadn't anticipated spending so much time there, but she discovered the faucets she liked wouldn't fit the old sinks, and she didn't care for any that *did*. So, she had no choice but to pick new sinks *and* faucets. They needed updating anyway, as half of them were discolored, so she figured she might as well replace them all at once. She placed her order and drove back to the lodge.

As she entered the kitchen, her neighbor's empty vegetable basket caught her eye. She needed to return it. She couldn't put it off any longer. Although the first encounter with Joseph had been awkward, her lack of manners at this point was embarrassing. Hoping she could leave it on his doorstep, she walked across the lawn.

She groaned inwardly as she caught sight of him in his gigantic garden.

"Hi, Joseph."

He raised his hand and waved.

"Here's your basket." She swung it while she walked. "The tomatoes were delicious. Thanks again."

He nodded and wiped his forehead with the back of his hand, spreading a smudge of dirt across it. Scant traces of gray were mingled in his dark hair and beard. If his hair was much longer, he really would be a dead ringer for the Jesus picture she'd had in her room as a child.

She handed him the basket.

He took it with a bashful nod.

The silence made Cora uncomfortable, so she added, "Your garden's huge."

"Yes." He gave her his full attention instead of gazing around at the plants.

She scrambled for something else to say. "Do you have any critters that come and eat your vegetables?"

"Some."

This was too hard. It was like pulling teeth to get this guy to talk, and she didn't have the energy for it. "I should get back to work. Thanks again." Clearly, this man would be one of those neighbors she would wave to from a distance but never speak to. They'd be cordial strangers.

She could live with that.

The next morning, as she stepped out to the porch, she spotted a basket overflowing with tomatoes, zucchini, and lettuce.

She stared at it, amazed at the generosity.

Apparently, cordial strangers made kind neighbors. She couldn't quite figure him out, but she was appreciative of the vegetables.

She carried the basket into the kitchen and stopped abruptly at the horrendous smell that accosted her. Wrinkling her nose, she looked around for something obviously rotting but couldn't find the source. She opened the back door to help air out the room and gasped at the pile of reeking dead fish stacked at the entry.

*What the heck? Who would—*

Then she remembered the one person she had been getting nasty glares from every time she passed his property when he was outside.

*Rolf.*

She even thought she'd seen him snooping on her from the thicket of trees between their properties a couple times. His displeasure for her presence at the lodge was palpable.

It had to be him. And she had just started to believe Sam that the old man was all talk. Clearly, Rolf was also a man of action. He must have been watching the lodge and saw that Widgy wasn't here to catch him this morning. Sneaky. And he had done it in a way that Cora wouldn't be able to prove it was him. Lining a trash can with a black plastic bag, she shoveled up the fish. The scent was powerful enough to make her gag. Pulling her T-shirt up over her nose didn't weaken the smell. With every scoop, she got angrier.

At the bottom of the slimy stinky pile was a piece of paper. The blurry writing was still legible: "You're not wanted here."

Her shoulders sank.

*I'm not a fan of you either, Mr. Johansson.*

# *Eight*

Cora leaned against the wall, her shoulders and back aching with fatigue. Stripping wallpaper, even with a steamer, was harder than she'd imagined. The four downstairs rooms facing the lake had been wallpapered, while the other three were painted a peach color that had faded to a dirty beige. She listened to Widgy clamoring away in the bathroom.

True to her word, Widgy always arrived a little after dawn and left promptly at five. In between the banging and trips back and forth to her truck for tools, she'd shout in frustration, "Lord have mercy, what a mess!"

The woman approached the day like a general approached a battle. She appeared determined to wrestle and conquer this massive project. A habit of Widgy's, which Cora found endearing, was that she'd holler from whatever room she was working in: "I'm not sure if it was God or the devil that possessed you to save this shack from the wreckin' ball. No rational mind would ever do such a thing!"

Widgy was right. Cora was in way over her head in restoring the place, propelled by some kind of personal mission to fill in the "lost" years, as she'd been calling them. In cleaning out the lodge, she'd found boxes of photos and papers from her grandparents. There were photo albums that included her mother as a child and even pictures of her as a child here at the lodge. But everything ended when Cora was seven. Had her grandparents just stopped cataloging life at that point? There weren't even photos of them in their later years. It was as if life wasn't worth remembering for them after she and her mother disappeared from it. What happened in the gap of time after they left was a conundrum. When she tried to get information from Sam, he shrugged his shoulders and said only that her grandparents got quieter and kept to themselves. He offered no clarity to the murkiness of her past. He was as tight-lipped about what had happened as her mother had been.

Since Widgy was her only companion in the house, Cora tried to engage her in chitchat, but Widgy would have none of it. She claimed to barely have known her grandparents and was annoyed to be distracted from her work. Ultimately, that kept Cora attentive to her own tasks. On those rare mornings she barely overslept, she bounded from bed as soon as she heard Widgy pounding, and then she worked until she fell back into bed from exhaustion. And yet, though the renovation was steadily progressing, the place *still* looked miserable. Widgy reassured her, several times, "It's gotta get worse 'fore it gets better!" Apparently *worse* meant gutted to bare bones.

From down the hall, Cora heard a weak call.

"Miss Matthews? Are you here?"

"Kitty?" she called back.

Sure enough, her elderly neighbor poked her head around the corner and came into the bedroom. She cradled a small bouquet of freshly picked wildflowers. "There you are! I'm sorry for walking in, but I knocked and you didn't answer. I ran into Ms. McQuire outside, and—"

"Who?"

"Ms. McQuire," Kitty repeated. "I believe she goes by Widgy. She told me where I could find you, so I came to pick you up for the tea. It's close enough that we can walk."

Cora wilted. "I totally forgot that I agreed to come this week!

I'm losing track of the days." She looked down at her dirty clothes. "I can't go looking like this!" She wiped her hands on a rag.

"Honey, the women you are about to meet are not interested in how you look but who you are. I told them you were coming, and they're all thrilled to finally get to meet you."

Guilt pricked Cora's conscience. Kitty was so sweet to her, and she hadn't even known her that long. She didn't want to disappoint her. Besides, how formal could this get-together be? Kitty looked the same except she'd put on a red gingham blouse with her jean skirt.

Kitty's eyes twinkled. "Those overalls suit your spirit. I like them on you."

"I've never dressed like this before."

"That doesn't surprise me. People change when they come to Moonberry Lake. They shed their old skin and emerge into something new."

Cora wasn't sure how to respond to that. "Give me five minutes to wash my face and throw on a sundress or something. These clothes are filthy." She spun and ran up the stairs.

Cora changed quickly and ran a brush through her hair. She grimaced at her reflection in the mirror. She hadn't had a haircut since before the funeral. So far, she'd gotten away with putting it up into a messy bun.

She pulled her hair into a low ponytail, then slipped on a pair of sandals and headed downstairs. On her way out, she passed Widgy and paused.

"Where do you get your hair cut?"

Widgy didn't look up. "From Billy down at the barbershop. He does crew cuts and your run-of-the-mill cut for men—nothin' fancy. Works magic with a buzzer and has the best selection of motor magazines in town."

*I had to ask.* Crazy considering she'd never seen Widgy without a hat. The woman always wore the greasy red baseball cap. "Thanks, I'll uh . . . keep him in mind."

Widgy's voice followed Cora down the hall. "For every tenth cut, he'll give you a free shave. It keeps the hairs on my chin under control. No need for that waxin' some women do."

Cora made a face. Now there was an image. "I'm going out with Kitty. See you later."

She found Kitty sitting at one of the dining room tables.

"I'm ready," she said, then froze. "No, wait! I don't have anything to bring!"

Kitty stood. "All you need is your charming self."

"I have to bring a gift for the hostess."

"Why don't we say these flowers are from the both of us, if that'll make you feel better?"

"I can't do that."

Kitty waved away her objection. "It's done. Let's go."

"I promise I'll make it up to you," Cora said as they headed out the door.

"No need."

They walked down the middle of the dirt road. Cora carried the flowers and tried to shorten her steps so Kitty wouldn't notice she was slowing her pace. The wind brushed her face. The sky was a translucent blue with a few puffy white clouds speckling it like spots on a robin's egg.

Kitty closed her eyes and tilted her face to the sun's warmth, reaching out as if she could gather it into her arms. "What a magnificent August day. Take it all in, my dear, because at this moment, God is giving us a glimpse into heaven."

Cora's smile disappeared as they passed Rolf Johansson's property. "Can I ask you a question?" she whispered to Kitty, as if Rolf could hear them.

"Of course."

"How well do you know Rolf Johansson?"

Kitty shook her head. "Is that grumpy billy goat giving you a hard time?"

Cora nodded.

"Pay him no heed. He's got nothing better to do than complain and spread misery."

"He claims to own the land the lodge is on."

Kitty scoffed. "Absurd. That argument was settled years ago. I was here long before your grandparents, and I know it was bought fair and square. Rolf is simply testing your resilience—feeling you out to see if you've got any fight in you." She echoed almost exactly what Sam had said.

"What should I do?"

"Do the hardest thing, which goes against our nature."

"What's that?"

"Kill him with kindness. Be a light in the dark. Resist reacting in a way that will only encourage him."

Cora took a big breath. "You're right. That doesn't come naturally."

"Not to any of us, darlin'. I've tried to be a good neighbor and have shared vegetables from my garden with him since he moved in after his father died, and I have yet to receive a thank-you."

"Then why do you keep doing it?"

"Because a constant sprinkling of water will eventually smooth any stone." Kitty winked.

Cora grinned. "Okay, lesson learned. Now, tell me something about the women I'm about to meet."

Kitty's face lit up. "Well, there's a difference in our ages. I'm the old-timer of the group. Arielle was the youngest, until you. It doesn't matter, though. Friendship crosses all boundaries. Every person brings something unique to the group. You're going to blend in perfectly. I've told them what a strong woman you are."

The comment surprised Cora. "You think I'm strong?"

"It takes a special kind of person to take on a project like you have. The fact that you chose to plant roots here tells me you're a survivor. Most cannot handle the solitude and quiet. The city allows an individual to run. Out here, you're forced to reflect. You become who your soul wants you to be."

Cora didn't say anything about the contract or inheritance, not wanting to disappoint her. But she felt complimented that Kitty viewed her in such a positive light. And there was truth in what she said. Even though most days she still felt overwhelmed by the tasks ahead of her, she was content. She was getting used to the solitude and quiet of the lodge. She felt a calm returning that she'd thought she lost long ago.

As the road curved, they approached a pale-yellow Victorian house. With intricate white gingerbread trim adorning the wraparound porch and window boxes bursting with pink flowers, it was a sight out of a storybook. An elaborate flower garden on both sides enhanced the charming architecture and created a picturesque scene.

Kitty didn't have to knock. A woman opened the door the moment they approached. "Welcome."

They entered the house, where two more women waited in the foyer. Kitty made the introductions. "Cora, allow me to introduce Ms. Sofia Bennett, Ms. Arielle Witherspoon, and Madame Mimi Morgan."

Cora smiled. "It's nice to meet all of you. These are for you." She handed the flowers to the hostess, Sofia. "Kitty—"

"I told her she didn't have to bring anything, but she insisted," Kitty interrupted, patting Cora's arm. "She's so sweet."

"They're beautiful," Sofia said.

"It's wonderful to meet you!" Arielle burst forward and shook Cora's hand with gusto.

"Let's go into the living room, so we can get to know our guest," Sofia said.

Cora couldn't help but stare at Sofia's striking beauty. A tall, willowy woman with dark brown hair loosely pulled back, she wore little makeup against her alabaster skin, adding greater contrast to her hazel eyes. She wore a long, wispy chiffon dress with a watercolor print splashed on it.

Sofia led Cora to one of the two high-back, pink velvet Victorian-style sofas facing each other, an oval coffee table between them.

A silver tea set in the center of the table gleamed as if it had been recently polished, and dessert plates of sugar cookies and lemon bars surrounded it.

Cora felt self-conscious and sat down daintily, then relaxed when she looked across the coffee table and saw Arielle on the opposite couch. Arielle embodied the antithesis of Sofia's effortless elegance. She was average height and build and had an unbelievable head full of long, curly, blond hair. The wild mane stuck straight out. Her eye color flipped from blue to green depending on the light and how she tilted her head. Her long, sleeveless dress was badly wrinkled and hung on her in a haphazard sort of way. Although the young woman appeared rumpled as if she had just rolled out of bed, Arielle's smile captured Cora. It shone with sincerity and kindness. Even as she sat, she seemed to have a hard time restraining the inner joy ready to bubble over onto anyone in close proximity.

Cora looked over at Mimi who had sat down in a chair positioned between the two sofas as if she were at the head of a table. The middle-aged woman had medium-length, fiery-red hair with tightly defined curls. Leopard-framed glasses with rose-tinted lenses took up a large portion of her face, slipping down her pointed nose. The only time her mouth changed from its pursed-together position was when she opened it to snap the piece of gum she chomped, exposing some gold-capped molars. She wore a leopard-print dress with long sleeves, despite the heat. Three heavy gold chains draped her chest, one featuring a pendant of a cat head. She had matching pendants for earrings. Her wrists jingled with half a dozen bangles on each, and every finger except her thumbs had rings with different stones audacious in size.

"We were ecstatic when Kitty told us she invited you," Sofia explained.

Cora turned to the hostess, who had taken the seat beside her on the sofa. "Thank you for having me."

"Everyone wants to meet the newcomer on the lake."

Cora smiled. "I'm not so much of a newcomer. I spent most of my time here as a young child with my grandparents before moving away. I'm now trying to restore the lodge."

Arielle leaned in closer. "Restoration projects are such fun."

"I've seen the lodge, and the task would be too staggering for me. It takes someone of your youth and endurance." Mimi made the statement with a cluck of her tongue.

"I'm sure the improvements will be lovely." Sofia countered Mimi's negative tone, giving Cora a conspiratorial wink.

Kitty sat grinning, looking as proud as a peacock for bringing such entertainment.

Cora crossed her legs, trying to relax and balance her little dessert plate on her knee. "I apologize for my appearance. I was stripping wallpaper when Kitty came to get me."

"Nonsense! There are days I get so wrapped up in my work, I forget to brush my hair or change my clothes." Arielle giggled.

"Take my word for it, she's telling you the truth," Mimi said, giving Cora a pointed look.

"Oh, stop, Mimi." Arielle turned to Cora. "Don't mind her. She teases to cover up that sunny disposition." All the other women laughed—except Mimi.

"Arielle's an artist." Kitty beamed like a proud parent.

That piqued Cora's interest. "What's your medium?"

Arielle sat up straighter. "I do a lot of things, but painting's my focus. I'll show you sometime."

"I'd love that." And she would. Having a friend somewhat close to her age—well, at least compared to the others—would be nice.

As the conversation continued, Cora realized how lonely she'd been. These women were so hospitable and interesting, and the discussion flowed naturally.

When the gathering ended, each of the women asked her to come again. Cora promised she would and meant it. On her way out, she passed a wall of bookshelves and paused for a moment, studying the variety of titles. There had to be a couple hundred of them.

"I have a soft spot for romance. You may borrow any that interest you," Sofia said from behind her.

Cora smiled. "I may take you up on that once I have a better handle on my work."

"Oh, there will always be work to do. Reading is a wonderful way to relax at the end of a hard day." Sofia selected two books and handed them to Cora. "Here, take these. I have double copies."

Cora stared at the brand-new hardcovers. "Savannah MacArthur. I haven't read anything by her."

"You'll have to let me know what you think of her writing."

Cora nodded. "I will. Thank you for the tea and the books. It was so gracious of you to have me."

"Cora, wait!" Arielle hurried over. "I want to make you some bread as a welcome present. Do you like bolillos? They're crusty Mexican rolls. If you don't like that, I could make you challah, a Jewish bread."

"I've never had either," Cora confessed.

"I'm learning how to bake different cultural breads as I try to connect with that primal need we all share for basic sustenance. The act of creating and baking bread can be meditative. It centers your spirit in the present moment."

Mimi turned to Cora. "Arielle is a hippie at heart. It's a quirk we've all come to accept."

"And *love*," Kitty added.

Arielle went on. "I study one kind of bread a month and make it over and over until I've mastered it. Last month was challah, and this month it's conchas and bolillos. For next month, I can't decide between South Indian dosas or the crepe-like flatbread, socca, a specialty of Southern France."

"I'd be happy to be your taste tester anytime," Cora told her.

Arielle's eyes lit up, and she threw her arms around Cora in a strong hug. "A kindred spirit added to our clan! I love it!"

They said their goodbyes, and Kitty intertwined her arm with Cora's as they left. Back on the road, Kitty nudged Cora with an elbow. "Well, it's obvious you're in. The ladies loved you, just as I predicted."

"I would love to go again next week. Thanks for not giving up on me and encouraging me to go."

"We all need a little push now and then." She winked.

"Tell me another story while we walk home."

Kitty laughed. "I've never met anyone so interested in my stories."

"It's *how* you tell your stories and the unique traits you remember about the people that interest me. Your characters seem so familiar—like I know them."

"They're familiar because, deep down inside, we're all the same. We all need love, grow from love, search endlessly for love, and end up living to feel loved. That's what connects us to one another. Everything else just keeps things interesting. The people I talk about are the same people who lived next door to you growing up or who came to fix the dishwasher. I simply took the time to notice them."

Cora smiled. "How do you always have the perfect answers?"

Kitty squeezed in closer as if she was about to divulge a secret. "Because I'm old," she whispered. "When you don't have distractions like youth and vitality, God gives insight to make up for it."

Cora held Kitty's arm as she walked her to the front door. Passing the graves, Kitty greeted each resident. "Hello, Werner. Good afternoon, Maggie. Hello, dear Beatrice." One after another, she bowed her head and acknowledged them.

When they reached the door, Kitty squeezed Cora's hand. "Thank you for walking with me."

"It was my pleasure." Cora turned to leave.

"Do you ever talk to your lost ones?"

Cora froze.

"You're too young to have that sadness in your eyes."

Cora turned back toward Kitty. "Do I come off as sad?"

"Not to others, but I can see it. Even today, with the ladies, with all the cookies and conversation, there was something missing. A sparkle that should be there . . . isn't."

Cora peered down for a moment before meeting Kitty's sympathetic eyes. "I've lost all my family. My mother knew she was going to die but didn't tell me. I was taken away from my grandparents when I was a little girl, and I don't know why. And now, living at the lodge, I'm reminded of all I missed."

"Do you ever talk to them?"

"You mean the way you talk to the people here in the cemetery? No, that's not me."

"You know, they never leave us," Kitty said with a knowing look. "We have a connection to those who have been part of our lives. It can never be broken. They're still with us, only now they make better listeners."

Cora gave a small smile. "Thanks for today."

# Nine

Her first morning with Mr. Wells had finally arrived. Cora waited in her car until the clock read 8:09, then she ran up to the door and knocked.

Nothing.

She knocked again. The curtain swished and the lock clicked open. Upon entering, she was prompted to remove her shoes, leave them by the door, and squirt sanitizer onto her hands.

"Good morning, Mr. Wells," she said. "What would you like me to do today?"

Looking at her with his usual deadpan expression, he handed her a sheet of paper. It was a neatly typed list of food items. Each item was categorized by the brand, size, cost, and the grocery aisle in which it could be found.

"You are to purchase the items on the list. Do not deviate from it *at all*. Get the exact sizes and brands cited." He took a white envelope out of his shirt pocket and handed it to her. "Here is the money."

Cora ran the errand promptly. When the store clerk told her the purchase came to $69.91 and she opened the envelope to find $69.91 in cash, she smiled.

Later, Mr. Wells instructed her on the proper way to put away the groceries. "I have a specific method of storage." He opened a cabinet door. The shelves were as neat as the grocery store. "I categorize everything by food group and then by alphabetical order. There is a shelf for fruit, domestic to the right, tropical to the left, and mixed in the center. This is the shelf for vegetables and legumes." He went on and on about his system of inventory.

Putting the food away carefully under his direction was going to take longer than her visit to the store. But he seemed pleased when she asked for a clean rag to wipe the shelves before filling them.

She stayed in the kitchen another two hours, cleaning and washing the floors, counters, and every other surface with antibacterial cleaner—all under his supervision. Although the kitchen had obviously been wiped down and all the surfaces were shiny, she redid it all, which earned her a nod of approval. She decided not to ask any questions since he was paying her to redo everything, and it wasn't a hard job. She tried to make conversation, but he never responded with words.

Whenever she tried to connect by asking him something that didn't pertain to her job, he got nervous and took out his ever-present pocket calculator or notepad and took notes. When she finished for the day, he stopped her in the dining room and handed her some papers.

"What's this?"

"Your homework."

She blinked at him confused. "My what?"

"I want to teach you algebra."

"*Algebra*?" She could hardly sputter the word. "No thanks." She shook her head and put the papers down on the table, backing away as if they were poisonous. "I didn't understand it at fifteen, and I'm pretty sure I wouldn't understand it now. Besides, I don't have time for that."

"It's part of your job."

Cora flinched. "Learning algebra is part of my job?"

"Yes."

Her mind was reeling. "What? No. No. No." Each no came out

more adamant. She shook her head vigorously. "My job is to help you, which includes going on errands and cleaning up the house. That's it."

"I'll pay you for your time."

Her mouth dropped open. "Why on earth would you want to spend your time and money teaching me algebra?" She was completely bewildered. "It would be a complete waste on both accounts."

He hesitated, looking down as he fidgeted with his trouser material. "I can't sleep." His answer came out in a whisper.

"What?"

Mr. Wells cleared his throat. "I can't sleep from thinking about what you said in your interview about getting a C in Algebra. I need to know what you didn't understand so I can rectify it. Math is nothing more than problem-solving using different methods to achieve the desired outcome. It's not difficult once you understand it."

Cora stared at him wide-eyed, trying to take in his argument. "But . . . I don't *want* to understand it. I have no *need* for it."

Apparently, her adamant rejection was jarring to him. He began rubbing his index fingers in circular motions against his thumbs. "Math is not about desire. It is about necessity and survival. Math is in all of life. It's nothing more than thinking analytically and critically, using fundamental methods and language for the creation and solution of mathematical models."

Cora made a face. "There was nothing simple even in that sentence you just said! Hence the reason why I'm horrible at math. I can't do it. I won't do it."

Mr. Wells lifted his chin, looking at her through the bottom of his glasses. "It's going to be a part of your job." The firm words brooked no argument. His mind was set and locked. He picked up the papers and handed them to her. "Complete these to the best of your ability, then I will discuss my findings with you. I've designed it so your area of weakness will be illuminated by your inability to reach the correct solution at different stages of the problem."

"Trust me, it's not going to be hard to find my area of weakness. I have *no* ability with this stuff."

Mr. Wells's chest puffed out. "This *stuff* is more accurately called algebraic expressions, such as variables, coefficients, and constants. That can be your first lesson."

"Mr. Wells—"

He stopped her midsentence. "I will see you every Monday, Wednesday, and Friday at precisely 8:10. You are dismissed for today."

When Cora returned to the lodge, she found Sam in the shed out back. Before he could speak, she blurted out, "I can't do it. He gave me algebra homework!"

Sam let out a chuckle. "That so?"

She was not amused. "He wants to teach me math because— get this—*he* can't sleep knowing *I* don't understand it. What is he thinking?"

Sam shot her a look.

Cora held up a hand. "Listen, I don't have the patience or desire to go through high school math all over again. I can't. I wasn't a good student the first time around."

Sam shrugged. "Why don't you let him teach you? What could it hurt?"

Her mouth dropped open. "Come on. It makes no sense!"

Sam put down what he was working on and looked her square in the eyes. "You're right. It doesn't make sense to us that a man with such a brilliant mind never leaves the house. It doesn't make sense to us that a brain that exceptional would be so stressed by the outside world that it caused him to have a breakdown. It doesn't make sense that anyone should have to live that lonely of an existence when they mean no harm to anyone. Many things in life don't make sense."

Cora was silenced by his passion.

"It doesn't make sense that your mother died relatively young," he continued. "Or that you're trying to restore this old place. Or that you're only the second person Jon has ever trusted to come into his home and help him."

His expression grew thoughtful. "You're not simply doing his errands, Cora. You're giving him human contact. He is paying for some small connection to life beyond his door."

Sam picked up the box he'd set down earlier. "When something makes absolutely no sense, the only thing you can do is see what sense comes from it. You might learn something besides a little algebra."

Cora sighed before heading inside the lodge, knowing he was right and that she had some homework to do.

When she returned to Mr. Wells's home on Wednesday, his face lit up as she handed him her completed homework. He took it with the eagerness of a child with a new comic and began poring over it. He didn't supervise as she cleaned but sat at the dining table, making notes in the margins of the paper.

The cleaning supplies were lined up on the kitchen table for her in alphabetical order. She went to work on the windows. If they were going to be his sole looking glass to the outside world, then they had better be clear. When that task was done, she took all the withered, half-dead plants outside to get some sun and then went in search of the shirt in need of a button. To her surprise, she found eight.

When she had finished sewing buttons on his shirts, she found him waiting for her at the dining room table. He tried to appear patient, but his leg was jiggling. As promised, her first lesson was going over the accurate algebraic expressions. She made a sincere effort to listen and be respectful in her attempt to follow along. What amazed her was the transformation in him. He went from shy and guarded to exuberant.

Afterward, he handed her a new assignment. Her stomach sank at the sight of it, but she took the papers without comment. She studied him a moment. "Mr. Wells, may I ask what you used to do?"

He hesitated. "I was a scientist at one time and worked for a highly respected university, then for the government." He did not offer any further details.

"Do you have any hobbies?"

"I enjoy quantum physics."

She leaned in closer to make sure they made eye contact. "Mr. Wells, that is one hobby I don't want you to *ever* share with me."

Through his thick glasses, his eyes softened. The corners of his mouth curved slightly, as if he was suppressing a chuckle. He gave a small nod. "Algebra first."

By Friday, they were already in a rhythm. Cora did the shopping, replaced the plants, made a salad, and prepared a casserole. Her time in his home always ended with math. It was apparent how much he looked forward to it.

Some people got a pet, did a craft, or started a project if they were bored or lonely. She understood now that Jonathan Wells's project was *her*.

As soon as Cora parked her Jeep and placed one foot on the ground that afternoon, she recognized the disgusting scent permeating the air. Slamming the door shut, she went in pursuit of the rotting odor. Her nose led her to a line of bushes alongside the lodge. Rolf had scattered dead fish throughout them.

Fuming, she called Sam. "I've got a problem." She told him the situation.

"Want to involve the police? This is genuine harassment and a form of vandalism."

"I can't prove it's him. The decomposing fish aren't branded or anything."

Sam chuckled. "Want to retaliate? Maybe throw all the fish back onto his property?"

She remembered Kitty's words. "No."

"Did he leave another note?"

"Just a minute." Cora searched the bushes and saw the corner of a piece of paper. Holding her nose, she leaned over and grabbed it. The same blurred scroll read "Leave."

"Yep. He left another love note. This one says, 'Leave.' Short and sweet. What should I do?"

"Just keep proceeding on the renovation. It'll send the message you have no intention of leaving."

Her stomach sank. It *was* her intention to leave. Eventually.

"I'm going to confront him, but in a nice way."

"Hmm, not sure that's a good idea."

"Well, I can't have this place continue to be vandalized by dead fish."

"Dead fish don't hurt anything. My advice is don't feed the fire. Wait it out and he'll get tired."

"I don't know if I can do that. I've never been a patient person."

"Then there's a lesson to learn from this. Plus, you've got something he finds very threatening."

"What is that?"

"Youth. Wait him out."

She released a big breath. "I'll talk to you later. I've got to go fish some fish out of the bushes."

"Hang in there."

# *Ten*

The following week, while painting bedroom four a soft yellow, Cora heard her neighbor's voice.

"Knock, knock."

"Come on in." She smiled as Kitty peeked around the corner. "What's up?"

"I told you I'd make up some excuse to pop over. These are for you." She held out a plate of lumpy brown cookies packed with shredded carrot. "They're fresh from the oven."

"Thank you. I needed a break." She set the plate on a nearby dresser. "What do you think of this paint color?"

"It reminds me of a field of daffodils."

"That's exactly the feeling I'm going for! I'm going to paint a floral border with butterflies around the ceiling to make up for the fact that I can't afford crown molding. Then I'm going to hang sheer white curtains."

Kitty closed her eyes and smiled as if imagining the finished room. "It's going to be beautiful."

"Each room's going to have its own theme."

"It sounds like a lot of work but well worth it." Kitty's eyes crinkled as she smiled.

"It is, but I figure I have the time since Widgy's doing just about everything else. For now, I'm concentrating on the downstairs. The

102

floors have been refinished, and I had Widgy replace the baseboards to give it a fresh look."

"You possess quite an artistic flair, Miss Matthews. You remind me of Arielle."

Cora blushed. "I'm not sure about that, but I enjoy it."

"Well, I will let you get back to your masterpiece." Kitty waved goodbye.

Later that afternoon, as Cora was on her way to the kitchen, she passed the forgotten plate of cookies. Each one was about four inches in diameter and close to an inch thick. Taking a bite of one, she felt the rough textures in her mouth. It was hard, so she bit harder. As she clamped down, a surging pain came from her back tooth. She spit the cookie into her hand and saw the shell of a walnut and a strange rock. Picking up the rock and inspecting it, she realized it wasn't a rock but part of her tooth.

Running to the mirror, she discovered a gaping hole where part of her molar used to be. She placed the chewed-up mess in a napkin, afraid to throw anything out in case there were more pieces of her tooth in it. She quickly grabbed her phone and searched for dentists in her area. There was one listing.

She frantically called, and an elderly voice answered.

"Hello. Dr. Walker's office."

"Yes, hi. I broke a tooth and need to see a dentist immediately."

"Who is this?"

"My name is Cora Matthews."

"Laura Meadows?"

"No, Cora Matthews."

"Dora Matthew?"

"No, *Cora Matthews.*"

"Hold on a minute and let me turn on my hearing aid."

A *clunk* told Cora the woman had set down the receiver. Then came noises of more fumbling.

"Okay, one more time, honey."

Speaking slowly, she shouted, "MY NAME IS CORA MATTHEWS."

"I don't know a Cora Matthews. Have you been here before?"

"No. I'm a new patient."

"Oh, good! We get so excited about new patients."

Cora took a deep breath. "Is the dentist available?"

"Dr. Walker's busy with the Simpson twins. They're always a handful."

"Please, this is an emergency. I'm holding half my tooth in my hand."

"Which one did you break?"

"My back molar."

"Oh my, that's not good. Let me go talk to Dr. Walker and see if he can fit you in."

Several long, excruciating minutes went by before the woman returned on the other end of the phone. "Are you there, Ms. Mitten?"

Too exhausted to correct her again, Cora simply responded, "Yes."

"He said he would see you if you come immediately."

"Then I'm leaving now." Cora hung up, grabbed her keys, and raced to her Jeep.

The office was easy to find. The small waiting area had four chairs and simple decor. A woman who looked to be well into her eighties sat behind the counter.

Cora walked straight up to her, napkin still in hand. "Hi, I'm Cora Matthews."

"Do you have an appointment?"

Cora felt her mouth fall open. "I just talked to you twenty minutes ago. I'm the one with the broken tooth."

The woman frowned. "I'm sorry to hear that. I'm expecting a Nora Matten with the same problem. She sounded rather upset on the phone. Have a seat and let me see if Dr. Walker has time to see both of you. There's lots of drama in here today."

Cora was in too much pain to argue. Holding one hand to her left cheek, she clutched the napkin with the other. Luckily, she waited only a couple minutes before the woman returned.

"He's ready to see you. Since it's an emergency, I'll get your insurance and information on your way out. Follow me, honey."

Cora walked through the doorway and noticed the dentist seated with his back to her. He was writing something down.

"Hello," she mumbled with her hand to her mouth.

He spun around in his chair. "Hello!" He stood up to shake her hand.

For a moment, she felt as if all the air had been kicked out of her. *You've got to be kidding!* It was the man from the lake, the one who had helped her when she fell out of the boat. She stood there holding her jaw and wondering which was worse—the absolute mortification of running into him in a state of emergency *again*, or the surging pain from her tooth.

*Don't recognize me. Please don't recog—*

"So, we meet again!" His smile broadened. "I never did get to introduce myself. I'm Ben Walker." He put his hand out for a hearty handshake.

The embarrassment was more painful than the tooth.

"It's nice to meet you, Ms. Mahoney," he continued. "Let me get my instruments set up and I'll be right with you. Please, have a seat."

As he put on latex gloves and arranged the instruments on the tray in front of her, Cora got a better look at him now that he wasn't wearing a baseball cap or wading shoulder-deep in water. He had chestnut-brown hair, a strong jaw, and square shoulders. Even with the stereotypical white lab coat he had on, with his name embroidered on the pocket, his athletic build was evident.

Once again, his brown eyes transfixed her. They reminded her of . . . something. She shook the feeling away. "My name's Cora Matthews. I corrected your receptionist numerous times, but she didn't seem to hear me."

His nod was good-natured. "I apologize. Grace is hard of hearing and not the best with names. She tells me one of your fillings came out?"

"No. Half my back molar broke off!" She didn't mean to sound desperate, but good grief! Panic filled her as she worried about the quality of care she was going to get. Tears stung her eyes, and she willed herself to maintain control.

He shook his head. "Sorry. I'm glad you came in. How did you break it?"

Looking at him, she finally figured it out. "Chocolate." His eyes were the velvety color of melted chocolate, dark and rich. They had the same glisten as tempered chocolate in a pot over the stove.

"You broke your molar on some chocolate?"

She snapped back to reality. "Um . . . no. Sorry. I mean a cookie."

"It must have been some cookie," he said, giving her a small smile.

His attempt to make her feel more at ease actually worked. "My neighbor made them. They were carrot cookies with raisins and nuts."

Humor crossed his face. "Not a Kitty Bjornson cookie?"

Cora's eyebrows knit together. "Yes! How did you know that?"

He chuckled. "I'm afraid she's helped me not only establish my practice but maintain it. I've had many people in here with problems caused by her cookies. I should be paying her commission."

His reaction made her feel foolish and angry at the same time. A surprising surge of protectiveness of Kitty washed over her.

"Well, I've found her to be an incredibly sweet woman and have appreciated the kindness she's shown to me, including her cookies."

Dr. Walker sobered and met her gaze. "Please don't misunderstand me. I know she's one of the nicest people you'll ever meet." He cleared his throat and rolled his chair close to hers. "May I take a look in your mouth?"

Cora hesitated. Her jaw clamped shut. She still had a pool of tears ready to be shed at the slightest trigger. Even on the best of days, she hated going to the dentist. She looked to the doorway, and for a moment contemplated running out.

"Just a peek?" he asked softly.

She knew the trepidation on her face was clear as anxiety made it hard for her to breathe. She found it unbelievable that this was the second time this man had seen her at her absolute worst. However, between the sound of his gentle voice and the softness in his eyes, she found herself relaxing and trusting him. She eased down the hand that was clamped to her jaw and opened her mouth. He shined his light in and then sat back. "Do you have the rest of the tooth?"

"Yes." She handed him the napkin wad.

After he had extracted the tooth chip and examined it, he checked her mouth again. "You had two cracks coming from the filling, which is why your tooth broke so easily. You're going to need a crown. I'll make you comfortable now, do the prep work, and take an impression, but you're going to have to come back for the crown fitting. You'll leave with a cap today. Sound good to you?"

Cora nodded, not trusting herself to speak.

He began working on her teeth as tenderly as she could imagine, for a dentist. She found it so hard not to stare into his eyes that she closed her own for most of the procedure, opening them only when he asked if she was in any pain.

Two hours later, he announced he was done. She opened her eyes. His chair was rolled back, his gloves were off, and he stood making notes on her chart.

"I'm sorry for how long it took, but it was a bad break. I have to send the impression of your tooth to a lab in another town, so your new crown won't be ready for about two weeks."

She nodded.

"If you have any problems, call the office. I check messages regularly when I'm at home. Be careful not to chew on that side for the next few days, and no more of Kitty's cookies—at least until I finish my work." He winked.

"Thur." Cora cringed as drool seeped out of her half-numb mouth.

Walking out of the exam room and into the empty office, she saw through the front window how late it had gotten. He had stayed past closing for her.

Since Grace was long gone, he went behind the desk and took all her information. As he handed her insurance card back to her, he smiled and said, "It was nice to meet you again, Cora."

She'd be lying if she denied that her heart jumped a little as he said it.

Driving home, she replayed the whole scene in her head. *I looked absurd!* By the time she pulled into her driveway, she was exhausted. Thankfully she could head straight to bed and forget about the whole mess.

On her way to the stairs, she passed the hall mirror and took half a glance. Stopping with a jerk, she spun around and went back to it. Her mouth hung slack. She hadn't bothered changing her clothes or looking at her appearance before she drove off. Standing there in front of her reflection, she noted how her hair was half in and out of a ponytail. There were paint spots, dirt, and blotches of spaghetti sauce from her lunch on her shirt. She wore no makeup, and there was a streak of yellow paint on the side of her neck and on the tip of her nose.

She wasn't sure what upset her more—her tooth or the fact that Dr. Walker had seen her looking like this.

Groaning, she walked up the staircase. "No more chocolate . . . er, carrot cookies."

Early in the morning, Cora went down the front stairs to the foyer instead of taking the back staircase. She was trying to avoid Widgy. The pain from her tooth had subsided, but the humiliation of the dental visit still stung, and she was in no mood to talk.

She continued down the long hallway on tiptoe. It wasn't until she passed room number two that Widgy spoke from behind her.

"Aww, Sleeping Beauty is finally awake. Did you get up for your appointment at the spa, or did you want to see how the common folk earn a livin'?"

"Leave me alone, Widgy! I'm not in the mood." Cora stormed

off but made it only ten feet before stopping and going back. "I'm sorry. I'm grouchy this morning. I shouldn't take it out on you."

Widgy shrugged. "It's okay. I'm man enough to take it. As a matter of fact, you may not be as much of a pushover as I pegged you for."

Cora rolled her eyes. "There's a compliment in there somewhere."

"What's wrong with ya?"

"I broke a tooth yesterday and had to get a temporary crown."

Widgy gave a gap-toothed grin. "Ah, that's nothin'. The solution is to lose most of 'em like me."

Cora turned to leave.

"Hang on. First, I have to show ya somethin'." Widgy walked to the middle of the bedroom. "New water damage has rotted these floorboards. It's not safe. We need to make sure whatever caused this is taken care of and then replace most of the floor."

Cora's shoulders sank as she let out an aggravated huff. "This place is going to kill me." She continued down the hall.

"I'll handle it," Widgy yelled after her.

After taking a couple aspirin, Cora decided to take a walk. Last night, she wasn't sure how she was going to feel in the morning so she texted Mr. Wells and told him about her dental emergency and canceled for the day. She knew that would throw him off a bit, but she figured he would be more agitated that she hadn't had time to complete her homework. Arriving Friday with a better attitude and papers in hand would be worth it to both of them.

She needed to clear her head and escape the problems of the lodge, at least momentarily. The place was a total money pit. Everywhere she turned, there was something wrong, broken, or needing to be replaced. Cora didn't know how she'd possibly make it through the full year. The roof would probably fall in on her by October.

Plus, her irritation and humiliation from her dental visit hadn't diminished with a night's sleep. Adding the cost of the crown and dental work to the list of all her other expenses was enough to make her hyperventilate. Life was feeling too overwhelming again, and she needed to walk out that itch to run away or else she would.

The temptation to call it quits was strong enough that she knew she had to get out of the lodge and get perspective.

Even though Widgy had teased her about waking up late, it was only eight o'clock. She began at a brisk walk and slowed as she passed Rolf's driveway. His home was as hidden as hers with all the trees. A phantom whiff of rotten fish filled her nostrils, even though she'd cleaned up his second "gift" over a week ago. She was going to have to talk to him at some point but was certainly not in the mood for it now.

Half a mile down, she stopped to stare at her favorite house on the lake. It was a narrow two-story, aquamarine house with pastel-blue windowsills, yellow flower boxes, and a pink front door. It was like something out of a Disney movie.

The yard was always cluttered with mismatched lawn furniture, and she could see from the road that the dock was painted the same color aqua, except at the end where a rainbow of colors made it look like a xylophone. Wind chimes made an orchestra of sound as they swayed in the trees.

The front of the house still had Christmas lights attached to the trim, and there was a collection of about fifteen birdhouses perched on top of poles to one side. On the other side of the house, a patch of sunflowers took up most of the lawn, most of which were dead.

"Cora?"

She turned to find her new friend coming around the side of the house, dressed in a long, tattered pink robe and furry slippers.

"Arielle?"

"Good morning!"

"I didn't know this was your house!" Cora looked between the wild house and the wild woman. *It all makes sense.*

Arielle shuffled toward her, holding a wooden bowl filled with acorns. "I was spreading some extra food for the squirrels. I want to make sure they have enough for winter."

"That's nice of you."

"I've done it since I was a young girl." She stopped and gave Cora an appraising look. "Something's wrong."

"How can you tell?"

"I can sense people's energy. What is it? What brought you here this morning?"

Cora shrugged. "Nothing. I'm just taking a walk."

"There's no such thing as a coincidence." Arielle dumped out the rest of the acorns. "Come paint with me." She interlocked her arm with Cora's and started for the house.

"What? Oh, no, I don't paint like you."

"From what Kitty tells me, you're doing an outstanding job at the lodge."

"Those are walls, not canvases."

Arielle swung her arm out. "Life is our canvas! It doesn't matter what you paint on. It's the feeling it evokes in you and the emotion portrayed in your work that matters."

The inside of Arielle's house was exactly what one would expect. Dozens of paintings covered nearly every inch of wall space, except one wall that had the most magnificent mural painted directly on it. It depicted angels among the clouds. The glow of colors and the intricately embellished detail took Cora's breath away.

A turning wheel for pottery stood near the window, with packed shelves of various vases next to it. An inviting overstuffed chair and an easel stood by the fireplace, and a life-size statue of a naked man wearing a crown of leaves on his head stood sentinel on the other side. Papers, books, and magazines cluttered the wood floor. All the tables were covered with sculptures and candles, jars filled with sand, and half-burnt incense sticks.

Cora counted eight baskets overflowing with art supplies, dried flowers, or yarn. There was a narrow path to walk. Arielle moved through the space with a fluid grace, as if none of the mess existed.

"Come to the porch. We can look out on the lake as we paint."

"What do you do besides painting and pottery?"

"I meditate. I love to weave. I have a two-hundred-pound loom

in one of the bedrooms upstairs. I have also begun to learn photography and tai chi this year as part of my resolution for turning
thirty-eight."

"What's special about thirty-eight?"

"Nothing and everything." Arielle smiled. "Every year I choose
to learn something new. I celebrate each year as if it were a new
start in life. For my thirties, I've gone scuba diving in the coral
reefs, learned how to salsa dance, traveled to Paris, and tried sky-
diving." She shrugged.

"Wow. What did you do for your twenties?"

"Let's see." Arielle tapped her chin, deep in thought. "I traveled
to the Inca ruins, built my own sweat lodge, learned macramé,
and practiced drawing henna tattoos. My goal is not to become an
expert but to try as many experiences as possible. I may or may
not like them all, but at least I've tried new things. I don't ever
make excuses or tell myself no."

"That's incredible."

Arielle waved away Cora's reaction. "I simply give myself permission to try anything that fascinates me. It's the same as a buffet
at a restaurant. People approach the abundance of choices with
the idea they will take a little of this and a little of that. There's
no hesitation in trying something new because you can decide if
you want to eat it all or go to the next thing. I apply that same
concept to life."

As Arielle talked, she set up a new canvas on an easel in front
of Cora's chair and handed her a paintbrush.

Cora looked down at it. "I don't want to waste your materials."

"Nonsense. We shall create together!" She pulled her own blank
canvas onto an easel. "Take a deep breath and play with the colors.
Free yourself from inhibitions. I'm not judging. This is only for you."

Cora closed her eyes, let out a breath, and began with a couple
hesitant strokes. Soon, she became immersed in the vibrant hues
against the white background, amazed at how much fun she was
having mixing shades together and creating fluid rainbows.

Arielle came to sit beside her. "That's beautiful."

"They're the colors I imagine when I'm dreaming at night."

As Cora applied a few strokes of a cobalt blue, Arielle moved her chair closer to her. "Now, tell me," she said, "why were our two spirits pulled together this morning?"

"I was out for a walk."

"And I *happened* to be out at that same moment? I told you, there's no such thing as coincidence. Everything is for a reason. Now, tell me."

Cora gave a frustrated sigh. "The problems at the lodge are never-ending. But my biggest annoyance right now is that I made a fool of myself."

Arielle waved her hand. "We all do that."

Cora shook her head. "No, I looked stupid. In fact, I made a fool out of myself *twice* in front of the same person."

"Wow. The universe desperately wants you to cross paths with this person."

Cora let out a short laugh. "Yeah, somehow that doesn't make me feel any better."

"You know, I think one of the tragedies of life is that we're taught, from the time we are children, never to laugh at ourselves. Pride can be a slow death to the spirit. We need to take ourselves less seriously. Instead of replaying embarrassing scenes over in your head, laugh them off. Stop torturing yourself over something that has already happened and move on."

"That's easier said than done. I'm going to have to see this person again."

"You can't let a little embarrassment take hold of you."

"You don't even know what happened."

"I don't need to. All that matters is that you don't let it keep you from moving forward. Today, you didn't want to make a fool of yourself painting, so you almost didn't try something you ended up liking. Whatever embarrassment you're carrying, realize that you're the only one lugging it around. Life is about learning, exploring, and taking risks. I do things that make me look ridiculous all the time. Imagine *me* on a surfboard. Now, *that* was funny."

Cora chuckled. "Mimi was right—you *are* a free spirit hippie."

"I consider that high praise." Arielle's triumphant grin drew a smile from Cora as well.

"You're a good influence on me," Cora said, thankful for this new friend.

Arielle beamed. "Oh, goodness! Don't ever tell Mimi that or she'll lose all respect for you."

Both women laughed.

"Now, you paint while I get us some bread to eat. Lord knows I have enough to feed all the Israelites."

# Eleven

One of the indulgent pleasures of living in Moonberry Lake was the local newspaper. Unlike city newspapers laden with serious and heavy world news, *The Town Times* made most world events into sidenotes. Discerning local readers seeking somber information were aware that government corruption and human suffering were hidden at the end, tucked between the garage sale listings and classified ads.

The paper focused on the dynamic "happenings" of the town and people of Moonberry Lake. Reading about neighbors, the coffee shop conversations, or the hearsay in the hair salon seemed to start the day off right for folks.

Cora knew from her time in Moonberry as a kid that summer visitors loved the levity of the paper. The hilarious quotes and pictures, detailed sightings of who was dating whom, lengthy stories of new marriages or deaths all made the paper a priceless lifeline to the community.

Today the front page featured a picture of a man in his eighties raising his cane in victory. The caption read, "Hal Nordstrom breaks the bank at penny bingo!"

Cora flipped to her favorite section, "Sightings and Satire." It was basically a gossip column commenting on the more salacious matters of Moonberry society.

## SIGHTINGS AND SATIRE

Congratulations to longtime Moonberry Lake resident Dorothea Svenson who is thrilled to announce the birth of her eighteenth grandchild! She now holds the record of most grandchildren of any living grandparent in town. The beaming grandmother boasts that the success of her family's procreation is due to long winters and few hobbies.

Do you have a hankering for haddock? Craving cod? Biting for bass? Longing for lutefisk? Salivating for salmon? Wanting walleye? Betty's Fish Shack is teeming with your choice! This week's special is 13 percent off your order if you say you have high cholesterol. Betty says, "My fish will swim through your arteries, and your heart will be happier for it!"
*\*Reminder: Every Tuesday, kids get one free fried Mystery Fish on a Stick!*

The people of On Our Knees Methodist Church are doing just that. Congregation members will be on their knees for the yearly fall cleaning of the church and landscape next Saturday. They're giving this advance notice so there will be NO EXCUSES. The same four people are tired of being the only ones to show up, so the project is being called, "Create in me a clean heart, O God." WIPE CLEAN THE CHURCH AND YOUR CONSCIENCE ALL IN ONE DAY!

Moonberry Lake's Little League championship game was so close that many players and fans wanted to pull their hair out. Literally. Itching for the sectional title, the pint-size boys were tickled to win. The tradition of throwing their caps in the air before every game spread not only their luck but head lice too! All the boys and their parents caught the glory of winning while tiny critters clung to their hair follicles. The victory celebration afterward included ice cream, hot dogs, and hairnets.

The State Health Board did a surprise inspection of one of our local diners (name withheld). Sadly, the local hub lost its license and is no longer permitted to serve meat. Any other details are being withheld for privacy.

Big news! Mike's Steak Wagon is closing, but he said he is thinking of turning the restaurant into a soup-and-salad buffet under new management.

"Stop readin' that smut!"

Cora jumped and looked up to see Widgy had entered the family room.

"It's not smut—it's the town paper. Don't you read it?"

She scowled. "I try not to. It didn't do *any* of my husbands justice in their obituaries. All it focused on was how I go through men like water. That's where the nickname Marry-Em-and-Bury-Em Widgy came from."

"Sorry." Cora put down the paper. "What can I do for you?"

Widgy set a brown jug on the coffee table.

"What's this?"

"Some of George's moonshine."

"George?"

"My third husband."

"Of course." Cora unscrewed the top and took a sniff of the concoction. The powerful fumes made her head jerk back. It was worse-smelling than rubbing alcohol.

"It's somethin' to keep under the medicine cabinet."

"To drink when I'm sick?"

Widgy's eyes widened. "Dear Lord, no! It'll kill you! This is from his most potent batch. You soak your feet in a diluted solution every six months, and any athlete's foot, calluses, or warts are guaranteed to disappear. Don't soak too long, though, or your skin will get raw and peel."

"I'll remember that. Thank you for the gift."

Widgy pushed her hands into her pockets. "It's nothin'. I've got six more barrels in the basement when you run out. It also works for sterilizin' things or cleanin' paintbrushes if you run out of turpentine."

"It sounds . . . useful." Widgy still hadn't moved, so Cora took another stab at conversation. "How's Beast?"

Widgy shrugged. "Fine. He's sheddin' his coat."

"His fur's thinning this time of year?"

"Yeah, his system's all screwed up. He loses big chunks of his fur, leavin' bald spots. I have to put lotion on the spots at night so the skin doesn't chap and then put two sweaters on him durin' the winter. It all grows back by early July. But, by then, the poor thing's so hot that I shave his whole body—except for his head. He doesn't let me touch him there."

Cora chose her words carefully. "His condition sounds unusual."

"It makes him misunderstood. Everyone thinks he's rabid or has some sort of contagious disease. No one wants to come close to the house once they catch a glimpse of him. The paperboy leaves the paper at the curb, and the mailman puts the mail in the back of my truck. On the upside, Beast keeps solicitors away."

Cora nodded. "Having a dog with a bad reputation does have benefits."

Widgy cracked a small smile, and Cora couldn't help but stare. The woman's roughness seemed to disappear, replaced by a softer look. Widgy turned to go back through the kitchen but added before leaving, "The moonshine also takes off rust and can be used to clean tar off your boots."

"I'll remember that. Thanks."

The overcast late-August day was thick with humidity, making Cora's shirt stick to her back. She huffed a little deeper as she worked. With all the mildewed curtains taken down and thrown out, light poured through the bare windows. Cora had been cleaning and clearing out with the same aggressive determination as Widgy and could feel new strength in her body.

She was busy painting when a cat leapt up from outside and sat on the window ledge. It was full-grown with splotches of brown, black, and orange all over its white fur.

"Hello, kitty-cat." She stepped down from the ladder, and the cat jumped to her side, leaning against her and purring. She reached down to pet the cat and saw it had a collar but no tag.

"I'll go get you some tuna." She hoped her new furry friend wouldn't run away as soon as she left the room. To her surprise, it followed her.

Widgy was in the kitchen with all her tools spread out on the table. Cora bit her lip at the sight of her new dish towels covered with grease and heaped in a pile on a chair.

"I can't find my—" Widgy stopped as soon as she caught a glimpse of the cat. Her lip curled. "Who let that mangy thing in here?"

"Do you recognize it?" Maybe she escaped from a neighbor's house. "She doesn't have any ID."

Widgy narrowed her eyes. "I've never seen it before, but you should get rid of it."

Cora frowned. "Be nice. It came to the window where I was working. Cats don't typically like me, but this one seems so sweet. I'm going to give her some tuna." She went to the pantry to get a can.

Widgy shook her head. "That's a mistake. You're teachin' it to come back beggin' for more."

"She could be lost."

"It's got a collar."

"She could be frightened."

"It's too friendly."

"She could have been wandering around for days."

"It's too clean."

"She could be hungry."

"It's too fat."

"She could be hurt and unable to get back home."

"It's walking fine."

"She could be *lonely*."

"Now, who are we talkin' about, you or the cat?"

Cora looked up from the cat, who was devouring the tuna, to see Widgy smiling at her own clever rebuttal. "Very funny! There's nothing wrong with showing a little kindness." She tenderly stroked the cat.

"Like when I showed some kindness to one stray, and now five come barkin' at my back door every night? I go through more dog food than the county pound. You're startin' somethin' here, take my word for it."

"It might be nice to have a pet around here."

"What does the collar say?"

"There's no stitching on it that gives a name or phone number. I think I'll call her Patchwork."

"It's not yours."

"I like the name," Cora said, ignoring Widgy. "Her coat resembles a quilt of autumn leaves."

"Try, Go Home. See if it responds to that. Or how about Scram. Try shoutin' that and see what it does."

Cora glared at Widgy. "Why don't you like her?"

She shrugged. "I prefer dogs. If the animal can't hunt, fetch the paper, or scare people from my property, it's no use to me."

"You take Beast hunting?"

"I haven't gone huntin' since my first Harry died, but I'm pretty sure Beast would make a fine bird dog."

"Does he fetch the paper?"

"Yeah. He may chew it up and pee on it, but it still counts if he gets it to the house."

The woman was one contradiction after another. "Why do you keep feeding all those stray dogs if you don't like them?"

"They're dependent on me now." Widgy's nostrils flared. "They would die from confusion. They think I'm their mama. Anyway, it's none of your business."

Cora held back the smile tugging at her mouth. "So, feeding one cat is wrong, but it's fine to enable a *pack* of dogs?"

Widgy sneered. "You have a way of turnin' things around, ya know that? Go on and kidnap the thing for all I care!" She wiped her greasy hands on the last clean dish towel, then threw it in the pile with the others.

"You have a good heart underneath all that flannel, Widgy. You'd do the same thing I'm doing if this cat came to you."

Widgy shook her head, letting out a huff. "Don't touch my tools. I'm goin' for a pop break." She stormed out the back door, leaving it open. Patchwork ran out the door too.

*Oh well. At least it's leaving with a full tummy.* Cora went to the fridge for some lunch and found nothing appealing. She had to either take a trip to the store or settle for a jar of sweet pickles from Kitty and one of Joseph's wrinkly tomatoes. Her stomach growled.

On her way to the car, Cora peeked over into Joseph's garden. Seeing he wasn't there, she went back to the kitchen and retrieved the empty basket that had been sitting for a few days. They had developed an unspoken understanding over the last couple months. She left the basket in his garden, and he refilled it and returned it to her porch.

It was a nice arrangement, and she didn't feel as though she was taking advantage of his generosity because she always left a little present in the empty basket as a thank-you. No better gift for a gardener than gardening supplies. The first time, she left new gardening gloves. Then a trowel, a kneeling pad, and another digging tool. This time, it was a few packets of organic seeds.

Dropping the basket in the same place she always did, she

hurried back to the car. On her way to the store, she smiled at the ways she was learning to adapt to her new surroundings.

While looking at the cheese options at the grocery store later that afternoon, Cora heard someone call her name. She turned around.

"Miss Matthews, over here!"

Cora glanced over the counter and saw the same worker who had served her the log-size sandwich. The hot pink–bespectacled woman was waving her hand frantically, so Cora pushed her cart over.

"Do you remember me? I'm Ruth Ann. I was wondering how you've been doing. We don't get many new folks in town, and I wanted to make sure you've been settling okay these first few months."

"That's nice of you. I'm fine, thank you."

"You need to give yourself time for *acc*"—Ruth Ann held up a finger, then glanced at the page of her *Reader's Digest*—"*acclimation.* That means settling in, adapting, or adjusting." She looked up with a proud smile. "I try to go through the vocabulary section in every issue and learn a couple new words. As soon as I read the definition of that word, you came to mind."

"Ah."

"Can I get you anything? We have a *myriad* of choices."

"Actually, I just came in for a few things."

"You can't leave without some of this sliced turkey. It's so fresh and savory. One could also describe it as appetizing or delectable."

Cora chuckled. "You talked me into it." She got a kick out of Ruth Ann and wanted to support her vocabulary endeavor. "Give me a pound. I'll have it for my lunches this week. If I don't eat it, my repairwoman will."

Ruth Ann stopped midway through putting on her gloves. "Repairwoman? You don't mean Widgy, do you?"

"Yes."

Ruth Ann rolled her eyes. "Oh, honey, with her in your house, you're going to need two full pounds! Have you ever seen that woman eat? Every potluck and buffet in town knows they're going to come up short when she arrives."

Cora laughed.

"Let me cut some ham for you too. Now that I know Widgy's at your place, I've got to look after you or you're likely to starve."

Cora crossed her arms, tilting her head to the side. "Do you always add to people's orders like this, or are you simply trying to drum up business for the deli?"

Ruth Ann giggled. "No, I want you to have plenty. That way, I won't worry about you." She got to work on the meat, then handed over the two wrapped packages.

"Thanks. I'm sure Widgy will enjoy it as much as I do." She set the items in her cart. "It was nice running into you, Ruth Ann."

"Adieu, goodbye, farewell!"

At the checkout, Cora set the last item on the conveyor belt and looked up. Her stomach sank at the sight of the clerk. It was the woman who had an opinion on everything. Cora pretended to be fully engrossed in which candy to select from the rack beside her. Maybe if she didn't make eye contact, she'd avoid advice on how to prevent constipation or high cholesterol.

No such luck.

"You don't want to fill your body with *this* junk!" the cashier exclaimed, holding up a package of brownie mix. She threw it under the counter. "It'll put on padding you'll never get off. It might be a little cushion now, but believe me, when you reach my age, that cushion hangs so far down, you'll think you've grown extra body parts. A cake I ate in 1995 went straight to my tummy, and today it's in my knees."

Cora moved away from the candy bars as the woman critiqued everything she'd purchased. She didn't know what to say about the discarded brownies. *What kind of grocery clerk doesn't let you buy the food you want?*

She cleared her throat. "I like that brownie mix."

The woman shook her head. "I'm only trying to help you. I didn't make up that cake story, I can lift my pant leg and show you if you want."

Cora stared at her with wide eyes.

The clerk held up a small container. "You're wasting money on this facial cleanser. What they make in labs is never as good as what God gave us. You need lemon—the citrus will clear away the dirt and tighten the skin. Let me get you one." Without waiting for an answer, she grabbed her microphone and spoke into the intercom in a booming voice. "Two lemons to line six. Put a rush on it—customer is waiting." She gave a firm nod. "Lemons should do the trick. Cut one in half and rub it all over your face. Leave it on for a couple minutes. If it stings, that's okay. That means it's making your pores smaller and cleaning deep down. You want to start doing this now because, by the time you reach my age, it'll be too late."

A few minutes later, the rest of Cora's food had been added up, including the lemons she didn't want but now, out of curiosity, would try.

"How much?"

"It comes to forty-one eleven. Do you have any coupons?"

Cora cringed. "No."

The cashier clicked her tongue. "You're throwing away money if you don't use coupons! Young folks today don't appreciate the value of a dollar. When I was your age, I'd save all my money so I could treat myself to a new pair of pantyhose."

Cora swiped her card and helped pack the bags, throwing in the food and not caring if the heavier stuff squashed the lighter. Pushing the cart away, she glanced back when she heard the clerk berate the next customer, lecturing a man on the horrors of hydrogenated oils found in the box of cupcakes he was trying to buy.

Back at the lodge, she put everything away and then decided to take Kitty something she had picked up at the gas station on her way home. Though they charged twice the price of a grocery store, Cora knew she could buy it without anyone judging her or taking it away.

Kitty was brushing leaves off the cemetery markers with a small broom.

"Hi, Kitty! I see you're busy as usual."

The elderly woman looked over at Cora and smiled. "I'm always doing something around here, but more importantly, I always have time for friends. Come and visit with me."

"I brought you some cookies."

Kitty's face lit up. "A treat? How thoughtful of you."

"They're a thank-you for the flowers you let me give to Sofia a few weeks back, and for the carrot cookies. I know all your cookies are homemade, but I bet these are different from anything in your kitchen. They're chocolate-covered marshmallow cookies."

"Ooh, they sound sinful."

Cora opened the wrapping and offered the container of billowy cookies.

Kitty took one and examined it carefully. "I love the shape. They look like tiny chocolate Bundt cakes, but they're so light." She bit into it, and her eyes got wide. "Mm, it's extraordinary! If I had to imagine what biting into a cloud tasted like, it would be this—soft, fluffy, and a little bit gooey."

Cora grinned. "I'm glad you like them."

"If I had known anything like this existed, I would've purchased these to eat alongside my carrot cookies years ago. I don't drive anymore, but I'd hike to town for these. I might die coming back, but at least I will have had my puffs of heaven!"

They both laughed. What a wonderful world Kitty lived in. Her delight for the simple things went all the way to her soul.

Cora was still smiling as she crossed the road. However, as she approached the lodge, her joy transformed into a wave of panic when she noticed a familiar car in the driveway. She clutched her stomach, feeling as though she'd been punched in the gut.

She had forgotten the one rule of running away: never stop, or the past will catch up with you.

Cora reached the front of the lodge, where he stood in the yard looking out to the lake.

She swallowed hard.

"Hello, Kyle."

# *Twelve*

Kyle appeared neat and ironed after hours of driving. His angular build wasn't so much physically strong as arrogant. All Cora could think about was her unbrushed hair and that she was wearing an old T-shirt and jeans.

"Hey, there's my girl." He came to give her a hug.

Her arms remained motionless at her sides. "What are you doing here?"

"You didn't answer any of my calls or texts. I've left a hundred messages."

It was an exaggeration, but he had left a lot. "There's bad reception here."

"It's been three months, I wanted to make sure you were okay." He cocked his head and put on the half smile she used to consider flirtatious. "I missed you."

She stepped back. "How did you find me?"

"I read in the obituary that your mom was buried here. I looked up the name Matthews and came up with this address. I didn't have to do much else. The guy at the gas station was more than happy to fill me in on where you lived. Is this whole thing really yours?"

And there it was. That glimmer of greed in his Realtor eye.

"Sort of," she mumbled.

"It's a sweet deal. You're going to make a killing flipping this place."

It sounded so wrong when he said it aloud. She drew in a deep breath, wishing he would leave. "Kyle, why did you come here?"

He acted like he hadn't heard the question. "Let's go inside and talk. You can show me around."

She didn't want him in the lodge. She didn't want him in Moonberry Lake. This was *her* place, not his. But he had already started walking in. She followed him through the porch and into the dining room, where Widgy had lined up her toolboxes on a table and was cleaning something. As they drew closer, Cora saw it was an enormous hunting knife. Widgy was polishing the blade.

If Kyle found Widgy intimidating, he didn't show it.

"Kyle, this is Widgy, my repairperson. Widgy, this is Kyle, my . . ." She cleared her throat. "My ex-fiancé."

Kyle put his hand out, but Widgy didn't shake it. She continued to glare at him while wiping the sizeable machete. After an uncomfortable silence, he lowered his hand and, in the same motion, put his arm around Cora's shoulders, squeezing her in closer. "We're working on the *ex* part," he said with a wink.

Widgy grunted, unimpressed. Dropping the knife into the toolbox, she crossed her arms and stood with all the dominance of a lioness defending her cub. Cora had to restrain a smile by biting her lip hard.

She would never say it aloud, but it appeared as if Widgy was being *protective* of her. That realization shocked Cora even more than Kyle's arrival. Widgy's stature and less-than-sunny welcome did have an effect, because Kyle's demeanor deflated. He stepped behind Cora, putting her in front for the kill.

Cora found it hilarious how much Widgy scared him. "Kyle came for a visit."

"I don't remember you mentionin' invitin' anyone," Widgy responded.

"It was a surprise," Kyle piped up. "If you'll excuse us, we have a lot to discuss. It was nice to meet you. Let's start with that tour you promised, Cora." His hands tightened on her shoulders and propelled her forward.

Cora shrugged off his grip and walked ahead of him. She hurried through the lodge, pointing to rooms as she talked.

"That was the dining room. The kitchen is in the back," she stated in a flat voice. "These are the downstairs bedrooms." She stopped in the foyer. "Here's the family room."

"The great room," he corrected her.

Cora stepped into the room and waited for Kyle to follow. He closed the French doors behind him, then turned to face her. "Why would you hire that Neanderthal of a woman? She looks like a criminal."

"Don't talk about her like that. You have no idea who she is and what she's capable of."

He put his hands on his hips. "Is she even certified to make repairs?"

Cora knew the fact that Widgy came from generations of repairmen would mean very little to Kyle. She plopped down on the couch, ignoring his tirade. "What are you doing here?" she asked again, already exhausted by his visit.

He sat on the edge of the coffee table so he was knee to knee with her. "I think we should get back together. Now that you've had a chance to mourn the death of your mother, I think it's time to get back on track."

Cora gawked at him. *Is he serious?* "We broke up!"

"Because your mother passed away and you couldn't handle the stress. I still have feelings for you. And my family forgives you. It was costly to cancel the wedding so close to the date, but they understand, considering how your mother was all you had."

Cora straightened. "I'm sorry I hurt you and your family, but we broke up because I couldn't go through with it. I wasn't ready to get married, and I wasn't ready to make that commitment to you. I told you all this before I left. And having distance from you has only made me realize more how different we are from each other. It would have never worked out."

When he started to shake his head, she dug in deeper. "We are wrong for each other, Kyle, and have been from the beginning." As she stared at him, it all clicked into place. Instead of seeing his perfections, all she saw were his insecurities. That was what had drawn them together. "You were trying to fulfill some image of the right woman for you. I was trying to do what my mother wanted for me. We were both wrong. I saved us from a dreadful mistake. This isn't love. It's convenience. You want a perfect life, and that's not me."

As usual, Kyle only heard what he wanted to hear. "You were scared. I get it." He rubbed her knee. "But you know I'm the most stable relationship you've ever had, and we care for each other. We should get back together." He was firm, resolute in his pronouncement, acting as if she hadn't spoken. Like every other decision in his life, once the train was on the track, it never deviated, not even when it was bound to crash. All the memories of how controlling he was about every aspect of their life together came back to her.

She rubbed her forehead. It was time to be brutally honest. She didn't love him. She wasn't sure she had *ever* loved him. What she had liked was that she'd found someone who knew what he wanted in life when she didn't have a clue. "No, we can't, Kyle. I don't want to."

He shook his head. "You don't mean that."

"Yes, I do. Please, just go and don't come back. Find someone who's truly right for you, because deep down, you know it's not me."

For the first time, he didn't have a comeback. He just stared at her.

She got up off the couch and began walking to the door.

"And *this* is the life you want?" he said, standing and motioning to the room.

His disbelieving expression almost made her laugh.

She nodded. And as she did, she realized she was admitting it to herself for the first time. She wanted every bit of this messy, surprising, exhausting, lovely life she was carving out every day.

His face hardened. "You're going to regret this," he said, nearly stomping to the door. "I'm a great catch."

"And I'm releasing you and throwing you back into the water."

His eyes narrowed and his jaw jutted forward. "Goodbye, Cora. Good luck finding anyone who will take care of you like I could've." With that, he stormed out.

She watched him evaluate the gravel driveway and overgrown landscape on the way to his car with a look of repugnance, reminding her of how he judged everything.

She trudged upstairs to her bedroom and curled up with a blanket, wanting to block out the world. Seeing him had thrown her off and she needed a minute.

However, that was impossible in a world with Widgy. The thud of footsteps announced her approach.

"I see your Prince Charming left."

"He's *not* my Prince Charming," Cora said from under her pillow. "I don't like him."

"You don't have to like him, he's not coming back."

Widgy scrunched her face. "He was eyeballin' this place like it was *his* while he was waitin' for ya. And he looks like he wouldn't know how to grout tile or work a chain saw."

Cora chuckled as she pushed her pillow away and turned to lay on her side, facing the doorway where Widgy stood. "Interesting analysis. It's actually pretty accurate. You should become a detective. You've got a nose for the dangerous, khaki-and-polo-wearing types."

Widgy pointed a finger at her. "I knew I was right."

Cora fiddled with the corner of the blanket. "My past never seems to completely leave me alone," she added quietly, keeping her eyes on the blanket.

Widgy frowned. "It's not supposed to. How can ya move forward if you don't got nothin' behind ya?"

Cora didn't have an answer. Maybe there was more to her rough-around-the-edges repairwoman than what met the eye. The corner of Cora's mouth raised in a half smile. "Cleaning that knife was a nice touch."

Widgy smirked. "I'm bringin' out my gun next time any of your old boyfriends show up."

That made Cora grin more widely, but only momentarily. Even Widgy's humor and veiled threats couldn't cheer her up.

Widgy came closer. "Okay, shoot. What else is wrong?"

"Forget about it."

"Spit it out. I don't like you mopin' around."

Maybe it was from being exhausted from all the endless work, maybe it was from seeing Kyle and being reminded of the poor choices she made in her old life and how she was always fleeing from them, but she couldn't suppress the swell of emotion rising. Her chest felt heavy with tears that wanted to be released. "Things just feel hard."

"Like what?"

Cora sat up, hugging her pillow tightly. "Fixing this place, my job with Mr. Wells, Kyle showing up, Rolf—"

"Rolf?" Widgy repeated, her face twisted. "You mean Johansson next door? What's he got to do with anything?"

"He's left a few piles of dead fish with notes telling me to leave."

Widgy's eyes widened. She opened her mouth as if to say something and then shut it. She took off her baseball cap, snapped it against her thigh, then put it back on her head. "I was wonderin' where they were comin' from."

"You found some?"

Widgy nodded. "Yep. I've just been scoopin' 'em up and takin' 'em home to bury in my garden. I didn't know they were dumped to send you a message."

Cora scoffed. "How did you *think* piles of fish got there?"

Widgy shrugged. "I don't know. Luck."

Cora fell back on her pillow. "You're unbelievable."

Widgy walked into the room until she loomed over Cora's bed.

She put her hands on her hips. "First of all, this place is comin' along just fine. Progress may be slow, but we're movin' ahead. And that's the right direction to be headin'. Second, from what I hear from Sam, you don't suck at your job with Jonathan Wells, so there's that. Third, that ninny Kyle showin' up has got nothin' to do with where you are or where you're goin'—only where you were.

"And lastly," she said with the stern voice and stance of a soldier, "you're gonna show old Rolf he's met his match. If he wants war, we'll give him war." With that, she gave a hard nod as if it sealed her commitment to the fight.

Cora sighed. "*We* are not doing anything. This is *my* problem, and I'll handle it."

"How?"

"I'm going to take Kitty's advice and shower him with kindness."

Widgy rolled her eyes. "That sounds awful. Now, are you gonna lay in bed all day and wallow in a pity party or get some work done? There're dead mice to clean up from the traps I set out."

"Well, when you put it like that . . ."

Widgy shook her head as she was leaving. "Sass, sass, sass."

Reinvigorated, Cora got up to get rid of the mice and wash floors. The exertion of scrubbing would feel good and give her time to think. She wasn't finding the answers that she needed. So far, all she had found in the other bedrooms were handmade quilts, old clothes, and embroidery. Nothing that seemed out of the ordinary or revealed clues about why her mother had left.

She still had the attic to explore. The one glaring truth about the lodge was that everything was old. Chipped dishes, worn blankets, threadbare sheets and towels, outdated household items, and little memorabilia among old photos. The lodge held all the scuff marks of a life lived here but not the imprint that indicated this was where her family had laughed and loved and fought.

Whenever she felt discouraged, she reminded herself that she had nearly an entire year left to figure it all out.

This time, she wasn't going to run from the unknown.

# *Thirteen*

Mr. Wells, we need to talk. I can't do this math. I never could." Cora's head hurt as she stared down at the mix of numbers, letters, and symbols. She heard the whining in her voice but didn't care. "I've always been terrible at math."

"Quitters never get ahead."

Cora threw her hands in the air. "I'm not looking to get ahead. I'll gladly step aside and let anyone who knows how to do this pass me right on by."

Mr. Wells fervently shook his head. "No. I'll explain it again, and you *will* persevere."

She crossed her arms. *Time to negotiate.* "If I continue to try at math, you have to let me organize these newspapers."

Mr. Wells stared at her. "They *are* organized. I have them all categorized. I've developed my own system of orderliness."

"I'm sure you have." She eyed the piles. "Tell me, why do you need them?"

"I like to keep records and information I find interesting."

"But you can get any information that's in these papers online. You can even read the newspaper online. These fill up your house and smell musty."

He was quiet.

"Life's about give-and-take," Cora continued. "If you want to teach me, you have to clear away these piles. Right now, we're only able to use a quarter of your dining room table. They also take up most of the floor space. Pretty soon you're not going to have any place to walk or live."

He still didn't respond. She thought about what would get him to change. And then it came to her as she glanced at his plastic-covered sofa. "Think of all the dust mites you'll be eliminating. These deteriorating papers are not only dirty, they're also polluting the air. We'll go one room at a time, and today, we'll start here in the dining room. We will fill a couple bags, and I'll take them with me to recycle."

She retrieved a trash bag from the kitchen and handed it to him. "You simply have to focus on filling one bag at a time. We'll take it nice and slow." She spoke in the gentlest tone. These papers were part of the fortress he had built to hide from the world. By the sheer volume, it was obvious Nona hadn't been successful in nudging him to purge any of it. Cora figured she'd push until he pushed back. She wanted Mr. Wells to have a nice home if this was to be his whole world.

Without a word, he took the bag and tentatively placed a newspaper into it.

Cora walked into the living room, pushed aside the curtains, lifted the shades, and opened the window.

He instinctively stepped back. "What are you doing?"

"I'm letting in light and some fresh air."

"No. I like them shut."

"Mr. Wells, for your health, you should *want* to air out this place. Cleaning is as important to me as teaching algebra is to you. I promise to shut them again before I leave."

He nodded but kept fidgeting with his glasses.

His discomfort saddened her. Perhaps talking about math would help distract him. "Maybe you can explain coefficients again while we move these papers. Then I can wipe down the area we cleaned so we can get back to working on algebra." She handed him another newspaper from the table and flashed her sunniest smile.

He nodded. "Then, you can learn the difference between rational and irrational numbers."

"Yes, we'll have plenty of time for math," she added. "I'm even looking forward to having you teach me on this nice space you created. And I have a feeling that irrational numbers will come easily to me, since that pretty much sums up my experience and understanding of many things."

He narrowed his eyes. "Was that a joke?"

The corner of her mouth turned up. "Yes. Apparently a poor one."

He frowned. "I've never understood sarcasm."

"I'll remember that."

After the math lesson, Cora lugged the bags to her Jeep and could barely lift them up into the trunk. Taking out a couple hundred pounds of newspaper had hardly made a dent. She'd underestimated how many bags and how much time it would take to clean the place. And she couldn't believe how Mr. Wells was allowing her to clean up when he hadn't allowed Nona. Then again, she had learned that Nona had refused any math instruction.

Maybe the key for Mr. Wells was the even swap—newspapers for math homework.

Whatever it was, the sacrifice on her part was well worth the small victory. She'd adopt Mr. Wells's motto of perseverance to get the job done.

When the phone rang in the dining room, Cora picked it up on the fifth ring. "Hello?"

No response.

"Hello?"

"Yes, I'm calling for— Wait a minute, I lost the name."

Cora immediately recognized the voice.

"Here it is," Grace continued. "This is Dr. Walker's office calling for Mr. Matthews."

"This is Cora Matthews."

"I'm sorry, can I please speak to your husband? There was an accident with the impression made for his dentures."

"There is no Mr. Matthews. There's only me."

"Well, then, you need to come in so we can make another cast for your dentures."

"I don't have dentures. I'm waiting for my permanent crown."

"Maybe that's what I lost. You need to come in for a new impression."

Cora looked at the clock. "I could be there around twelve thirty."

"That's my lunchtime. Let me ask Dr. Walker."

Cora heard Grace put the phone down and shuffle papers before the line went silent for a couple of minutes.

Finally, the woman returned. "That's fine. Dr. Walker said he would handle it."

She hung up. *How can he maintain a practice with that woman as a receptionist?*

After running a brush through her hair, she did a final look in the mirror. No paint, no spaghetti stains, no dirt.

When she arrived, the office was empty.

"Hello?"

Dr. Walker appeared from the back. "Hi, Cora. Sorry you had to come in again. It seems there was a mix-up with the impression sent to the lab. Grace mailed them another patient's night guard by mistake, and she's pretty positive the original impression is lost." He gestured apologetically to the messy reception desk. "I have another receptionist, but she's on maternity leave for two more months, so right now it's just Grace—who kind of came with the practice when I bought it. My hygienist suddenly eloped and moved away about three weeks ago, and I haven't found a replacement. I apologize if you've gotten the wrong idea about this office. Normally, we're very efficient and professional."

She gave him a smile. "No problem."

"Come on back."

She followed him without saying a word. She studied his profile as he prepped his station. He had a chiseled look to him that might seem intimidating if his smile didn't soften it.

There seemed to be something shy about his demeanor today. He examined her tooth. "How's it feeling?"

"Fine for the most part. A little sore now and then."

He did some adjustments and made the impression.

"I'll send this out by Express Mail, so your final crown will arrive as soon as possible. Again, I apologize for the inconvenience."

"Don't worry about it. Accidents happen—although it appears they happen to me more often than most people."

He grinned.

"Actually, I'm relieved. I was dreading the appointment."

That seemed to bother him, so she hurried to explain.

"I mean the procedure, not you. I'm not dreading seeing you. You're nothing to dread." Her cheeks burned. She sounded like an idiot. "That didn't come out right."

He laughed and his smile brightened. "Here—I'll walk you out." He led the way back to the lobby and held the door for her. "I look forward to seeing you at the dreaded appointment," he teased, "and I promise it won't be that bad."

"That's easy for you to say. How about we switch places?"

They shared a smile, and she headed home.

⁓

Whatever it was that had put Widgy in such a foul mood later that afternoon, Cora had no idea, but she was over it. The two were upstairs, chiseling out tiny squares of tile in one of the bathrooms. They were supposed to be working as a team, but when Widgy wasn't giving orders, she was criticizing Cora's work.

Cora had had enough. "Okay, what is wrong? Why are you being so nasty?"

Widgy was quiet.

"Is it something to do with Beast?"

She gave a small nod.

It was unsettling to see Widgy so upset. Cora moved closer. "What happened?"

"He bit my neighbor's dog."

Cora let out a little gasp. She thought back to Widgy's description of the animal. "Was it bad?"

"The dog had to have a few stitches, but the bite wasn't deep. Beast was prob'ly just trying to mate with it. I paid for the vet bill, but my neighbor is tryin' to get animal control involved." Her voice quivered. "He wants Beast taken away."

"Oh, Widgy, I'm so sorry. What are you going to do?"

"I have to prove he's not a danger to the community."

"How are you going to do that?"

"I'm not sure yet. I don't like leaving Beast alone though. You wouldn't mind if I brought him here, would ya?"

*Oh dear.* The lodge was the last place she'd ever want that dog to be, but seeing the desperation in Widgy's eyes, Cora couldn't refuse.

"Sure. That's . . . fine."

Widgy's disposition changed immediately. "You'll like him. He can be a real sweetheart." She cleared her throat. "Just don't wear anything yellow—for some reason, that color sets him off."

Cora closed her eyes. *What have I agreed to?*

⁓

Widgy's description of Beast proved accurate. Cora's first glimpse of him the next morning was both shocking and disturbing. The poor thing did have some sort of skin condition that made him half-bald. The patchy fur stood straight out like a cartoon creature that had been electrocuted. Anyone with a heart would feel compassion for the animal, but then his personality came out, and all that empathy evaporated.

Though he showed his teeth and growled anytime Cora got

near, Widgy insisted Beast was fond of her. The proof was that he lost control of his bladder whenever she tried to pet him, which apparently was a positive sign.

At the moment, the dog was on the porch peacefully asleep, an unusual occurrence. Typically he barked and whined while he slept.

One Tuesday, Cora noticed Beast's water bowl was filled with a dark liquid, so she went to the foyer, where Widgy was perched on a ladder fixing the light. "There's brown stuff in Beast's water dish. Want me to put some fresh water in it?"

"Nope. That's his Dr Pepper."

Cora flinched. "You give your dog Dr Pepper?"

"He needs caffeine in the morning or he gets all jittery. The vet said it was worth a try since the tranquilizers didn't work. I wouldn't have given it to him, but you're all out of coffee. Usually, a bowl of coffee does the trick and keeps him regular for a bonus."

Cora shook her head. "You lead a very unusual life."

Widgy shrugged and went back to work on the light.

Cora decided to stop by Arielle's since she hadn't been able to talk to her friend one-on-one at the last couple teas. She went to the pantry and grabbed an unopened container of meringues she'd hidden from Widgy in a soup pot. She knew Arielle would love them.

Five minutes later, she knocked on her friend's door. "Arielle? Are you here?" she shouted through the screen door.

"Come on in. I'm in the living room."

Cora found Arielle painting. All the furniture had been pushed aside. There were six canvases, each about six feet long, set up in a circle. The paintings were amazing. There were sunbursts of pinks and oranges, splashes of yellow, and horizons of blues and purples.

Arielle offered a quick smile. Her hair seemed more out of control than usual, looking as if it hadn't been tamed in a week.

"What's up?" She made a swipe of the brush as she spoke.

Cora was astounded by the sight before her. "These are gorgeous!"

Arielle's eyes brightened. "I call the collection *Ethereal Awakenings*."

"The colors are spectacular."

"You were my inspiration. After you left, your picture gave me an idea. I began working on one, and soon I had a roomful."

"How could *my* picture give you inspiration? All I did was smear some colors together."

"It's what you told me. When you said they were the colors you thought of at night, I got a fabulous idea about painting what lies so deep within us that it's actually *outside* of us. Does that make sense?"

"Um . . ."

Arielle turned back to the images as she spoke. "I imagine what exists beyond our consciousness but then is perceived in reality. This portrait is called *A Walk in the Ethereal Realms*. I'm trying to evoke the feeling that came to you as you remembered dreaming. I want my paintings to be a reawakening." She turned to Cora. "It's been a long time since I've painted with such passion. I watched as you created, and it reminded me of what I need to get back to."

"All I did was listen to you and then paint."

"You closed your eyes, took a breath, and let your inner self pour onto the canvas. After you left, I closed my eyes, took slow, deep breaths, and allowed myself to dream. The vision of this collection is what came to me. I was so excited to begin, I didn't stop until I had something on each canvas."

"It's unlike anything I've ever seen," Cora said with genuine astonishment.

"I have a dozen ideas of what I want to include in this grouping. The creativity and colors are bursting out of my soul. I'm letting this beautiful energy flow through me."

"Well, get back to painting. I just came by for a quick visit and to give you some meringues."

"I'm famished. Thank you!" Arielle opened the package and popped one into her mouth. "You see, we're so connected that you even know when I need nourishment or, in this case, a sugar high."

Cora laughed. "I'm happy to provide sweets whenever you need them."

Arielle was a whirlwind of energy. Watching her paint in her pigment-splattered clothes, with her hair all tangled, Cora was amazed at how happy and beautiful her friend was. Arielle was the embodiment of what she wished for herself. She lived joyfully in the present.

The more Cora thought about it, the more she realized how her present could be fuller and feel different if she just had answers to her past. The blatant lie her mother had told her about her grandparents' deaths only made her wonder what other lies were woven into her life. Every time she felt like giving up from having no leads, Widgy's words echoed in her mind, *"How can ya move forward if you don't got nothin' behind ya?"*

And that was the problem—Cora didn't feel as though she could move forward without uncovering what really happened to her family.

# *Fourteen*

## SIGHTINGS AND SATIRE

Be on the lookout for Donna Patterson's Pomeranian, Fluffy. She says the pooch jumped out of her car as they were going to the vet's office and that she's sure Fluffy, who had an appointment to be spayed, is on the prowl. "I have a terrible feeling she's in heat and looking for a hookup," a distraught Donna told us. As a precaution, we suggest keeping available suitors inside until frisky Fluffy is captured.

Pucker problem? Misplaced part of your mandible? Is there a change in your chops? A pair of teeth was found at the Our Last Saving Grace Lutheran Church potluck two Sundays ago. If you've noticed anyone with no teeth who can only gum their food, call Joyce at the church office. She said she cleaned them up, and they are in a little baggie in the lost and found box. Owner must come in and try them on.

To the relief of many, Mary Mackie's absence from church last week was not due to illness but to a bad hair day. When a friend went to check on her, Mary reportedly said, "There was no way I was going to enter the house of God with my roots showing so bad. Sin is one thing, but two inches of gray outgrowth seemed sacrilegious!" She has been taken off the prayer chain and says she needs the miracle only her hairdresser can perform.

Rodents run loose! Teddy Bear Hamsters escaped their cages at Lulu's Little Loves Pet Shop. "Their mischievous cavorting resulted in them multiplying faster than rabbits," says Lulu. The amorous critters are on a Super Sale. "Buy one, get THREE free! Come in and benefit from the prolific procreation of hot hamster love!"

Moonberry Lake's own Marci Seither won the Midwest Regional Bake-Off! Her recipe for Fudge Mocha Mint Brownie Bites with Salted Caramel Sauce beat out over one thousand other contestants from across the country. This win entitles her to go to Washington, DC and bake her sumptuous creation for the national prize. Her recipe will be printed with other top contenders in a cookbook, and Marci has graciously agreed to have a book signing when it comes out. Be sure to congratulate Marci when you see her around town. You can't miss her—she's wearing the sash that reads "Dessert Diva."

Cora folded up the paper, smiling. In the mood for more stories, she decided to visit her favorite storyteller. Stepping outside, she admired the beauty of the lake before turning to walk to her neighbor's. Looking out to the lake had become a habit. It was her compass in starting and ending the day, pointing her mindset in the right direction.

It was too early in September for the leaves to change into majestic colors, but she noticed the beginning of the turnover in the lake. The churning happening underneath the surface made the lake appear deeper and darker. The steely cool breeze made the tips of the whitecaps glint in the sun, giving the illusion of bits of broken glass sparkling on the water.

Cora crossed to the cemetery and found Kitty pulling the weeds creeping up her precious gravestones.

"I brought a homemade treat for today," Cora called to her, holding her gift high. "Take a break and have some pie with me."

Kitty clapped her hands together. "Goodness, what have I done to deserve so many treats? You have indulged my sweet tooth so often I could hardly zip up my skirt this morning."

Delight spread through Cora. It felt wonderful to love on her elderly friend. "By the way," Kitty continued, "I found a treasure in my mailbox yesterday. You wouldn't know anything about that, would you?"

Cora shook her head. "If it's a treasure, it was probably left by one of your gnomes."

"Yes, and I suspect I have one living across the road from me." Kitty winked. "I have to keep my chocolate treats out of sight so I don't eat them all at once. I haven't had any today."

"Then you are entitled to a treat now." Cora opened the picnic basket and took out the fresh pie.

Kitty's eyes grew wide. "What kind is it?"

"Apple, of course. 'Tis the season."

Kitty's mouth formed into a small circle. "Ooh, my favorite! I had the last piece of my own pie two nights ago. I snuck into the kitchen in the middle of the night and brought it back to bed with me. Nothing feels as scandalous as eating pie right out of the tin! It was a thin slice, so it left me dreaming of more the rest of the night."

Cora grinned. "Sometimes the smallest pleasures feel the most decadent." She couldn't resist serving an extra-large slice to Kitty to see the glee in her eyes. "Who are you working on today?"

Kitty swallowed a bite before answering. "This is Rose Stewart."

"Hello, Rose. It's nice to meet you." Cora nodded to the marker.

"She was a lovely woman but, unfortunately, she anguished over her lack of gardening skills. She felt compelled to grow roses because of her name, but success eluded her. Her flower garden was pathetic, and her trees and shrubbery were even worse. She desperately wanted to have a green thumb, but hers was absolutely black. People joked that all she had to do was look at a plant for it to die. She was so saddened by it, so I etched roses all over the marker—front, back, and sides. What she didn't have in life, I gave her in death."

"The roses are gorgeous. You've made them so lifelike." Cora traced over them with her fingers. "Tell me more about her."

"Rose had two daughters and wanted to pass on the tradition of flower names, so she named them Lily and Violet. Unfortunately, she passed on her black thumb as well. Her girls are as proficient in killing plants as she was. It's rumored that their mere presence can even stop mold from growing in basements."

Cora chuckled. "I don't know how you come up with your stories."

"They are not *my* stories, Miss Matthews. I am simply telling you *their* stories." Kitty took another bite of pie. "Mmm, this is delicious." She set down the plate. "You spend all your time in the lodge or over here indulging an old lady. When are you going to make some friends?"

"I *have* made friends. I have you, Arielle, Sofia, Mimi, and even Widgy. But don't tell Widgy that—she'd deny it."

Kitty eyed her. "What about male friends?"

Cora knew exactly what Kitty was hinting at but dodged it. No way was she sharing her disastrous dating past. "There's always Sam, and I work with Mr. Wells."

Kitty arched a brow but didn't push the subject.

Time to turn the tables. "What about you? Why don't *you* have gentlemen calling? You can't tell me it's never gotten lonely here."

Kitty paused. "It's time I introduced you to Peter. Come with me." She wiped her hands on her apron, then put her hands out to Cora. Cora helped her stand and then followed her through the yard to the front of her tiny home, which faced a small lake. Cora had never been to the other side of the property.

Kitty crossed to an oak tree and sat down in front of a marker. "I didn't know there were plots in front of the house."

Kitty was wiping off the top of the stone in an oddly tender fashion. "Miss Matthews, I would like to introduce you to the love of my life, my husband, Peter."

Cora's breath caught. "Oh . . . I'm sorry." She read the inscription. *Beyond the walls of life, beyond the bounds of time, I will love you. Heaven is only a whisper away.*

Kitty smiled at the stone. "He chose the inscription before he passed. I didn't know about it until the marker was placed in the ground. Peter knew I would see his grave daily and wanted it to be a source of comfort. And it has been. When I read his words, I feel close to him. I am reminded how fleeting this life is and how soon I'll be with him." She began tidying up the area around the stone. "Some people are gifted with a love that not only fills this lifetime but carries them into the next. It happens when the heart's so full that the moments, whether in memory or reality, keep you going and comforted forever."

Kitty turned her tender gaze to Cora. "What you need to know, my dear, is that true love doesn't ever leave you—it *leads* you. Like a beacon of light, it shepherds you through life, drawing you closer, filling you with a warmth that never goes cold."

In that moment, hearing the love in Kitty's voice, Cora understood where that twinkle in her friend's eyes came from.

"How long were you married?"

"A little less than forever, but long enough to fill a lifetime." Kitty grinned.

"What do you miss the most?"

"Oh my, there were a million things that made each moment memorable." She peered out at the lake. "I guess . . . holding his hand. It was a little turned around, because his hands were soft and mine were always dry and rough." She chuckled. "I react to certain soaps and don't wear gloves like I should, so I've always had eczema. He felt sorry for me and would gently take my hands, kiss them, and then hold them tenderly. I felt embarrassed at how cut up and red they were, but he never let go and always made me feel beautiful."

Cora watched as Kitty examined her hands, lost in thought for a moment.

Kitty looked up and smiled softly. "We held hands whenever we walked together or sat down to talk. He was left-handed and I'm right-handed, so we could even hold hands during meals. We went to sleep that way too. It's that gentle grasp I miss."

She stared at the marker and her voice grew distant. "I've often imagined he will take my hand again during my departure from this world—that I'll feel his touch and know it's time to go, like an angel escorting me into heaven. Sometimes, when a breeze touches my arm, I think it's him letting me know he's near." Kitty rubbed her arms as if to bring herself back to the present. "I bring him up on the business of the day and tell him my troubles. My conversations are all one-sided, but it makes me feel as if he's close by. We found true love in each other, and that never dies."

Cora leaned against the tall oak. "How did you meet?"

"It was love at first sight. I knew the second our eyes met. It's a long story I'll save for another day"—she threw Cora a playful grin—"over some more of your delicious pie."

"That's a deal. I have to say, the little cherub statues surrounding him are beautiful. Did you place them there so they would watch over him?"

She paused. "Those are my children."

Cora gasped and put a hand to her heart. "Oh, I'm so sorry, Kitty. I didn't mean—"

"Take off your shoes." Kitty's command was kind, though surprising. She gestured to Cora's feet.

"W-what?"

"You'll see. Just take them off."

Cora did as she was told.

Kitty led her to the water, where she removed her own shoes and walked into the lake a couple feet from shore.

"Your skirt's getting wet!" Cora cried.

"Hush now. Close your eyes and take a deep breath."

Cora watched Kitty close her eyes first, then started taking slow, deep breaths. She did the same.

Kitty's soft voice flowed over her. "I come out here to be with my family. I breathe them in. I feel them. Once you are in touch with the life force that pulsates all around you, another world opens up. It's the greatest gift to discover because then you understand you're never alone. Most people think I live the loneliest existence. If they only knew the company that surrounds me."

After another minute of listening to the waves and feeling the water slosh around her ankles, Cora felt Kitty take her hand. She followed her back to Peter's grave.

"May I ask what happened to your children?"

Kitty laid a hand on one of the cherubs. "I miscarried three of them. I set these tiny cherubs on the ground, though there were no bodies to bury. Once I carried life within me, even if it was for a short time, losing them was as real as any other death. I had the privilege of holding their spirits inside me, and I wanted to give the same respect to them that I would have if they had lived many years. It was too painful for Peter, so I had my own private ceremony. It brought me healing and was something I needed to do to release my grief."

She moved her hand to the statue of a small boy. "Our son, Scott, died from pneumonia when he was three. So precious but, sadly, born with weak lungs and no strength to fight infection. In those days, they didn't have the medicine they do today. We were devastated by his death, and Peter was never able to move on. He adored Scotty, and a part of him died along with our boy. It was years later the doctors said Peter had congestive heart failure, but I think he died from a broken heart. I understood because that's what I felt when Peter passed away. I became disconnected from the world."

Cora was taken aback by the sadness in Kitty's life. "What helped you through your grief?"

"At first, it was all I could do to get out of bed and make myself some toast and broth. I neglected everything in my grief, including this cemetery. It took all my strength to get through the day. And then as time passed, I noticed weeds creeping up around Peter's stone, so I began pulling them. I wanted his stone to stay nice. At the time, I believed it was my only connection to Peter. But after a while, I started on the markers next to his because they deserved the same care. As you can see, it grew from there, and I've been doing it ever since."

The ache of Kitty's pain was nearly palpable. "I think you're one of the strongest and most remarkable people I've ever met. You lost so much but kept going."

Kitty peered up to the tree overhead, pausing to take in its beauty before speaking. "Grief is a journey that keeps unfolding. It was a process for me and a process for the cemetery to become what it is today. But it was remembering the lives of these people that forced me to reflect on my own. There are endless examples of successes and failures, heartache and lost dreams buried here. It taught me to choose not to be swallowed up in sorrow but instead to make myself useful and try to be happy no matter what. The end result is that I've met extraordinary people. I've discovered a whole world, both above and below ground." She gave Cora a wink.

"One of the truths of life is that you have to keep yourself open. You never know who will cross your path who may share the wisdom which explains your own existence. Contemplating other people's stories has given me an insight I wouldn't have gained otherwise. Now, with every new sunrise, I get out of bed, make my broth, and know I have a job to do. It doesn't affect the rest of the world, but it's opened up eternity for me. I'm more mindful of the journey and have no fear of the destination."

For someone who was constantly surrounded by death, Kitty knew more about life than any other person Cora had ever met. She found meaning in life and purpose in her day from reaching deep inside herself and summoning the courage to go on.

Cora woke with a smile. Her mountain of tasks was being checked off systematically with the help of Widgy and Sam. Even projects she took on by herself didn't escape their watchful eyes. Sam kept busy on the outside of the lodge, while Widgy took ownership of the inside. Cora couldn't ask for two people more dedicated to the restoration. A definite metamorphosis was taking place in every scrub of a brush or turn of a screw. The charm and simple comfort of the old building was being reborn.

Even now Sam was outside, whistling his way through the task of painting, while the sound of pounding told her Widgy was hard at work transforming the bathrooms into what she called "downright respectable." Widgy grumbled less these days and even initiated conversations.

Something Cora had never felt before washed over her—a bone-deep contentment. She slid from the bed, pulled a blanket free and wrapped it around herself, then headed outside. She went to sit by the lake, bundled up snugly. It was going to be a picturesque September day. Staring out at the lake, she soaked up the glorious surroundings, thankful to be immersed in such divine nature.

Fall was her favorite time of year—the sound of rustling leaves, the blaze of color, and harvest of pumpkins and squash. Autumn meant hot, bubbling casseroles, thick soups, and apple crisp.

Gazing at the water, Cora closed her eyes, trying to etch the sight and feeling into her memory.

"Wake up! We've got work to do!"

She opened her eyes to find Sam leaning over her, decked out in his painting clothes and carrying a bucket of paint.

Cora groaned. "I'm too tired to work, Sam. You guys are making me old."

He chuckled. "That makes me prehistoric." He plopped into the chair next to hers.

"There isn't a part of my body that doesn't ache. I *cannot* look at those bedrooms today. Besides, what are you doing here this morning? It's Saturday. Don't you take any days off?"

"I need to finish some painting. With my classes, I can't come by during the week."

*Classes?* She'd forgotten about his day job. Aside from helping her, he was a professor of anthropology during the academic year. Of course. That's why she had seen less of him. "When did the semester start?"

"Three weeks ago."

She bolted up in her chair. "What? I don't want you doing this anymore. You're too busy. You should be spending your free time with your wife. Forget about the painting."

Sam shook his head. "Nope. I'm a man of my word, and I told you I would finish the north and east sides. Georgie doesn't mind. Besides, I'm almost done."

Kitty was spot-on when she had described him as "steady as an oak."

"Fine." She settled back into her chair. "How are the classes going?"

Sam's grin spread from ear to ear. "The students don't know it, but I'm sucking the youth right out of them. Teaching actually makes me younger. It breathes life into me." With that, he got up and went back to work.

After getting dressed, Cora walked outside and noticed a fresh basket of produce waiting for her: long green beans in plentitude. Joseph may not be one for conversation, but he grew the most beautiful vegetables, and she enjoyed his generosity.

From the scaffolding, Sam called down, "I saw your neighbor."

"Yep."

"He brought over another basket."

"Yep." She busied herself with stirring paint.

"He sure has kept you supplied the whole summer."

"Yep."

"And now into fall."

She paused her stirring. "Mm-hmm."

"Awfully generous of a neighbor to look after you like that."

She looked up at him. He was up to something.

"Have you had many conversations with him?" he asked.

"Nope."

"Who has a hard time with conversation, him or you?"

She put her hands on his hips. "What are you getting at?"

Sam stopped painting to look at her. "I think it would be nice to thank him personally rather than leave small tokens and then dodge out of there like one of the rabbits who steal his food."

"I'm not dodging him like a thieving rabbit. And how do you know about the gifts I leave?"

Sam shrugged. "I talk to my neighbors."

"He's not *your* neighbor, he's mine. You don't even live near him!"

"I'm being friendly, unlike some people." He said that last bit under his breath but still loud enough for her to hear.

She stormed past him, heading for the garden. *No one's going to accuse me of being an unfriendly, stealing vermin!*

Sure enough, Joseph was in the garden, watering. When he saw her approach, he turned off the hose. Concern etched his features.

"Is everything all right, Cora?"

She was so taken aback by his use of a complete sentence that, for a moment, she forgot why she was there. "I-I'm fine."

"You looked upset and were walking in such a hurry, I was afraid something was wrong."

She shook her head. "I was coming over to thank you for the vegetables."

"I see." He didn't look convinced.

"So . . . thank you for all the vegetables you've given me this entire summer." Now that she had blurted out her gratitude, she didn't know what else to say.

"You're welcome." He eyed her as though still trying to discern what was going on. "I've enjoyed giving them to you. And you don't need to continue leaving gifts. Having the ability and abundance to share is the blessing."

She studied him. "I don't even know how to respond to that."

"Is something wrong?"

Now that he was talking, she figured she had nothing to lose. "Has anyone ever told you that you look like Jesus?"

Joseph stared at her for a moment and then started laughing so hard, he had to wipe tears from his eyes. It was a full minute before he regained control.

"I'm serious," Cora continued. "You're spooky-similar to those old caricatures in the storybooks from when I was a kid. I realize they're not quite accurate to what He looked like, but still. You wear sandals, you share a freaky facial resemblance, you always appear so peaceful in the garden, and that thing you said about 'sharing is the blessing'—that's a very Jesus-like thing to say."

Joseph's face tightened into a modest grin as if he were struggling not to burst out laughing again. "No, no one has ever told me that. But I'll take it as a compliment."

Cora grew more perplexed. "What *do* you do?"

A huge smile spread across his face. "I'm a pastor. And I'm *not* joking."

She gasped. "Oh my gosh, you *are* Jesus!"

Deep laughter resonated from his chest. "No. I'm hardly the Messiah, but any resemblance in my line of work is highly regarded, so thank you."

"Where do you preach?"

"I'm the hospital chaplain, as well as the chaplain for hospice.

You could say I moonlight my services for Moonberry Lake. My calling has always been to serve the sick and dying."

Cora shook her head. "A pastor. I should have known. It explains the whole not-talking thing."

He gave her a crooked grin. "I'm a pastor, Cora, not a monk. I *do* talk."

"But you never put more than two words together when I spoke to you before."

"I enjoy listening more. And I talk when I know I can improve the silence."

She stared at him, gobsmacked. *How do I respond to that?*

Joseph beamed. "I've heard how nice you are from Sam. I was hoping that you'd eventually come over to talk. When you didn't, I was afraid I'd done something to offend you."

Oh, how wrong she'd been. She had misjudged him, avoided him, and acted rudely. "I'm sorry. I should've come over personally. It was rude of me."

"And I could've been more engaging when you first inquired about the garden. Why don't we start fresh?" He put out his hand. "Hi, I'm Joseph."

She paused, seeing her neighbor in a new way. "I'm Cora Matthews, your new neighbor. It's nice to meet you." She shook his hand.

Ten minutes later, she walked back over to Sam.

He was whistling a happy tune. "Have a nice chat?"

"You could've told me Jesus was a pastor!" she hissed in a loud whisper.

"You've got to figure some things out for yourself. It's all a part of settling in." Sam didn't even try to hide the mischievous gleam in his eyes.

"No more surprises," she warned, walking back to the paint cans.

When he didn't respond, she glanced over at him. He had a sad, troubled look on his face, just like on the first day she had met him, when he gave her the blue envelope. Something told her he didn't answer because he had no intention of making that promise. She could feel in her gut that he wasn't being completely honest with her.

He knew a secret to her past.

# *Fifteen*

s Cora was rushing out to go to the ladies tea the following
Thursday, her phone rang.

"Hello?" she answered as she headed outside.

"Can I speak to a Miss Mellows?"

Cora sighed. *Grace.* "Yes, this is Miss Mellows."

"Your mouthpiece is ready."

"Do you mean crown?"

"No. We have a night guard for you, so you stop grinding your
teeth at night."

*Unbelievable.* Cora closed her eyes and took a deep breath. "I'm
waiting for a crown. Can you please check to see if it's come in?"

"As a matter of fact, there has been one here for days. There
was a funny name on the box, something to do with the ocean. I
think it said *Coral.*"

"That's mine. May I come in this afternoon?"

"I'm leaving early to go to the Boy Scout pancake dinner over
at the church, but I'm pretty sure Dr. Walker isn't going. I don't
think he likes breakfast food for dinner. It doesn't matter to me. I
could eat pancakes any time of the day."

"Is there an opening around four?"

"The dinner is open to anyone. You don't need a reservation, and it's only five dollars. It's all-you-can-eat, so I'm sneaking in a container for leftovers."

Cora was ready to pull out her hair. "I meant is there an opening with Dr. Walker at four?"

"Why, yes, there is! And you might have time to run over for pancakes afterward."

"Thank you. I'll be there."

After enjoying treats, salacious town gossip, and laughter at tea with the ladies, Cora rushed home to brush her teeth before heading to her dentist appointment.

When she arrived at the office shortly before four, she found Grace emptying the contents of her purse onto the desk so she could fit a rather large plastic container into it. The container was the size of a small casserole, big enough to fit two or three helpings from the Boy Scout dinner. The woman was definitely going to smuggle enough leftovers for a couple days.

Cora approached the desk. "I'm here for my appointment."

Not even looking up, Grace shooed her toward the chairs. "Have a seat and I'll see if Dr. Walker has time to squeeze you in."

There was no use in pursuing the conversation. Grace was concentrating too hard on her purse. She had managed to jam the container in and was now working on adding a supersize travel mug.

"Okay, let's see what we have down on the calendar." She sat back in her chair. "I found you in the book, Mary. I'll tell Dr. Walker you're here."

"My name isn't Mary."

"Are you sure?"

"Yes. It's Cora."

Grace eyed her up and down. "You look like a Mary. Have you ever considered going by that? It's such a pretty name."

"Yes, it is. But no, I haven't."

"No, you haven't what, dear?"

"No, I haven't considered going by the name Mary."

"Why would you?" Grace asked, looking at Cora as though *she* were the one this side of senile.

"I wouldn't."

"I think I'll call you Mary. It fits you nicely."

Cora sighed. Conversation with Grace was exhausting. "Okay," she surrendered."

Dr. Walker entered the reception area, and Grace returned to her purse-stuffing.

"Ready for the big day?" Dr. Walker asked Cora.

All she could do was nod. She didn't know if her anxiety was from getting the crown or seeing the handsome dentist. Butterflies pirouetted in her stomach.

His smile put her slightly more at ease. "How are you doing?" he asked.

"Fine," she responded a little too quickly.

He studied her as if trying to decipher if she was telling the truth. "Yeah?"

"If I give a different answer, will it change the outcome of me having to do this?"

He shook his head, clearly amused. "No."

"Then let's stick with fine."

He chuckled. "This shouldn't take long. And I'll be as gentle as I can." He paused. "I wouldn't want to scare you off from coming back."

Though Cora was sure he meant that in a professional sense, her heart did a little flip and she had to keep herself from blushing. What was it about this guy that turned her completely senseless? *Pull yourself together, Cora.*

When he motioned her into the exam room, she was relieved for the distraction. She followed him back, then sat down in the chair and closed her eyes, taking a few deep breaths.

Twenty minutes later, Dr. Walker sat back. "How does that feel?"

She ran her tongue over the new crown. "Good."

"Do you feel it when you bite down?"

"No," she said, moving her jaw up and down a couple times.

"That should do it, then." He rolled his chair back and took off his gloves. "Was it as bad as you imagined?"

"No. I imagined it to be far worse."

He laughed. "Don't forget to call tomorrow and make an appointment for sometime in the next couple weeks."

Cora recoiled. "What? Why?"

"For your teeth."

She scowled. "What's wrong with them now?"

Dr. Walker's mouth twitched. "I meant for your cleaning and X-rays. You can't keep ignoring your teeth. They need routine care."

Cora's shoulders slumped. "Okay, but after all this, I think I deserve more than a free toothbrush."

He burst out laughing. "I'll try to think of something."

His chocolate eyes sparkled and crinkled in the corners, and she couldn't help but smile back.

There was an undeniable current zinging between the two of them, making Cora wonder if he felt it as strong as she did. She felt breathless and excited, something she'd never experienced with Kyle. Whatever was happening here felt good.

On her way home that evening, Cora stopped at the grocery store. Ruth Ann looked up from the deli counter as she came in.

"Hello, Miss Matthews. How are you acclimating to your new life?"

"Fine, thank you. It's nice of you to remember my name."

Ruth Ann looked at her like she had just said the most absurd thing. "How could I forget you? You've been in my prayers since you told me you were all alone. The last thing I would ever wish is that someone so pretty be"—she took out a little piece of paper from her apron and read— "ostracized."

Cora couldn't help but laugh. "I hardly think I'm being ostracized."

Ruth Ann's brows creased. "Hold on and let me look at the definition again. You know, if you don't use the words in conversation, they'll never stick in your brain. Now, let's see . . ." She peered at the paper. "Oh, you're right. Saying that you are being 'ignored, separated, excluded, isolated, banished, or dispelled' is a bit harsh."

Cora felt her lips twitch. "A bit."

"I'll continue to hope for the best and keep you in my prayers."

"That's kind of you. I appreciate that." And it was. She couldn't remember the last time someone had said that to her, and it was lovely, especially since this woman was virtually a stranger.

Ruth Ann put on a new pair of plastic gloves. "What can I get for you? Turkey? Potato salad?"

"What do you recommend?"

Ruth Ann frowned. "I can't say. The manager says I'm too opinionated and am steering the customers away from the food that needs to move."

"What if I weren't a customer but a friend passing by who happened to ask you what you made most recently?"

"Hmm." Ruth Ann tapped a finger on her chin. "He didn't say anything about *that*. I suppose I could talk to you as my friend, pal, buddy, and chum." She grinned. "Well, *friend*—"

"Cora."

"Okay, *Cora*—who happens to be passing by and may or may not be shopping—I made the most delicious egg salad an hour ago. I put a little secret ingredient in it that gives it some zip. And nobody makes better fried chicken than I do, and that's cooking right now."

"Anything else?"

"If you take a close look at the meatloaf, you will see that the cat food on aisle seven looks more appetizing and has better color."

Cora grinned. "Point taken."

"And the baby back ribs have about as much meat on them as a mouse. It's simply an overabundance, excess, and surplus of sauce covering bones."

*Opinionated* was a good word for Ruth Ann.

"Thank you for the chat. I'm going to go look around the store, and when I come back as a customer, I'll order a large container of egg salad and six fried chicken breasts."

"And, if I see you again in about ten minutes as a customer"— Ruth Ann winked—"I'll have that food ready for you."

The store was pretty empty, so Cora got through her shopping quickly. She stopped in the snack aisle to pick up a fresh package of marshmallow cookies for Kitty and two cases of Dr Pepper for Widgy. Then she circled back to the deli for the chicken, which both Widgy and Sam would like, and the egg salad for sandwiches tomorrow. As promised, Ruth Ann had the order waiting.

"Thank you."

Ruth Ann had her vocabulary paper ready. "Luxuriate, savor, delight in, and relish the chicken and salad! Or simply *enjoy.*" She tucked the paper back in her pocket. "Bye, honey!"

There was one checkout line open. The food police clerk was working. It didn't matter how fast Cora unloaded; the woman thoroughly inspected all her selections.

"This tomato sauce has sugar in it. You should choose a brand that uses natural ingredients. I read in a magazine that tomato sauce helps prevent certain cancers. All these additives are unnecessary and leave less room for the tomato. You don't want to dilute the tomato sauce but go full strength with a hint of garlic. That reminds me, you don't have garlic. Garlic should be a staple in your diet. Pop those cloves into everything you make." She pulled the microphone close and switched it on.

"I need two jars of the natural tomato sauce on the top shelf of aisle three—the one with no sugar in it—and three heads of garlic." She placed the offending, sugar-laden tomato sauce under the counter.

Cora glanced at the next person in line and was relieved they were captivated with a magazine and didn't seem concerned by the wait. "They don't have to go through all that trouble. I just won't get any sauce this trip."

The clerk waved off her concern. "It's no trouble. You should insist on the best when it comes to your health. When I was your age, I believed I'd live forever. Now, death is all I think about. I could drop at any moment, and we'd never know if it was from all the pie I ate when I was young. You should start asking yourself now, 'Am I shaving an hour off my life by eating this?' Ninety percent of your diet should be raw. The roughage will keep the polyps away and—"

The woman choked out a gasp.

She'd spotted Kitty's marshmallow cookies.

With a horrified expression, she reached for the toxic material, and Cora knew they were going straight under the counter with the other contraband. Kitty's precious gooey cloud puffs from heaven would disappear forever into the no-no vault.

Cora placed her hand on the package. "They're for a friend. I am *not* leaving the store without them, and I don't want some granola, high-fiber, fat-free, organic, flaxseed substitute."

The woman's face hardened, and her lips pressed together so tightly they began to turn white. She finished scanning the rest of the food, including the natural tomato sauce and heads of garlic, with silent agitation.

She gave Cora a withering look. "Any coupons?"

~

It was time.

Cora decided to go over to Rolf Johansson's home and introduce herself. Perhaps even ask for a truce. Walking onto the property, she crossed the cluttered yard to the open back door that gave her a clear view inside through the screen. She could hear the faint white noise of a TV, but above that was something else. Something unfamiliar. Something wild.

The sound of birds.

Many of them.

Holding her breath, she approached the entrance quietly. Too curious to knock, she peered through the screen and saw tall cages lining the living room. Inside them were brilliantly colored birds, chattering in metallic tones and loud song. There were too many to count, and she couldn't even see them all.

A cough from inside made her jump. It would be awful to be found spying.

She knocked and waited anxiously, not sure what to expect. She swallowed hard as she spotted the towering figure coming toward the door.

He stopped briefly at the sight of her and then approached the screen door, not opening it. He wore baggy pajama pants and a gray sweatshirt with food stains on the front. Cora stepped down from the stoop and stood back a couple feet. Staring down at her, he loomed larger than ever. What Rolf lacked in social skills, he made up for in intimidation.

She cleared her throat. "I never got to introduce myself."

"I know who you are. The Matthews resemblance is undeniable."

"Um, well, my name is Cora. I thought it would be nice if we got to know each other. What type of birds are those I hear?"

"You never mind those. They're none of your business. I told you before that you're not wanted here. I almost got back my family's property before you came, but the guy wouldn't sell."

*Guy? My grandfather?* "Look, I'm sorry for past misunderstandings, but it has been settled. I was hoping we could put it behind us, start fresh, and be more neighborly to one another." She offered a wobbly smile.

He opened the creaking screen door slowly and stared at her with an expression that made the hair on the back of her neck prickle.

"Over my dead body," he said in a calm, cold voice.

Cora stood frozen with fear for a moment. Her mind told her to run, but her legs wouldn't move.

"I ain't giving up till I leave this property in a body bag. You remember that, missy." His death stare sealed the promise. "Now, git off my property."

Cora could only give a shaky nod before she hurried back to

the road. She didn't start to breathe normally until she was inside the lodge. *Kill him with kindness.* What a joke! Rolf looked like he wanted to kill *her*. So much for burying the hatchet. The only thing her visit had done was guarantee more dead fish dumped on her doorstep.

Winning over Rolf Johansson was impossible.

# *Sixteen*

Getting up at an hour even Widgy would consider early, Cora went to the kitchen and began making biscuits using a recipe from Arielle. By the time Widgy came in, Cora was pulling the fourth batch out of the oven. Widgy paid no attention to the table set with warm biscuits, butter, and a new jar of honey until Cora turned her back to wash dishes. Then she glanced over and saw Widgy consuming the biscuits at an indigestible rate—a sign they met her approval.

Cora zipped up her polar-fleece jacket, tucked her garden gloves into the pockets of her work jeans, and slipped on her boots. Her once-oiled, unblemished, brown leather boots were now paint-speckled, scuffed, and caked in dirt. She smiled when she realized they were almost as scratched and muddy as Widgy's.

These boots had become an indicator she had the grit and gumption to attack the day's work with fervor. But, more importantly, they showed she'd earned the right to work next to Widgy.

Cora headed to the door as Widgy devoured her tenth biscuit and washed it down with a swig of Dr Pepper. Cora arched a brow at the two biscuits in the dog dish next to a bowl full of coffee.

"Hey, did you notice my flannel shirt?" Cora proudly held out her shirttails to show off the print.

Widgy made a face. "You're not tryin' to dress like me, are you? 'Cause I've never been into that girly junk. I don't need a twin."

"No! I just thought you'd like it, that's all."

"Why would I like it?"

"Because it's flannel! Your precious flannel—the only thing you wear!"

Widgy looked at her like she was crazy. "What other kind of shirt is there?"

Cora sighed. "Forget I said anything."

"I will, because half the time I don't know what you're talkin' 'bout anyway."

"I'm heading to Kitty's."

"Uh-huh. You're almost outta biscuits. You should've made more. And bigger! These are the size of mouse turds."

Cora walked out while Widgy continued to gripe. Taking a deep breath, she blew out her annoyance and focused on her plan to help Kitty.

Her neighbor was not outside yet, so Cora began picking weeds. Kneeling on the damp grass soaked the knees of her jeans, but she didn't mind. When Kitty came out, Cora pointed at the sizable mound of weeds she had accumulated.

"Well, aren't you the eager beaver this morning!" Kitty smiled.

"I was up early, and I came to get a jump on the weeds."

"I normally wait until the dew dries. Look at how your pants are soiled!"

"It's fine. I also brought you some biscuits and honey to have with your broth later." She pointed to a basket with biscuits wrapped in flour sack towels.

"Thank you." Her lips pursed. "Oh, please be careful of that little marker behind you."

Cora looked from side to side. "What marker?"

"It's covered by that pile of leaves."

Cora felt around the ground until she discovered the small stone.

It wasn't smooth and polished but rough. "It's so small and plain compared to the rest of them."

"That was all the man's wife could afford. She was an immigrant and didn't have a lot of money."

Cora lightly wiped away the leaves and dirt. "That's sad. Why haven't you decorated it like the others?"

"There's nothing in the grave."

"What?"

"I take that back. There is a pot of flour down there but not anyone's remains."

"Why?"

"The story of that grave begins with the wife of the man who is supposed to be buried there. Her name was Daria, and she was from Russia. She met and married Earl, who absolutely adored her. Daria worked hard as a seamstress and was talented at her trade. She was shy but so sweet and won the hearts of everyone she met.

"Although she and Earl were deeply in love, there was always a sadness about her. Even when life was going well, you could see it in her eyes."

Cora frowned. "Do you know why?"

Kitty nodded. "She missed her homeland. Earl promised they would save money to go and visit, but they never had enough. Then, tragically, Earl was killed in a car crash. Before his ashes were to be buried, Daria emptied the urn and filled it with flour."

Cora's brows knit together. "Why would she do that?"

"She wanted to return to Russia. But she loved Earl and wanted to be buried with him. She couldn't imagine being separated from the man who had been so devoted and kind to her all those years."

"What did she do with his real ashes?"

"She transferred them to an empty two-liter Coke bottle. She used his life insurance money and the proceeds from selling their house and flew back home, carrying Earl on the airplane, tucked away in her carry-on. No one in town ever heard from her again."

Cora felt like she was missing part of the story. "Why did she go through all that trouble? Why did she have to hide the fact that she was taking his ashes with her?"

"Earl had a nasty old sister, his only living relative, and she insisted he be buried in Moonberry Lake with other generations of their family. Daria was so meek, she felt she couldn't disobey."

"How did she pull it off without anyone knowing?"

"It wasn't that hard. All it took was a little help and distraction from a friend." Kitty winked.

Cora's mouth dropped. "You?"

"My dear Miss Matthews, there are some secrets that are going to die with me in this graveyard." She chuckled. "I think you've done enough work. It's chilly. How about we go inside and have a snack?"

"Sure," Cora said, getting up quickly when she saw Kitty shiver. The two made their way toward the house. Kitty was walking slower than usual and leaned more of her weight on Cora's arm.

"Are you feeling okay?" Cora's heart tugged as she watched Kitty struggle.

Kitty chuckled. "Do my bones creak that loudly?"

"Not at all."

"Sweetie, I'm old enough to be biblical. There is always going to be *something*. The cold weather makes me stiff, that's all. My lungs and bones hurt in the autumn until I get used to the temperature change. I'll be fine once I get some broth into me."

As they entered the kitchen, the same waft of thick air she remembered from her first visit greeted them. She tried to decipher the various aromas. It was a blend of spices, moist soil, and the musty smell that accompanies old houses. As strange as the combination was, somehow it all worked together—a blend of sustenance, earth, and the passage of time, resulting in a nostalgic sense of home.

"Have a seat, dear, and I'll get us some mugs for the broth."

"Can I help?"

"No, no. I rarely have guests, so let me enjoy playing hostess. Make yourself comfortable."

Kitty's kitchen was the same jungle, though the greenery had grown more. The plants on the table not only touched the floor but were crawling up the legs of the chairs. Cora slid one of the chairs back far enough so she could squeeze in without breaking the vines.

"I can't even see your gnomes with the lushness of your greenery."

Kitty carried two cups of hot broth to the table. "I know, it's getting a bit out of control, but I love the beauty of the plants. They're good company, and the steam from the soups and broths simmering on the stove makes them flourish even this time of year."

Kitty gave the mug with no chips to Cora. "Plants are like people—if you give them some warmth and conversation, you renew their life."

"Thank you," Cora said after she took a sip of broth. "What's in this batch?"

"Oh, a little of this and a little of that." There was that twinkle in her eyes again.

"Are you ever going to tell me?"

"When the time's right, I will share the recipe. For now, it remains my secret." Kitty settled into her chair and held the mug with both hands to warm them. She looked so small sitting in the chair. The mountains of greenery all around made her appear gnome-like herself.

"Tell me what you've been up to." Kitty took a sip, then reached for a biscuit, dipping a corner into the broth before taking a bite.

"Well, I went to try to talk to Rolf a couple days ago, and he basically made it clear that he hates my guts."

"Stubborn fool." Kitty shook her head. "Like I said before, you've just got to wear him down. Be glad you're the water and not the stone. He has far more lessons to learn. I remember back when he and your grandfather were close friends, and then one day they weren't. I have no idea what happened. The man has been the neighborhood curmudgeon ever since."

Cora tucked that little nugget of information away along with all the other mysteries this town held.

"Now, what else? I see a difference in you. There's something you're not telling me."

Cora maintained a poker face, careful not to give anything away. "There's not much to say. My life is working on the lodge and visiting you."

"You have more going on than that. You have a light about you I've not seen before."

Cora shrugged. "Maybe it's because I'm feeling more settled."

"Or maybe it's because you are feeling at *home*, and there is something else in the making."

"Maybe," Cora repeated before taking a sip.

Kitty didn't push the subject, so they sat enjoying the warm broth.

But Cora's thoughts were stuck on Kitty's words. Something had crept into her heart and life. Happiness and genuine contentment—both were new to her.

After Cora's mug was empty, she excused herself and left with the promise of returning to help finish the work on the markers. Crossing back over to her property, she hummed all the way up to the door and greeted Beast, waiting for him to get into his usual barking fit and chomp at her ankles. His little dagger teeth often left imprints on her boots but never punctured flesh. That was the main reason she had switched to work boots—to protect herself from all Beast's "friendly nips."

The nasty critter was busy chewing off the corner of the outside step. Accustomed to his behavior, she greeted him but never attempted to actually pet the little psycho mutt. The sound of her voice always resulted in the same outcome, a large puddle of urine. As Widgy stated, "If the dog pees, he likes ya."

Stepping over his sign of affection, Cora found Widgy patching a wall where there had been water damage.

"Hey, Widgy, Beast chewed up the stair on the front steps."

Widgy stopped her work. "Sorry, I'll fix it," she said in a quiet voice.

Cora shook her head. "Don't worry about it. The wood was probably rotting anyway. Let him finish—it's a good chew toy for now. Anyway, he peed again when he saw me, so our relationship is definitely improving."

Widgy peered over at her, and Cora gave her a nod.

She went on with her work, and Widgy seemed uncommonly pleasant the rest of the day.

Now Cora understood.

There were two things that brought Widgy happiness—driving her crazy and that monster of a dog.

# Seventeen

What are your plans for Thanksgiving?"

Cora and Sam had been going from room to room upstairs all morning, sealing the windows with thick plastic sheeting in preparation for winter. The temperature had dropped as soon as they hit November, and Widgy had warned that her ankles were hurting, which, she said, meant snow was on its way.

"Same as always," Sam said. "I'll volunteer in the morning down at the VFW, and in the afternoon, Georgie and I have a potluck over at our place for anyone who doesn't have somewhere to go."

"Who do you usually have over?"

"It changes year to year, according to who has family visiting, but Kitty's usually there. And Arielle and Mimi come if they're not traveling." He lifted a brow. "I'm sure Joseph will be included."

She busied herself with the plastic sheeting. "Do you think you guys would have room for me? I mean, it's okay if you don't," she added hurriedly.

Sam gave an incredulous stare. "I was counting on it! You know you're always welcome at my table, holiday or not."

Cora's shoulders relaxed. "Thanks. What can I bring?"

"How about a dessert? The main dishes fill up fast."

"I can do that," she responded quickly, grateful she wouldn't be spending the holiday alone.

"It looks like we're covering the windows in the nick of time."

A few snowflakes flew around in the wind. Nothing heavy, but enough to stir Cora's excitement about the snowfall to come.

"Have you ever known Widgy's ankles to be wrong?"

"No, but don't tell her that. It encourages her to be an authority on too many other subjects."

The two worked the rest of the afternoon finishing the upstairs windows. When Cora was ready to call it quits, Sam gave her a hard clap on the shoulder. "We work well as a team. We can probably do most of the rooms downstairs when you get home from Mr. Wells's tomorrow afternoon."

"Thanks for all your help. You do so much for me, I wish there was something I could do for you."

Sam dismissed her statement with a wave. "Don't worry about it. It makes me feel better knowing you'll be warm this winter. Sealing up the windows will help with the draft. Most of these windows should actually be replaced."

Cora didn't want to think what *that* would cost. "The new furnace should keep me snug as a bug. I've also gotten pretty good at building a fire."

"Hold on to that pioneer spirit. You'll need it when it hits twenty below!" He gave a nod goodbye.

She watched as he turned up the collar of his jacket and tucked his head low, making his way to his truck against the biting wind.

Widgy was out back cutting wood. The sleeves of her flannel shirt were rolled up, and her cheeks were bright red from the cold. Cora observed the strength and force the woman put into every blow of the axe.

"Widgy," Cora called out to her, "why are you chopping wood?"

The woman stopped for a moment to wipe the sweat from her forehead. With a slight pant in her voice, she responded, "We have to start buildin' up your woodpile for winter or you're gonna run out by January. I knew you wouldn't know how to use an axe, and I wanted to take advantage of the weather."

"It's cold and windy." Cora wrapped her arms tightly around herself.

"It's cool, and I like doin' physical activity with a breeze."

"It's *snowing*."

Widgy snorted. "The ground is barely dusted. You've got to toughen up, Matthews, or you'll never survive what's comin'." With that, she turned back to the chopping block.

How was it that Widgy's words always managed to cut her? Not deep, but enough to hurt. The woman gave her no slack. No matter what Cora did, Widgy constantly gave her two options: toughen up or get out of the way.

*Okay, then. Toughen up it is.*

Cora started to stack the wood against the side of the house. Widgy glanced over at her, took a pair of gloves out of her back pocket, threw them down on the ground near Cora, then went back to work. The two worked in the howling wind for an hour.

As Widgy got ready to leave for the day, Cora asked, "Hey, what are you doing for Thanksgiving?"

"My boys can't make it home, so I was gonna go over to Sam and Georgie's if they have room. I haven't asked yet. Their place can't hold a lotta people." She slammed the tailgate of her truck shut. "Why?"

She shrugged. "Just wondering."

"What about you?"

"Same as you."

"My advice is to get there early, or you're gonna be eatin' standin' up." She threw the axe in the back of the truck and opened the door to the driver's side, letting out a loud whistle. "Beast!"

The dog came running. As he passed Cora, she noticed he had one of her favorite dress shoes in his mouth. When he jumped up into the cab, Widgy took it from him. The heel and toe had been completely chewed off.

Widgy gave it a disgusted look. "What a ridiculous shoe. Tell me how much they cost and I'll take it off my labor this month. See ya in the mornin.'" She tossed the shoe back to Beast, who was foaming at the mouth at the sight of it.

The next morning, Cora got an idea of what she could do for Sam. She called him as soon as the clock struck six.

"Good morning. It's Cora."

Sam answered on the second ring, his voice groggy. "Anything wrong? It's early for you."

Cora made a face. "You sound like Widgy. Nothing's wrong, and I always get up early. I'm just slow to get dressed."

Sam laughed. "Fair enough. What can I do for you?"

"It's what *I* can do for *you*. I would like to host the Thanksgiving potluck at the lodge."

There was a pause before Sam answered. "That's nice of you, but are you sure you want to take on all those people?"

"Absolutely! It's why this place was built. The dining hall can easily fit forty people. It'll be fun to entertain and meet some more neighbors. If it's okay with you and Georgie, you can call all your usual people, and we'll have a party!"

Sam chuckled. "All right, then. We have a short list so far. I'll let you know the final count."

"Great. I'll see you later. I've got to get ready for work."

"Actually, now that I know you're up, I'll come over right away and get started. I don't have class until tomorrow. We need to get a jump on those downstairs windows. It's going to be even colder today." Sam hung up.

Cora gave a shriek of excitement. Preparing for the party was going to be as much fun as the event itself.

Over the next week and a half, she worked on making the dining room look nice. The two long dining tables, with their benches tucked underneath and chairs at both ends, were repainted white. It brightened the room and made everything look clean.

"I don't understand all the fuss you're makin' over a dinner." Widgy shook her head. "People don't notice if the seat they're sittin' on has recently been painted or not. You don't have to gussy up the place. People come to *eat*. The food's all anyone cares about."

"The room had to be painted anyway. I'm merely rearranging my to-do list for the holidays." She waved her paintbrush.

Widgy sighed. "Whatever tickles your fancy little backside. All I'm sayin' is the food better look as good as these tables. Well, ya know what I mean. There better be a lot of it, and it better taste decent."

"I'll do my part, but remember, it's a potluck. I don't have any control over what others bring."

"I'll bring the Dr Pepper, and ya can count on my three-meat hot dish."

Cora was afraid to ask, but curiosity got the better of her. "What are the three types of meat?"

"Venison, rabbit, and squirrel. Beast loves it."

Cora turned and continued painting. *Like I said, I don't have any control over what others bring.*

"I'm gonna be workin' upstairs if ya need me." Widgy headed for the hallway. "Beast's up there sleepin' next to one of the toilets."

"Why?" Cora yelled the question toward Widgy's loud footsteps on the back staircase.

Widgy hollered back, "The sound of flushin' puts him to sleep. I was doin' my mornin' business, and by the third flush he was out." Her voice trailed off and she was gone.

*I had to ask.*

Joseph and all the tea ladies, except for Sofia who was heading out of town to visit family, accepted the invitation to Thanksgiving dinner and volunteered to bring their favorite dishes. Mimi wanted to bring candied yams with marshmallows, Kitty was bringing a pie, Arielle insisted on supplying all the rolls and floral centerpieces for the tables, and Joseph offered a green bean casserole. Sam was set on doing a fried turkey to give people a choice other than regular roast turkey, and there would be Widgy's Squirrel Surprise.

As the day approached, Cora took out a tall stack of plates and a box of silverware and washed them. She set up a couple small tables in the corner of the dining room for drinks and appetizers. Everything was coming together seamlessly.

The night before the event, she was making a Jell-O salad and homemade cranberry sauce when Widgy stopped by the kitchen on her way out. She took one look in each of the bowls and made a face. "What on earth are you cookin'? It looks like somethin' that came out of Beast a while back."

"Homemade cranberry sauce and a Jell-O fruit salad."

Widgy scowled. "Cranberry sauce comes from a can. It's supposed to be thick enough to cut, like meatloaf."

Cora continued stirring. "There is also such a thing as making it from scratch. It's delicious, trust me."

"You can serve your foo-foo salad, but I'm bringin' a can of jellied cranberry sauce to plop on a plate."

Cora rolled her eyes. "If you insist."

That night, she went to bed dreaming of the holiday with her new friends. She woke up extra early and got a jump on cleaning the dining room and preparing the turkey for Sam. Arielle arrived at breakfast time with all the rolls and centerpieces. She wore a coat over her pajamas, her hair went in all directions, and her feet were shod in dirty fur slippers.

"I got up around three to make these from scratch," she said, setting the rolls on the counter. "I think it's one of my best batches." Arielle beamed.

"We better taste them to make sure. I mean, what would Thanksgiving be without testing some of the food first to make sure it's good?"

The two sat at the kitchen table and ate the fresh rolls slathered with butter, laughing and talking.

Cora pushed back from the table. "I better start the coffee for Sam. He'll be here soon. Would you like some?"

"No, thanks, I always carry my own caffeine." Arielle lifted her tumbler.

As Cora was setting up the coffee maker, she poured yesterday's leftovers in the dog dish before washing out the pot.

Arielle frowned. "What are you doing?"

"It's for Beast. He likes to drink coffee or Dr Pepper in the morning."

"You can't give that to a dog!"

Cora angled a look at her. "Have you ever met Beast?"

"No, but he's legendary."

"Well, you'll get your chance today. Widgy's bringing him to dinner, but she promised to keep him tied up outside. I'm hoping that between the caffeine, which has the opposite effect on him than it has on humans, and some of Widgy's hot dish, he'll be calm and not so psycho."

"What's in the hot dish?"

"You don't want to know. Just be glad you're a vegetarian."

Arielle laughed. "Thanks for the tip."

After Arielle left to get ready, Cora took one of the extra pumpkin pies and walked over to Rolf's. Placing it on a dish towel on his doorstep, she knocked loudly and then hightailed it out of there, jumping over a rusty push mower hidden in the tall grass. She didn't look back until she had reached the road, but when she did, she saw the pie was gone.

A few hours later, Cora gave a final inspection of the food in the kitchen and the tables in the dining room, foyer, and family room. Appetizers were set out, the fireplace lit, the lodge was clean, and Arielle's flowers and sparkling apple cider were situated exactly as she had envisioned. As Cora headed to her room to get ready, she felt she might burst from the mixture of excitement and pride.

Walking back downstairs, she saw that the party had begun without her.

Sam was the official greeter at the door, ushering people inside with a smile. Some mingled near the fireplace, others walked down the hall to the dining room, peeking in rooms and commenting on the renovations.

Cora smiled. *Good.* That's exactly why she'd left the doors open.

Before she made her way to the dining hall, she popped into the kitchen to check on the progress. Arielle was busy arranging the food. Mimi sat in the corner of the kitchen with Kitty, watching the activity. What a blessing these women were.

When everything was ready, Sam called the guests together and Joseph said a prayer. As all the heads lifted after the collective "amen," people dug in as if they hadn't eaten in a week. With her fork poised to take her first bite, Cora heard the front doorbell. She scooched back from the table and went to answer it. When she opened it, her breath caught.

"Hello. Sorry I'm late." Dr. Walker's smile was warm. "Here's the pie I promised Sam. It's my mother's recipe. I hope you don't have too many pumpkin pies." He extended the plate out to her.

She stood staring.

He waited, holding out the pie and looking nervous. "Sam told me Thanksgiving was here this year."

Clearing her senses with a shake of her head, she took the pie with a smile. "Yes, it is. Come in. Welcome, and thank you for the pie. There's no such thing as too many pumpkin pies. I usually hide some away for the morning after Thanksgiving. Somehow it tastes even better a day later."

His face lit up. "I do the same thing! Leftover pumpkin pie for breakfast is my favorite tradition." He stepped into the foyer and took in the empty room. "It looks like I missed the party."

Despite still feeling flustered, Cora was determined to sound coherent. It didn't matter that this man had the superpower to turn her insides to mush; she wanted to appear calm and collected. "Not at all, Dr. Walker. Your timing's perfect. Everyone's in the dining room. Follow me."

"You can call me Ben, you know?" he said, his eyes twinkling.

She smiled as they walked down the long hallway. "Okay," she said, "Ben." She felt a thrill saying his name aloud. She glanced at him and was delighted to see he was grinning at her too.

"This is an awesome building," he said, turning his gaze to scan the inside of the bedrooms they passed. "I've never been inside before. It's huge."

"Thanks, I'm trying to bring it back to its former glory."

Ben gave a low whistle. "That's an immense undertaking."

"It is, but well worth it." Before Cora could say anything else, they entered the dining room. If the noise level was any indication, everyone was having a wonderful time. Sam looked up, saw Ben, and came right over to greet him. As the two talked, Cora slipped away to take the pie into the kitchen. Pushing through the swinging door, she encountered a different kind of chaos. There was no one in the room, but Beast was barking up a storm out back. Cora walked over to the screen door to look out. The dog was barking insanely and growling at a bush.

"Beast, stop that! Stop! Shh!"

The dog didn't listen, so Cora grabbed his food bowl and went to the bottom oven, where Widgy's hot dish was hidden. She had told Kitty to put it there, and if Widgy ever questioned where it was, Cora planned on saying it had been forgotten in the warmer. Better a little white lie than sending her guests home sick.

Cora scooped some into the bowl and took it outside.

Whistling, she tried to beckon the dog over. "Come, Beast." She slapped her leg a couple times and set the bowl by her feet.

She jumped back when a skunk came out of the bush and headed toward the aromatic three-meat concoction. Beast lunged toward the animal, biting at it. The skunk was almost the same size as Beast, and it snapped back.

Cora retreated closer to the door, hissing for Beast to come, but he ignored her. The two animals launched into a vicious fight. When the dog yelped, Cora didn't stop to think. She ran and picked up poor Beast and cradled him close.

It was then that the skunk lifted its tail and sprayed them both.

# Eighteen

With the injured dog safe in Cora's arms, the skunk toddled away. Georgie came to the door, and her hand flew to her nose. "What happened?"

Cora had to stop holding her breath to respond. "Get Widgy. Beast is hurt."

Thirty seconds later, Widgy came running out. "My poor baby!" She lifted the dog out of Cora's arms, completely unfazed by the pungent odor. Sam followed Widgy outside, and the two of them examined Beast, though Sam held a handkerchief over his nose. The dog had a nasty bite on one of his legs that would no doubt need to get checked by a veterinarian.

Beast lay in Widgy's arms, whimpering softly. "I've got some bandages in my truck." She sniffled as she headed toward it.

Sam and Cora followed.

"How'd dis happid?" Sam asked through the handkerchief.

"I was bringing him some food to stop his barking. The skunk came out of the bushes, and they started fighting. Then, like a fool, I ran over to rescue the dog."

"Dat skuk coulda dud a lot worse dabbage. Beast is pretty spall to take on a fight like dat."

Cora's eyes ran like faucets. "I think we both learned our lesson. You go back inside. Someone has to play host. And can you ask

Joseph and Arielle to take care of the food, please? I don't want the party ruined, so I'll stay out here."

Sam nodded and left.

Cora headed over to Widgy, who put Beast in Cora's arms while she cleaned the wound and wrapped it with the utmost care. The skunk stench didn't even make Widgy wince. All her attention was on her precious dog.

"I'll take him home and call the vet." Widgy's eyes were brimming with tears.

Cora was rendered speechless by Widgy's display of emotion. Her usual rock-hard exterior had crumbled. Widgy made a bed in the front seat of the truck with her coat, and Cora carefully placed Beast on it. Before getting into the truck, Widgy walked over to Cora and put her arms around her, squeezing tightly.

Feeling the force of the embrace and knowing how Widgy felt about any signs of affection, Cora knew how much her help meant to her friend. She felt she could call her that now. Cora and Widgy's friendship had been forged by a ten-pound balding dog and a decrepit lodge. Who knew such things could create this sense of loyalty and love.

Cora smiled as she watched Widgy's vehicle pull away.

Rather than putting a damper on the party, it seemed the skunk drama had added an element of fun for the dinner guests. At least, that's what Cora assumed from the roaring laughter she heard coming from the lodge. She listened to the hilarity as she sat shivering in an old flannel work jacket of Widgy's. With every breeze, she fought the revolting stench emanating off of her. Not even a shower would take care of the skunk vapor rising from her body. She'd already thrown out her sweater, shoes, and socks, which had gotten the worst of it, but she still reeked. Her pants and shirt would be tossed also. She refused to go inside until everyone had left. She didn't want to sour the party by the stench she would leave.

An hour later, the sun was going down, and she was chilled to the bone.

A voice called from behind her. "Care for a piece of pie, or would you like me to hide it away for tomorrow morning?"

*Ben.*

She turned to find him at the other end of the dock, holding a plate in one hand, a blanket in the other.

"Is it pumpkin?"

He smiled. "Of course."

"It's tempting, but I don't ever want to associate that taste with this stink."

He started toward her, but she put up her hand. "Please don't. The smell's making me faint. Save yourself and run away."

"I'll take the risk." He drew closer, not even covering his nose. Standing over her, he placed the plate of pie on the dock and wrapped a blanket around her. "Think of it as a reward . . . although *I* made this pie, so it may not qualify."

"I don't deserve a reward, but I would appreciate a long bath to wash off this stink."

He squatted down so they were eye to eye. "Not many people would intervene where there's a skunk involved, not to mention when it's for Beast. That dog is not liked."

"Beast isn't so bad. You have to take time to understand him."

Ben studied her. "You seem to be a woman of many talents. Sam has been singing your praises about what you've done to turn this place around. Widgy was starting to brag about you, too, right before all the excitement."

She threw back her head, laughing. "Now I know you're lying. Widgy would never do that."

He met her smile. "It can't be denied, since Kitty, Ms. Witherspoon, and Ms. Morgan all agreed and shared their own stories about you. You've made quite an impression on the people of Moonberry."

Cora closed her eyes for a moment to rein in her feelings. It had been a long, emotional day. Her voice came out in a whisper. "They've become dear friends. I adore them all."

Ben was silent until she looked back up at him. "I hope to be privileged enough to be included in that circle one day."

Her breath caught.

"Is there anything else I can get for you?"

She swallowed, struggling to keep her voice light. "I'm taking donations of hydrogen peroxide, baking soda, and dish soap. It's going to take a barrel of each to wash this off."

"I'm intrigued. Not tomato juice?"

Cora shook her head. "No. That's an old wives' tale, like applying butter to a burn. Sam told me what really works."

"Well, until you get your supplies, you could jump in the lake." A corner of his mouth twitched as he struggled to remain serious.

She cocked her head to one side. "You know the answer to that. I don't swim in lakes."

His mouth lifted on one side. "You're also a woman of great irony. You live on the water yet never go in."

She shrugged. "I'm complicated."

He burst out laughing. "By the way, everyone had a great time. Your heroic act made this holiday memorable."

"Then it was worth it. I'm thinking next year maybe I'll wrestle a bear. Anything to add a little drama." She nodded toward the plate. "Thanks for the pie."

He smiled and walked back to the lodge.

Half an hour later, almost everyone had gone. Guests had waved goodbye to her from the porch, shouting their thanks but keeping their distance. All the ladies, even Mimi, stayed behind to help put away food and wash the dishes.

As they finished cleaning, Sam called Cora to come inside.

He held the door for her. "I managed to get a couple bottles of each ingredient to de-skunk you. It's a start. I put it all in the bathroom. Pour it all over yourself and marinate in it for a while, then scrub-a-dub-dub."

"Thanks, Sam."

As she made her way upstairs, he added, "Leave your clothes outside the bathroom, and I'll throw them out."

Cora nodded and continued up the stairs. After an hour in the tub, during which she felt remarkably like a preserved biology specimen, she found her friends sitting in the family room in front of the fire, having a second helping of pie and warm conversation. She entered the room and found a cup of tea waiting for her. Still feeling pungent, she took a chair from the card tables in the foyer and sat across from her friends, putting a little distance between them. Enough time had passed that she was able to laugh about the whole skunk event and enjoyed hearing about what had transpired inside.

"Widgy called while you were upstairs and wanted you to know Beast is eating and doing well," Sam said, "but she wondered where her hot dish went."

Cora and Arielle exchanged looks, then burst into laughter until tears ran down their faces.

Sam looked at Cora for an explanation, but before she could say anything, Mimi launched into her review of the dishes that had been served. She raved about the rolls and whatever else she knew the other women had brought but went on and on about how she couldn't comprehend someone bringing macaroni and cheese—out of a box, no less—to a Thanksgiving dinner. In her opinion, it was simply not appropriate holiday fare.

After five minutes of this, Arielle interrupted her. "Um, Mimi, *I* brought the macaroni and cheese."

Everyone roared with laughter, except Mimi, who apologized profusely and tried to explain her reasoning.

Cora's sides hurt from all the laughter. These people—these friends—were changing her.

The next day, Cora walked up to Mr. Wells's door, feeling as if invisible vapors were still coming off her body like Pigpen from

*Peanuts.* Another bath this morning seemed to have taken the stink down one more notch. It began as overwhelming and repulsive, went to obnoxious and foul, and was now at the merely unpleasant stage. Only time would expunge the remaining odor.

She knocked and opened the door. The last few times she had come, Mr. Wells had left the door unlocked as he sat in the living room waiting for her. She had not taken more than three steps inside when he covered his nose. "You smell horrid!"

She frowned. So much for merely unpleasant.

"I'm sorry. I was involved in a skunk accident yesterday and got sprayed. I've scrubbed myself raw, but the stench is taking its time going away. I understand if you want to skip today. I could do the shopping and leave the bags inside the door."

"No, no. I don't want you to leave." He waved her inside. "I have a surprise for you."

She took off her shoes and put hand sanitizer on her hands. Glancing into the dining room, she saw the table was set for two. Over the last few months, she had carried out countless bags of newspapers and magazines, leaving the dining room and living room spacious and tidy.

She followed Mr. Wells to the table.

He straightened his carefully folded napkins. "We can have an early lunch together and take a day off from math."

Her eyes widened. "You want me to fix you lunch and *not* do any math?"

"No, I've already made lunch."

Cora stepped into the kitchen and was taken aback at the sight of the stove and the cooking pots along the counter. Something had exploded or boiled over and then oozed down to the floor. She walked closer to investigate the mess. It was red, frothy, and sticky.

"I tried to make homemade cranberry sauce, but it boiled all over. I haven't had a chance to clean it up."

She peeked into the other pots without saying a word. The first had peas that were wrinkly and brownish from being overcooked.

Another had potatoes that had been slightly mashed. The last pot contained what she guessed was some sort of stuffing. She put a fork in and tried to stir, but it was stuck to the bottom.

"It didn't turn out as I expected. There were too many factors going on at the same time, and I lost track of the proper calculations of timing, cooking, and accurate temperatures." His scowl showed how disappointed and frazzled he was with multitasking.

She gave an encouraging smile. "You did a fine job, Mr. Wells."

"There are no rolls. I forgot to put them on the list earlier this week." He mumbled mostly to himself, annoyed, as he fidgeted with something in his pocket.

"You have a loaf of bread. I can put a couple pieces on a plate or toast them for you."

He shook his head. "That's a poor substitute. You're not supposed to have toast on Thanksgiving!"

His words smacked her. *This is his Thanksgiving dinner.*

In her busyness of rushing around to make sure everything was taken care of at the lodge, she had forgotten that he would spend Thanksgiving alone, like every other day of the year. He had waited until today to celebrate the holiday . . . with *her.*

Cora wanted to weep as she remembered her own lonely Thanksgivings with her mother. She blinked back tears as it hit her how much effort Mr. Wells had gone through to cook this meal.

She let her appreciation shine. "Oh, but that's not true! Charlie Brown had toast at his Thanksgiving meal, and you know how much I like Charlie Brown." She reached over to him and took his hand. To her surprise, he did not recoil. "Thanksgiving's about counting your blessings and being thankful. And I'm thankful we've become friends."

He gave a bashful nod. "The turkey's in the oven."

She went over and took a peek at the foil pan warming in the oven. The turkey slices looked like gray rubber floating in milky sauce. She turned back to him and smiled. "Yummy."

*A Charlie Brown Thanksgiving meal.*

One more blessing.

# Nineteen

While doing errands in town, Cora found herself meandering down Main Street and window shopping. She was standing in front of Delphinium's Flora Emporium looking at the beautiful floral arrangements in the showcase when a familiar voice startled her. "Delphinium's bouquets are like no other." Cora turned to find Ben standing behind her.

"Hi." He smiled.

"Oh . . . um, hi."

They stood staring at each other a moment, before Ben broke the awkward silence. "I saw you here as I was walking back from lunch. It's nice to see you out and about, which means you must have fully recovered from your skunk encounter."

She groaned. "I still feel as though there is a light scent lingering on my skin. I wouldn't get too close. On the plus side, I've exfoliated my skin enough for the next year. If I scrub any more, I think I'll draw blood."

He laughed, and she felt her cheeks heat up.

Ben pointed to the window. "Have you gone inside this shop?"

Cora shook her head.

"Delphinium is wonderful at what she does."

"You talk about her as if you know her well."

"I know most everyone in town. I've lived here my whole life, except when I went to college and dental school. It's a small place and everyone needs to go to the dentist eventually." He waggled his eyebrows, and she couldn't help but smile.

"Are you teasing me?"

"Never," he said with mock seriousness. "I would never try to scare you off from returning to my office."

She held onto his gaze a bit too long before looking back to the bouquets.

"You should go in and check out her shop. Delphinium is a unique person."

"How so?"

"Let's just say she definitely embraces her profession as a florist. She seems to embody everything floral." He opened the door and held it for her. "Come on. I'll introduce you quickly before I go back to the office."

"Okay, thanks."

Entering the shop was like walking into the most beautiful garden. Cora turned slowly to take it all in.

A back door swung open, and out walked a woman with outrageously curly red hair pulled up into a messy bun. Flower earrings dangled from her ears, and she had on a rose-print apron over her floral-patterned shirt and cropped jeans. Even her canvas tennis shoes had tiny flowers embroidered on them.

*Ben wasn't kidding about this woman embodying her work.*

Ben raised a hand to wave her over. "Hey, Delphinium."

"Hi, Ben."

"This is Cora Matthews. She's kind of a newcomer in town, and I wanted to introduce her to you."

"It's nice to meet you, Cora," Delphinium said, coming over and shaking her hand.

Cora couldn't be sure, but it seemed as if the florist leaned in and smelled her. The movement was so quick, it could have just been her imagination.

"Yes, just *lovely*," she added with emphasis and a brighter smile.

"Thank you," Cora answered, feeling a bit confused on what had just occurred. "Your shop is absolutely stunning. The floral arrangements are so creative and different."

Delphinium grinned. "I like to have fun with flowers."

Cora could see it wasn't simply a mixture of flowers. There were fairy houses and little figurines interspersed among them to help create a more magical feeling within the shop.

"Well, I need to get back to the office but couldn't resist bringing Cora in when I ran into her outside," Ben said.

"I should be going too," Cora added hastily. "It was great to meet you, Delphinium."

The woman nodded. "Likewise. I'm sure we'll run into each other again."

As Cora made her way to the exit, she heard Delphinium whisper to Ben, "Your scents match beautifully. She's a pink camellia."

Ben murmured something in response, then followed Cora to the door.

Once outside, Cora turned and saw that this time it was Ben who looked a bit red in the face. "Everything okay?" she asked.

He nodded. "Like I said, Delphinium is unique. She identifies a flower for every person and was just telling me what flower you smell like."

"I hope it wasn't skunkweed."

He burst out laughing. "No."

"What flower was it?"

"Pink camellia."

Cora's eyebrows scrunched together. "I don't know that one."

Ben shrugged. "Neither do I. Delphinium is a walking ency-clopedia of flowers. She didn't tell me what it represents, but it sounded like a good thing."

"Okay." Cora was ready to drop the subject since he seemed uncomfortable about it.

Ben shoved his hands into his pockets as he looked up and down the street. "Would you like to walk toward my office?" He nodded to the right.

"Ah, sure. I left my car parked at the hardware store."

As they began to walk, he didn't seem to get any less uncomfortable. Odd. He was typically so confident.

"I-I am running late, and I don't want to leave Grace alone too long," he said.

"That does sound risky," Cora agreed.

He glanced over at her.

"I mean, she's a sweetheart and everything, don't get me wrong," Cora added. "She's just unique in her own way, like Delphinium."

He chuckled. "Grace makes quite a few slipups, but she's been coming to that same office for over half a century, and I'm certainly not going to be the one to tell her she can't keep coming. She says it gives her a reason to get up in the morning."

Cora's heart melted. She shook her head. "You are . . ."

When she didn't finish, he looked over at her. "I am . . . what?"

How could she ever convey what a sweet and decent thing that was to do? Afraid of what she would say, she shook her head again. "You are late and need to hurry."

His eyes narrowed for an instant, studying her curiously. He seemed to decide not to push for more. "I hope to see you again soon, Cora Matthews."

She nodded. "I'd like that too." She smiled, feeling her heart bloom.

As they parted ways at the intersection, with him turning to go up the street and her going one more block, she couldn't stop herself from glancing back.

And wouldn't you know, he was looking back at her also.

# *Twenty*

The first major snowfall came while Cora slept. It had descended in the dark of night, erasing the landscape and creating a blank canvas. The winds sculpted the heights and angles of snowdrifts, softening the world's edges.

She felt cozy, thanks to warm socks and flannel pajamas, despite the draft making the tip of her nose pink. The chill of the lodge didn't matter. It had *snowed*.

Cora felt there was nothing more beautiful than a fresh snow covering. It was bright white and clean, powdery, and thick, clinging to even the smallest branches. The season of snow boots, gloves, scarves, and ice scrapers officially was upon them. It was time to reach into the cedar chest, where all her wool sweaters were waiting to hug her body like old friends.

She had completed most of the lodge winterization, so what occupied her mind now was getting ready for Christmas.

Sam was excited when he walked in that morning. "I've got something fun you can do."

"What are you talking about?"

"Come to the winter dance down at the town hall on Sunday night. I'm playing my harmonica in the band, and it's a chance for you to meet people. You've been too cooped up, hidden away from everything. Come, and I'll introduce you to some new faces."

Cora considered the proposition. "All right."

His face lit up.

"It'll be fun to do something different," she said. "What time does it start?"

"Meet me there at seven thirty. And don't be late—you don't want to miss my solo!"

⁓

Sunday night, Cora checked her watch and then scanned the parking lot for Sam's vehicle. There were a lot of people here already. Apparently the winter dance was a big deal for Moonberry Lake. It was too cold to sit in the car, so she went inside. Walking into the crowded room, she smiled politely and said the customary holiday greetings as she searched the room for Sam—or anyone else she recognized.

Not one familiar face.

She found an empty chair against the wall in the back and set her coat down. After standing by the dessert table and listening to one woman describe the horrors of her gall bladder surgery to a couple eager listeners, Cora wandered over to the punch table. As she poured a glass, she spotted a place to wait and made her way over to chairs lining the back wall. She sat and watched everyone dance and mingle. Some women wore dresses, but the majority of people dressed casually in winter sweaters and jeans. When people glanced at her, she made exaggerated movements like she was looking for someone in particular.

After thirty minutes, she'd had enough. As she headed for the door, she heard the music stop.

"Excuse me, everyone," the band leader said into the microphone. "Can I have your attention for a moment, and then we'll return to playing."

Cora stopped since everyone else did.

"I see the same faces here tonight, but there's one pretty lady here that some of you have pointed out to me. She's new in town, and we want to give her a proper welcome. It looks like she's missing an escort, so would any gentleman be willing to leave his partner for one spin on the floor with her?"

The room grew silent as all eyes turned to look at her. Cora gasped. *They're talking about me!* When nobody moved, the announcer redoubled his efforts.

"Come on. Surely there must be one eligible bachelor out there. And if not, what lady here is willing to share her man for a dance?"

Heat crept up Cora's face. She prayed for some great distraction so she could bolt.

*Lightning.*

*Fire.*

*Roof caving in.*

*Death.*

"That's okay." She spoke loud enough so the man on the stage could hear.

A young boy around eight years old inched toward her. With his head down, his hands in his pockets, and his ears bright red, he mumbled, "Wanna dance?"

The women all cooed a collective *aww*, and the men chortled. She couldn't say no to this poor boy, so she nodded. Everyone clapped. With a fake smile frozen on her face, she began to dance. His head came to her stomach, and they lumbered about like statues. He stared down at the floor, apparently in an effort not to step on her toes but failing miserably.

*Will this song never end?*

Cora was certain the band kept playing to keep the two of them dancing. Finally, the song ended, and she thanked the boy as he made a grand bow, which evoked more chuckles from the crowd.

Strolling in the direction of the punch bowl, she saw a side door with an exit sign above it. *Forget my coat. I'll buy another one.* She didn't look back but stepped outside. The cold winter air immediately stole her breath.

Wrapping her arms around herself, she began the trek to her car when she heard her name.

"Cora!"

Turning her head, she saw Ben hurrying toward her.

"I just got here and saw you coming outside." Suddenly his face fell. "You're not leaving, are you?"

She nodded. "Yes. I was supposed to meet Sam, but he never came."

"Come back inside, and I'll wait with you."

"Thanks, but no. I'm going to head home." She shivered.

"Wait! Could I get a dance with you?" The words tumbled out quickly. The slight tremor in his voice suggested more nervousness than cold.

"Sorry. I'm done for the evening. My dance card was filled by an eight-year-old."

"Hold on." He touched her arm. "It couldn't have been that bad."

"Believe me, this tops the boat incident, the broken tooth, *and* the skunk. I got far more publicity on this one. In fact, I'm surprised you missed it, since you're typically present whenever I embarrass myself. But if you go in now, I'm sure you'll hear all the highlights."

"You're shaking." Ben took off his coat and put it around her. "Where's your coat?"

"Inside. I had to sacrifice it in my escape."

He broke into laughter, shaking his head. "You're so funny. May I at least walk you to your car?"

His infectious smile was making her feel better and she found herself smiling back at him. "Thanks, but I'm parked around the corner. You should go inside and enjoy yourself."

He shrugged. "These social functions are never much fun. I don't know why I go. I usually end up standing around listening to a bunch of guys talk about work."

"If you hang out at the dessert table, you can hear a woman describe her gall bladder surgery. That was my thrill for the evening." She handed him his coat. "Thank you."

He pushed it back gently. "Take it. I have my suit jacket."

197

It struck her how handsome he looked in a suit. He followed her stare. "Don't recognize me all dressed up?"

"You look very handsome."

She saw something change in his eyes. Excitement?

"I'll walk you to your car, but first take a short stroll with me."

"Ben! It's ten degrees and dark. What's so important?"

His smile dissolved any fight in her. "I want to take you to the gazebo. Come with me?"

Before she could answer, he hooked his arm securely around her and began leading her in the opposite direction of the town hall, to the park situated in the center of town.

She slipped on the icy path, but Ben tightened the arm around her waist, guiding and protecting her. "I've got you." His tone was reassuring.

The words shot warmth through her body. No man had ever said that to her before. Her instinct told her to be more guarded, but whenever she was around him, she wanted to do the opposite.

The gazebo was close, and the pathway leading to it had been shoveled. Still, Ben didn't let go as they climbed the dark stairs to the top. Once inside, they stood across from each other awkwardly.

Cora studied him. "Okay, we're at the gazebo. Now what?"

He extended his hand. "May I have this dance?"

Her mouth dropped open. "What?"

"I don't want the evening to be a total disappointment. You came for a dance, and you should get one."

"Here?"

He nodded, grinning.

Astonished by the gesture and spontaneity of it all, she peered around. "There's no music or light."

"We have the moonlight, and sometimes the best music is silence." His hand remained extended.

"I don't know what to say."

"You don't have to say anything. Just take my hand and dance."

Before she could hesitate again, he pulled her into his arms, drawing her close as they began to sway in the moonlight.

The nervousness she typically experienced around him vanished. She relaxed into his touch and let him hold her. His arms were strong, his chest a shield that erased the embarrassment of her first dance of the night. Standing so close to him felt wonderful—natural even, as if she were returning to where she had always belonged.

He smelled of soap and fresh snow. Inhaling deeply, she melted against him, letting her head rest on his shoulder. He welcomed her, tightening his hold until she could hear his heart beating. The outside world faded. Nothing mattered in this moment but his touch.

In a gentle voice, he whispered, "I'm sorry you had a miserable night."

She looked up at him. "It turned out to be not so bad after all."

His gaze was intense, and she didn't look away. They danced for a few minutes, not saying anything. Her vision adapted to the darkness, and she was able to see clearly as the moon cast its glow upon the glistening snow. Ben's dark-mocha eyes swallowed her. The contours of his face were exaggerated and cut sharp by the shadows. The steam of breath barely escaped from his mouth, his lips parted slightly, as if he were about to whisper. She lifted her own lips to the beckoning claim of his as they drew closer.

The feel of his warm lips against hers was soft and inviting. She drew closer and clung to him as the kiss deepened. He responded with a low moan and strengthened his hold. She was about to lose herself in him when a cold wind sprayed snow against her face, like droplets of water on a hot griddle, bringing her back to reality.

She pulled away with a gasp, separating from the warmth of his embrace.

They stared at each other, Ben regaining his breath as well. The winter chill against her skin caused her to shiver, and she remembered she was wearing his coat.

"You must be freezing," she said.

"I'm fine. I don't even notice the cold." He took a step closer.

Cora backed up a step, overcome by the feelings spiraling inside her. It was such an automatic response, she surprised herself.

But Ben noticed the step back.

Sensing the frailty of the moment, or perhaps not wanting to break the spell that had bewitched them both, he reached out his hand. "Let's finish our dance." With slow and tender movements, he took her hand, holding her more at a distance. It seemed he understood how deeply she'd been affected by their kiss and was careful to reassure her of his gentleness and respect.

The serenity of the frosty air enveloped them.

She cleared her throat, hoping to steady her voice. "Is this where you bring all your patients to dance?"

He chuckled. "You'd be the first."

"So, you're going out on a limb for me."

"Yes," he said, gazing into her eyes. "But something tells me you're worth it."

His confident, kind words stirred something uneasy inside her. *What am I doing?* She took two steps back as pricks of panic crept up inside her.

Ben studied her. "What's wrong?"

"I-I can't do this. I'm sorry, Ben, but I can't allow myself to get carried away. I've never had a healthy relationship and the common denominator in all of them is . . . me."

There was silence for a moment as Ben took in her words. "What if I'm not like other men you've dated?"

He wasn't. She could already tell that was true. And she couldn't come up with an argument to that. She only thought of how much she loved being in his presence and never wanted to leave—which scared her to death. The feeling made her want to run, not only from him but from Moonberry too. That was what she typically did when the rush of emotions was too much—cut ties and ran.

"You should go inside before you start to turn blue," she said, trying to lighten the mood. "Thank you for the dance." She turned, ready to bolt, but he moved in front of her.

"Cora, don't do this. Not before you give what's happening between us a chance. We can take it as slowly as you want, but stay in it. This feels different than anything I've ever felt, and I'm going to fight for it."

She refused to meet his eyes, afraid of the intensity and promise she'd see. Her breaths were shallow. "We should go before we both freeze to death."

He stepped close and lifted her chin, keeping his hand there. He waited.

She raised her gaze to his and not only saw but felt the truth behind his oath.

"This is not over before it's even begun." With one finger, he traced the outline of her jaw and then the bow of her upper lip, bringing back feelings of the kiss, which must have been his intention. "We're going to finish this conversation another time." Letting those resolute words be the final statement, he walked her back.

At her Jeep, she offered a quick "thank you," but she avoided meeting his eyes. She couldn't risk it.

Without a word, he lifted her hand and kissed it. Her breath caught when his lips touched her skin. She got into her car and drove away. Though she didn't look back, she knew he was watching.

Cora trembled all the way home, and not from the cold. Once she was ready for bed, she sat in the darkness of her room, staring out at the quiet lake. The frozen surface sparkled by the light of the same moon she and Ben had danced under. She finally drifted into a slumber in the wee hours, dreaming of their dance and the kiss.

*Oh, that kiss.*

The next morning, Cora woke early, not the slightest bit tired from getting so little sleep. Her mind was still on the kiss. Ben's persistence in wanting more and the look in his eyes made her

201

feel cautiously optimistic. Even a little giddy. She couldn't forget the feeling of being in his arms. The shelter, warmth, and safety of his embrace.

She arrived at Mr. Wells's home on an adrenaline high and finished her work in record time. He didn't even mind her leaving early when he had homework to grade, so she had the afternoon free.

She was keeping warm by eating lunch in front of the fire, when she heard familiar booming steps. Widgy appeared, wearing her typical husky overalls, flannel shirt, and scowl.

"Have you seen the paper?"

Cora shook her head. "No. I just got home from work. Why?"

"Appears you're the Ginger Rogers of Moonberry." She threw the paper down on the coffee table in front of her.

Cora did a double take. The front page featured a picture of her and the boy dancing. The image showed her face, clear as day, while it only showed the back of the boy. What made it even worse was the caption underneath: "Big date night for the single ladies."

Her mouth dropped open.

"Consider yourself an instant celebrity." Widgy grinned. "I hear they're also gonna run it in the *North Woods Weekly* in the next county."

Cora gaped at the paper. "I'm the laughingstock of Moonberry Lake! I can't ever show my face in town again!"

Widgy blew through her lips like a horse. "Nah, it'll all blow over in a couple months. People will chew on it while they're hibernatin' and then, come spring, they'll move on to somethin' else. Believe me, this'll all be forgot by May or June, possibly through summer, but for sure by September."

Cora buried her face in her hands, wishing she could run away. She grabbed her cup of cocoa and collected her plate that still had half a sandwich before heading to the kitchen.

Sam walked in the front door as she was passing the foyer. She spun around and glared at him. He knew.

Sam put his hands up. "My truck battery died, and I had to get a jump. I didn't reach the hall until nine. I called ahead and asked the guys to look after you."

"They looked after me all right. Check the front page of the newspaper. My date was a kid! Your pals down there made sure we had a nice long dance."

"I'm sorry!" Sam called after her as she stomped down the hallway in a huff. "But I've got your coat!"

*I need to talk to Kitty. She'll put this into perspective.* As she put her dishes in the sink, she heard a commotion outside. Opening the back door, she saw a delivery van had gotten stuck in the driveway. Widgy was yelling directions to the driver as the wheels spun on the ice. Cora slipped on her boots and coat, then ran out to join Widgy and Sam. Between the three of them, they got the van unstuck.

As it drove away, Cora glanced around. "What was it doing here?"

"There's somethin' for ya in the entry," Widgy responded.

Sam gave Widgy a hard pat on the back. "Come on, Widge, help me spread some sand over this area. Cora, you go on inside and see your package."

Cora looked at Widgy, who nodded. "We're okay out here."

"I'll put some coffee on to warm you both up when you're done," she said, leaving them. In the foyer on the table stood a long box with a bow. Cora opened it, and her face lit up at the sight of a dozen long-stemmed, red roses. Beautiful, fresh roses in wintertime. *Wow.* The lovely vision made her smile. She gently touched the velvety petals and then brought them to her face to inhale. The attached card read, "I saw the paper. I'm sorry. –Ben."

Her heart fluttered at the sight of his name. She no longer cared about the picture in the paper. After looking from the flowers to the card again, she decided to thank him in person and return his coat, which he'd insisted she wear home last night. She needed to apologize for her abrupt departure. She didn't want things to be awkward between them.

After doing her hair and makeup, she threw on a pot of coffee, then went to the dental office. She was relieved to see that no one was in the waiting room. Grace sat behind the desk knitting.

Cora put on a bright smile. "Hi, Grace!"

The old woman jumped. "Good heavens! You don't have to shout."

"I'm sorry, I didn't mean to."

"The doc tinkered with my hearing aids, and now they're supersonic or something, because I can hear a baby breathe. The downside is I feel like I'm in a tunnel with this echo. Do you hear it?"

Silence.

"There it is again! What can I do for you . . . you . . . you? Do you hear the echo now?"

"Yes." Maybe if she agreed, Grace would change the subject.

"I think you're making it worse."

Cora bit her tongue. "Is Be— Dr. Walker free? I'd like to talk to him for a minute."

"Free? Have mercy, no doctor is *free*. Even in my day, we had to pay them with what we had. My father once paid the family bill with a steer. Give me your insurance card, and I'll let you know how much it will be."

"No, I don't have an appointment. I just want to talk."

"You don't have an appointment? We can't have people walking in off the street. Go back home and give us a call." She gave an irritated flick of her hand.

Grace was never short with her. Something was bothering her.

"I only need to talk to him for one minute. Can you please tell him Cora Matthews is here?" she pleaded, smiling sweetly.

"If you want someone to talk to you, I suppose you can stay here and keep me company. The snow's made it a slow day. Put your hand out."

When Cora obeyed, Grace slipped on a mitten she had knitted. "Hold still. I'm trying to get the right fit for a niece of mine. I'm having the darndest time with these. I think I've started and restarted ten times. Her sixtieth birthday is on Friday, and I need to get these done. I don't know what the young ladies are into these days but figured everyone needs mittens."

"You know what"—Cora slid her hand out of the mitten—"I'm going to leave this here." She handed Grace the coat.

The woman frowned. "Why would you leave it here? It doesn't belong to me."

"It's Dr. Walker's."

"What did you say your name was?"

"Cora Matthews."

Grace put down the mittens for a moment and scanned the schedule. "No, I don't see you here."

Cora rolled her eyes. "Don't worry about it. I'm sure I'll see Dr. Walker sometime. I'll let you get back to your mittens." She walked outside and then stopped in front of a newsstand and stared at the front page.

"It's a good picture of you, but it doesn't show how beautiful you are."

She spun around and saw Ben behind her, smiling.

"What are you doing out here?"

"I had time before my next appointment and went to get a cup of coffee." He lifted the to-go cup in his hand. "What are you doing here?"

His smile was making her flustered.

"Um, I-I came to return your coat and thank you for the roses. They're gorgeous."

"I'm glad you liked them. I felt terrible when I saw the morning paper. I was wondering if you—"

Before he could finish, a woman with long, strawberry-blond hair approached and threw her arms around his neck.

"There you are! I wanted to thank you for last night." She kissed him on the cheek. "Are we on for dinner tomorrow? This time, I'm not letting you leave early." She nuzzled in next to him.

Cora felt like she'd been kicked in the gut.

Ben tried to pull the woman's arms off his neck. "Cora, this is—"

205

"Oh, am I interrupting?" the woman asked with wide eyes, keeping a vise grip on him.

"Aubrey, please."

He peeled her hands away, but Cora had seen enough.

"I need to get going."

"Hey, aren't you that girl from the paper?"

Cora didn't answer or move her wounded stare away from Ben.

"Your coat's in your office."

Back in her car, she forced herself to concentrate on the road. *"Thank you for last night." What did she mean by that?* Had Ben gotten together with another woman after she left? She had no right to feel jealous. She and Ben were friends. Sort of. They danced together once. But the kiss . . .

*Let it go.*

*Let him go.*

A few tears trickled down her cheeks, and she tried to swallow the emotion choking her. Her breath felt ragged as the old, familiar feeling of disappointment crushed her chest. She gripped the steering wheel as she took small sips of air. The desire to keep driving past the boundaries of Moonberry Lake for good felt almost irresistible. The urge to run away felt both instinctual and safe.

*What was I thinking getting involved with someone again?* The compelling thought continued to niggle at her. *What if I just left?*

She let out a frustrated grunt. She'd lose the lodge, that was what.

Either way she looked at it, she'd lose—her heart or her inheritance. *Why do I always have to be on the losing ends of things?*

She made it to the next town before she turned the car around.

# *Twenty-One*

After another restless night, but for opposite reasons than the night before, Cora walked downstairs, yawning. She had to bite her lip to keep from crying at the presence of the flowers on the table. The roses in the entry were such a bittersweet sight that she had to get rid of them. It seemed awful to throw out such a vision of beauty, especially this time of year.

Then she got an idea. *Kitty would love them.* It would make her day to receive fresh flowers.

Cora hadn't seen Kitty in over a week, which was the longest she'd gone without visiting the rock house since she'd moved in. A heavy blanket of snow had resulted in the two inevitable facts of wintertime: hibernation and isolation. Being sequestered with work and Widgy filled Cora's days.

The last time she'd planned to visit, Kitty had come down with the same cold as Sofia and Mimi, which had canceled their Thursday tea. Cora had taken over some soup but was quickly shooed away, as Kitty worried Cora would catch the bug.

She wrapped the rose bouquet with newspaper to protect it from the cold and headed for the rock house. Stopping at Kitty's mailbox, she frowned. It was packed full. *This hasn't been emptied in days.* She pulled out the envelopes and junk mail.

The snow had made the cemetery a cluster of small hills and

valleys. With her arms full, Cora struggled to keep her balance. No path had been trodden. When she finally made it to the stairs, she was out of breath. Her pants were caked with snow. She sighed. It would be a miserable trudge back to the lodge with wet jeans once the snow layer melted.

A hump of snow against the door proved it hadn't been opened in a few days. After banging on the door twice with no answer, she used the extra key Kitty had given her.

*She's got to be here. There are no footprints in the snow.*

Opening the door, she called out, "Kitty? It's Cora." No answer. "I brought you a surprise and I grabbed your mail." Upon entering the kitchen, she gasped. All the plants were drooping. There was no broth on the stove. The house was still and silent. A combination of fear and dread prickled her skin.

Dropping the roses and mail on the table, she ran into the next room.

She scanned the tiny living room. Nothing.

"Kitty!"

She rushed down the hall and into a small sewing room. It was empty. She ran into the next room. Kitty was lying on the floor in her nightgown, next to the bed.

She gasped. "Kitty!" She rushed to the older woman's side. Kitty didn't respond to her voice. She felt cold to the touch, and a horrible rasping sound came from her chest. "I'm here. It's going to be okay. I'll call for help." She ran to the phone and picked it up. There was no dial tone. What a day to have left her cell phone at home!

She went back to Kitty's side. "I have to go for help. I'll be right back. I promise." She grabbed two blankets from the bed and covered Kitty, then hurried back to the lodge, screaming for Sam.

She was almost to the lodge when Sam and Widgy came running toward her. "Kitty is on the floor and unconscious! Call an ambulance!"

Widgy nodded and ran back to the lodge.

"I'll start clearing a path," Sam said.

Cora hurried back and sat with Kitty, putting two more blankets over her and whispering prayers. What if she hadn't come when she did? She wiped away a stray tear as she watched Kitty struggle to breathe. *Please be okay.*

Cora paced the waiting room, unable to sit still. When the ambulance had arrived at Kitty's, she'd insisted on riding along, holding Kitty's hand the whole time, even though her friend seemed unaware of her presence.

Now, the doors to the waiting area swooshed open and Sam came in. Cora ran to him and collapsed into tears. "I should've checked on her earlier!"

Sam held her and let her cry. "You're not to blame. I could've checked on her also. All we can do is wait for the doctors to do their work."

After an hour, the doctor came with a report. Sam had been Kitty's emergency contact, so he was allowed the information.

"Along with severe dehydration, she has double pneumonia." The doctor paused and then looked at Cora. "Her condition is critical. Between her age and the illness, her prognosis is not good."

Sam put his arm around Cora.

Cora was relieved for the support because her legs felt as if they would give out.

Later, when Kitty had been moved to a room, they were allowed to visit. Cora stood in the doorway staring at her. Kitty lay motionless. The white sheets and harsh lighting accentuated her wrinkles and sunspots. Without her sparkling eyes and big smile, she appeared fragile. Ancient.

Tears streamed down Cora's cheeks. Losing her mother hadn't hurt this badly. It was as if something inside her was ripping open. The pain went deeper than flesh and muscle. *Why does it hurt so much?*

Then she remembered: old scars didn't open cleanly. They tore in jagged slits, releasing the hurt behind them. Cora wrapped her arms around herself, wanting to close off the pain and make it stop by sheer force. With a hiccup, she choked back what she was most afraid of saying.

*Goodbye.*

Later that week, Joseph came to the hospital room. He looked different than when he worked in his garden, dressed more formally as a chaplain, but his gentle demeanor remained. He stood beside Kitty's bed, bowed his head, and said a prayer. Then he moved to kneel next to the chair where Cora sat. She was too tired and drained of emotion to speak.

He seemed to understand what was churning inside of her because he began to pray again. Cora didn't close her eyes but studied him while he spoke of the strength, love, and healing he wished for her as well. She had never had anyone pray out loud for her. It was fascinating to watch him. He emitted an aura of peace and she was surprised at the soothing effect his words had. When he finished, he sat with her, requiring no conversation. His presence felt comforting. She appreciated his quiet spirit and the support of him simply sitting by her side.

In the following days, she only left Kitty to go home and shower and then returned to the chair by her bed. She called Mr. Wells and told him the situation, and he agreed that she should stay with Kitty. He told her not to worry, and Sam said he would get any groceries he needed this week.

Cora covered Kitty with an extra homemade quilt from the lodge and gently smoothed her hair while talking to her. After four days of continual sleep and being hooked up to oxygen and IVs, Kitty finally opened her eyes.

Cora sprang up and went to her dear neighbor, who was looking around the room in drowsy confusion.

"You're in the hospital, Kitty, and you're going to be fine."

Kitty gave a weak smile.

"I went over to your house for a visit and found you unconscious. The doctors say you developed double pneumonia. They've been pumping medicine and fluids into you for days. Sam and Joseph and the ladies have been by to visit, and we've all been waiting for you to wake up."

Kitty raised her hand high enough to touch Cora's face.

Cora took it and held it. "Is there anything I can get for you?"

Kitty stared at Cora and then the corners of her mouth turned up. In a small, raspy voice, the old woman whispered, "Marshmallow cloud."

Cora started laughing and crying at the same time.

Kitty would fight back.

She would live.

After Kitty had been moved out of intensive care and was feeling stronger, Cora asked her what had happened.

"I wanted to call you for help, but my phone went dead, and I didn't have the strength to walk over to the lodge."

Guilt shrouded Cora. "I'm sorry I didn't come by sooner."

"Dear child, you're not my guardian. Possibly a guardian angel, but it's not your job to take care of me. Besides, I wasn't alone. Peter was with me. He was as handsome as the day we met." She closed her eyes. "I miss him so much, and I wanted to go with him, but he told me it wasn't time—that I still have some work to do, though I can't imagine what! I'm as old and useless as they come."

Cora's face fell. "Don't say that! I can think of a lot of people who need you."

"Are we talking about the company lying in my yard?" she said with a small smile.

"I'm including everyone standing up *and* lying down."

Kitty chuckled.

Cora held her friend's hand. "Widgy's going nuts with the number of people calling her for an update. She keeps threatening to charge me for her secretarial services."

"I'm touched," Kitty said before falling asleep.

The old woman looked fragile and small, almost childlike in the bed. With a ginger touch, Cora traced the blue and green veins jutting out from underneath the skin on Kitty's hand, skin as thin as tissue paper. Staring at the transparency and softness of Kitty's skin, at her long white hair cascading down the pillows, Cora saw the beauty of a soul who had lived a full life. Kitty looked like a delicate earth angel who had grown old and weary. The image broke her heart.

It was late, and the road was dark as Cora drove home. She pulled up to the lodge, turned off the engine, and sat in the Jeep. The last week and a half had been an emotional roller coaster, and she needed to breathe. She grabbed the flashlight from the emergency kit in the trunk and headed for Kitty's stone house. She'd make sure it was locked and all the lights were turned off. It would make her feel better knowing the place was closed properly. Some of the plants no doubt needed watering.

With the moonlight reflecting off the snow, there was plenty of light to find her way through the cemetery. Using her key, she unlocked the door and went in.

The house was cold and musty. She flipped the switch, but no lights came on. *That's odd.* Turning on the flashlight, she scanned the room. Without the greenery pouring over every surface and the smell of simmering broth, the place seemed to have lost its warmth and charm. The living room was neat with minimal furnishings. There was a small sofa and chair in faded tapestry fabric and a coffee table decorated with gnomes. On each side of the sofa were wilted plants. The centerpiece on the fireplace mantel was a large, blue-gray urn. Spilling over the top of the urn and onto the mantel were folded pieces of paper, like fortunes from Chinese cookies.

She opened one and read it. "Sam came to check on me today and brought a loaf of bread from the mission."

The blessings jar. Kitty had talked about it during her first visit. Cora peeked at some of the other slips of paper.

*"I could bend my fingers easily today, and I was able to work on the gravestones without pain."*

*"A bird sang a song to me the entire time I was outside to keep me company."*

*"I wore a sweater Peter gave me, which kept me warm in the wind."*

*"My lovely new neighbor brought me a chocolate wonder I call 'marshmallow clouds.'"*

*"I've been watching a spider make the most intricate web outside my window. I'm in awe."*

*"I loved the conversation at the ladies tea. I always leave smiling."*

*"Spent time praying in the middle of the night when I couldn't sleep. God had lots to say."*

Kitty's blessings were simple. She took delight in the most basic things. Perhaps it was from living alone all those years, or sitting in daily quietness at the cemetery markers, but she seemed to have discovered how to extract pleasure from everything around her.

Cora walked back to the lodge, opening her eyes to the serene, moonlit world. She inhaled the smell of snow. It helped clear her mind and prepare her for the blessing she needed the most at that moment—sleep.

The next morning, Cora sat in the dining hall with a cold cup of tea as she stared out the window to the lake. The sound of the kitchen door told her Arielle had come early.

"Good morning." Arielle shivered as she took off her mittens and coat. "How long have you been sitting here?"

Cora stretched. "I don't know. I got up around five. What time is it now?"

"A little after eight. You've been sitting here staring out the window for three hours?"

Cora didn't take her eyes off the frozen expanse. "That image of Kitty on the floor keeps haunting me. I can't get it out of my head. I keep thinking, What if I had gone over there sooner? Or worse, What if I had gone over any later?"

Arielle sat down. "You're not responsible. We all could've checked on her."

"I've been trying to figure out why I feel such a connection to a woman I haven't even known that long. Then I think about all the people she's told me about in the cemetery. Every person buried there has a story. Kitty recognizes the best qualities in every person and then memorializes them in the most beautiful way. Their stories live on." Cora took an unsteady breath. "When I saw her lying on the floor, my panic was not that she was dead but that I never got to tell her what an impact she's had on me. To thank her for being the family I always wanted. To say, 'I love you.'"

Arielle nodded and wiped away a tear.

Cora shook her head. "I know it's selfish, but I'm not ready to let go. And when it comes time for Kitty to go, she shouldn't be lying on the cold floor, forgotten and alone. Someone should be with her, like the way she was with Peter. She deserves more, and I want to give her that."

Arielle reached over the table and put her hands over Cora's. "We all want to give her that. Mimi's going to the hospital to sit with her all day. Let's go over to Kitty's house and find some things to cheer her up. I'm sure she would like her own nightgown and hairbrush—things like that."

That lifted Cora's mood. "That's a great idea. With some luck, she'll be ready to come home in another week. We could bring in some new plants and brighten the place up, get it ready for her homecoming."

Arielle nodded. "I'm ready when you are."

The two trudged through the snow to Kitty's house. As Cora opened the door, the hinges let out a long, sad moan that echoed her emotions. They stood staring at the shriveling brown vines and dead plants in the kitchen.

"It's freezing in here." Cora looked around for a thermostat.

"The heat must be off. When was the last time you were here?" Arielle asked.

"Last night, but I couldn't see much with just a flashlight. What about you?"

Arielle shook her head. "I haven't been inside for months."

The sink filled with a dead herb garden caught Cora's attention. "We need to get this place cleaned up. It would break Kitty's heart to see this. Some of these plants can be saved."

"You check for garbage to be thrown out and food that's expired, and I'll go to her bedroom and see what I can find to take to her."

Cora nodded and glanced around for a trash can. She began opening the cupboards to search for trash bags. Her heart sank at the sight of how bare those cupboards were. There was little food, mainly jars of spices and a meager assortment of canned goods. The refrigerator wasn't much better. It held a couple jars of homemade jam, pickles, butter, a casserole container of broth and noodles, and expired milk. The freezer was filled with plastic bags of vegetables, all defrosted thanks to the power being out.

"Arielle, come here!"

Her friend returned holding a scrap of cloth that was too thread-bare to be used as a rag.

Cora frowned. "What's that?"

"Her nightgown." Arielle shook her head. "She has nothing warm or in decent condition."

"The electricity is off. The freezer is defrosted. And there's almost no food in the kitchen."

Moments ticked by as the truth surfaced in their minds.

"How long do you think she's been living like this?" Arielle asked.

"I don't know. I'm getting the feeling there's a lot we didn't know." She took a big breath. "Let's go get Sam and Widgy."

Within a couple hours, Widgy was in the basement, Arielle was in the bedroom packing a small suitcase, and Sam was on his cell phone talking to the utility company.

Cora remained in the kitchen, throwing out the contents of the freezer and refrigerator and deciding which plants could be nursed back to life. She lined up all the gnomes she found along the counter: thirty-two so far, not including those on top of the cabinets.

Cora heard the heavy thud of Widgy's boots on the basement stairs. Judging from her long face, she didn't have good news.

She gave a heavy sigh. "It's worse than I expected. This place has all the original plumbin', and it's in horrible shape. There's nothin' to fix. It all has to be replaced, and it's too big a job for me. I could make a couple calls and get some guys out here, but you're still talkin' about a lotta money. If the county ever saw this place, they'd condemn it."

Cora rubbed her forehead. "If Kitty had the money, she would've fixed it."

"Well, until everything's replaced or repaired, this house is unlivable. She has no heat, water, or electricity." Widgy ticked off the deficiencies on her fingers.

Cora nodded. "Okay, then she can live with me until it's fixed. It's not like I don't have the room."

Sam came into the kitchen, tucking his cell phone into his pocket. "I talked to the electric company, and they agreed to turn on the power if I drop off a personal check. She hasn't paid her bill for months."

Arielle entered, looking as sad as everyone else. "I packed a few belongings, but she doesn't have much. I'm going to buy her a couple new nightgowns and a robe on my way to the hospital."

Cora fought back tears. "There's basically no food here. She was living mostly on broth."

They all stood in heavy silence.

In a whisper, Cora asked, "Why didn't we know how bad things were?"

Widgy blew out a sharp breath. "Kitty's a proud woman. She's not one to ask for help and probably wanted to do things her way, which meant standin' on her own feet."

"I should've known," Sam said. "I should have made it my business to know how she was living and not assume everything was fine." His voice cracked on the last word.

Arielle wiped her nose with a paper towel, her eyes red. "For someone who spent time with her, I certainly am no friend. A friend would have known about *this*." She gestured to the kitchen around her. "She must have been cold and hungry."

Cora straightened her shoulders. "Well, we can be here for her now and change all this. Whatever it takes, Kitty will never live like this again. Widgy, can you get the repairs started?"

Widgy stepped forward. "I'll call in some favors to get an estimate."

Cora nodded. "Sam?"

"I'll keep working with the phone and electric companies."

Cora took a deep breath. "I'll start cleaning this place since Arielle is going over to the hospital. It needs a hard scrubbing, and it'll feel good to do something physical."

Arielle brushed a dead leaf from the kitchen table. "I'll take shifts sitting with Kitty, and I'll take the dying plants and empty planters over to my house and start putting new plants in them." She offered a wry grin. "I'm going to have to create an indoor greenhouse to get these up to Kitty's standards."

It felt good to have a plan and friends to help. "Let's get started, then meet over at the lodge around five o'clock tomorrow to see what we've discovered."

"I'll bring a casserole and some bread."

Everyone looked at Arielle.

"It'll be dinnertime, and we all have to eat."

As they went to work on their tasks, Cora pushed back the shame that cloaked her. It was the time to act.

For Kitty.

# Twenty-Two

S omeone wise once told me that warmth and conversation renew life, so that's precisely what I plan to give you." Cora leaned over Kitty's hospital bed. "I need one important thing from you though."

Kitty grinned. "What is that?"

Cora raised an eyebrow. "It's time you gave me your secret broth recipe."

Kitty chuckled. "Not yet. Have you gone over to my house?"

Cora knew to choose her words carefully. "Yes."

"How are my precious plants doing?"

Cora hesitated. "I'll be honest with you. We have a problem."

Worry knitted the old woman's brows.

"The gnomes have taken over."

Kitty burst into laughter.

"Don't worry. I'm taking care of everything," Cora continued. "And when you leave here, you're going to come stay with me until you're stronger."

Kitty shook her head. "Nonsense."

"I insist."

Kitty frowned. "I've become a burden, and that is precisely what I never wanted to be. It's time I took my place next to Peter."

"Don't say that. You're never a burden."

Kitty looked at her pointedly. "Miss Matthews, I have no fear of death. I look forward to seeing my Maker, in addition to dear Peter again. In my long life, the one truth I've come to believe is that there's not a beginning or end to life, but simply a sigh as we move on. The action of breath is present at both times, acting as a means of tying the two ends together. At birth, we inhale, and at death, we exhale. That's it. I've seen people die, and it always looks as if they're taking a pause."

Cora gave a small smile at the calming thought.

"Death is not as frightening as everyone makes it out to be," Kitty continued. "I was holding Peter's hand when he passed. The moment he left this life, stillness fell upon the room. There was impenetrable pain and sickness one moment and then only peace." A tear escaped her eye and ran onto the pillow. She placed her hand on top of Cora's. "None of us came here to stay. There's a time to be born and a time to die. Our purpose is to leave an imprint of love behind."

Cora rested her head against Kitty's arm, fighting back her own tears. "There are people who love you and still need you around. Peter was right—it's not time to go yet."

Kitty eyes twinkled. "Although I don't think the decision is up to you, I appreciate your sentiment."

That evening, everyone met at the lodge at precisely five o'clock to share what they'd learned. Each face looked more sullen than the next. Just as Widgy sat down, Mimi came bursting in.

"Did I miss anything?" she asked, out of breath. "Kitty said she wanted to sleep and would be fine with just the nurses, and I wanted to be here for the meeting."

"You haven't missed anything." Cora gestured to an empty spot.

Mimi dropped into a chair. "Sofia told me about the situation with the house, and I feel terrible! There are so many things I wish I could do over." She blurted out the words as if she were in a confessional and cleansing herself of past sins.

Arielle passed a plate of casserole and bread to Widgy, but the repairwoman put them down in front of her and looked at the others. "I can't eat 'til I say what I have to, and I'm afraid that once I tell ya what I've found, you won't be that hungry." She cleared her throat. "The house has been deterioratin' for some time. There's extensive water damage, but that's another story. For starters, all the plumbin' and electrical work needs to be redone. I can oversee the job and do some myself, but I'd need to bring in help. The bid I got from a couple guys I trust was a lot—more than Kitty has."

Silence.

Mimi shifted in her seat. "I want to help financially."

Everyone gaped at her.

Mimi huffed. "What? Kitty's one of my dearest friends, and it would make me happy to help her out. I'm getting older and have money. If I don't spend it now, when will I? Heaven knows I can't take it with me."

"Oh, Mimi!" Arielle jumped up and threw her arms around her.

"Get off me! Your wild hair's going to get caught in my jewelry!" Mimi pushed Arielle away.

Arielle let go. "Fine, but now I know you're a softie like the rest of us."

Mimi rolled her eyes. "Don't hold your breath, hippie girl." She puckered her lips, probably to deny Arielle the satisfaction of a smile.

"I ain't done." All attention returned to Widgy. "That's the tip of the iceberg. We're a far cry from makin' the place livable. Some beams are rotted and need to be replaced, the windows let in more than they keep out, the roof's leakin' like a strainer, and two interior walls need fixin' from water damage. The house is in such bad condition, it needs a huge pot of money for a complete overhaul."

This time, the silence was much heavier and longer. Mimi looked helpless.

It was Sam's turn to speak up. "I know we're all willing to help, but don't you think we need to assess whether or not the cottage is worth such extensive repairs?"

"But we all know how much she loves that cemetery," Arielle said. "She'd never move."

Sofia cleared her throat. "In searching through Kitty's papers, Sam and I found some discrepancies in her social security that don't make sense. I'm not saying anything else until I do some more investigating, but there may be a silver lining in this mess."

"What should we do until then?" Mimi asked.

Widgy leaned her elbows on the table and rested her head on her clasped hands. "Nothin'. We have to let the house sit 'til spring. This kind of renovation needs warmer weather and no snow."

"What do we tell Kitty?" Arielle asked.

Taking a deep breath, Sam folded his hands in his lap. "Kitty would want the truth."

Cora shook her head. "I disagree. I say we treat this with the utmost discretion—say we're sending Widgy over to fix a couple things when the weather gets warmer, which is the truth. We don't have to hurt her pride and say how extensive it's going to be. Let her get well first and then Widgy can explain all that needs to be done. In the meantime, she'll stay with me in one of the downstairs rooms. That way, she'll feel close to her own house and not have to struggle with steps."

Everyone agreed that was the best plan. They ate and spent the rest of the time brainstorming how each of them could do something for Kitty during her recuperation.

⁓

The following day as Cora was exiting Kitty's hospital room, she stopped short at the sight of Ben walking toward her in the hallway, holding a bouquet of flowers. Her stomach dropped.

He looked just as surprised and uncomfortable as she felt.

"Cora," he began.

"Don't," she said, putting her hand up. "Please. I'm too tired and too emotional."

"If you'd just let me explain."

She shook her head. "I don't want to hear it."

The hurt in his eyes was unmistakable.

"My focus is on Kitty. That's all that matters to me at this moment."

Ben gave a stiff nod. "I brought her some flowers."

"She'll love them. I was just stepping out to get some food. I haven't eaten all day."

"I could—"

"Kitty will love the visit and flowers," Cora said, cutting him off. "Bye, Ben," she said, then walked past him.

He didn't respond or try to stop her.

And she didn't look back.

Kitty was set to be discharged that afternoon, after two weeks in the hospital. Though she was still weak, the doctors felt she would be fine since she would be well cared for. Cora was planning to take Sofia's car to pick her up so she wouldn't have to climb up into the Jeep. Before Cora left, the group gathered over at the lodge to check the progress on Kitty's temporary room.

Sofia had been in charge of the project. She had Sam and Widgy bring over Kitty's dresser, end table, and bed frame to make the room feel more like home. Widgy commented on how dilapidated her mattress was, so Sofia purchased a new mattress, box spring, and pretty bedding. After Sam cleaned and oiled the furniture and Sofia made up the bed with the fresh linens, they stood back and reassessed.

"It's too empty in here." Arielle squinted her eyes as if trying to see the room through a different lens. "It needs something in the corner."

Sam's face lit up. "I've got a rocking chair at home we never use. I'll run and get it!"

"I've got a little table and lamp." Arielle scurried after him.

Later, with the rocking chair, lamp, and table nestled in the corner, topped off by one of Arielle's watercolor paintings hanging above them, the room looked cozy. They were standing in the doorway admiring it when Mimi slid between them.

"Excuse me." She carried a vase bursting with fresh flowers and placed it on the table. She hurried out of the room again. A minute later, she came back carrying a robe, nightgown, and slippers. She laid the robe and nightgown across the foot of the bed and placed the slippers on the floor beneath them. She stood back and assessed her contribution. "Perfect."

No one said a word about the fact that the entire ensemble was in a tiger print.

As if reading their thoughts, Mimi grinned. "The store had animal-print pajamas on sale. They're so soft and plush, I couldn't resist. Don't you simply love them? I doubt Kitty has ever slept in anything this soft. I went wild and picked up two sets for myself."

Before anyone had time to respond, Widgy barged into the group and placed a picture frame on the end table next to the bed. It was a photo of Peter.

"*Now* everything's perfect," Sam said.

"I've got to get back to work," Widgy mumbled and left the room. One by one, everyone else did the same.

Widgy shoveled and salted the walkway heavily so Kitty wouldn't slip. Sam and Sofia went back to the rock house to bring over any other belongings that would make her feel more comfortable. Arielle worked busily in the kitchen making a huge pot of vegetable soup and a couple loaves of multigrain herb bread. Everyone had their task.

When Cora entered the hospital room that afternoon, Kitty was sitting up and looking cheerful. "I'm going home today!"

"You're simply too healthy to stick around this place." Cora bent down to give her a hug. "We've set up a beautiful bedroom for you at the lodge. Sofia's putting the final touches on it as we speak."

Kitty placed her hand on Cora's. "Thank you for your kindness. I simply don't know what I'd do without you in my life."

Cora gave a wobbly smile. "That's something you're never going to have to worry about."

When they arrived at the lodge, the whole crew was waiting to greet them at the door and help Kitty inside to her new living quarters. Cora found herself holding her breath, anticipating Kitty's reaction to the special room they'd prepared.

Kitty began to cry as soon as she saw the room. Cora watched with pleasure as Kitty took in her bed and dresser, the picture of Peter, her time-worn blanket draped over the rocking chair, plants below the windows with little gnomes around them. She grinned at everything, especially the little bowl of chocolates on the nightstand.

"I'm overwhelmed." Kitty wiped her eyes with a tissue. Holding on to Cora's arm, she slowly walked over to the edge of the bed and sat, running her hands over the new bedding. She chuckled at the robe and nightgown. "I see each one of you added a special touch. Thank you for being my family and showing me so much love."

Widgy and Sam bowed their heads, Cora and Arielle wiped their eyes, Mimi had to leave the room, and Sofia gingerly sat on the bed and hugged Kitty. After more gentle hugs, everyone but Cora left the room. She helped Kitty get situated and propped up on pillows in her new bed. Then she brought her some of Arielle's soup and bread. With the warm, hearty food in her, Kitty's eyelids began to droop. Cora rearranged the pillows so she could lie down, and Kitty was asleep in minutes.

As she tiptoed out of the room, Cora glanced back and couldn't help but smile at the sight of her diminutive neighbor nearly lost in the sea of blankets and mountains of pillows. All she could see was her face and her shoulders wrapped in the tiger-print pajamas.

Kitty now had what Cora believed every person had the God-given right to—warmth, good food, and love.

Later that night, Cora checked on Kitty again and found her awake, staring at the ceiling.

"Hey there, roomie. What are you thinking about?"

"My friends."

Cora sat on the edge of the bed. "Who would you like me to have come and visit you tomorrow?"

"I meant the ones surrounding my home."

"Oh." Kitty was talking about her precious cemetery.

"Have I ever told you about Eleanor?"

Cora shook her head, adjusting her position on the bed to get more comfortable. "Who's that?"

"She's the third one down from the Mary figure on the right."

"Is she the one with birds and feathers on her marker?"

"No, that's Sarah. Eleanor is next to her."

Cora tried to envision the stone. "I can't picture her marker. What's on it?"

"Let me tell you about her first." Kitty's warm smile rested on Cora. "I wish there was some way you could have met her," Kitty started. "She owned a bread shop in town and made the most heavenly bread you've ever tasted. This was before the nuns started baking, mind you, and people came from miles for her bread. There was a quality and taste that nobody could match. Some said that it was the love she put into every loaf."

"Sounds delicious," Cora added.

"Mm-hmm." Kitty licked her lips at the memory. "Every evening, when the shop closed, she would pull out a basket filled with bread. Not the bread that was unfit to be sold, but the most beautiful loaves of the day. Then she'd take the basket to struggling families, asking if they would do her the favor of taking this unsold bread so she wouldn't have to throw it out. She apologized if it was stale or burned, which of course it wasn't."

A wistfulness took over Kitty's expression. "I remember this vividly because my home was one of those she visited. For me, it meant not going to bed hungry. As a child, I was able to fill my tummy with fresh, soft bread when there was nothing else. It was sustenance. It fed both the giver and receiver."

She turned shining eyes to Cora. "That's what you have given me. Your friendship has given me sustenance."

Cora took Kitty's hand. "I know the marker; it's the one with wisps of wheat on it."

Kitty nodded. "Sustenance."

It was like Kitty's words broke something open inside Cora, or maybe it was salve to an old wound. Whatever it was, love filled her. She couldn't express it any other way but to lightly squeeze Kitty's hand and repeat, "Sustenance."

In the morning, Cora knew she had to talk to Widgy. Working for Mr. Wells just twice a week since Kitty went to the hospital had made things tight financially. She crept into bedroom eight where Widgy was working, dreading each step. She took a deep breath and blurted it out. "Widgy, you have to stop working."

The repairwoman didn't even look up. "What are you yakkin' about?"

"I can't afford to keep paying you."

"Don't worry about it. You can pay me when things get better."

Cora wrung her hands. "I can't do that. I don't have any idea when I'll get the money to pay you. You've given me the bills for the materials, but I haven't even seen anything for your labor for the past two months."

Widgy finally stilled. "You're takin' care of Kitty. You love her like she was blood. It's a nice thing you're doin'. I'm not stoppin' my work. I can get you wholesale prices on the materials."

"Even if I can pay for the supplies, I can't afford *you*. I'm barely making it between what I earn from Mr. Wells and dipping into my savings."

Widgy shrugged. "I accept monthly installments. Can you afford ten dollars a week?"

Cora made a face. "How do you expect to live on forty dollars a month? You couldn't even feed Beast for that!"

Widgy turned and pointed at Cora, waggling her finger. "Listen here. I started this job 'cause Samuel asked me. I kept doin' it 'cause I saw how much this place needs help, and, well . . . you've kinda grown on me. Like a puppy. Truth is, before this, I wasn't workin' much. No need to. The life insurance from five husbands left me with enough money to keep me and Beast comfortable. But retirement doesn't suit me—and there's not much for me to do all alone. It was drivin' me nuts sittin' there doin' nothin'. That's when Sam told me you needed help."

Cora didn't know what to say.

"Fact is," Widgy continued, "I don't know what I'd be doin' if you hadn't moved here. I've gotten accustomed to gettin' up and comin' over here every mornin'. I like havin' a routine, and you're not that annoyin' most days, and you need someone lookin' after ya. So, this conversation's over. Leave me to my business. There's a rat's nest behind this outlet and the wirin' has been chewed. It's gonna take me the rest of the mornin' to clean it up."

Cora stood there, gaping. There it was—the truth of who Widgy really was.

Somehow, she and Widgy had come to each other's rescue.

Cora tried to wrap her mind around that profound—and utterly shocking—truth. "I-I don't know what to say. Thank you, Widgy." She moved toward her with open arms.

"Stop right there." Widgy put up a hand. "This confession wasn't an open invitation to blubber. Don't start the waterworks, 'cause I'm *not* gettin' up to hug ya. All I've ever asked is that a Dr Pepper be waitin' for me in the fridge. I don't need gratitude. A cold pop will do."

"It'll always be there." Cora sniffled.

"What did I say? No waterworks! Now, get out of here and let me work."

Cora did as she was told, but as she walked away, it felt as though a burden had been lifted and an enormous blessing bestowed.

She peeked in on Kitty and saw she was still asleep. *Good.* She needed rest to recover. She inched the door shut and went to the kitchen to heat some water for tea. Kitty loved mint tea in the morning, and there were cinnamon rolls in the refrigerator to warm up.

What extraordinary people had come into her life. The emptiness that had plagued her for so long was being filled with a love she never expected from the most unexpected people.

These people were so different from anyone she would have chosen as friends before coming to Moonberry Lake. It was amazing how, in stepping out of her comfort zone and getting to know people who lived a bit "outside the box," she was discovering a new self.

A better self.

# Twenty-Three

Cora sat at the side of her bed looking out the window to the beautiful snowy landscape. The pristine whiteness and frozen stillness filled her with gratitude. Walking downstairs, she peeked in on Kitty and was glad to see she was sleeping peacefully. As she made her way to the kitchen, she met Widgy in the dining hall. It was no surprise that Widgy always beat her at greeting the sunrise. The repairwoman kept a key to the lodge on her grapefruit-size key ring. Which felt right.

Widgy sat drinking a Dr Pepper with Beast sleeping beside her on the sheepskin seat cover that Cora had given the repairwoman as an early Christmas present.

Widgy lifted her can of pop. "Merry Christmas."

Cora smiled and sat down across from her. "Merry Christmas to you. Why aren't you home with your boys? You can't think I would've expected you to work today or this week."

Widgy shrugged. "I came by to check on a couple things. I like to make sure everythin' is workin'." She looked to her snoring dog. "Beast sure loves the sheepskin."

Cora stared at Beast enjoying the car seat cushion as his personal bed mat. The dog was lying on his back, legs sprawled out and twitching. "I'm glad he likes it, but it was supposed to be for you to put in your truck."

"Nah, Beast deserves somethin' this nice. It puts him to sleep right away. You can see how he's dreamin' now. He must be chasin' a squirrel." She stroked his tummy to stop the muscles from jerking. "Beast also loves the slippers you left him."

"I didn't leave him any slippers."

"Then I probably should apologize for them now before you go into the kitchen."

Cora shook her head. "We'll count them as an extra gift from Santa." She began to get up from the table.

"Wait a minute. I wanted to give you somethin'." Widgy motioned for her to sit back down, then reached underneath the table and pulled up a brown grocery bag. "This is for you," she said, placing the bag down with a thump.

"You didn't have to give me anything."

"Stop yappin' and open it."

As Cora scooched it closer to her, she was surprised by how heavy and solid it was. Reaching inside, she pulled out a bulky cloth sack and placed it on the table with a thud.

Widgy couldn't contain her excitement. "It's twenty pounds of sausage mix! All you need to do is add some ground-up meat, and you'll have the best sausage you've ever tasted."

Cora's mouth dropped open. What did one say to a giant bag of sausage mix? "Wow, this is a big . . . big bag."

Widgy's chest swelled. "That's the same mix the fancy restaurants use. Instead of payin' money for breakfast sausage at restaurants, you can make your own. It'll also help to put some meat on your bones, no pun intended. You're lookin' scrawny."

"Thanks, Widge. This is very generous of you."

She gave a curt nod. "I better get back. The boys will be expectin' somethin' for Christmas breakfast." She lifted Beast, wrapped in the sheepskin as if he were a newborn. "Tell Kitty I'll be checkin' on her tomorrow, and there's somethin' for her in the family room. I put it with the other things." With that, she was out the door.

*Other things?* Cora headed back down the long hallway, past

Kitty's room, and saw the miniature Christmas tree that Sam had set up before Kitty arrived, decked out with tiny lights and ornaments and placed in the center of the coffee table. Presents were lined up along the fireplace. Feeling like a kid who discovered Santa had come, she knelt down and saw they were all for her and Kitty. Too excited to wait, she started to open her presents.

Without looking at the tag, she guessed from the Santa cat wrapping paper that the first gift was from Mimi. Inside were pajamas exactly like the ones Mimi had given Kitty, but Cora's were leopard print. The idea of her and Kitty walking around the lodge in their animal pajamas made her chuckle.

The next box was wrapped in elegant pink paper with Victorian angels on it. The name tag dangling by a gold thread was signed by Sofia. Underneath an array of pink tissue paper was a beautiful teacup and saucer set made of ivory bone china, with a gold rim and delicate rosebuds adorning it. Inside was a note, "A starter for all the ladies teas to come!"

Behind Sofia's present was a badly wrinkled snowman bag overflowing with newspaper. Inside was a large clay bowl Arielle had made on her pottery wheel. It was glazed in a multitude of blues.

The last gift was from Sam. It was a small photo album. Cora opened it to the first page and saw a picture of her whole family posing in front of the lodge. Her mother, so young and beautiful, stood next to Cora's grandparents. Genuine joy shone on each person's face. Joy she never saw on her mother's face later on. Cora traced her finger over their images.

As she turned the pages, memories flooded back to her. Hot summer days spent in a swimsuit, which she wore from morning 'til night. In the pictures she was grinning with crooked teeth, messy hair, and tanned legs and arms. She was unkempt and caked with sand, looking so happy. Another photo was of her in a boat wearing a life jacket and grasping a fishing pole as her grandfather held up the catch of the day. She never had summers like those at the lodge after they left. Occasionally, her mother would take her to a community pool, but the carefreeness and sense of contentment was gone. No other home they moved to ever felt like it was truly hers.

The last page was a picture of two tiny figures. *That's me and Sam!* They were sitting at the end of the dock together. He was baiting a hook for her to throw out a line to catch some perch. Their faces were turned toward the camera, squinting in the sun.

Lost in the past, she jumped when she heard Kitty say good morning.

"You startled me."

"You look as if you're a thousand miles away."

Cora held up the picture for Kitty to see.

She studied it. "Is that you?"

"It's Sam and me sitting on the dock."

"Well, aren't you the most adorable thing! I wish I would've known you back then. We could've had all this history together."

A corner of Cora's mouth pulled up. "We do. Though you didn't know me, I used to watch you from behind trees while you sat at the graves."

Kitty clapped her hands together. "Not you too! I used to see children sneaking around the property and wished they'd walk up and say hello."

"I wish I had. Instead, I listened to all the other kids who convinced me that you were a witch listening to the whispers of the dead."

"What?" Kitty giggled and bent over slapping her knee and laughing. "How fun! I had no idea I brought such imagination to your summer days. I'm tickled you all came up with something so creative. If I had known, I would've played up the part a little and hung some plastic bats or ghosts in the trees. I could've even worn a pointed hat. What great fun that would've been!" Her eyes sparkled, and Cora could almost see the wheels turning in her mind with other ideas. "It would've been nice to have visitors."

Cora frowned when she realized Kitty had already been a widow back then, and how wonderful it would have been to give her some distraction from the loneliness. She swallowed around the lump in her throat. "I much prefer knowing you now."

Kitty nodded.

"I'm going to pretend you just walked in so I can greet you properly." Cora stood up, opened her arms wide and shouted cheerily, "Merry Christmas!"

"Merry Christmas, sweetheart."

"Some elves left some presents for you. Would you like to open them now or wait until after you've had breakfast?"

Kitty's eyes widened. "For me? Oh, my! Presents are the same as sweets, I have no self-control and must indulge in them immediately!"

As the two of them laughed and smiled over the gifts, Cora felt herself getting choked up over the shower of love. Christmas at the lodge. Something she had always wanted to experience again and now she was back.

# Twenty-Four

T he rest of the winter with Kitty living at the lodge flew by. Kitty blended in as though she'd always been there. Widgy continued renovating the upstairs, and life went on as usual, with Kitty right in the middle of it. Cora found she actually got more work done with Kitty at the lodge rather than across the road. She moved the rocking chair to whatever room she was working in and had Kitty sit and keep her company when one of the other women was visiting. Which was often.

Kitty thrived with all the attention. She was gaining weight *and* getting her spunk back.

After months of sitting inside, Kitty finally got permission from her doctor to do small tasks as she worked on regaining her strength. Kitty translated that to mean she could return to her beloved cemetery.

"I have to see my stones. The snow has melted enough, and I must see how they've weathered the winter."

Cora helped her slip on her coat, then grabbed her own. "I'll come with you."

The snow was melting under the March sunshine, and the ground was slushy. Cora marveled at the pace Kitty was able to walk as they crossed over to her property. "Slow down. Don't tire yourself. You need the energy to walk back."

"I've been cooped up too long." Kitty inhaled the outside fragrance. "Smell the air! Everything is so fresh and clean. What a glorious day."

Cora held on to her friend's arm to make sure she didn't slip. She frowned when Kitty began breathing a bit hard. The rasping in her lungs still wasn't completely gone.

They reached the front yard of the cemetery.

"Oh my . . ." She put her hand over her heart. Every marker had been wiped clean of snow and debris. The statues were uncovered from their winter wrappings.

Cora slid her arm around Kitty's frail shoulders. "I've been coming over and taking care of them for you. I kept the snow and ice from building up and didn't take the coverings off until last week so they would stay protected and not get dirty. In case anyone ever did visit, I shoveled little pathways for them to walk."

Tears spilled from Kitty's eyes.

Cora gasped. "Have I upset you? I'm so sorry. Should I not have worked on them?"

Kitty shook her head. "I'm not upset. To the contrary. I've never been more touched. By caring for the markers, you didn't allow my family or my life to be forgotten." More tears poured down her cheeks. "Thank you. Thank you from the bottom of my heart."

"I enjoyed doing it. After learning all their stories, I feel as if I know them. I made sure to introduce myself too."

Kitty's eyebrows flew up. "You talked to them?"

"Of course."

"Goodness! I have had an influence on you." She laughed.

"More than you'll ever know."

Kitty leaned closer against Cora.

"I think you'll find all of them in good shape. I didn't notice any damage."

"They look perfect."

"I do have questions about a couple of these." Cora pointed to a grouping of various religious statues crowded together. "Were these supposed to be clustered so closely?"

"Yes—they're all for one person. Beverly was the garage sale addict. If there was a deal to be found, she'd find it. She bought those statues at a going-out-of-business sale. She couldn't decide which was her favorite, so she took them all home. She figured she was covered in terms of faith by putting a cross, a statue of Mary, an angel, and a Jewish star above her. 'Better safe than sorry,' she always said."

Cora shook her head.

"She even bought her coffin on clearance," Kitty went on. "It was the floor model that had been sitting out for years, so she got it for eighty percent off. After being open so long, it was pretty dusty. Since it couldn't be dry-cleaned, she had the carpet people steam-clean it. She swore it was like new when they were done. She paid extra for the stain protector and then finished it off by putting a couple car air fresheners in it."

"Oh, come on," Cora said.

Kitty grinned. "She chose pine scent because it reminded her of the North Woods. However, there was one problem with the coffin. It was a foot shorter than Beverly."

Cora winced. "I don't think I want to know how she fit in."

"She left instructions in her will to be laid on her side with her knees bent. She said she always slept best in that position anyway."

Cora couldn't hold in her laugh. "I wasn't expecting that."

Kitty's expression was all wide-eyed innocence. "It's true. She wasn't about to let her height get in the way of a bargain."

"I wouldn't want that to be the story people remembered about me."

"Oh, it's only a peek into the character of the person. We are so much more, but I think it's wonderful when a funny quirk or characteristic makes us different and memorable."

Cora pointed to another stone. "What about this one? Why does it say 'I WON' in capital letters?"

Kitty craned her neck to see where Cora pointed. "That's Dotty. She had those words engraved above her name because she was an avid quilter. She had a sign in her home that read 'Whoever Dies with the Most Fabric Wins.' She always said she was the winner and declared herself that. I put some of her favorite patterns along the sides and back of her marker."

"I see that." Cora fingered the patterns. "It looks like a quilt is surrounding her. You did an excellent job. Except . . . what are those two lines?" She pointed.

"Those are knitting needles. I figured if I put sewing needles there, people would think they were scratches."

"That makes sense."

"Dotty made quilts for anyone getting married, baptized, or confirmed, and anyone having a baby. They're considered heirlooms and have already been passed on to second and third generations. I have the privilege of owning three. I treasure them. There is such craftsmanship and stories within every square."

"I'd love to see them sometime."

"You will." Kitty winked at her. "Dotty requested to be buried with her two most favorite shawls and then covered with one quilt she had made from all the fabrics she had ever used. Each square was two inches in diameter on the finished quilt. She resembled a mummy by the time they fit the whole thing in the coffin."

"These stories," Cora said, shaking her head. "No one would ever believe you."

"Would it make them less real to you if some people didn't believe them?"

Cora smiled. "Not at all."

Kitty nodded. "Each person is a dear soul deserving to be remembered."

"Why don't you write these stories down?"

Kitty shrugged. "I didn't think others would be interested in hearing about folks who are gone. It seems like people are focused so much on the future that they barely have time for the present. The past is old news."

"I would be interested."

Kitty's smile was tender. "You've been far too patient in humoring an old lady for reasons I'll never know." She gave Cora's arm a little squeeze. "Let's go see my house."

Cora held her back. There was no way she could let Kitty see the devastation of her empty kitchen, gutted bathroom, and basement. "Don't worry. Everything's being taken care of. Let's head back before you wear yourself out. Would you like a cup of broth?"

The corners of Kitty's mouth turned up. "Isn't it funny how life turns around? It seems like just yesterday I asked you that same question."

Cora tucked Kitty's hand into the crook of her arm as they walked arm in arm back to the lodge. "Maybe it doesn't turn around but keeps going in a circle. You're receiving back what you gave."

"Perhaps you're right, Cora. Perhaps you're right."

Cora slipped out early to go to the mission one morning. She had been craving fresh bread smeared with jam for breakfast. The warmer temperatures in April still hadn't completely melted the ice on the lake, so she took her Jeep.

Sam had convinced her to hike across the lake with him, back when the ice had been thick enough. It was exhilarating to stand at the frozen shore of the mission, loaded down with backpacks as if they were travelers from afar, then walking into the modest building and filling their bags to capacity with blessed bread as the reward for their adventure.

This time, as she opened the door to the mission, she saw the bread on the table, but there wasn't a nun present for a blessing. The emptiness gave the room a strange feeling. Going over to the tiny altar and worn kneeling bench where the nun usually prayed, Cora stared up at the cross. Emotion rose in her chest. Layers of weariness and worry fell away while something that could no longer be suppressed emerged. She couldn't define it, but something stirred deep within.

Cora knelt down, closed her eyes, and prayed for Kitty and the dilemma about her home. She thanked God for meeting people who were not only changing her life but also her outlook on it. And she prayed for her faith, as Joseph had promised he was doing as well.

A peace washed over her like a warm rain.

After a few minutes, she stood and turned around to see Ben at the entrance. She'd been so absorbed in her prayer that she hadn't heard the door open. It had been almost four months since she'd seen him. She had managed to not even run into him in town. So much had happened since their brief encounter in the hospital hallway. She pushed away thoughts of the night in the gazebo and his embrace for the sake of her own self-preservation. She needed to see him as a friend, as her dentist. Taking a shaky breath, she summoned all her inner strength.

He took a few steps into the room. "I'm sorry. I didn't mean to disturb you." He gestured toward the bread on the table. "I haven't come here all winter and was missing fresh bread."

"You didn't disturb me." She managed to speak without her voice shaking. "When I saw the place was empty, I . . ."

Ben rescued her. "It's a good place to think and pray."

She nodded.

"You missed your cleaning appointment. I was hoping to see you."

She had canceled, not ready to face him. "I've been busy."

"How's Kitty?"

"She's getting stronger."

"It was kind of you to take her in." His tone was gentle and sincere.

She cocked her head. "How did you know about that?"

He gave a small shrug. "Nothing stays a secret in this town." Although he tried to say it with humor, it fell flat with the sadness in his eyes.

With heartache washing over her, she could barely get a corner of her mouth to turn up. "I'm learning that."

Silence.

Cora found the unspoken words between them almost too painful to stand and take.

They stared at each other, and just as she was going to leave, he drew a breath. "I've wanted to talk to you ever since that morning on the sidewalk. I wanted to explain," he blurted out.

"You don't have to." *Time to get out of here.* She headed across the room to the door.

"Yes, I do. I need to." He stepped to the side and blocked the doorway. "It's important you don't get the wrong idea. I'm not involved with that woman and haven't seen her since that day. We dated a couple years ago. I ran into her after I walked you to your car at the dance, and we spoke for a few minutes before I went home." He was talking rapid-fire, as if he couldn't get the words out fast enough. "She was hoping to get together again, but I'm not interested." He looked at her with sincerity. "She interrupted something between us. I was going to come over to the lodge and explain, and then I heard you were taking care of Kitty, and I didn't want to make your life any more complicated. But I haven't stopped thinking about that night in the gazebo."

"Like I said, you don't have to explain. It's fine. I haven't given it much thought." *Liar.*

"I see." His brown eyes lowered to the floor.

Cora's stomach clenched. She couldn't stand to see him hurting, no matter her own feelings. "What I mean is, I haven't forgotten about you." She hesitated and then said what was on the tip of her tongue. "I could never forget you," she confessed. "But between working for Mr. Wells, caring for Kitty, and restoring the lodge, life has been crazy. I'm exhausted."

Concern shadowed his face. "If I can help in any way, please let me."

Cora's heart raced as she felt all the emotions she had choked down resurface. The magnetic pull to him was almost painful. She gave him a quick nod, then backtracked to the table and selected her bread, and left her donation in the basket. When she crossed back to the door, he stepped aside to let her exit. As she left, she turned back. "It was nice seeing you, Ben." The words came out breathless and fast.

Before he could respond, she hurried out. As she walked to the Jeep, she didn't have to look back to know he was watching her.

Work on Kitty's house was arduous. Everyone felt impatient for the soggy weather to end so they could start the larger renovations. In the meantime, Widgy and Sam were doing what they could. Mimi had given the money she promised to get things started.

Arielle was finishing her final canvas in the sizable collection she had created. Though her pieces were going to be shipped to New York, she insisted on first having a showing for Moonberry Lake at the end of the month.

After Sofia had nudged Kitty about the truth of her finances and the dire situation she was in, with Kitty's permission, Sofia and Mimi went to work immediately trying to find a solution.

Cora was making sandwiches for Widgy and Kitty when she heard a car pull up to the lodge. A minute later, Mimi and Sofia came bursting in the back door.

"We've got it!" Mimi announced, waving a fistful of papers in the air and holding her head almost as high in triumph.

Sofia clasped her hands together. "You're not going to believe what I discovered about Kitty's house!"

"First tell her the news, before the big announcement," Mimi demanded, her voice almost shrill. All her jewelry jingled as she moved, and her smile was wide enough to shine gold from her back molars

Sofia took a big breath and straightened her shoulders on her already-erect posture. "After looking over all Kitty's finances, I couldn't figure out why there was such a huge discrepancy between when Peter was living versus when he was gone. There was something other than her social security and his retirement I was missing. After going through more papers, we discovered Kitty has not been receiving compensation for maintaining the cemetery! The property was in Peter's name, and when he died, the payment for managing a county cemetery stopped. Kitty should have continued to receive a monthly stipend for being the caretaker of public property."

That was what was causing all this excitement? Surely it couldn't be much money. "How much is she owed?" Cora asked.

Mimi and Sofia exchanged looks before Sofia spoke. "This is the back payment for her services."

Sofia pointed to a figure at the bottom of the page.

Cora put her hands over her mouth, not sure if she was about to scream or cry. "That's a lot of zeros!"

"That's not all." Sofia grabbed her hand. "As I was looking over the deed to the house, the name of the previous owner seemed so familiar that I couldn't get it out of my head. It kept me up one night until I finally got out of bed and started looking through my own library. Around four in the morning, I stumbled across it. The name matched the author of a book I had. After a little more digging, I discovered the original owner was a poet who used the house as a vacation getaway before it became a cemetery. He even wrote about the house in a couple of his books. Kitty's house could be considered a historical landmark!"

Cora's mouth dropped open.

Mimi did a little jig that made her stiff red curls bounce and her tiger pendant jump up and down on her chest. "That means the county *has* to give her money to maintain the structure and original look of the house to keep it historically accurate. She'll receive an additional stipend for the upkeep of the property. I should know—I'm on the town arts council!"

They all screamed and hugged each other.

Kitty entered the room, her brows knitted. "What's all the commotion?"

"You're going to have to sit down for this." Sofia pulled out a chair from the table.

After hearing everything explained, Kitty was still as a statue. They all sat around the kitchen table letting the information sink in.

Kitty finally looked up at them. "First, I want to pay everyone back. I know there are things going on over there you haven't told me about, and I want to make sure nobody but me pays for it." Her expression said she meant business and would brook no argument. "Then I want to clear the hospital bill, get the house fixed, and pay any other debts I owe."

Cora reached over and placed her hand on top of Kitty's. "That won't be a problem."

Widgy walked in at that moment and, after hearing the news about Kitty's reimbursement, promised to go full throttle on getting the house in the best shape it had ever been. "It's going to be as strong as when it was built!" She gave Kitty a broad grin. "Now that we've got cash behind the whole kit and caboodle, it shouldn't take as long before you can move back into your home. I'll give the team I've assembled the go-ahead. There's nothing like money to light a fire under people."

Kitty looked at Cora with a teary smile. She was going to be able to go home.

# Twenty-Five

Springtime carried with it a renewed energy. Everything hibernating in a winter slumber came back to life. The water hitting the lakeshore sang a song of rebirth.

Cora kept busy trying not to think of Ben. She couldn't bring herself to call him. She had left so many things unsaid at the mission about her true feelings, so she knew he would be uncomfortable showing up at the lodge.

Arielle had graciously offered her artistic talent in making the downstairs bedrooms something special. The finished result was striking. Thanks to the array of paint colors, every room had its own dramatic look. Arielle got carried away stenciling borders and was soon painting all over the walls. Each one became a work of art.

Before they knew it, the day had finally come for Arielle's art show. All the ladies were going to support her. Cora frowned at her reflection in the mirror. She didn't look right. An old dress that used to fit every curve now hung like a rag. With all her hard work, she'd lost weight. Even worse, she had dark circles under her eyes from lack of sleep. As it turned out, it was far easier to keep Ben from entering her thoughts during the day than at night. She tossed and turned every night thinking of him.

Her hair had grown long these past months, and she didn't know what to do with it. She ended up putting it into a messy bun.

"You clean up pretty good."

She turned to find Widgy standing in the doorway of her room. "The dress is quite a change from the overalls. You're not half-bad-lookin' once you wash the paint off and change clothes."

Cora gave a half smile. "Thanks, Widge."

"But you do look a little green around the gills. Are ya feelin' okay?"

Cora shrugged. "I'm tired. I haven't been able to sleep." She turned back to study the dark circles under her eyes more closely.

"Or eat, from the way that dress fits you." Widgy shook her head. "You need to stop workin' long enough to chow down and get some meat on those bones and sun on that pale skin."

"Between caring for Kitty and working on this broken-down old building—"

"It's not that broken down anymore," Widgy interrupted. "Look what you've done in nearly ten months' time."

She turned back to her friend. "You're the one to thank for that. I simply cleaned the corners and added the frills." Cora crossed the room to give her burly friend a hug. "I don't know what I would've done without you." She kept her arms wrapped around her for a good minute.

Widgy stood like a rock, not hugging her back but not pushing her away either. "It was nothin'." She finally gave Cora a hard thump on the back and then rearranged her baseball cap.

"Are you going to Arielle's art show?"

Widgy nodded. "Yeah, I'm gonna get cleaned up first. I stopped by to snake a toilet."

"I haven't noticed any clogged toilets."

"It's the one at the far end of the hall up here."

"But that one's never used."

"I've been using it as my own *personal* one. I plugged it up and didn't have my snake in the truck."

Cora held up her hand. "Enough said."

"Those burritos down at the gas station are killers."

"Again, no need for details. I'll see you at the art show."

Widgy nodded and left.

"Wait!" Cora went to the doorway. "I've never seen you in anything but overalls. What are you wearing to the show?"

Widgy shrugged. "My Sunday trousers, of course."

*Of course.*

The town hall was packed. Squeezing through the crowd, Cora saw a stunning display of Arielle's paintings with Arielle standing in the center of it all.

The exhibit was extraordinary. Everybody was amazed by her talent, and rightfully so. Arielle herself was breathtaking. Her typically unruly hair lay like spun gold with small sparkling stones woven within it. She looked as ethereal as her artwork. She always stood out from the crowd, but tonight it was as if every light in the room pointed toward her.

When Arielle spotted Cora, she came over and wrapped her in a tight hug. "Thank you for coming."

"You look gorgeous!"

Arielle's smile dazzled. "Thanks. It's such fun to show my work before it's shipped off."

"It's captivating, as are you. This is your day, and you deserve every accolade. Enjoy it."

Arielle's eyes shone. "It all came about because of you. You were my inspiration, so I think you can take some of the credit."

"I'll take none. These could have come from your soul only."

Arielle's expression went from pride to concern. "Hey, are you okay? You look a little pale."

*Do I really look that bad?* Cora started to reply, but someone who wanted to talk to Arielle came up behind them. Cora waved goodbye and made her way through the crowd.

Everyone was mingling and happy. Cora made her way into another room that held a photography exhibit by a different artist.

She saw Sofia walking toward her. Sofia noticed her and smiled, but then worry etched her face.

"Are you okay? You don't look well."

This was getting ridiculous. "Everyone keeps saying that. I'm fine." Cora looked around the room. "Isn't this entire exhibit fantastic?"

"It's awe-inspiring! Have you seen the pictures by this debut photographer?"

Cora shook her head. "No, not yet. I'm looking for Kitty. I want to make sure she's all right."

"I'm sure she's in a corner talking to someone, but I'll help you search. In the meantime, take a quick peek at these photos." She pointed. "The one in the center is my favorite. The artist says it was taken here in town. I was thinking of buying it, but it's already sold."

"I'll take a look and catch up with you later." Cora squeezed her way through the crowd to the front of the display.

She gasped.

*Silhouettes of Love* was a black-and-white photo of two dark figures under a gazebo at night.

There was no doubt.

It was her and Ben.

The light from the moon illuminated the falling snowflakes. The faces of the figures couldn't be seen, only their embrace.

All the emotions from that evening came rushing back. She turned to leave and spotted Ben across the room. He was staring at her and began to make his way toward her through the crowd. His expression was serious. Desperate even. He must have seen the photograph.

She didn't want to talk to him, not in front of everyone.

The room was too hot, and there wasn't enough air to breathe. She felt dizzy and had to get out. Her stomach churned and sweat broke out on her forehead.

*I need air.*

Fighting her way through the crowd, she kept her eyes on the floor. The world felt like it was tilting. Once she broke free of the throng, she headed for the exit.

At last she was outside, holding on to the railing for support as she descended the stairs. She walked to the side of the building where she could avoid being noticed. Light-headed, she leaned against the wall and closed her eyes.

She tried to will the spinning to stop.

Her face tingled.

A pair of strong hands grasped her shoulders. Opening her eyes, she saw Sam.

"Cora, what's wrong?"

His words sounded far away. She couldn't get through the tingling and light-headedness to answer. The pressure of his hands increased as she leaned into them, and then . . .

Cora opened her eyes. Sam was kneeling over her. She was on the ground.

"You're fine." Sam's voice was low, soothing. "You fainted. Take some deep breaths."

She followed his instructions and concentrated on the fresh air filling her lungs and the solid ground beneath her. Sam brushed the hair away from her forehead, looking down at her with those worried eyes.

An old memory flashed into her mind of her grandfather sweeping the hair from her face when she was a little girl.

After a minute, she could think well enough to talk. "What are you doing here?"

"I saw you leave the building. You looked terrible."

Cora managed a nod. "Yeah, that seems to be the general consensus." She closed her eyes. "I needed some air. It was too hot in there, and I didn't eat much today. I'm going to go back to the lodge."

Sam slid an arm around her shoulders and helped her sit up. At that moment Ben came and knelt by her.

"What's wrong? Are you sick?" he asked, reaching out and touching her shoulder.

Cora nodded, still feeling woozy.

"She fainted, and I'm going to bring her home," Sam said.

"I can take her," Ben offered.

"No. It's fine," Cora said. She couldn't handle being alone with him now.

Kitty and Widgy hurried toward her. Kitty looked at Sam. "How is she?"

"*She* is fine." Cora softened her response with a smile.

Sam talked over her. "She passed out. I caught her as she was going down. She needs to get home."

"You were peaked when we left the lodge. You need some broth," declared Kitty.

"You've been so busy takin' care of everybody else that you've let yourself become weak as a baby bird." Widgy shook her head. "Come on, I'll take you home."

Cora saw that more surrounding eyes were staring at her, and a crowd was beginning to form. "I'm fine. I just got overheated. I'm feeling better and can drive myself."

"Absolutely not! We don't need you passin' out at the wheel!" Widgy was nearly yelling. "I've got my pickup 'round the corner. You can sit on top of my toolbox."

Sam held up a hand. "I'll give her a ride. I was leaving anyway."

Cora looked at Kitty. "What about you?"

Kitty waved her concern away. "Don't worry about me, honey. I'll find a ride. I would like to stay a bit longer. I'm having a wonderful time."

Sam turned to Kitty. "I'll come back to get you."

"Don't worry, Sam. I'll take her home whenever she's ready," Ben said.

Widgy gave Cora a hard pat on the shoulder, which made Cora wince. "I'll get someone to drive your car back too."

"Okay. Just let me say goodbye to Arielle."

"I'll say it for you. Go lie down." Kitty's tone was not to be argued with.

Sam took Cora's arm and helped her stand. She swayed but managed to walk to the parking lot with his help. She glanced back and saw Ben watching her with concerned eyes. She allowed Sam to help her into the car and then into the lodge once they arrived home.

"Will you be okay here alone?" he asked her.

"I'm fine, Sam. I simply need to go to bed."

Sinking into bed never felt so wonderful. Slipping between the covers, she closed her eyes and fell asleep immediately.

She slept soundly all night and woke the next morning feeling a little better. Going downstairs, she didn't hear Widgy hammering and making her usual noise. Instead, the repairwoman had taken over the kitchen.

"Have a seat." Widgy waved the spoon she was using at the chair at the table. "I've almost got it ready."

Cora was almost afraid to ask. "Got *what* ready?"

"A hearty meal to put the spunk back into you."

Cora had seen this nurturing side of Widgy once before with Beast, but never with a human. She was sure few people besides her sons and late husbands ever saw it.

"Iron's what your body needs." Widgy scooped some food into a bowl and put it in front of Cora. The stew was loaded with meat, potatoes, and vegetables and was thick enough to remain in a clump.

Cora made a face. "I can't eat this for breakfast."

"This is what I made each of my husbands when they were sick."

Cora poked at the food with a fork. "Yeah, but they're all dead."

"Eat!" Widgy commanded, drill sergeant in her nursing skills. "No comments are welcome. This straightened up Beast's stomach after he got a bad case of ringworm."

"You have a real knack for presenting food in an appetizing way." She didn't miss that Widgy cracked a half smile. "There better not be any squirrel in this."

"There ain't, you big baby."

On the morning of the third day, Cora finally felt like her old self. All it had taken was sleeping for long periods and eating more of Widgy's magic stew.

Arielle came into Cora's room holding a coffee tumbler. "How are you feeling?" she asked.

"Much better. I think it was the flu."

"I think it's called complete exhaustion. You pushed yourself too hard."

Cora plucked at her blanket. "You work crazy hours when you're in the middle of a project. I'm younger than you. How do you get these bursts of energy?"

Arielle sat on the edge of the bed. "My bursts are short. I don't push myself continually like you do. And I don't work so hard that I forget about eating and taking care of myself. *And* I always have this." She held up the tumbler. "This will give you some energy."

"Thanks, but I don't drink coffee."

"Neither do I. Try it." Arielle gave her the mug.

"What's in here? Tea?"

"Just try it. It's happiness in a cup."

"Happiness?" Cora took a taste. "It's chocolatey and something else. What is it?"

"Matcha hot chocolate."

Cora lifted the lid of the tumbler. "It's green."

"And it's good for you," Arielle said, sitting up proudly. "Chocolate feeds the soul, and I believe in feeding my soul daily. And the matcha is an amazing healing and energizing superfood."

Cora took another sip. "You're one of a kind."

"I like to think so," Arielle agreed with a gleam in her eyes.

Cora looked at the bouquet of flowers Arielle had brought in and put on the dresser. The arrangement was gorgeous. It was a collection of all her favorite flowers with sprigs of greens, eucalyptus, and tiny berries. She loved the eucalyptus and berries as much

HOLLY VARNI

as the flowers. It was exactly the kind of arrangement she would pick for herself. "You didn't have to get me flowers."

"I didn't. They were on the front steps when I came over. It appears you have a secret admirer." She raised an eyebrow. "Any idea who that might be?"

Cora slumped back onto her pillows and moaned as she covered her face with one arm. "He's persistent."

Arielle shook her head. "I don't understand why you're fighting it."

"It's complicated." She sighed.

"It doesn't have to be."

"You don't understand. I ran away from my own wedding in my last relationship. I used my mother's death as an excuse, but in reality, I would have found some other reason to bolt. The fact that I could have let that toxic relationship go as far as it did with Kyle makes me question my judge of character when it comes to romance."

"I'm glad that you bolted and that the wedding didn't happen. If you had gotten married, you wouldn't have come to live here, and I would've never met you."

Cora smiled at her friend. "So, what do I do?"

"How about letting what's trying to happen, simply *happen.*"

# *Twenty-Six*

Cora was back to working on the lodge by the following Tuesday. Although she had enjoyed taking a few days to rest and chip away at the pile of books on her end table, she knew she needed to get back on her feet when she couldn't even look at Widgy's clumpy stew anymore. She was busy painting one of the bathrooms when she heard Kitty call for her. "I'm in here!"

Kitty peeked in.

"What's up? Are you okay?"

"Yes, but I was wondering if you would do me a tremendous favor."

"Anything and always."

Kitty smiled. "I have a friend who I've not been able to check up on, and I wanted to bring him this pie, but I don't have the strength to do it myself. Would you deliver it for me?"

"Sure. Where does your friend live?"

"Just down the road."

Cora put down her brush. "How about if I drive you there?"

Kitty shook her head. "No, I don't feel up to it. I'd like to rest."

"Okay. Let me finish up this corner, and then I'll go."

"Thank you." Kitty turned to leave, then angled back toward Cora. "Why don't you wear that pretty sundress you have? That would be nice on a day like today."

Cora's brow furrowed. "You want me to change clothes for your friend?"

"I like seeing it on you, and it'll give a better presentation to my pie if you look nice."

It was an odd request, but it was so rare Kitty asked Cora to do anything. "Your pie doesn't need any better presentation, but I'll be glad to do it."

A half hour later, with the pie wrapped in a blue gingham dish towel, Cora followed Kitty's directions, pleased to see her destination was a mere half-mile drive down the road. It was the opposite direction she typically took when going for walks. This house was along a road with many other smaller cabins and was on the way into town.

The address was clearly marked on the mailbox. The homes on this end of the road had cleared the trees to make wide driveways. The lawns were cut short, and Cora could see the lake from the road.

She parked, gathered up the pie, and went to knock on the door. No answer. She walked around to the lakefront to see if anyone was there. Sure enough, a man in a baseball hat was sitting in a lawn chair. Cora started walking toward him. "Hello? Excuse me, I'm . . ."

The man turned around.

She stopped.

*Ben.*

"Cora? What are you doing here?" He stood, and she took in his appearance. The stubble on his face suggested he hadn't shaved for a couple days, and he wore shorts and a T-shirt.

"Kitty wanted me to deliver this pie to her friend who lives here. What are *you* doing here?"

"I live here."

"What? She didn't tell me it was you." Cora shook her head. *Kitty.* "Anyway, here." She handed him the pie. "Kitty baked it fresh this morning."

"Er . . . thanks." He seemed as flustered as she. "Would you stay for a minute and have a slice with me? There's no way I can eat this all by myself."

She hesitated.

"One piece?" he asked. "Please? You can't say no to Kitty's pie."

Cora gave a reluctant nod.

"I'll go get a couple plates and forks, and we can eat out here."

While he was inside, she looked around. It was a small yard but had a pretty view of the lake. She went to the dock to look at his boat, which was up on a lift. It was a lot nicer than her old fishing boat.

"I'd love to take you for a ride sometime," he called out, dishes in hand.

She walked back toward him.

He handed her a slice of pie and a fork.

"Thank you." She sat in the lawn chair next to his.

"Kitty's apple pie is famous."

Cora smiled. "It's a terrible weakness of mine. There's always one cooling on the stove at the lodge. It's become one of the major food groups for me. Plus, it doesn't have nuts in it, so I can eat it without worrying about having to make another trip to your office."

"That's my loss."

He held her gaze for a second too long. The butterflies were back in her stomach. She gulped.

"You're looking better," he went on.

"I didn't know I looked bad."

He laughed. "You don't ever give a guy a break, do you?"

She blushed. "Sorry. Sarcasm is a family trait. It comes out when I'm nervous."

"So I make you nervous?"

"So I look bad?"

He chuckled. "I was really worried about you at the art show. You scared everyone when you fainted."

"I'm feeling better. I got caught up on sleep and have eaten lots of pie. It has better healing powers than chicken soup."

"It seems to have worked. You look lovely."

"Thank you." *Bless Kitty for telling me to wear the sundress.* "I also received some beautiful flowers."

"Flowers helped your recovery?" His eyes sparkled with amusement.

She nodded. "Immensely. They brightened both my room *and* my disposition. However, there was no note, so I couldn't thank the sender."

"Hmm. No note. That's mysterious."

"Yes, it is." She peered at him.

"Maybe you have a secret admirer."

A movement caught Cora's eyes. The wandering cat who had come back to the lodge repeatedly came up and started rubbing against her legs and purring.

"Patchwork," Cora cooed as she set down her plate and lifted the cat into her arms. "Where did you come from, sweetheart?" She stroked its back.

Ben swallowed his bite of pie. "You know my cat?"

"*Your* cat? I didn't know she belonged to anyone. I assumed she was a stray. I've been feeding her off and on for months—whenever she visits me at the lodge."

He shook his head. "That explains why she's gotten so fat."

The cat had settled into her lap and expressed contentment by purring loudly.

Cora chuckled. "I'm sorry. I shouldn't have assumed she was a stray, and I should've listened to Widgy about not encouraging her to keep coming back. But don't ever tell her that."

Ben grinned. "It's obvious she adores you. I've never seen her act this way around anyone. I don't think it was the food drawing her back."

"What's her name?"

"I call her Trouble because that's what she usually gets into."

"Oh, I can't imagine that." Cora lifted the cat to give her a kiss on the head. "You're no trouble, are you?" She snuggled the furry bundle, but seconds later, the cat jumped down and began licking the pie. "It looks like I spoke too soon." Cora laughed.

"I'm sorry. Let me get you another piece."

"I'm fine—the pie was for you anyway. Please sit. There's more at the lodge."

They sat in comfortable silence. In fact, Cora couldn't believe just how lovely it was to sit and watch the lake with him. Being with Ben felt nothing like being with Kyle.

"How's Kitty?" he ventured.

Cora felt relieved to talk about a subject she loved. "She's happy and getting stronger with each day. She seems pretty much like the old Kitty to me."

"That's great. I've been meaning to visit her for some time, but I didn't know when she would be moving back to her house."

"Pretty soon, I think. The restoration is nearly complete. But that shouldn't stop you from visiting. Feel free to stop by the lodge anytime."

"I'll do that. How's your remodel coming?"

She felt a pride bloom inside her. "It's turning out better than I could've ever hoped."

"Then I definitely have to come by and see what you've done. That's what neighbors do."

"That's what neighbors do," she agreed, but even as she repeated the words, her heartbeat increased. "I better get back." She stood.

Ben set his plate aside and stood with her. "Thank you for the pie and the visit."

"You're welcome. I enjoyed myself." She walked away with a spring in her step.

"I'll have to somehow return the favor," he called after her.

She turned and winked. "The flowers make us even."

Back at the lodge, Cora went directly to Kitty's room. "Your *friend* liked the pie."

Kitty didn't look up from the blanket she was knitting. "That's nice."

"You forgot to mention your friend was Ben Walker."

Kitty feigned surprise, making a little circle with her mouth. "Did I?"

"Yes, you did. There wasn't any reason for that, was there?"

"No, no. I'm simply a forgetful old lady. It must've slipped my mind."

Cora crossed her arms over her chest and lowered her gaze. "Of course, because I can't imagine you'd have a hidden agenda in sending me over there alone."

"No, no. Not me."

"And the sundress suggestion?"

Kitty nodded too quickly. "It was for the pie. It made the *pie* look better."

"Uh-huh."

Kitty continued to appear absorbed with her knitting.

"Well, your friend Ben asked about you and may come over here to see how you're doing." Cora turned to leave but caught Kitty's whisper as she did so.

"Well, then, the pie worked."

The area around the gravesites had been blocked off with yellow "Do Not Cross" tape. The work on the exterior of Kitty's house was done and in beautiful shape. Now they were waiting for the final touches on the inside. To beautify the surroundings even more, Cora had agreed to "gussy up," as Kitty called it, the markers. But planting flowers all morning was more work than Cora had anticipated.

She straightened her aching back and took a long stretch. "I need a break," she moaned and fell backward onto the grass. "I don't know how you do this for so many hours."

"Practice." Kitty sat nearby, resting comfortably on a blanket.

"I'm like a broken-in horse. At this point, you either let me do what has become instinct or lead me to the glue factory."

"You're a long way off from the glue factory." Cora laughed. "You have more endurance and strength than anyone I've ever met."

"Apparently not, because you only let me plant one flat of marigolds!" Kitty frowned. "I never dreamed I would see the day someone else would plant flowers in my yard while I sat back and watched. You know how much I love to run my fingers through the soil."

"Yes, I know, but I don't want you to overdo it."

"It's not work. It's a privilege." Her look grew tender. "I've had the honor of spending most of my life on my knees, forced to confront what others run from. I hope, many years down the road, when someone stumbles across this cemetery and notices the drawings on the markers, they try to imagine the spirit of each of these people. This has been my life's passion. It's brought me deep joy."

Cora couldn't resist the question weighing heavy on her heart. "What if you don't know what your life's passion is?"

"It's there inside you. It may not be something big that draws a lot of attention, but something that's small and privately yours. It's what makes your heart sing and makes you feel alive. When you're doing it, time ceases to exist because you're so consumed by the joy of it."

Cora gaped at her, blinking. "How on earth am I supposed to find *that*?"

Kitty chuckled. "You're making it too complicated. My advice is to simply look for what makes you happy." They sat in comfortable silence for a while. When Cora looked back at Kitty, she saw her friend was watching the workers going in and out of the cottage.

"What are you thinking?" she asked.

"I'm thinking about my favorite Bible verse," Kitty answered, not taking her eyes off of the bustling people. "Psalm 91:11. 'For he will command his angels concerning you to guard you in all your ways." I've loved that verse since I was a child because it brought me comfort in so many situations. The idea that there's a group of angels specifically assigned to me has always made me feel special. I've never questioned that there are angels in the spiritual realm, but now I see that they walk around earth as well." Kitty looked at Cora. "Many of the angels who guard me are right here. All of you are my precious angels." Her voice caught.

Cora went over and wrapped her arm gently around the elderly woman. "It would be a privilege to be considered one of your angels, but I'm not sure how that works since I consider you one of mine."

Kitty's eyes glistened. "That's precisely how it's intended to work."

When the reconstruction of Kitty's home was finally complete, Cora was stunned at the transformation from old and decrepit to new and sturdy. Widgy's work and leadership were impressive. Keeping the image and integrity the town arts council required, she had made the house look clean, solid, and stable, even as it was reminiscent of a bygone era. The new roof and windows were the only improvements that looked current. Everything else kept its period charm.

Kitty's new bed had been moved from the lodge. The walls had been painted, new linoleum in the same checkered pattern had been put in the kitchen, the cupboards had been refinished, and the worn carpeting had been replaced.

All the ladies added homecoming gifts. Mimi had flowers and a fruit basket delivered. Sofia had filled the refrigerator with prepared meals. Arielle had replaced all the plants and put them back in the same locations as the ones that had died. She also left a fresh loaf of bread on the table and two more in the freezer. Cora had packed one cupboard with nothing but marshmallow clouds and left a box of chocolates by Kitty's bed.

They crowded around as Kitty opened the screen door, which

no longer squealed when it opened, and watched as she stood with her mouth open and her eyes wide, gazing at her beautiful kitchen.

"Oh my." Kitty reached out and touched one of the plants that adorned the redone space. "My old kitchen has new life!"

Insisting on keeping the original sink and appliances, Kitty had wanted only the walls and cupboards "spiffed up," as she said. She went around exploring each surface, running her hand over the new counters, fussing over the beauty of it all, until she had thoroughly embarrassed Widgy.

"And don't forget to check all your cupboards and your freezer too," Cora spoke up. "We've left you a few treats to help sweeten your homecoming."

Kitty's eyes lit up at the abundance of goodies. She smiled, lovingly touched the plants Arielle had stocked, and gushed over the bathroom remodel. Kitty's face shone with immense gratitude. Making her way down the line of friends, she hugged each one. "Thank you for giving me back my home and making it more lovely than I could ever imagine."

Her home—her haven—had been restored.

# Twenty-Seven

Cora had a sense of uneasiness one morning in early June. Something she couldn't pinpoint felt different even though everything appeared normal. She sat outside, listening and watching. The nagging feeling didn't subside.

She walked to the middle of the dock and stood to face the lodge, searching for something that would give her a clue or reassurance. She focused on what was in front of her.

An eerie calm had descended on the lake. The leaves were not rustling. She didn't hear a single bird. The water looked like glass. It was so . . . still. The air felt strange.

Sam had mentioned once that if she watched animals closely enough, they'd reveal warnings or communicate if life was out of balance. "Every animal has an innate sense of when danger approaches, and their behavior can alert us." He said humans had that same instinct, but few listened to or trusted that feeling.

"Sam!" she called out.

Sam came out of the shed. "Yeah?"

"Does anything seem *off* to you?"

Sam looked around, and Cora noticed his expression alter the moment realization dawned. "A storm's coming. Let me go turn on the radio. Will you please secure the boat with a second tie?"

Cora worked quickly as Sam went inside. It was one of those times she wished she had a television for the news and weather reports.

Going into the kitchen, she found Sam listening to the weather report on the ancient radio. She could kick herself for not updating that.

Sam's face had turned grave. "One has already touched down in the next county."

"One what?"

"Tornado."

Her stomach dropped and anxiety set in. As if on cue, the distant wail of the tornado siren sounded in the distance. Looking out the kitchen window, she saw that the quiet sky was turning an ominous gray. It took only a few minutes for the wind to begin howling and blowing violently, making the trees sway and the leaves swirl.

Cora raced outside to put away the lawn chairs.

Sam burst through the patio door with such force that the screen door stayed open. "We have to get to shelter now! The tornado has changed direction and is headed our way!"

"I don't understand. How can this be happening so fast?" she said, following Sam around the side of the house. He had already opened the doors to the storm cellar. Panic gripped her chest.

She stopped abruptly. "Wait! Where's Widgy?"

"She took off in her truck twenty minutes ago."

"What about Joseph?"

"He's out of town. Now, come on!" He waved her forward.

Cora looked at the end of the driveway toward Kitty's house. "Did you call Kitty?"

"She didn't pick up. She's a smart woman and has been through this before. I'm sure she's in her basement," Sam assured her, taking hold of her arm and pulling her forward. "Come on! Get in!"

They both went down the steps, descending into the darkness, and closed the doors behind them. Sam turned on a flashlight and gave her one to hold.

She scanned the dingy room with her beam of light. Wooden racks lined a wall. There were some crates and a bench to sit on. "I've never been down here."

Sam led the way farther into the musty room. "This was intended to be both a wine and storm cellar. Those crates are supposed to be full of emergency supplies for situations like this, but with nobody living here for so many years, I didn't keep up with it. I'm sorry."

"I wouldn't expect this room to take priority. When was the last time there was a tornado in Moonberry?"

"They're not common. The last one was a couple decades ago, but we've had strong windstorms that did major damage."

The air was stale and thick with dust. Cora stopped speaking and listened to the wild noises above.

Sam motioned to her. "Come sit."

Joining him on the bench, she sat close to him. The screams of the wind were piercing enough to indicate this was the real thing. She winced at the loud crashes and glass shattering above.

Cora jumped when a hard thump hit the door. Sam took her hand and patted it, his solid touch reassuring. She gripped his hand, praying for everyone's safety.

"I've never experienced an actual tornado."

Sam put his arm around her shoulders and pulled her closer. More glass shattered, followed by a thunderous crash that shook the ground.

"The worst is coming now. Hold on."

A deafening roar rolled above them as though a train were passing overhead. Sam put both arms around her, holding her tightly. The walls trembled, stirring up dirt and encircling them in a cloud of dust, making her cough. The air was thick and gritty.

Just as she was positive the ceiling was going to come down on them, the roars and trembling abruptly ceased.

As quickly and violently as the storm had come, it just . . . stopped. Everything went still. Cora didn't move or say a word. She had dropped her flashlight. It was lying a few feet away, shining a light on the murky air.

"It's passed." Sam's shoulders visibly lowered, and he released his grip on her.

Cora took a deep breath in relief. She regretted it immediately, because the polluted air set off a coughing fit. She wiped her cheek and noticed it was wet with tears she wasn't even aware she had shed.

"That was terrifying."

"Yeah," Sam said, his tone shaky.

Cora retrieved her flashlight. "What do we do now? When is it safe to go out?"

He tried opening the doors. "The doors won't open. There's something on top of them. Someone's bound to come looking for us."

After twenty minutes of sitting in the dark, they heard yelling from the outside. "Cora! Cora! Where are you?"

*Widgy.*

Cora yelled as loudly as her scratchy throat would allow. "Down here in the cellar!"

Sam joined in. "We're in the cellar!"

Widgy's voice came closer. "Cora!"

"Here! Down here!"

"There are branches blockin' the doors." Widgy's voice was right above them. "I'll have you out in a minute."

After a few minutes of rustling, the storm doors flew open.

"Are you okay?" Widgy looked them over and extended her hand to help them up the stairs.

Cora stepped outside, coughing again as she tried to clear her lungs. She spit out the terrible taste coating her mouth. When she was able to take a deep breath and straighten, the sight before her stopped her cold.

It was a world she didn't recognize.

Pine and oak trees littered the ground, along with wood and trash scattered everywhere, covering the yard like a blanket. Cora walked to the front of the building. So much was coming at her all at once. Everything felt surreal. A numbness set in as she stared at the mangled aftermath. She felt oddly calm and detached as she took it all in.

The lodge was destroyed.

All her work was gone.

Her life was in shambles.

Again.

Her breath caught at the sight of pieces of the porch strewn across the lawn, the majority of it floating in the water and littering the shoreline.

Widgy was the first to speak. "Looks like the porch was suctioned out, along with some of the bedrooms facing the lake. Most of the damage is to the west end with chunks of the roof missin.'"

The center of the lodge had been ripped out, leaving an enormous cavity.

"It's gone. Destroyed," Cora whispered, feeling as though she was going to collapse.

Sam spoke, his voice sure and strong. "It can be rebuilt."

Cora shook her head and put her face in her hands. "It's gone. It's been taken away from me—again."

At the sound of her name, Cora looked up and saw Kitty picking her way across the yard. Cora ran to her.

"Are you okay?"

The old woman nodded. "I'm fine. When I heard the siren, I headed for the basement."

Tears spilled down Cora's cheeks. "The lodge is ruined."

"*You* survived. That's what matters." Kitty took Cora's face in her hands. "Try not to focus on what you have lost but instead on what you still have, and that is a gathering of people who deeply care for you. We all love you and only care that you're safe." She stroked Cora's hair with a mother's touch.

"She's right, you know," Sam added.

Widgy stood next to her and gave a hard nod in silent agreement.

And that's when it hit Cora. She finally had the family she had desperately yearned for.

Eventually, the rest of the ladies came and joined in circling the property, surveying the damage. Everyone had their comments and opinions on what could be done to fix the lodge. As the group started to disband and everyone was going back to their own homes, Arielle sidled up next to Cora. "Come on, you can stay with me."

"That's a good idea," Sam said.

"She's welcome at my place too," added Widgy. "I just have to move a few stuffed animals out of the extra bedroom. It's where Clyde did most of his taxidermy."

"Or she could be my roomie now," Kitty piped in. "I've got my sewing room. It would be nice to repay the favor."

"Thank you," Cora said, "but I think I'll stay with Arielle." She knew with the chaos of Arielle's house, she would not be an inconvenience.

She locked arms with Arielle, and as they walked away, she kept looking back over her shoulder.

Widgy directed a stern look at Cora. "It's gonna be a couple days before anyone can come out here and take a look at the place. Until then, you can't go pokin' around inside. It's not safe."

Cora glanced at Sam, and he nodded his agreement.

"Are you going to go check on your place?" Cora asked him.

"Widgy was over there getting something from my shed when the tornado hit us. It skipped right over." He stepped to her other side and put a hand on her back. "It's going to be okay. There isn't anything here that can't be rebuilt."

Cora could only nod at his assurance, not sure if she truly believed it.

Arielle spoke up. "Anyone who's hungry can come over to my house. I made some Danish rye and German bauernbrot bread earlier."

Mimi let out a quiet groan.

Cora and the others couldn't help but smile. Some things in life never changed.

And that was a good thing.

# Twenty-Eight

Cora stared into the darkness of Arielle's guest room, unable to sleep. She'd expected to feel a heavy ache of sadness over the magnitude of her loss once again but instead felt strangely at peace.

Lying in a bed of mismatched sheets, a cozy blanket, and a quilt of wild colors and patterns, she felt comforted. The smell of incense that permeated the wallpaper and curtains gave the room a spicy, woodsy feel. The softness of the worn bedding wrapped her in a warm cocoon. Arielle had taken out a quilt that she had made—for a special birthday, of course—and insisted Cora sleep with it, believing it would bring solace.

With the faint glow of the sun's first light, Cora got out of bed, took off Arielle's pajamas, and changed back into her clothes from the previous day. Careful not to wake Arielle, she crept out of the house. She'd taken this walk along the road many times before, but it had never been this solemn.

There was no movement in the trees, and a hush had settled over the land as if everything were in mourning.

She slowed her steps as she approached the opening to her property. A mammoth tree had fallen in front of the entrance, blocking the driveway, as if trying to keep people from seeing what lay ahead.

Cora climbed over it and kept walking.

Thick debris blanketed the ground. Up close, the once formidable lodge, an unbeatable fortress in her childhood memory, looked as if it were folding in on itself to hide the ruin. Piles of wreckage poured out, sprawling in all directions.

*It's destroyed. What am I going to do?* She couldn't fathom the work and effort it would take to rebuild. It would be easier to start over somewhere else. That was what her mother would do and had done. When things got hard, they moved, believing a fresh start would wash the old slate clean.

It was too much to wrap her head around at this point. Making her way to the water's edge, she noticed her beloved dock was gone. Sections of it floated along the shore. The water seemed to be cleansing itself of the storm's rage, pushing pieces of wood off the lake's surface and onto the land. Taking off her shoes, she took two steps into the water and reached down to pick up one of the chunks. As she did, she noticed her reflection with clouds in the background.

She stared at her watery image. As gently as she could, she touched the surface without breaking through the mirror.

Pressing her hand deeper into the water, she embraced the feeling of the smooth, cool wetness. Her hair was a mess and her clothes wrinkled and dirty. Straightening up, she dropped the piece of wood and removed her outer layer, letting the grimy overshirt fall into the water. With her eyes fixed on the horizon, she began to walk farther into the lake, beyond the debris.

Her body didn't resist the gradual submersion but leaned into it. When the water came to her chest, she turned onto her back and began to float. Breathing deeply, she took in the sky, seeing it like it was in the reflection of the water. Relaxing, she let the movement of the water carry her.

Her heart opened to the gentle caress. Everything that had held her back before—the fear and trepidation of the lake, the terror of the unknown with nothing to hold on to—was being washed away.

She let go of her inhibitions. She rested in the embrace of the water and the encouragement of the rising sun. She relished the sensation of being light within heaviness and weightless within such density. She lowered her head enough for her ears to fill with water, so all sound became muffled. Within the silence, her breath slowed, and she felt herself touching the edges of a peaceful dream state.

The exhaustion and emotional pain that had gripped her body seemed to loosen and dissipate as each tiny lap of water washed over her, cleansing and healing her wounds, past and present. She closed her eyes and saw the colors within Arielle's paintings.

Immersed in the quietness of this other world, she was rocked as gently as a newborn. Like a renewal of baptism, she was being transformed and given new life by the sense of God all around. Strength replaced fear, happiness erased despair, and loneliness transformed into Presence. Tears streamed out of her eyes and joined the waters that bathed her in love.

She wasn't alone. She had never been.

Floating and tranquil, she didn't feel tethered to the earth until something touched her arm and jerked her back to reality. She went under briefly and began to kick and thrash.

"Stop! Cora, it's me!"

*Ben?*

She opened her eyes. He had swum out to her. She spit out water, choking.

"What are you doing here?" She treaded water clumsily as she wiped her eyes but kept sinking. Ben came closer and put an arm around her waist, supporting her. She relaxed enough to catch her breath.

"What am *I* doing here? What are *you* doing all the way out here? I saw your shirt in the water and then spotted you way out here. You looked dead! Didn't you hear me calling your name?"

"No." She took in her surroundings. She had floated over a hundred yards from shore. "I didn't realize I'd come so far out. Let's swim back."

Ben didn't leave her side as they did so. When they reached the shore, Ben matched his stride to hers. With every step, she walked further away from that other world and back to the present.

They sat on the shore to catch their breath. She was chilled to the bone.

Ben studied her. "What were you doing out there?"

She shrugged, looking away. "I don't know. I saw in my reflection how messy I was and decided to wash off." She picked up a stray stick and began scratching the sand with it.

He scoffed. "Yeah right. You don't go into the lake. Don't forget that the first time we met, you clung to me for dear life because you fell in. And as for washing up, you could have used Arielle's shower."

She looked at him. "How did you know I was staying at Arielle's?"

"I don't disclose my sources. Now, tell me why you were out there."

His expression told her this was not a time to make jokes. His eyes begged her to share. Cora struggled with how to explain what had just happened. After a minute, she took a deep breath and stared out to the water. "The lake was the one thing the storm wasn't able to touch or take away from me. I was picking up some driftwood and then . . . then I was floating, totally at peace with being in the water. It felt like a beautiful dream." She peered back at him. "I wasn't at all afraid. I felt . . . brave. Like I was in the middle of something God had created just for me."

The intensity of his gaze hadn't shifted. He was taking in her every word.

"I felt like God was right there with me. It's the first time I've ever felt that presence. It was transforming."

The meaningful words dropped and neither one of them spoke for what seemed a long time.

"It's barely seven o'clock in the morning," she said finally, breaking the silence. "What are *you* doing over here?"

He gave a slight shrug. "I couldn't sleep, so I went for a walk to inspect all the damage along this side of the lake. Then I came

272

here and saw a shirt floating in the water and looked out farther and spotted something. At first, I thought it was a piece of wood, and then, when I realized that it was you, I lunged in." His voice caught. "I thought you were dead."

"But . . . why?"

"You're the one who's afraid of what's lurking beneath the water, remember? You're the last person I'd expect to be alone and that far out. And with the extensive damage to the lodge, I didn't know what state of mind you'd be in. Other than that, I suppose I had no reason to worry."

She couldn't help but smile.

Ben didn't take his eyes off her. "When did you get so brave about the water anyway?"

"Just now." She got up and walked over to one of the downed trees. She sat on the trunk, facing the lodge. Ben came and stood in front of her.

"I'm sorry about the lodge. I know how much work you put into it."

The kindness in his voice and compassion in his eyes overwhelmed her. She had to look away and take a breath to clear her head. "The soul of the building is standing. The rest can be rebuilt."

His eyebrows went up. "That's a remarkable attitude considering the storm was less than twenty-four hours ago."

"Oh, don't get me wrong, I stayed up most of the night thinking about all I've lost. But Kitty and the others helped me put it into perspective. Everyone's safe—that's what matters."

"Exactly," he agreed softly. He touched her arm. "You're shivering. You need to get out of those wet clothes."

It wasn't until he mentioned it that she became acutely aware of the goose bumps covering her body. Of course, she wasn't sure if it was because of her wet clothing or the way Ben was looking at her. "These are all I have. I'll go back to Arielle's and borrow something of hers. You need to go home and change too."

"Why don't you come with me back to my house? I'll give you

dry clothes and some coffee to help you warm up. After yesterday, I doubt anyone's getting up early this morning."

"You mean besides you?"

"And you." He smiled.

"Arielle probably won't be up for another couple hours, so I'll take you up on your offer." As they stood and started toward his house, she rubbed her chilled arms. "You should know, I don't drink coffee. I make it every morning for the fragrance, but I never actually drink it."

"That's . . . interesting."

"My mother always had a pot of coffee on in case a neighbor stopped by. I do it for Sam. Widgy won't touch it."

"Why not?"

"I wash the pot after every use, and she drinks a special blend that she makes with a pot she never washes. If she ever offers you some, take my word for it—don't accept."

"I'll remember that," he said with a chuckle.

Their conversation was light and easy as they went along. She told stories of her experiences with Widgy and Kitty, and he laughed the whole way. She loved sharing her crazy life and seeing his reaction to it.

When she walked through his front door, Patchwork came running and coiled herself around Cora's legs.

Cora bent down to rub the creature's belly. "There's my sweetie."

"She never greets me that way when I come in," Ben complained with fake outrage.

"That's because I'm her favorite," Cora teased with a grin.

He shook his head. "I'll go get you some clothes."

She looked around the kitchen. It was tidy. No plates in the sink, a clean dish towel hanging from the oven door, and bananas ripening on the counter. The table and chairs showed signs of age, adding to the coziness of the room.

He returned, offering her a pair of sweatpants and a sweatshirt. "They're going to be large, but they're clean and dry. The bathroom is down the hall. I put some towels out if you want to take a shower."

"Thanks." She felt her heart expand over how easy it was to be around him.

The hot shower felt wonderful. After putting on the oversize clothes, she found Ben in the kitchen making breakfast. He had changed into jeans and a long-sleeve shirt. She loved this look on him.

He glanced over at her. She had cuffed the sweatpants a couple times, and the baggy sweatshirt hung below her hips.

Ben gave an approving nod. "My clothes don't look too big on you."

She cocked her head to one side and put her hands on her hips. "That's *exactly* what every woman wants to hear."

He laughed.

She gestured to the hot stove that was covered in pans and various food items. "Can I help?"

"Nope. Have a seat. Bacon, eggs, and French toast will be ready in a minute. There's some coffee brewing—to give you the aroma." He winked at her. "And juice is on the table."

"Thank you," she said as she sat down, relaxing into the wooden chair. Between the homeyness of the setting, the aromas in the kitchen, and the sight of Ben, she had the overwhelming desire to snuggle in and stay.

He placed the food on the table a few minutes later. There had to be ten pieces of French toast stacked on a plate and what looked like a dozen scrambled eggs on another.

"Look at all of this food!"

His ears reddened. "I didn't know how much you'd eat."

"If it tastes as delicious as it looks, I will probably eat it all." She couldn't stop smiling as she served herself and then drizzled maple syrup over her French toast.

After breakfast, Ben insisted she leave the mess for him to clean up later and invited her to sit on the front porch.

Patchwork curled up on Cora's lap. She stroked the cat and watched as the morning light sparkled on the lake.

He sat down next to her with a cup of coffee.

"Thank you, Ben."

He shrugged. "Making eggs is no big deal."

"No. Breakfast was great, but I meant thank you for checking on me this morning."

He crossed his legs and brushed some crumbs from his pants. "I hardly slept last night, thinking about what had happened to you," he said, still not meeting her eye. "I went to the lodge to feel . . . to feel closer to you somehow. I didn't expect to find you there, but I'm glad I did. I needed to see for myself that you were okay."

"You have a habit of doing that."

A corner of his mouth tugged up. "Well, we're neighbors, and we do share custody of Trouble. I'm looking after you for her interest."

Her heart filled as he teased. *He's a good man.*

They sat taking in the morning glory. The loons were calling and gliding across the water not far from his dock.

"Can I ask you something?" he said, breaking the silence.

"Sure."

"What were you thinking after the tornado?"

She considered how to explain what she felt, and he waited patiently. Finally, she said, "I was devastated when I saw the damage to the lodge. But surviving the tornado and having friends gathered around me afterward helped me see how it could've been a lot worse. I realized nothing in life is ever perfect. Buildings crumble, friends get sick, people leave you, tragedies happen . . . but you have to go on."

Ben gave her an encouraging nod, so she continued.

"As I approached the water this morning, a peace came over me. When I stepped into the lake, for the first time, I didn't think about what was lurking beneath it. I became connected to everything around me. I realized I've never been alone. All this time God has been with me—I simply chose not to open myself up to Him. In the lake, I felt Him surround me."

She took a deep breath before the rest came tumbling out. "I've spent my life running away from something I couldn't explain. I pushed people away, and I held onto anger that destroyed my relationship with my mother. I felt alone, but now I know it was because I isolated myself. I came to Moonberry Lake out of duty, but then . . . everything changed." She paused. "When I began the renovation, I wasn't sure I'd be able to do it. But sometime during all the painting and working and talking and sharing, I built a life. When I least expected it, the most amazing people became a part of my life. They gave me something I've always wanted—a home."

Her eyes pooled with tears, and her voice caught. Ben reached over and placed his hand on hers, giving it a gentle squeeze.

"I arrived here with nothing," she said, "and I've ended up receiving everything—happiness and a family." A tear rolled down her cheek, which she quickly swiped away. "They are all such inspiring examples of strength, and I've finally found my own. I don't want to be held back by fear anymore, including swimming in a lake right outside my door."

Ben was watching her intensely, listening to every word. She was grateful that he was giving her space to talk.

"Am I making any sense?" she said finally.

Without saying a word, he lifted her hand and kissed it lightly, which made her breath catch. He didn't let go, and she didn't want him to. Looking out to the shimmering water and the awakening of a new day, they held hands, sharing the magical moment.

After a while, she maneuvered Patchwork off her lap so she could get up. "I better get going. Arielle's probably up and wondering where I am."

"Let me drive you back."

She shook her head. "You don't have to do that. It's less than a mile. I can walk."

"I insist. I'll go grab my keys." He got up from his chair.

When he returned, they walked together to the car. As he opened the door for her, she turned to face him. "Thank you for the clothes."

He grinned. "Do me a favor and don't go floating out in the water next time a tornado destroys your place."

She bit down on her lip. "I'll try to remember that." Without letting herself think about it, she reached up and kissed him. It felt so right. The kiss was short and sweet, his lips were warm and tasted like maple syrup. As she began to pull away, his hand reached within the tangle of her hair and drew her closer.

In a flash, sweet turned to desperate and yearning. The kiss held all the desire and passion as the one in the gazebo.

Breaking for a breath, she smiled, and Ben's face lit up.

"Cora Matthews, I like you brave."

Heat flooded her cheeks, and she slid into the car. The drive took only a minute. She thanked him again as she climbed out. When she reached Arielle's front door, she turned to wave at Ben as he left. She sighed happily and walked inside.

Arielle was at her pottery wheel, throwing clay.

"Hey." Cora tried to sound casual though her heart was still pounding fast.

Arielle gave a big smile. "There you are! I figured you went to survey the damage this morning."

"I did." She sank into an overstuffed chair across from her friend. "What are you making?"

"A bowl. It's going to be my housewarming gift to you when you're done rebuilding the front of the lodge."

"I already love it."

Arielle eyed her. "You look different. Your cheeks are full of color."

Cora shrugged innocently.

"Are you hungry? I have some bran muffins and tofu cheesecake."

"No, thanks, I already ate. I ran into Ben at the lodge and we went back to his place for breakfast."

Arielle stopped her wheel and looked up from the mass of clay. "Oh, *really*?" She raised one eyebrow.

"He made me French toasts and eggs."

"Oh, *really*." Arielle studied her. "And are those his clothes?"

"He gave them to me to wear after I took a shower."

Her eyes widened. "Oh, *really.*"

"My clothes were wet from going into the lake, and so were his from swimming out to me, so we both had to change."

Both eyebrows shot up. "Oh, *really.*"

"Will you stop that! It's not how it sounds! I was floating in the water, and he came out to rescue me, even though I didn't need rescuing. He assumed I was drowning. We were both soaked and cold, so he invited me to his house to change and eat. That's it."

Her mouth dropped open. "Oh, *reeeally.*"

"That's it, Arielle. Put your eyebrows back down and close your mouth. I'm going upstairs to borrow some of *your* clothes." With that, she stood. "Keep working on your bowl. And I would love a vase that matches it!" She gave her friend a wink.

Once in her room with the door closed, Cora sat on the bed and pulled the sweatshirt up to her nose. She closed her eyes and inhaled, smiling as she breathed in Ben's familiar scent. It smelled like soap and . . . *him.* She could bury herself in this fragrance. She sighed and imagined Arielle's response. *Oh, really.*

"Yes, *really.*" She brushed the soft, oversize cuffs against her face and let another sigh escape.

# Twenty-Nine

Later that day, Cora walked back to the lodge and found Rolf standing at the entrance of the driveway, looking at the mess.

"Hello, Mr. Johansson."

He stared her down as she approached him and then gestured at the debris. "If this isn't a sign, I don't know what is. Are you ready to pack your things?"

"Are you?"

His head jerked back. "I told you before, I'm only leaving in a body bag. This is my home."

"And this is *my* home. I'm not going anywhere."

"You're not welcome here, and you never will be."

Studying his face, Cora could only feel sorry for the bitter old man. To be so angry and unhappy all the time must be miserable.

"Look, whatever argument and misunderstanding you are holding on to is not my fight. And it's not yours either. It was between your father and my grandfather and was lawfully settled. I have every right to be here, and I'm staying. The community and neighbors have become my family, and I would like to be friends with you. Whatever feud our families had doesn't have to continue with us."

He took a step toward her so that he was looking down at her, but she stood her ground this time. "I'll never want you here," he said in his gravelly voice.

And that's when she saw it in his eyes. Behind that hard, intimidating glare, she saw loss, emptiness, even uncertainty. He could try to cut her down with his stares all he wanted, but she saw the truth. The only thing Cora could do was continue to be the water that washed over and softened his rock-hard exterior.

She offered a small smile. "Then I'll just have to keep trying to change your mind."

Rolf scowled and stomped off, mumbling to himself.

The next few days passed with all hands on deck to clean up the property around the lodge. Cora scheduled a tree-cutting company to come and haul away the debris, but Widgy insisted they first separate the good from the bad so usable wood didn't go to waste.

Many of the large oaks, because of their size and age, had created a domino effect as they fell. Widgy stood with a chain saw in hand among the massive fallen trees, looking like a kid in a candy store.

Sam wasn't much better, talking about all the tables he was going to make from such huge trees. He went at the ones he wanted with his own chain saw, with Joseph hauling away the pieces as fast as they were cut.

Cora's job was to collect smaller pieces of wood and trash that lined the shore and water. To her delight, Ben offered to help. But Widgy immediately took advantage of having another man's strength and assigned him to putting all the logs she was cutting into a pile to be split into firewood and stacked.

Though Cora and Ben didn't have time to talk, she often caught him looking over at her. He'd give her a nod as if saying, "You can do this," and she'd give a small smile back. She found his very presence to be a comfort.

Taking a moment to rest, she watched everyone work with the same heartfelt focus and intensity they had at Kitty's house.

Little by little, Cora could see some organization to the mess, but with every tree taken away, she felt saddened by the bareness. The lodge was no longer a secret hideaway tucked within a blanket of evergreen and a canopy of oaks, like some magical Camelot.

It was exposed.

By late afternoon, everyone was exhausted and ready to call it quits for the day. Cora had gone from the shore over to help Ben stack the final pieces of wood he had cut. He rubbed one shoulder, fatigue evident on his face.

"Thank you so much for all of your hard work."

Ben took off his work gloves. "It's no problem. I want to help." He paused. "I would do anything for you."

Cora stilled. Without thinking she stepped closer and wrapped her arms around him.

He was rigid at first, clearly not expecting it, but then relaxed into her embrace and tightened his hold. When she peered up at him, he was smiling broadly.

"I'll definitely be back to work more."

She laughed.

He looked down at her with eyes gleaming with happiness and gently stroked the side of her cheek. "I like us working side by side," he whispered.

His hushed voice made her all but swoon, and she snuggled back into his embrace for a bit longer. She was in no hurry to leave his arms.

Joseph said his goodbyes, too, then walked across the yard with one hand on his lower back. Sam was already driving off in his truck, the bed loaded with choice wood.

Widgy came over, looking equally worn out. "We got a lotta work done today. Sam has enough wood to keep him busy for a long time in his workshop. I'm takin' my share of what I can use, and Dr. Walker set you up for the next two winters with firewood stacked on the side of the property. Sam and I can build a shelter over it." She scanned the spotless shoreline and the pile of debris

Cora had been working on all day. "You should feel proud 'bout puttin' in a decent day's work."

Cora smiled. "Thanks, Widge. For everything."

The woman gave a nod, then turned and ambled to her truck a bit more slowly than usual.

It had been five days since the tornado and five days since Cora had seen Mr. Wells. She had called him the day after the storm and asked for a couple days off, which of course he agreed to. Sam said he would pick up groceries for him, but Mr. Wells assured them he had enough until Cora came again. Her heart was not in it to go, but he needed supplies. It wasn't like she could quit her job because her life had been turned upside down. He needed her.

When she arrived, she slipped off her sandals and squirted sanitizer on her hands per usual. But when she turned to head into the living room, she stopped at the sight of Mr. Wells standing there waiting for her.

Something was wrong.

The typically manicured, buttoned-up, clean-shaven man with neatly ironed clothes was gone. Standing before her was a man she didn't recognize. His shirt was untucked and wrinkled, his face rough with the prickling of a white beard, and his hair was tousled instead of neatly combed. He looked disheveled, tired, and old. His shirt pocket bulged with pens, and papers were scattered all over the coffee and dining room tables behind him.

She approached slowly, not wanting to startle him. Every instinct told her to be calm and soothing. As she drew closer, her alarm increased. His eyes were weary and glazed over. "Mr. Wells, are you okay?"

He looked down, checking the pens in his pocket with a trembling hand.

She took his free hand and had him sit while she knelt on the floor in front of him. Keeping her gaze on him, she stroked his hand and spoke softly. "Mr. Wells, talk to me."

His voice cracked from lack of use, so he cleared his throat and tried again. "I . . . I should have been able to warn you. I monitor weather patterns and statistically calculate the possibility of disaster. I keep graphed data on my computer from the last fifty years, and I was wrong. My calculations were wrong." He rubbed his forehead, looking agitated. He didn't pull his other hand away from her grasp. "The tornado should have never come near you, but it did. Its irregular pattern jumped out of my estimated prediction."

Cora took both his hands and held them in his lap, then placed her cheek against them. This was the closest she could get to giving him physical comfort.

*You're the sweetest, most misunderstood, gentlest person I've ever met.*

Looking up, she said, "Mr. Wells, it's not your responsibility to track the possibility of a tornado hitting the lodge. No one could have predicted it would touch down in that spot. I'm fine. It's all over."

"It could have been worse. You could've been killed!"

"You're right, it could have been worse, but it wasn't. All of this was out of your control. You can do all the math calculations and estimations in the world, but in real life, things sometimes happen that don't make sense. You could not have predicted it or prevented it. A natural disaster is one burden you cannot carry."

He stared at her hands over his. "Are you going to continue working for me?"

Cora nodded. "Yes. I'm not going anywhere. Nothing has changed."

"I could have lost you." His voice quivered.

Eyes glistening and smile wavering, she responded, "But you didn't." She gave his hand a gentle squeeze, released it, and stood. "Now, go take a shower, shave, and put on fresh clothes while I get this place cleaned up and run to the store. Then I'll make you some lunch. We'll spend the whole day together."

He nodded, got off the couch, and started toward the bathroom. She called after him, "We'll have to find something else to do today. Sadly, my homework was destroyed in the tornado." She didn't bother masking the happiness in her voice.

"That's fine. You've mastered the basics this past year. I think you're ready to stop studying algebra and move up to the next step."

Her eyes narrowed suspiciously. "What do you mean, move up?"

"I was saving it for a surprise. It's on the table." He motioned before disappearing into the other room.

She went to the dining room table and rummaged through papers filled with math equations and graphs. Underneath the stack she felt something hard and bulky. Moving everything aside, she lifted an enormous, two-inch-thick book with bold letters across the front: *General Geometry*.

She shook her head. *Lord, help me. This man's going to kill me long before any natural disaster.*

Then she laughed at what a unique family had come into her life.

~

Cora stopped in the grocery store on her way out of town and walked over to the deli counter. Without even greeting her, Ruth Ann immediately began pouring out her sympathies.

"Honey, I am so sorry about your place! I mean, it's absolutely tragic, dreadful, unfortunate, appalling, and sad. As soon as I heard about your lodge, I felt sickened. I mean, truly upset, distressed, grieved, and disturbed." She put a hand over her heart. "Such an unfair, inequitable, wrong, unreasonable thing to happen to someone so pleasant, lovely, and friendly."

Cora waited patiently for her to finish. "Wow, you said all that without looking at your notebook."

Ruth Ann shook her head. "I go off on these tangents whenever I feel flustered or emotional. You should hear me at funerals. It drives my family crazy. I start to prattle, chatter, jabber, and blather on."

Cora smiled. "I don't mind. I think it's incredible you have all those words at the tip of your tongue every time you speak."

Ruth Ann waved her off. "Enough about me and my quirky, odd, peculiar, eccentric habit. How are you doing?"

"I'm doing okay. I'm staying with a neighbor, who just so happens to be a vegetarian. I'm all for salads, beans, and nuts, but I was craving one of your colossal creations."

"It would be my pleasure and delight!" The woman went to work, cramming every ingredient at her disposal onto a full loaf of Vienna bread.

When she handed the sub over, it was the size and weight of a newborn baby. Cora could only laugh.

Before checking out, she stopped at the small garden display in the floral department of the grocery story. She had forgotten to buy Kitty's marshmallow cookies the last time she was in, and she needed the right ammo to get them past the check-out clerk. An idea had come to her that she was eager to try.

As Cora approached the counter, she held her head high and purposely lifted her chin. She set the boxes of cookies on the conveyor belt, and before the woman could say anything, she reached into the cart and lifted out a potted plant and handed it to her.

"I'd like to buy this for you," Cora told the clerk. "It's an aloe plant that has healing qualities. If you have a small burn, all you do is cut open one of the leaves and rub the aloe on the burn to take the pain away. I think it's best to have it in the kitchen so it's right there when you need it."

The woman looked bewildered. The gift had obviously thrown her off her game. She appeared unsure where to put the plant once she'd scanned it, but then she gently set it down next to the register. She cleared her throat. "You know, real aloe is better than any cream."

Cora nodded. "I'm sure it is."

The woman scanned the cookies without a blink. At the end, before hitting total, the clerk reached into the pocket of her apron and pulled out two coupons and swiped them, saving Cora $1.20. When she handed Cora her receipt, she leaned over and whispered, "Thank you."

Cora leaned in closer and whispered back, "You're welcome. My name's Cora."

The woman gave a curt nod. "Mine's Alma."

# Thirty

When Cora returned to the lodge that afternoon, she found the insurance agent waiting for her.

"I came early to take a few more pictures and get your signature on a couple papers," he told her.

They sat at a picnic table Widgy had brought over so they'd have a place to sit and eat while cleaning up.

Cora began looking over the papers and stopped. "What's this?"

He scanned the paper she held up. "That's a copy of the deed passed to you by the last owner."

She shook her head. "This can't be right. My mother's name isn't on it."

"No. I double-checked your information, and Lydia Matthews was not the last owner. As a matter of fact, she never was. The previous owner had the lodge up until last June and then deeded it to you."

Cora's hands trembled as she reread the name at the bottom of the deed. *Joseph Manz.* Her heart skipped a beat when the listed address confirmed her suspicions.

She took a quick breath and tried to steady her voice. "Um . . . I'd like to look these over a little more. Would it be all right if I brought them to your office tomorrow morning?"

The agent shrugged. "Sure. But know we cannot proceed with any reimbursement until the paperwork is finalized."

"I understand." She didn't take her eyes off the paper.

As soon as he left, she walked over to Joseph's house, her heart beating hard in her chest. He wasn't in the garden, so she went to his back door and pounded on it. When he approached the door, she had already stepped back and was pacing his deck.

She stopped and gave him a bewildered look. "Your name is on the deed to the lodge as the previous owner." She waved the paper she'd brought over. "Your name is on the deed!"

He hesitated before answering. "Yes."

Cora balked at the acknowledgment. "*Yes*? This is really not the time to go monosyllabic on me!" Her volume rose slightly. "You owned the lodge, not my mother. She was *never* the owner. Who are you to my grandparents, and why would you give the lodge to me? Are we related somehow?" The conflicting feelings churning inside her made her feel ill.

"Explain! Say something!" she demanded.

Joseph's shoulders dropped as he released the breath he'd been holding. He looked at her with eyes full of sadness. "Cora, I'm your uncle."

The words hung awkwardly in the air. She couldn't even comprehend them.

"Your mother was my half sister. Your grandfather was my father. I inherited the lodge when he died."

She stiffened. "What? I don't believe you. My mother never mentioned you."

Another sigh. "You should sit down."

She crossed her arms. "I prefer standing."

Joseph took a deep breath. "Your grandfather had an affair with my mother." He said it with such release, as if confessing the sin lightened a heavy burden he'd been carrying. "It was impulsive and happened at a vulnerable time when he and your grandmother were going through a rocky time in their marriage. Your grandfather regretted it immediately and apparently ended it as quickly as it began. His intention was never to leave your grandmother or your mother. However, like with most bad choices, there was a consequence." He paused. "Me. He had already recommitted himself to your grandmother and was devastated for the shame and complication he created. Instead of keeping it a secret and walking away from me, he told your grandmother and begged for her forgiveness. She did forgive him, although the healing process took much longer, I was told years later."

Cora was not prepared for anything he said. She opened her mouth to say something, but when nothing came out, she closed it and let him continue.

"Your grandfather didn't want me to suffer, so he agreed to support me. Growing up, I saw him a couple times a month. My mother and I lived an hour away. Your grandmother requested that the misdeed remain private. Your mother was a small child at the time. In a small town, even one as lovely as Moonberry Lake, gossip can be vicious. So your grandmother helped him hide it from everyone, including your mother, so he could spend more time with me. I knew from the time I was young that my father had two families but was told to never speak of it or I wouldn't be able to see him again.

"They kept it a secret my whole life until, one day, when I was over at the lodge visiting from college, you and your mother came for an unplanned visit. Feeling the time for transparency had come, your grandfather tried to explain the situation to your mother and reconcile with the truth in his own heart. She was stunned, but even more so furious. The transgression of fathering me was one thing, but your mother could not forgive the double life he had lived for most of her life. She never forgave him." Fresh pain filled his eyes. "Or me. I saw you once, and then you never came back. You were about—"

"Seven." She put her hand to her chest as if to hold in the pain that was spilling out. She sank into one of the two chairs on his porch.

He came close to her and sat, then scooched his chair so he sat directly across from her. "I tried contacting your mother for years, but she would have nothing to do with me. It wasn't until one month before her death that she called me and expressed her deep regret for letting all those years pass. She said she was sorry for what she had taken away from you and asked if I would someday get in touch with you and explain everything. She hinted at how you two were not close and how she knew you never forgave her for taking you away from this place. She said you never found your footing again." He looked at her with such sympathetic eyes. "I think your mother was afraid of how you would react to the truth. Some people do not feel brave enough to confront their mistakes like your grandfather did."

Cora slumped against the chair as if all the energy was being drained from her body. "I— I can't believe it."

He leaned in, his face full of anguish. "I'm sorry I didn't tell you the truth. I was afraid you wouldn't have anything to do with me if I revealed everything. I was avoiding the inevitable, which wasn't right. I hope you can forgive me."

So many questions swirled in her head that she had a hard time choosing one. "But why did you give me the lodge?"

Joseph gave a shy smile. "Like you, I have no one. I was an only child like your mother. When I heard she'd passed away, I wanted you to have the lodge but wasn't sure how to go about it or explain it. I needed help to do it."

"Sam," she whispered. It was all coming together now. That was why he couldn't look her in the eyes when he told her about the inheritance.

Joseph nodded. "He hated lying to you, but we figured if we got you here, even if it were for a short time, I would be able to meet you. He was the one who came up with the idea that you had to live here for one year. We just switched out your mother's letter with the deed he had drawn up."

"And of course I never read the fine print," she said, shaking her head.

"Sam knew of your mother's blue envelopes because he had received one too, asking that he tell you about your family. Before the funeral, he put the title to the property in his envelope and then handed it to you instead of telling you about the truth of your grandfather and me."

*My mother.* Cora's brain felt scrambled with so many different emotions whirling within her. Her strongest emotion, however, was anger. It bubbled up and burned inside her.

"I can't believe it," she spat the words out.

"I know it's a lot to take in."

She stood from the chair and placed her hands on her hips. Her breath came out hard and fast. "No, you don't understand. I can't believe my mother never told me. I can't believe she deprived me of grandparents—of a *family*! She would never discuss what happened, never tell me why she cut them off. Mom and I were never close, and this was one of the biggest reasons why. When she shut them out, something in her shut me out as well. I was always . . . alone." Her fury was building. "I could have had many more years with my grandparents! I could have had an uncle!" Her fists clenched, and her heart pounded.

Joseph was quiet for a minute, then he said, "You *do* have an uncle. It's not too late. That's why I gave you the lodge. I wanted to see you. I never imagined you would stay, and when you agreed to do so, I was so nervous I nearly blew my chance at getting to know you. I wanted to take it slow."

She tunneled her hands through her hair and turned to face the lake. She turned back around.

"Are you really a pastor?"

"Yes."

She put her hand on her forehead, pressing against the headache that was forming. "I have so many questions."

"And I have all the time in the world to answer them for you."

His words acted like water thrown upon the fire within her, melting her anger.

She sat back down and stared at him. *He's family.*

He gave her a couple minutes before speaking again. "What are you thinking?"

She shook her head in amazement. "I can't believe Jesus is my uncle."

He let out a hearty laugh. "I'm so relieved you finally know the truth. It feels as if a tremendous burden has been lifted off me."

"This is so much to take in. I thought I had gotten over the loneliness of losing it all, but if there's one thing I've learned in coming here, it's that I had only gotten accustomed to the ache. Maybe my heart was always pulling me back here. I ran in every direction looking for home—until the funeral. That space deep inside me finally stopped hurting—not simply from being back here but by coming back and being welcomed and loved by this community."

He grasped her hand and squeezed it. "I'll be right back."

He went into the house and came back with a blue envelope. "This is what Sam was supposed to hand you that day."

She stared at it, almost afraid to touch it, as he held it out for her. Slowly inhaling, she reached out with a shaky hand. "I need a minute."

"Of course."

If this held her mother's last words to her, she knew she needed to open it privately. She turned and walked a few feet away.

Keeping her back to him, she opened the letter and inhaled sharply at the sight of her mother's writing. On the first page, there was a short note.

*Sam,*

*I've made a lot of mistakes in my life, and the biggest was not being able to forgive my parents. I know Cora suffered for this. When you see her, I ask that you give her this letter and introduce her to her family. That includes you. You were always there for my parents, and I imagine you still were after I left.*

*Lydia*

The second page was as brief as the first.

*Dear Cora,*
*These last four on the checklist are going to be harder than the others.*
*And I'm sorry for that. I'm sorry for a lot.*

*Mom*

7. *Spend time in Moonberry Lake. It was my true home and I think it's yours too.*
8. *Visit the lodge your grandparents owned for much of their life.*
9. *Ask the next-door neighbor, Joseph, to tell you about your family.*

And at the bottom of the page—

10. *Please forgive me.*

Tears streamed down her cheeks and sobs escaped, releasing pain that had been sealed up inside her for so long. She felt a hand on her shoulder. Joseph.

*My uncle.*

She turned around and accepted his hug.

When her sobs finally eased, Joseph left to get tissues. Head pounding, nose stuffed up, and body utterly exhausted, Cora read number 10 again and made the decision.

She was done letting the past dictate her life. Her mother's death had given her a new beginning. It was different than she'd planned or expected, but it was hers.

It was time to let go of loss, to move forward, embracing what was right in front of her—the family she'd always wanted.

People funneled in and out of the lodge, evaluating the damage, determining structural safety, estimating needed repairs, and analyzing insurance coverage. Thankfully, the foundation and back end of the lodge had not been damaged. Widgy stayed glued to Cora's side throughout it all to make sure everything was valued correctly and fairly.

Finally, word came that it was safe to go inside the back of the house. Widgy had draped heavy plastic tarps across the openings where the wall facing the lake had been torn out. She wanted to protect anything exposed from the outside elements.

In a proud, strong voice, Widgy bellowed, "The one thing the tornado couldn't destroy was my plumbin'. I've said it before and I'll say it again: my plumbin' is good for life!"

"You got that right!" A low, gruff voice from behind surprised them both.

Cora turned to see a short, pudgy man with squinty little eyes and round cheeks covered with gray-white stubble. He wore a navy bucket with a couple fishing lure in it, a white short-sleeve shirt that had *Mobile* embroidered on the pocket and *Phil* embroidered below it, and dirt-stained navy pants. Half his face was drawn up so he could keep a clenched bite on the stub of a soggy, unlit cigar.

He walked over to them and gave a nod, mumbling "ma'am" through clenched square teeth so as not to move the cigar.

*Who on earth is this?*

Nobody said anything until Widgy cleared her throat. "Uh, Cora—er, um, Ms. Matthews—this here is, uh . . . Stan."

*Ms. Matthews? What is that about?* And was Widgy . . . *blushing*? She'd never seen Widgy so tongue-tied.

Widgy stuffed her hands into her pockets. "Gettin' this place back to normal is going to be a two-man job, so I was gonna have, um, Stan here . . . ah, help me. Kind of a second contractor to, uh, watch over the crews since there's a lot to be done."

"Oh, um, okay. Widgy, may I talk to you for a moment in private?"

She took Widgy's arm and pulled her out of earshot. "This guy? This is who you want to partner with?"

Widgy reddened and her nostrils flared. "I'm not makin' him my *partner*. Geez, the way your mind works," she hissed, giving her a disgusted look. "He's the best man for the job. He only hires good men, always puts in an honest day's work, and doesn't cheat at poker."

Cora's eyes widened. "What does poker have to do with rebuilding the lodge?"

Widgy rolled her eyes as she let out an impatient breath. "If a man cheats at somethin' as petty as cards, you can bet he's gonna cheat at a lot bigger things in life."

Cora glanced over at him. "His shirt says *Phil*."

Widgy shrugged. "He likes to shop outta the community clothes bin. You're not gonna hire him 'cause he's a penny pincher?"

"Of course not. He's just—"

"He's worked in housin' and construction for thirty years. I know he won't build junk or allow it to be done wrong when we're not lookin.'"

Cora sighed. "Well, I trust you. If this is the guy you want, I'll go with him."

"I didn't say I *wanted* him, I said I'd *work* with him." Widgy gave an aggravated grunt. "Will you stop talkin' like that? We haven't even started and you're makin' this out to be somethin' dirty!"

Cora scrunched her face. "What are you talking about? And why are you so defensive and calling me Ms. Matthews all of a sudden?"

"I'm tryin' to be *pro-fes-sion-al*." Widgy emphasized every syllable. "You might want to try that yourself. You didn't exactly give the best first impression and welcome him right."

Cora flinched. "I haven't said anything to him!"

"Exactly. It's a poor first impression."

Cora blinked, not believing the track of the conversation. "Fine. What would you like me to say to Phil, er, I mean Stan?"

"Nothin'! You'll embarrass me. Keep your trap closed, and I'll handle it!"

"I'll have to talk to him at some point."

"No, you won't. You go through me, and I'll tell him what needs to be done. But look who I'm talkin' to. You didn't know half of what I was doin' before, and now most of the walls with all the fancy colors are gone, but my toilets are still standin'!"

Cora's jaw dropped. "I never said anything about your toilets. I know you do an excellent job. You're acting weird. This whole conversation is weird. What's up with you?"

"Nothin.'" Widgy's eyes darted back to Stan, who was studying the damage. "The man makes me nervous."

Cora looked from Stan to Widgy. "I didn't think that was possible. You aren't scared of anything or any*one*."

"I'm fine. Let's go back to how the rules were when I first got here—stay out of my way and lemme handle it."

Cora put her hands on her hips and leaned in closer, staring her in the eyes. "Here's the thing. I don't like those rules anymore, and that's *not* how we will operate. We're friends, and your dog likes me so much he loses his bladder every time he sees me. About a thousand gallons of Dr Pepper and saving Beast entitles me to some respect. Not to mention, I work as hard as you do. *I* am the boss. This is my home."

Widgy stared at her, eyes wide and a slight grin on her face. She cleared her throat again and gave a nod. "Glad to see you've developed some backbone. I've had a good influence on you. You're right, and I'm sorry." She looked at the ground and shifted a bit before speaking in a barely audible whisper. "I know we answer to you, but can we act like I'm the boss when he's around? I need to look tough in front of this guy."

Cora scoffed. "Believe me when I say no one would ever mistake you for a rose petal."

Then Widgy uttered the one word Cora didn't think was in her vocabulary. "Please."

The genuine plea crumbled Cora's defenses. Her shoulders fell with a sigh and she nodded.

Widgy took a sharp breath in to puff out her chest and walked—no, strutted—back to Stan to discuss the job.

# Thirty-One

Cora left Widgy and Stan inside, then found Sam in the back of the lot going through another pile of wood and sorting out what he was going to haul away.

"You lied to me about my mother and the deed."

Sam stopped for a minute, then continued his sorting. "I'm sorry. If it means anything, I felt terrible doing it. It wasn't right to bend the truth like that. I only did it because I thought it was for your own good and Joseph was desperate to bring you back."

She stood there, stewing, as he kept sorting. "I trusted you."

"I am sorry," he repeated. "I promise to never lie to you again."

She crossed her arms. "You could've told me about my grandfather."

"It was not my story to tell. It was family gossip I didn't want to stick my nose in."

Cora sighed. "And you could have told me about Joseph instead of introducing him to me as my *neighbor*."

"That was for him to tell you. *He's* your family."

"*You're* a part of my family."

Sam stopped and looked at her, then grinned. "All the more reason to protect you until the time was right. You weren't ready when you first arrived. Think back to that first day when I found you at the end of the dock. You were about ready to bolt right then. I couldn't predict how you'd take learning the truth about your family. None of us wanted you to run off when we've waited so long for you to come back."

Cora looked to the lake, chewing on her lip as she considered his words. After a minute, she turned back to him. "What other secrets are you keeping from me?"

"None, and that's the truth." He looked her square in the eyes.

She dropped her gaze, unsure what to say.

Sam drew her into a hug while her arms were still crossed. "Now that we have you, we're not letting you go."

She put her arms down and let him embrace her more tightly.

"Apparently I don't have any say in the matter," she mumbled against his shirt.

He chuckled. "Nope. Now, are you going to forgive me?"

She nodded, and he squeezed even tighter.

"Good, because I've kind of grown attached to you. Now go talk to your uncle." He gave her a gentle push in Joseph's direction.

Looking across the yard, she saw Joseph in his garden and walked over to him.

"Hello Joseph . . ." She paused. "Uncle . . . um, Pastor Joe." She shuddered at how awful that sounded. "Sorry. I don't know what to call you."

He chuckled. "I'll go by anything you like."

"I've never had either, but I think *uncle* trumps *pastor*, so I'll go with Uncle Joe."

Joseph smiled.

"What are you doing?"

"I was praying while pulling some weeds."

"Oh." She wondered if he ever included her in his prayers.

He seemed to read her mind. "I pray for many people, you being at the top of the list. I've been steadfast in my prayers for you, that your faith be strengthened since we spoke about it some months ago. Has there been any change?"

She paused. "Considerably. Has *your* faith been strengthened?"

"Considerably." He grinned.

Her heart swelled. She loved having a family.

⁓

After discussing plans for the lodge reconstruction with Widgy and all the possible alternatives, Cora's head throbbed. She needed time to think before committing to anything and let everyone know that. There were more things to consider than just the lodge. She was trying to imagine a permanent life in Moonberry—one that included all the ladies, Sam, Widgy, getting to know Joseph more, and . . . Ben. When everyone left, she stood in the front yard staring at the lodge. No clarification came to her, so she escaped the pressure with a walk.

Striding up the road felt good, but after some time, she went to the place she had always ended up. Kitty's cemetery.

After visiting her favorite markers, where Kitty's artwork was especially exquisite, she went to the front of the house. Turning the corner, she saw Kitty at Peter's gravesite.

"Hi, Kitty."

Kitty looked up and smiled. "Come for a visit?"

"I came to think."

"I did the same."

"We're alike."

"Indeed, we are." Kitty gave a nod. "I wanted to visit with Peter and bring him up-to-date on what's been going on."

"You could've done that from anywhere. His spirit is always with you."

Kitty burst out laughing. "Oh my, you've been around me too much."

Cora plunked down next to Kitty, taking in a long, slow breath.

"That was a heavy sigh."

"I have a lot of decisions to make about the lodge."

"You need to focus on what your heart's telling you about the lodge and other things."

Cora arched an eyebrow. "What other things?"

Kitty gave a mischievous smirk. "Like a certain man who is clearly taken with you."

Cora opened her mouth to say something, but Kitty put up a hand to stop her. "Hear me out. I've seen how you and Ben look at each other, and I know there's something pulling the two of you together."

"You've been watching Ben and me?"

"Yes, and the other ladies have noticed it also. We've all talked about it and are in total agreement."

"You've *all* talked about this?"

Kitty nodded. "Oh, you've been the topic of many discussions. We all see how you light up when you're near him."

"*All* of you?"

"Why yes, we discuss you in detail when you're not around. The ladies all agree with me, even Samuel and, I daresay, Ms. McGuire."

Cora let out a cough. "You've discussed my romantic life with Widgy?! I'm glad I've given you something to talk about."

"Sometimes you have to swallow the hesitation you feel and take a leap of faith. If you ever find anything in life that makes the light within you shine brighter, you know it's a part of God's plan. Don't reject a gift that's being offered to you."

Cora fiddled with the hem of her shirt. "I don't have a good track record with relationships."

"When it's the right time, with the right person, you no longer need to keep past records."

Cora was silent.

"All the ladies and I, Sam, Joseph, and Widgy treasure you. Ben wants to be added to the roster. He wants the chance to love you. Open your heart, my dear. Happiness is yours for the taking. Sometimes you just have to do things scared and see how they work out."

"And I suppose that wisdom pertains to the lodge as well."

Kitty nodded. "You'll be led." Then she gave her a pointed look. "Do you ever stop running around so you can be quiet and hear what that still, small voice inside is saying?"

"Not really."

"It took sitting here in silence for me to become aware of that voice, so deep inside and true. If you open yourself to it, you'll hear it over the chaos. The voice of God doesn't come in a scream but a whisper."

Cora didn't answer right away. "I love the book you put on the marker." She pointed to Peter's marker.

"That was my first etching. It became an unexpected turning point in my life."

"How so?"

"For the first twenty years I lived here with Peter, I didn't touch the markers except to clean them from leaves and bird droppings. I took pride in keeping the space beautiful and tidy. I mowed the grass with a push mower and planted flowers by every stone.

"When people stopped visiting because no one was being buried here anymore, I was not as meticulous with my work. I said to myself, 'What does it matter? Nobody cares. Life has moved on, new generations have been born, and these people are nothing but notations in family trees.'" She paused. "Then Peter died. The loneliness swallowed me up. All I could feel was his absence. Looking at his gravestone, I wanted something to symbolize who he was and came up with the idea of a book. I got up and went back into the kitchen. I searched all the junk drawers for something that would scratch the stone. I didn't find anything but a pair of scissors, which were too clumsy and didn't work well. I called Samuel and described to him what I was looking for. He brought me a small chisel.

"I worked for days etching a book by Peter's name. As I worked on it, the most extraordinary thing happened—I started to hear Peter talk to me. He told me how much he loved me and how he would always be with me. I began to feel better and started re-membering all the wonderful times we shared."

Kitty paused, closing her eyes and smiling at the memories. She sighed contentedly before continuing.

"After I completed the book, I could actually smile when I looked at the marker. It makes me think of him poring over his books in his study or reading while he drank his morning coffee. That small picture brought back warm memories and gave me comfort.

"I needed to concentrate on something other than my sorrow, and the carving brought me joy. That's when I got the idea of two hands intertwined, Peter's in mine, for the other side of the marker. The sketch took me months, but I didn't care. No matter how many hours I sat chiseling away, I felt comforted."

She smiled, and Cora smiled back.

"I know you've felt something since you first walked over here, or you wouldn't have kept coming back. It's a gift. You discovered the same thing I did all those many years ago—that the air seems to have breath and the wind whispers. You'll never be alone, no matter your age or circumstance, because by remembering these people we have invited them into our lives." Kitty folded her hands.

"Any answer I have ever needed, God has given to me. When I stopped filling my world with noise, I heard the truth. Stop and listen, my dear." She brought her hands folded in prayer to her chest, dipped her chin, and closed her eyes. "The answer is wait-ing to be heard."

# Thirty-Two

## SIGHTINGS AND SATIRE

Modern-day Tree of Life! Firefighters were amazed when they were called to rescue three cats, a Chihuahua, two guinea pigs, and five pet canaries that were stuck in an oak tree on Maple Drive. Apparently, the strong gusts of wind sent the miniature Animal Ark flying into the tree. While a bit shaken, all critters have been checked and hydrated by the vet and returned to their owners (none of whom are named Noah).

It's that time of year again for the fire department to check and flush the fire hydrants. As torrents of water are released, residents are encouraged to use the water wisely by participating in public bathing. Come wash your dogs, cars, and children. Note that nudity is prohibited. Although all creation is to be celebrated, some is better left covered.

The veterinary clinic has reported an outbreak of overweight stray dogs. The obesity of these animals has skyrocketed from generous people giving them scraps. Strangers are apparently killing them with kindness in snack form. Next Saturday, the animal shelter will be sponsoring "Save a Life—Adopt a Fat Dog" day in the park.

Praying Insomniacs is the new hip group in town! No, it's not a musical band but a prayer chain made up of people who have a hard time sleeping. The Catholic church came up with the idea, and it's a hit with the late-night owls that toss and turn all night. Their slogan is "God is up twenty-four hours a day, so celebrate your lack of snooze by praying!" Sign up for a time slot so even if you fall asleep, you'll receive a phone call to wake you.

You've wanted it. You've dreamt of it. You may even still be feeling the effects of it. Back by popular demand is the coveted Rhubarb Crisp ice cream at Freya's Candy Shop! The tangy treat with a bitter bite will have even the most cynical puckering up for more. The misunderstood and underrated backyard fruit has been turned into a sweet and sour sorbet. Hidden like little gems within cinnamon ice cream are dark pink chunks of locally grown rhubarb. Only served in the summer. Try it on a dare. Come back for the craving. It's only odd if you don't embrace it.

Cora couldn't get any enjoyment out of the newspaper when all she was thinking about was what Kitty said about taking a leap of faith and doing things scared. Acting on pure adrenaline, she got in her Jeep and went straight over to Ben's house.

Ben did not hide his shock when she knocked on his door, but he recovered quickly. "Good morning."

She held out a large bag. "I brought your clothes back. They're washed and ready to wear. I put extra softener in the rinse cycle so they'd be soft and smell like lavender." She was rambling.

"Thank you for looking out for me that day and letting me borrow them."

"You're welcome. I've never had clothes that smelled like lavender." He smiled, lifting the bag up to his nose to take a whiff. "I'd forgotten about them."

"Sorry I didn't return them to you sooner. I wanted to bring a dessert or something as a thank-you, but Arielle only had ingredients for rye or spelt bread, and I've never made either, and I didn't think you should be the guinea pig for *that* experiment."

"You don't have to make me anything." He seemed to be holding back a chuckle. "Would you like to come in for some . . . juice?"

She loved that he remembered her dislike of coffee. "Sure." She followed him to a closed-in porch that had two comfy chairs facing the lake.

"Have a seat. I'll be right back."

She nodded and sat down.

A minute later, Ben returned with drinks. "How's it going with the lodge?" He handed her a glass and sat down next to her.

"The lodge had good insurance, so I'll rebuild. With Widgy overseeing the construction, it'll be updated and probably end up looking better than it did in its former glory days. And I'll make sure that the charm and cozy feeling remain intact."

"What are you going to do with it when you're done?"

Cora looked down at her juice. "I love living on Moonface. The lake, the lodge, the people—I've fallen in love with them all. I want to build a life here in Moonberry Lake." Then she took a breath and blurted out the news she'd been keeping to herself. "I'm going to open the lodge again and run it as a retreat center."

His face brightened at her announcement.

The way his eyes crinkled in the corners distracted her for a moment. He was all warmth and tenderness—and he didn't even know it.

"That means you're going to have to continue putting up with me as your neighbor."

"I think I can handle that."

She felt as if his tone and piercing stare put her under a spell. "It also means I'll probably be visiting a lot more. You know, coming by if I need to borrow a cup of sugar."

"I'll go buy more sugar today." A grin spread across his face.

"Okay, then."

"Okay, then."

Her stomach fluttered. "I should let you get back to whatever you were doing." She set down the juice she hadn't even taken a sip of and stood.

"Wait." He stood too, blocking her exit. "Will you have dinner with me tonight?"

"Dinner?"

"Yes, dinner. I want to take you, Cora Matthews, out on an official date. I've wanted to take you out on a date since I first met you out on the lake—or, actually, *in* the lake." He put his hand through his hair, disheveling it.

Cora fought the urge to reach up and smooth it with her fingers. *Have mercy.*

"Well, how about now?"

His eyes widened. "Now?"

"I figure there's less chance of some disaster or accident happening to me if we go on a date now. The sky's clear, there doesn't appear to be a storm coming, I'm not in or near water, I haven't eaten any of Kitty's cookies today, and there isn't a roomful of people to watch me humiliate myself. However, I can't guarantee a skunk won't cross my path—even if we're inside. On second thought, I'm afraid there will always be the risk I'll get myself into predicaments that will require your rescue."

He came toe to toe with her. "I don't mind coming to your rescue."

"Well, at some point I'd like to come to *your* rescue."

Ben reached up and tucked some of her flyaway hair behind her ear. "You already have."

At his soft whisper she swallowed, clearing her throat. "Less drama would be okay with me."

He smiled. "What did you have in mind?"

"How about taking a walk first? It's a beautiful day, and walking will give us an opportunity to talk."

"I'd like that."

"It will also count as our first date, so I'll be much more relaxed for our second date tonight and actually eat. However, that does bring up the possibility of choking, but I assume you know how to perform the Heimlich maneuver."

He chuckled. "You're unforgettable, do you know that?" He put a finger under her chin and lifted it so their gazes locked. He lifted his other hand, and one finger lightly traced the outline of her jaw. As he took in a deep breath, Cora found herself matching his breath.

His warm eyes and intoxicating scent made her head spin.

Ben's voice was deep and rich. "I can't stop thinking about you. You make me laugh, and I relive every moment we've spent together when we're apart. You're the most remarkable, beautiful, stubborn, sweet, and strongest woman I've ever met. You're a wonderful, loyal friend to others and fun to be around. You're kind and generous to wandering cats and crazy dogs, and I've loved every so-called mess you've gotten yourself into because it's brought me closer to you."

She felt his breath on her face, and then his lips touched hers in a light kiss, and then another . . . and another, each a bit deeper and a lot longer. When he finally pulled away, he looked down at her so lovingly, she felt as if her heart was breaking wide open to receive all that he was offering.

"And you are . . ." she began, and then stopped, distracted by how happy he looked and how it mirrored how she felt.

"I am . . . what?" he asked, prompting her to continue, appearing bemused but also a little vulnerable.

Cora blinked to hide the building emotion. "You are . . . what I've been looking for—for a very long time."

Ben placed a trail of small kisses from her forehead to the tip

On Moonberry Lake

of her nose to her mouth. Then he stepped back and extended his hand. "Shall we go for that walk?"

For a moment, she was transported back to another time, remembering the scene Kitty had described with her Peter. It was as if history was repeating itself, but this time it was Ben extending his hand to Cora to lead her to a future together.

She glanced up at Ben, knowing she would remember this image for the rest of her life.

"Is something wrong?"

Cora shook her head. "No." She slipped her hand into his and held it tight. "For the first time, everything is as it should be."

Excited to return to

# Moonberry Lake?

Turn the page for a sneak peek at the next adventure in town!

**COMING SOON**

# *One*

Delphinium Hayes could identify the goodness—or wickedness—of a person by their scent. With the slightest passing whiff, she immediately knew someone's most admirable or weediest characteristic.

Generosity had the full-bodied boldness of lilies. Kindness possessed the reserved yet intense fragrance of pink azaleas. Humility smelled of lily of the valley. Those who had a great sense of humor or who were natural storytellers conspicuously reeked of poppies. And people who were good at keeping secrets were rose-scented.

When the odor of rhododendron wafted around a person, it was a dead giveaway that the individual was vain and selfish. Bullies who insisted on getting their way stunk of onion weed, liars were always oleander, and wisteria sprang up from hypochondriacs.

Delphinium used her ability to her advantage. She knew which buyer at her flower shop would be good to work with and which would try to cheat her. She had the dearest and most trustworthy friends. Customers marveled at her knack to give them exactly what they were seeking. Her acute sensitivity was her intuition and guide, telling her someone's true character before they even spoke. This perception never failed.

Until it did.

Lugging a ceramic planter she'd found hidden away on a bottom shelf in her favorite store in Moonberry Lake, Fine Antiques, Heirlooms & Collectibles, Delphinium calculated the number of steps left before she reached her shop and wondered if her sweaty grip would hold out. Her tangled mass of red hair refused to be tamed in the oppressive summer humidity and escaped in corkscrews from her messy bun, making the center look like a matted nest. She only needed bird eggs burrowed within it for her head to be the perfect home to a family of chickadees.

Though her namesake flower came from the azure shade of her eyes—her hair, compassion, and intuition came from her beloved grandmother, Annie. Delphinium could still picture the old woman's white hair springing out of her head like fusilli pasta, making a near-audible *boing* as she moved.

Delphinium smiled wistfully. How her grandmother would have loved to go antique shopping and find such a treasure. She let out a heavy sigh, which didn't come from lugging around the planter. The lingering grief from the absence of her kindred spirit pressed on her chest. Grandma Annie was the only person who had truly understood her—not only believing in Delphinium's ability but celebrating it.

Her grandmother had known what it was like to be different, or at least to feel that way. She had lived with a form of synesthesia where she saw color and even tasted flavor for every letter and number. The letter *A* was red, *O* was white, *P* was orange, and *E* was teal. The number *5* was blue, and the number *2* was green. When her grandmother bit into a brownie, she tasted purple. All the mundane components within ordinary life were an assault on the senses, an exploding rainbow always in front of her eyes or on her tongue.

As a little girl, Delphinium had wanted to be just like her grandma Annie and was devastated when the letter *K* didn't appear magenta or when she couldn't taste saffron when she saw the number *47*.

However, her consolation prize of genetics, or "gifting," as her grandmother insisted on calling it, was her ability to smell fragrances that were nearly imperceptible to everyone else. It was a scent not created by perfume or soap, but what a person emitted naturally.

In a small way, Delphinium felt like she had a superpower too, and that was her link to Annie. Instead of tasting colors, she smelled scents. No matter how faint, Delphinium was able to detect a fragrance linked to the person's most dominant characteristic. All she had to do was get a whiff for the insight.

Delphinium blew out a sharp breath to move a bouncing curl from her line of vision. The stagnant, muggy air melted not only her eyeliner but her patience as well. Every passerby looked as wilted as she felt. The humidity of the summer day made it hard to breathe. Her nose wrinkled as a puff of petunia emitted from a man who walked past her, appearing equally annoyed as she was with the foul weather. Petunia always indicated anger and resentment.

Feeling a trickle of sweat trail down the hollow of her back, she cradled the cumbersome ceramic planter, determined not to let it slip from her grasp. The front of her shirt was going to be badly wrinkled from dampness.

Delphinium groaned. *Why couldn't I have waited for it to be delivered? Why can't I ever simply wait?*

She knew the answer, of course. When it came to her beloved store, she possessed the tolerance of a toddler. As soon as she had seen the beautiful hand-painted planter abandoned on the bottom shelf in the antique store, she envisioned the exact plant she was going to put in it—bird-of-paradise—and the price she'd get for the match. The three-block jaunt to her shop would pay off.

Surely it would turn a nice profit.

That's why she was heaving this monstrosity down Main Street, she told herself. She'd rather be more creative and come up with lucrative arrangements customers couldn't resist than hike up all her prices to pay the mortgage on her corner property. Her dire financial state only meant she needed to up her game in presentation and quality.

Giving herself little pep talks calmed her down when she was anxious and helped her lift her head proudly in these moments when she knew she looked like a hot mess.

Literally.

Main Street was the heart of Moonberry Lake, and she knew carrying the oversize planter made her quite a spectacle. Having ogling eyes was known as perfect vision in the small town. Delphinium was accustomed to her family feeding the gossip mill.

Her grandmother had been a regular topic among coffee shop discussions. Being quirky, or rather, having an "artistic flair," as Grandma Annie called it, attracted stares. "The price for not being ordinary," she'd say, waving a bit too enthusiastically to scrutinizing eyes. "Be proud to be the spectacle, not the spectator, sweetheart."

Delphinium's shoulders relaxed a bit as she approached the shop. She pushed open the door, and it dragged, sticking halfway. With a grunt and a swift kick, she budged the door another inch, allowing her to escape the outside heat.

"Paavo! The door is sticking!"

After carefully setting the planter on the counter, she shouted again, "Paavo, where are you?"

Wiping away the strands of hair stuck to her sweaty forehead, she headed to the back storage and workroom. Paavo was standing at the worktable, pulling thorns out of a shipment of roses. Even though he had his earbuds in, she could hear the distant clamor of music from ten feet away. She walked closer and waved her arms. He pulled out one of the earbuds.

"Oh hey, Miz D. I didn't hear you come in."

Between his earnest smile and the chill of the air-conditioning, her annoyance dissipated. "Paavo, didn't you notice that the front door sticks?"

The teen shrugged. "Nope. I came in through the back door. There's nothing wrong with that one."

"Well, the *front* door, which coincidentally is the entrance to the business, drags like it's being pushed through taffy."

An ornery voice spoke from behind her. "It's because this horrid weather is making the wood expand. Everything swells up. My fingers are like sausages!" Henry, her right hand in this business, must have been one minute behind her. Even on his day off, he came in to check that everything was running "shipshape," as he called it.

"Good morning, Henry."

The elderly man tipped an imaginary hat in greeting. "That flowerpot out there is a pretty one. You'll get a good price with the right plant."

Delphinium smiled. *Great minds think alike.* "Checking on me this early?"

Tight-lipped, the man shook his head, his jowls swaying slightly with the motion.

She didn't miss the quick glance between Henry and Paavo. "What? What are you guys not telling me?"

Paavo grinned at Henry. "They're in the refrigerator."

"*What's* in the refrigerator?" But before they could respond, Delphinium strode over to the floor-to-ceiling door to the giant cooler. She pulled it open and stared at the contents, then turned around and marched back to her two employees, her hands on her hips.

"Does someone want to tell me why there are three *men* in my refrigerator?"

A huge smile spread across Paavo's face. "They're playing cards." She felt her mouth open.

"Now, Delphi, hold on a second," Henry began, but she was already marching back to the oversize refrigerator.

Opening the door again, she studied the three elderly, half-dressed men sitting on upside-down buckets. "Excuse me, gentlemen," she said, "but why are you playing cards in my walk-in fridge?"

Hunched in concentration, two of the men didn't even look up from their hands, and the one who did answered her question with a question. "Why do you look like a raccoon?" His face contorted into a look of repulsion.

Henry stepped beside her, draping an arm around her shoulders. "The answer to both questions is that it's blazing hot outside and we're all melting." He looked her in the eyes. "Your makeup runs clean down your face in this temperature, but for us, we're at risk of melting into a clump of wax. We needed a place to play poker where we wouldn't get heatstroke, and I suggested here. It's the coolest place in town."

"What's wrong with The Gardens?" Henry's typical hangout was the game room at the assisted living facility where all the men lived.

"The air-conditioning is out except for the dining hall, so they tried to herd us all in there like cattle. The room is a mass overcrowding of wheelchairs and sleepyheads. And the director only allows cards if we don't gamble. There's no fun if there ain't somethin' at stake."

"This is a free country, and I'll gamble if I want to," barked one of the other men, still not looking up from his cards. "It's my right!"

"We should know. We fought for this country. We fought to be able to gamble, and that director is unpatriotic for denying us that right!" a second man piped in. The other two grumbled in agreement.

"All right, boys, simmer down," Henry interjected. "Delphi is fine with us being here."

Delphinium whipped her head to the side to gawk at him. "I never said that!"

Henry gave her a pat on the back. "We just need to give her time to get used to having the walking dead in her cooler." All the men chuckled.

Poker Player Number One, the grumpy man who had pointed out what a mess she was, looked up at her again. "We're being *preserved* in here instead of turning into a liquefied mess and drooling all over ourselves like the others down at the home."

Delphinium scrutinized him. "So how long will this *preservation* take?"

"Forever!" the grumpy man shouted.

"Anarchy!" Poker Player Number Two added, raising one fist in the air.

"Jump ship!" Poker Player Number Three yelled.

Delphinium turned to Henry who smiled crookedly at the feisty behavior of his buddies. He shrugged as if to say he had no control over what was happening in her shop. "I guess that's your answer. Any other questions?" The goofy grin on his face indicated he was enjoying their rebellion.

She whispered in Henry's good ear, "Why must they all be in their *underwear* shirts?" She looked back at the men in their thin white tank tops. It gave her too vivid of a peek at their bodies, which did indeed sag like dripping candles. "Are they playing strip poker?"

"Oh no, it's just more comfortable this way." Henry winked, then stepped inside the giant cooler and began unbuttoning his own shirt. "The fact that this cooler only runs on half its cylinders makes it the ideal temp."

She frowned at the reminder of another expense. "It's on the list to fix."

"Don't. It's the perfect breeze in here." He smiled.

Delphinium sighed, her shoulders lowering in defeat, knowing this was no battle to fight. She felt totally drained and it wasn't even ten o'clock. With a roll of her eyes, she turned and let the men have their way.

"Shut the door!" the men yelled in unison.

She went back and closed the door, shaking her head. *What am I going to do with a refrigerator full of nursing home rebels?*

She let out a long sigh. "I need to find a person who's a hydrangea," she muttered, as she passed Paavo on her way to open the shop.

Paavo paused in putting his earbud back in. "What's a hydrangea?"

"Hydrangeas are always team players. I need someone to take my side and agree that this place is crazy!" she said over her shoulder.

Leaving the chaos behind her, Delphinium headed to the front counter. She absentmindedly opened the drawer where Henry always put the mail. The sight of three words stamped in red on the top envelope caused her to shut it just as fast.

*Notice of Foreclosure.*

The beating of her heart thumped loud, and her head began to swim.

*It's just the heat.* She drew in a breath and focused on the expansion of her lungs.

Opening the drawer again, she peeked at the envelope, willing the printed, red words to change.

They didn't.

They might as well have been stamped in blood by the way her heart ached. The reality of eviction was getting dire. Things were going from bad to worse.

She slammed the drawer shut.

*Breathe.*

*Just breathe.*

# Mabel's Famous Fudge

## Ingredients

2½ cups granulated sugar
1 pinch salt
1 (12 oz) can evaporated milk
2 tablespoons unsalted butter
12 oz (about 2 cups) semisweet chocolate chips
12 oz German sweet chocolate
1 (7 oz) jar marshmallow creme
1 teaspoon vanilla extract
2 cups chopped walnuts (optional)

## Instructions

1. Butter a heatproof pan (11x16-inch jelly roll pan or similar size). *9x13 for a thick hunk of fudge!
2. In a large saucepan, combine the sugar, salt, evaporated milk, and butter.
3. Bring to a vigorous boil, stirring often; then reduce heat and simmer for 7 minutes, stirring continuously.
4. In a large bowl, mix together the chocolate, marshmallow creme, and vanilla.
5. Gradually pour boiling syrup over the chocolate-marshmallow mixture while whisking.
6. Beat until chocolate is melted and mixture is smooth. Stir in nuts if using.
7. Pour into prepared pan and let sit for several hours at room temperature to harden before cutting into 1-inch squares.

# — Marci's Fudge Mocha Mint Brownie Bites — with Salted Caramel Sauce

## Ingredients

1 cup butter, melted
3 cups granulated sugar
1½ teaspoons vanilla extract
4 eggs
1½ cups all-purpose flour
1 cup unsweetened cocoa powder
1 tablespoon instant coffee granules
1 teaspoon salt
1½ cups mint chips or chopped Andes mints
1 (10 oz) jar premade salted caramel sauce

## Instructions

1. Preheat oven to 350 degrees.
2. Lightly grease a 9x13-inch baking dish.
3. Combine melted butter, sugar, and vanilla in a large bowl. Beat in the eggs one at a time until thoroughly blended.
4. In a separate bowl, sift together flour, cocoa powder, coffee granules, and salt. Fold dry ingredients into the egg mixture until just blended. DO NOT OVERMIX.
5. Stir in the mint morsels.
6. Spread the batter evenly into the prepared dish.
7. Bake in preheated oven for 30 to 35 minutes.
   *A great brownie has a crust at the edges and is soft in the middle. To check if done, insert toothpick into center and pull out. If there is batter, add a few more minutes. If it comes out dry, you have overbaked and it can be chopped up as an ice cream topping.
8. Remove pan to wire rack and cool before cutting.
9. Drizzle with caramel sauce.

# Kitty's Broth

*Sorry, top secret!*

# Acknowledgments

This book has been a journey. A long journey. It feels as though a lifetime has passed since these characters first came to me. In the process of creating this Moonberry Lake world, I've picked up so many sweet souls along the way, and I am thankful for each one of these people.

Thank you, Kelsey Bowen. I choose to believe our meeting, although a bit late, was meant to be. Your generosity, guidance, and belief in my writing made this book better. A big thank-you to the entire Revell team for their hard work and expertise. Robin Turici, you are a gift.

Tawny Johnson, it is a privilege to be included in your wolf pack. Your integrity will always make you my go-to person, and your heart will always make you a forever friend. I can't wait for our next adventure together.

Megan Basinger, thank you for your eagle eye, big brain, and sweet spirit.

Lauraine Snelling and Sarah Shepard, I love you. We are family. Your eagerness to hear all my stories means everything.

Friend and mentor, Ginny Yttrup, you are the loveliest teacher and encourager to so many. Your kind words have made such an impact, as have your examples of quality and class.

Geana Bassham, you are the most amazing prayer warrior whose demonstration of faith has literally changed my life. Your dedicated prayers over my health are imprinted on my soul. You are a true blessing and sister-friend. As the leader of the best Bible study, you've taught me never to question the power of a group of praying Texas women.

Rebecca Voss, Christine Limbers, and Heidi Wilson, thank you for your loyal friendship and steadfast prayers. I could not have gotten through cancer without any of you. Always know how much you are treasured.

Jennifer Templeton, I will never forget your role as my first reader and how you stayed up all night to read this book and fell in love with the characters. Thank you for your dogged enthusiasm through the years.

Marci Seither, thank you for your friendship, support, and wonderful baking skills. Your endless creativity and heart for serving are so inspiring.

Helen Arnold and Rosie Makinney, thank you for your genuine cheerleading and sweet friendship. Sharing our writers' journey has forged an unbreakable bond that I cherish.

My incredible family has trudged every step of the writing process with me. Thank you to my parents who have always encouraged me to hold onto my dream of becoming an author. To my amazing brother and sister by heart, Andrew Collins and Erica Schumacher, thank you for your love and support. You mean the world to me.

My beloved James, you are my smile, my calm, and my home—always. Our journey together has been God-led from day one. Beyond the walls of life, beyond the bounds of time, I will love you.

To Chocolate, Maple, and Honey, I will love you beyond my last breath. You are my light and happiness. No words can express how proud I am of the men you've become. Each of you are an example of the goodness in the world.

And most of all, to our God of creativity and healing. The Light in my darkness, my Guide when I am lost, and the true Storyteller always encouraging me to go on, distracting me from pain, and lifting me up in His strength.

**Holly Varni** is a native Minnesotan of strong Norwegian and Swedish descent, who was raised in the Lutheran Church that Garrison Keillor made a career depicting. Between the lutefisk, grumpy grandparents, and crazy neighbors who mowed their lawn wearing pajamas, the seed to becoming a storyteller was planted in Holly's heart. Though she and her husband and their three sons live along the Central Coast of California, her beloved Midwest roots continue to influence everything she writes. She is host and author of the podcast *Moments from Moonberry Lake*, where more stories of her characters from this sweet small town are shared.

# Meet Holly

Visit Holly online at **HollyVarni.com**
to read her blog or listen to her podcast.

f HollyVarniWriter 🐦 HollyVarni 📷 HollyVarni